CW00507026

# WE ARE
# ALWAYS
## WATCHING

PLEASE RETURN TO
LIBRARY
REH

WITHDRAWN

# HUNTER SHEA
# WE ARE ALWAYS WATCHING

## SINISTER GRIN PRESS
## MMXVII
### AUSTIN, TEXAS

Sinister Grin Press

Austin, TX

www.sinistergrinpress.com

March 2017

"We Are Always Watching" © 2017 Hunter Shea

This is a work of Fiction. All characters depicted in this book are fictitious, and any resemblance to actual events or persons, living or dead, is purely coincidental.

All rights reserved. No part of this book may be reproduced in whole or in part without the publisher's written consent, except for the purposes of review.

Edited by Erin Sweet-Al Mehairi

Cover Art by Zach McCain

Book Design by Travis Tarpley

ISBN: 978-1944044-41-1

*This one's for Tobi*

# CHAPTER ONE

When the money ran out, there was nowhere else to go but Grandpa Abraham's. The old man claimed his house was haunted; he'd said just as much to West several times during their one and only phone conversation. West had had no desire to talk to his absent grandfather, but his parents had insisted. Grandpa Abraham seemed just as unhappy to be thrust into the forced exchange.

He did light up a bit when he warned West about the possibly possessed house—for his own good, of course. West Ridley was old enough to know that was just his grandfather trying to scare them off. He was, after all, a cantankerous prick.

At least that's what his parents called him when they thought West was out of earshot.

"You grew up there, Dad. Did you ever see a ghost?"

The battered Ford F-150 made every pothole on Route 80 feel like they were blasted mine holes. It was about as uncomfortable a ride as possible, and that was including taking school trips on those ancient, yellow buses. His mother had to trade in her Camry for this rust bucket because they needed the extra cash to pay for the move. Besides, where they were going, pickup trucks with four-wheel-drive were a necessity.

His father's eyes were closed, head in his large, calloused hands as if he were trying to keep it from rolling off his neck. Faint black stubbles peppered his shaved head. His once perpetually tanned skin had faded to a shade of heavy cream, the sun no longer his constant companion.

"The only ghosts in that house are the spirits of all the field mice your grandfather's caught in his traps," he said through gritted teeth.

"You want the bag?" his mother said, eyes on the road, one hand on the narrow wheel, the other holding a yellow plastic shopping bag.

"Not yet," his father said.

"Why don't you hold onto it just in case?"

He pushed the bag away, daring to take a hand off his head. "I said not yet. I just want to get the hell out of this truck. Can't you go any faster?"

West's mother pursed her lips. "Not without the truck falling to pieces. And even if I could get it to go more than sixty, we can't afford to get a speeding ticket."

Plucking his headphones from his lap, West prepared to shut them out.

"Thank you for never failing to throw that in my face," his father growled. The nausea kept the usual bitterness from his voice.

"That was totally uncalled for. I was just trying to help."

His mother tossed the bag onto his father's lap. She fussed with the tight curls of her raven hair, pulling ringlets straight until they touched her shoulder, then let them spring back.

When he didn't reply, the bubble of rising tension in the car popped.

Good. Dad would retreat into his misery and Mom would concentrate on getting them to Pennsylvania. Lately, uncomfortable silence was best.

West sat in the back seat, crammed between boxes with clothes still on their hangers draped over them. Knees pressed together, he was just able to reach into his hoodie pocket to get his iPod. It was a first-generation Nano, a hand-me-down from his best friend, Anthony, when his parents upgraded him to a new iPhone.

He wondered when he'd see Anthony in person again. Sure, they could call each other on his mom's phone or maybe Skype on her computer, but he couldn't imagine not hanging out every day after school or chilling out at the outdoor mall on weekends. Of course, getting access to his mother's laptop was always an issue and who knew if there was such a thing as the Internet out in the sticks?

Everything about this move sucked.

And what kind of grandfather took delight in trying to scare his fourteen-year old grandson?

His parents told him that he saw his grandfather when he was four, but he had no recollection. That was back when his grandmother was still alive. His father only had one photo of them, a faded Polaroid taken some time in the seventies, his grandparents younger than his parents are now. They stood beside a green Chevy Impala, neither smiling, about a foot apart, no sign that they were a couple, happy or otherwise. It was a grim snapshot that looked more like something captured in the *1870s*.

*I'm surprised your father didn't tell you about the ghosts,* Grandpa Abraham had said to him the day his father made him pick up the phone because he wasn't in the right head space- his words – to talk.

*What ghosts?*

Plural. The house so nice it was haunted twice.

*They were here long before I was born. I've made my peace with them, but I don't know how you're going to feel about it.*

West knew he shocked him when he said, *Cool! Do you see full body apparitions, shadow people, hear voices, have stuff move around?*

He was answered by silence, then *get your father on the line.*

Because Grandpa Abraham didn't know him at all, he had no idea about West's fascination with all things horror. Anthony's father was a midlist horror writer, and their house was filled with all kinds of spooky memorabilia he collected from conventions over the years. After watching *Friday the 13th* at Anthony's one day after school when he was just nine, he was hooked.

His obsession deepened further when his parents expressed their dislike of the genre. According to them, he should be into sports, not werewolves and boogey men.

On the plus side, West devoured horror books like they were M&Ms. For that, his parents were somewhat happy.

"Any port in a storm when it comes to reading," his father said. "Back in my day, it was comic books. That's the only way I was able to make it through *The Odyssey* and *Moby Dick*."

For West, ghosts were mysterious but not creepy. From everything he'd read and watched, they were just people without an earthly body. It was really kind of sad when you thought about it. Like being lost and invisible all at the same time – every little kid's nightmare.

No, stories of ghosts were not a deterrent for him. He hoped there was some truth to it, but it was a slim hope. Everything about the last year was a shit show. Why should living in some old farmhouse in Pennsylvania make things better?

Watching the trees zip by, West looked for a podcast to listen to, settling for *Bloody Good Horror*, the movie review show that never failed to crack him up. The banter of the five guys, followed by a beer recommendation, word of the day, and review of a new slasher flick that just came out, did the trick and took his mind off his family's new low.

✠

His mother tapped his arm, his signal to take off his headphones.

"We there?" he asked.

He'd spied the sign for Buttermilk Creek from the corner of his eye when they jumped off Route 80. The town was just a few exits over the Delaware Memorial Gap Bridge, separating New Jersey from Pennsylvania. Before they left, he'd looked the place up on Wikipedia. It had been founded in the mid-1700s and had a population of a couple thousand people. Where West was coming from, that would fill a neighborhood.

It was still a mostly farming community just outside the Poconos. Everything about it looked boring as hell. The highlight of the year was the annual Apple Fest.

It looked like they were in a different world. This was the deep country, as far as he was concerned. His father had said there was an amazing pie shop not far from the bridge, hidden somewhere within the trees, jagged mountains on either side of the road. He'd promised to take them there once they settled in.

"You haven't lived until you've sat back with a slice of their shoo fly pie," he'd said, rubbing his stomach.

"Complete with flies buzzing all around it," his mother added. "I remember they were in need of better screening on their door and windows."

Pie. That was literally the only selling point they had to give when they talked about the move. It didn't do much to pique West's interest.

"It's just up there," his mother said, pointing to a dirt road to their left. The road they were on now was lined with thick-trunked trees in full bloom, their canopy blocking most of the sunlight. He didn't see any houses around.

His father was snoring, head leaning against the window.

"Are you sure? Maybe you should ask Dad."

"GPS works out here. It's not as remote as it looks."

"It *looks* like we're in Oklahoma."

From where they were coming from, a bustling New York suburb, this may as well have been Saturn. Going to the store to get a Red Bull would probably require a thirty-minute car ride. West slumped into his seat.

The long, narrow driveway seemed to stretch on forever. Huge gouges had been carved out of the hard-packed earth and gravel. The Ford wheezed and creaked, dipping from side to side. His father smacked his head against the window and woke up cursing.

"It's not like I'm doing this on purpose," his mother snapped, both hands gripping the wheel. She leaned forward as if that would help her find a more navigable route to the house.

Tall, golden stalks of ragweed swayed in the late afternoon breeze. West rolled down the window, took in a lungful of country air. It smelled sweet and pure, with a tang of onion. He wasn't sure if he liked his air this fresh. It just didn't seem right.

"Looks like you're going to have a lot of mowing in your future," his father said, trying to lighten the mood.

"Yeah, right. I'd need a tractor to whack these weeds."

When his father didn't say anything, his hopes dared to soar just a tad. "Am I going to get to drive a tractor?"

It was two years until he could get his driver's license, the Holy Grail for all teens. He'd sell his entire *Fangoria* Magazine collection for a chance to get behind the wheel of some heavy-duty farm equipment.

"Your grandfather hasn't worked the land since I was younger than you. He used to have a tractor. Big, blue sucker. If it's still around, I'll bet it's rusted solid."

West sighed.

So much for that.Back to everything sucking.

"Finally," his mother said, leaning back into her seat.

The ragweed pulled away like a stage curtain, the end of the rutted road in sight, and the faded white farmhouse dominating the small rise.

The house looked old.

*Was old.*

It was a flaking scab on a fleshy field of neglect. West took a breath, held it unconsciously, eyes roving over the bleak tableau.

If ever a house was haunted, this was it.

A brown picket fence, gaps in the slats like a rot-toothed smile, rose and fell along the side of the hulking structure. A lone tree loomed over the front yard like an expectant vulture, its denuded limbs casting gnarled finger shadows on the lawn. It looked like it had died years ago but forgot to fall. A rusted Dodge pickup looked like it was melting into the soft ground.

West dug it.

His mother's ESP was working, because she said, "Right up your alley, huh?"

"Straight out of central casting," he said, tucking his iPod away. "All it's missing is a tire swing with a frayed rope and a couple of creepy girls singing nursery rhymes."

"I used to bug your grandfather to put up a tire swing," his father said. "He told me I'd crack my skull open on it. So, I was left to my own devices, which led to me actually cracking my skull open when I thought I was The Human Torch and jumped off the shed out back."

"That'll teach him," his mother said with a nervous laugh.

None of them really wanted to be here. It didn't take a genius to figure out that some really bad stuff must have gone down for West's father to avoid coming back all these years. Whatever it was, they were going to have to suck it up, because in a few minutes, they were all going to be roommates.

The Ford's brakes squealed. West popped the door open, anxious to stretch his legs.

The farmhouse looked deserted.

There appeared to be three floors and nothing much of a porch – just a little space by the front door big enough for a couple of chairs. Weren't farmhouses supposed to have wraparound porches with rocking chairs and spittoons and wind chimes?

There wasn't another place in sight. His father had said there were homes on the edges of the property, but they were either too far away to see or concealed by trees. Even the sounds of traffic were missing way out here. It was as remote as being on a deserted island. In a world where strip malls, chain restaurants, and boxy hotels were popping up like chicken pox, this place was a throwback to pioneer days, at least to West. He wouldn't be surprised if Grandpa Abraham told him they'd have to churn their own butter.

West didn't hear his mother come up beside him. She draped an arm over his shoulder and squeezed.

"I know you're hating this right now," she said low enough so his father couldn't hear. "You've been amazing through all of this and I love you. I promise this is only temporary. You ever hear of the phrase grin and bear it?"

He shook his head.

"Well, just follow my lead."

The front door opened, the screen door banging against the frame. The old man was short but built like a fireplug. He had a full head of long, graying hair but his square jaw was clean-shaven. He stood with his hands on his hips, squinting at them.

"That you, Debi?" he said.

"Here we go," she said to West from the side of her mouth. She broke out in a big grin and waved. "Hi Abraham, it's been too long." West watched her stride to the porch, acting like this was a treasured family reunion.

"Is Matthew feeding you? You're all skin and bones."

"And you look great."

West's father said, "Can you find my cane?"

"Sure, Dad."

*So that was how you grin and bear it.* West's friends called it *being plastic.* It came in handy when dealing with teachers. And now, grandfathers.

"He looks like an old-time wrestler," West said, pulling the cane out from under a box of books.

His father chuckled. "You're right, he does. The long hair is a new thing. Guess he got tired of paying someone to cut it. He can be as cheap as the day is long. Here, help me get on my pegs."

He grabbed his father's arm, pulling him gently out of the car. He slipped the cane's handle into his other hand, steadying him as best he could.

"You mind walking with me?" he asked.

"Nope."

They ambled toward the house, Grandpa Abraham and Mom watching their unsteady approach.

"I thought you'd be in a wheelchair," Grandpa Abraham said with a tone that sounded like a mix of derision and disappointment.

"Not if I can help it."

Finally face-to-face, estranged father and son didn't shake hands or hug or say they were glad to see one another. West looked from one to the other, waiting for something, but he wasn't sure exactly what.

The old man broke his father's gaze and looked to West. "Looks like you got my genes there, kid," he said, patting his head roughly. "Pint sized just means folks will spend a lifetime underestimating you. It's fun to knock them on their asses from time to time." When he smiled, the lines around his eyes deepened, stained teeth peering out from behind his thin lips.

Before his father could protest, Grandpa Abraham barked, "No sense standing out here like a bunch of scarecrows. I have to feed this wife of yours. She's got the hips of a little boy. Hell, just like him."

18

He stormed into the house muttering to himself.

West looked to his mother, who had managed to keep her smile in place, though it had lost some of its initial dazzle. His father looked ready to spit nails. She took his hand in hers, a rare gesture lately.

"Come on, we knew it wouldn't be easy," she said. "Let's go inside and see how we can fatten me up."

# CHAPTER TWO

A long, narrow hallway led to a kitchen that was surprisingly filled with light. The threadbare runner had a pattern so worn down from years of foot traffic it resembled the faded Shroud of Turin. West Ridley noted that there were no pictures on the walls. The place had a funky odor – like old vegetation and dirty underwear. He prayed his mother's touch would at least improve the house's bouquet.

He walked past the living room, mismatched furniture clogging the space with barely enough room for a stand with an old tube TV.

"I have liverwurst and bologna. You pick," Grandpa Abraham said.

He gestured for them to take a seat around the old aluminum table, yellow padding poking out from cracks in the chairs. West helped his father sit, making sure he didn't fall.

"Thank you," he said, his eyes dancing a bit. That happened when the spins hit hard.

A loaf of off-brand bread landed on the table, followed by plastic bags of cold cuts. Next came a bottle of mustard, the top missing, with a thick brown crust on the spout.

"You so fancy you need plates?" his grandfather asked, rooting around a cabinet and coming up with a short glass.

"Never considered eating off a plate fancy," West's father said.

"It's just sandwiches."

"I don't need a plate. I'm not hungry," West said. There was no way he was eating liverwurst and he'd lost his taste for bologna somewhere around third grade.

His mother got up. "I'll not only get plates, but wash them when we're done."

"Suit yourself," Grandpa Abraham said. He reached under the sink for a bottle of amber booze and poured some in the glass. Leaning against the sink's stained skirt, he knocked the drink back in one gulp, then poured another.

While his mother made two sandwiches, West asked, "Have you lived here all your life?"

"I was born right there," he replied, pointing at the table. West pulled his hands off the table, as if bits of the old man's afterbirth were still jellying on the surface.

"In the kitchen?"

"Came out on my own terms. Been that way ever since."

"Was there a doctor?"

"That quack was miles away and we didn't have a car then. My older sister helped my mother deliver. She must have done something right because here I am and my mother was doing the

22

laundry the next day. Who needs a hospital when you have common sense? Dogs can do it all by themselves. I'll never understand why we like to complicate things."

His father dropped his sandwich. He looked like he was going to say something, then took a breath, picked it up and took a hard bite.

"God bless her," his mother said. "I could barely get my butt out of bed the day after this guy was born. There was a point I swore he'd decided not to come out. That labor is the reason he's an only child."

He'd heard her say that a hundred times. She chuckled, winking at West.

"I was the last of nine," Grandpa Abraham said. "They don't make them like my mother anymore."

No one knew what to say, so his parents ate while Grandpa Abraham drank and West willed himself to astrally project back to New York.

There was a soft thump that sounded as if it came from just under their feet. West looked at the scarred linoleum, then at his grandfather.

"What was that?"

"I told you on the phone."

Now his father spoke up. "There's no ghost in the basement. I'm sure there are living critters, though, and plenty of stuff to knock around."

"What makes you the expert?" Grandpa Abraham said, the edge of his voice dull and sloppy.

"Because I grew up here, too. Please, stop trying to fill West's head with ghost stories. He obsesses enough with that stuff as it is."

"You're not afraid of ghosts?"

West shook his head. "No way. My friend Anthony and I want to start our own paranormal investigation team some day. We'd love to spend a night in a haunted house."

His grandfather considered what he said, then grunted, rolling his eyes. "What lives here just might change your attitude."

"Come on, Dad."

The old man shrugged. "Suit yourself. You can't say I didn't warn you. When you're done cleaning up after yourselves, come get me and I'll show you to your rooms."

He shuffled into the living room, glass in one hand, bottle in the other.

West's mother touched his arm. "He's just trying to scare you."

"He's just a you-know-what," his father said, lowering his voice.

"It doesn't bother me. This house *looks* haunted..."

"You sure you don't want a sandwich? I could see if he has some cheese in the fridge."

"Nah, I'm good. I kinda want to see my room."

When he got up from the chair, the thump came again, this time so close, he could feel it through his sneakers. He stamped his foot down in reply.

"You may not have talked to a ghost, but I do think you just scared the heck out of a squirrel," his father said. He managed to get up on his own, using the cane to steady himself for a moment. "You want me to take my old room down here?" he called to Grandpa Abraham.

"Can't have you falling up and down the stairs now, can I?"

West had learned a lot about his grandfather is just a few minutes. He was an entertaining buzzard, in a cranky kind of way, but making light of his dad's condition showed the man had a deep, dark mean streak.

That could prove to be very important information somewhere down the line.

"You don't have a stereo, do you?" Grandpa Abraham asked. They were in one of the two upstairs bedrooms. West's bedroom was at the end of the hall. He could see into his grandfather's across the way, the heavy oak door partially open. He spotted an old bureau, a white doily on top, little bowls everywhere. He wondered what was in those bowls.

*Probably old pennies and leaking batteries.*

"No. Just my headphones," West said. He could hear his parents settling in to their room downstairs. Their voices carried through the floorboards, but he couldn't make out what they were saying.

"Good. Keep your loud music to yourself. Those things make you deaf, you know." He jabbed a thick, nicotine-tinged finger at the headphones wrapped around his neck.

"By the time that happens, they'll have discovered a way to reverse it," West replied, dropping his duffel bag on the four-poster bed. The box spring made an awful racket, the mattress sagging so much, he wondered if there was any stuffing left. "I read it in *Discover Magazine.*"

"Nobody likes a wise ass, kid." His grandfather ran a hand through his long, wild hair. Lifting his arm gave West a chance to catch a whiff of the b.o. that had been fermenting in his armpit. He tried not to cringe.

"I wasn't trying to be. Doctors are working on all these kinds of implants that will mimic the inner workings of the ear. Kind of like laser surgery for eyes."

Grandpa Abraham raised an eyebrow. "Well, I guess you just gotta hope you live to see that miracle come true. They told us twenty years ago that cancer would be cured after they found all that DNA-chromosome-genome crap. I see people dying every day from it. Even the rich bastards, like that Steve Jobs. Don't believe everything you read."

West turned his back to him, unzipping his bag. It was filled to bursting with clothes, books, and magazines.

"You hear what I said?"

West locked eyes with him. "Yeah."

"Okay, well, make yourself at home. Bathroom's down the hall. I'm in it a lot at night, so don't be surprised to hear me knocking around."

Now West smiled. "I'll assume it's either you or one of the ghosts."

He thought he saw the tiniest fraction of a smile start to curl the corner of his mouth. "Laugh now. You'll see."

He took a faltering step to the door, reaching for the handle to steady himself. "Guess your dad's not the only one with a case of the dizzies today. Maybe your dad and I should enter ourselves in one of those potato sack races. That would be a sight, wouldn't it?"

When he laughed, it sounded like there was a stormy sea of phlegm rattling in his lungs.

To his surprise, West chuckled, picturing the two of them bonding in a race where they would have been doomed from the start.

"I'll be watching the Phillies game downstairs. You like baseball?"

"I could take it or leave it. I guess the Mets are okay."

"The Mets? Do me a favor and don't bother me during the game." Grandpa Abraham went down the hall, wondering out loud how in the hell he had a grandson who didn't care about baseball and liked the Mets of all the goddamn teams. West watched him turn the corner, holding on to the newel post, and clomp down the stairs.

What the heck was he to make of the man? Was he always all over the place, or was it just the alcohol? It was painfully obvious he'd rather they weren't here, but they were family. How could you not welcome your family with open arms when they were down on their luck?

"Forget him," West said, plucking his stack of horror magazines and placing them on the dresser. There was a dusty shelf above it just the right size for his books. He had to get rid of a lot of stuff before the move, but his books were sacred. Most were packed in a box in the moving truck, but he kept his favorite authors with him – Bentley Little, Stephen King, Brian Keene, Brian Moreland, and Clive Barker. He'd gotten most of them at a second-hand bookshop in Harstdale, and even though they were beaten and battered, they were his most prized possessions.

After wiping the dust with his sleeve and sneezing four times, he settled them on the shelf. There was an old steamer trunk at the foot of the bed. It looked like something people would have brought with them on the Titanic. It had two brass clasps on the front. He tried to open them, but they were either locked or fused shut. He gave it a kick. It sounded full.

*I wonder what's in there.*

No sense asking Grandpa Abraham. Not now, while the Phillies were on. Maybe in a few days when he got used to them being here.

*Maybe he's just set in his ways, and we're screwing up his routine.*

But then, he and his father had had a falling out over something. It was one of the things West was determined to find out.

Grabbing an old copy of *Rue Morgue Magazine*, the one with the tribute to Barbara Steele on the cover, he plopped onto the bed. The ancient mattress sucked him in like quicksand. He kind of liked it. It was like being wrapped in a cocoon or a cushioned hammock.

The baseball game blared downstairs. He thought he heard his father yell something. It was a quick outburst. West paused, waiting for more. After a while, when all he could hear was the cheering of the crowd and steady warble of the analyst on TV, he flipped to an article about some 60s B-movie where sea monsters from the bottom of the ocean attacked Miami Beach.

*No arguing today Mom and Dad,* he thought. *Grandpa Abraham is enough fun for one day.*

He wondered what Anthony was doing right now. Probably going to the movies or out to an early dinner with his parents. They liked to skip lunch on weekends and go out to eat in the late afternoon.

*Lucky.*

A sharp breeze battered the house, rattling the warped frame of the room's sole window. West stiffened, dropping the magazine on his chest.

"Ha ha, maybe you are afraid of ghosts," he croaked, his heart thumping against his ribcage.

He stared up at the ceiling, scolding himself for being such a chicken shit.

There was something up there. It was faded and looked like it may have been painted over a long, long time ago. But the cheap paint had dried and flaked away, revealing crudely drawn words that hovered right over his face.

West squinted.

WE SEE YOU

✠

"Why don't you go watch the game with your father?" Debi said. She was busy stuffing drawers with their clothes, removing pungent mothballs and dropping them in the dented waste pail beside the dresser. They pinged against the metal pail, their odor singing the hairs in Matthew Ridley's nose. Christ, he hated the stench of mothballs. His mother and father kept the industry alive over the years, sticking them in every corner and pocket they could find.

"That should be a lot of fun, especially with him two sheets to the wind. A couple of more drinks and he'll make it the full three."

Matt sat on the edge of the bed, gripping the handle of his cane with both hands. The spins that had almost swept him off his feet when they first came into the room were starting to abate. He knew they'd never fully go away, but at least he didn't feel like tossing up that horrible sandwich.

"When do you think he bought those cold cuts anyway?" he said. "I'm pretty sure liverwurst isn't supposed to have crusty edges. Nothing like a little food poisoning to start our prison sentence."

Scooting the empty suitcase into the closet with her foot, Debi shook her head in exasperation. "You know, you're not doing a whole hell of a lot to make things any easier. Your father is an old man who was as crusty as that liverwurst on his best days. He's not going to change his spots now. That leaves being the bigger person in your court. The last thing West needs is more tension in the house."

Waving her off, Matt said, "He has his headphones on most of the time. I'm surprised he even remembers who we are."

Debi glared at him, slamming a drawer closed.

"Don't you dare turn our son into a teenage caricature just to make your lack of effort acceptable."

"Give me a break. We just got here."

"I'm not just talking about now."

Hi bit back his reply. They'd stepped into discord déjà vu. He wasn't up to it just now. And she was right about one thing – West didn't need them adding to the tension in the house. With all of the things he couldn't do anymore, that was something he was able to control. Why he didn't more often was a mystery even to him. He often thought that maybe people were right – misery really does love company.

"Baseball with my father without a drink. This should be fun," he said, pulling himself up from the bed by leveraging his weight against the cane.

His wife touched his shoulder before he left the bedroom, the same room he'd done his homework in, put together model battleships, and dreamed of one day getting out to New York.

Putting her arms around his neck, her deep amber eyes demanding all of his attention, she said, "We're going to get through this. I know it hasn't been easy and this is far from a step in the right direction, but if we work together, we can get out of here in no time and back on our feet."

Matt felt some of the tightness in his chest loosen. He hadn't realized how wound up he'd been until this moment. "I like the together part." Placing a hand on her hip, he pulled her closer. The little bit of extra padding she'd always carried had melted away over the past year. He'd never tell her, but he missed it.

She kissed the tip of his nose. "I wouldn't count us out yet."

"I guess I need to stop counting myself out." He breathed in the floral scent of her hair. "But it's getting harder and harder not to."

"Maybe what you need more than anything is to get out of your own head for a while. Spending time, quality or otherwise, with your father could be just what the doctor ordered."

He gave a small laugh. "If that's true, I want a second opinion."

Debi swatted his ass. "Now get out of here. I have work to do to get this room in shape."

When he leaned down to kiss her, the floor nearly slipped out from under him. Instead of launching into his usual string of invectives and bemoaning his situation, he closed his eyes, steadied his rolling brain, and smiled.

"Let's go Phillies!" he said, heading for the living room.

If life was a bitch, vertigo was the head bitch in charge. Walking to the living room was like stumbling down a shifting hallway on a ship at sea.

To be more precise, *central vertigo* was the bane of his existence. It had been three years since the car accident. Getting T-boned off that exit on the Taconic Parkway had nearly killed him. The other driver was drunk as hell, blowing a 1.2 when the state trooper pulled her out of the car. Naturally, she was fine, though her Nissan SUV was barely good for scrap metal.

Matt's seatbelt had kept him from bouncing around the car like a pinball on speed, but even the airbag couldn't stop the car from crushing him. He'd fractured his sternum, broken the arm and leg on his left side, punctured a lung, had internal bleeding and lost most of the teeth on the left side of his mouth. The left side is where the Nissan had tried to cleave his car in two.

But the humdinger was the head trauma. He still swore it was the airbag that did it. Apparently, his brain had smacked against the inside of his cranium good enough to cause permanent damage. His short-term memory wasn't as sharp as it had been before the accident, and now he had migraines that made him wish the drunk bitch had just ended him right there at the Fahnestock Park exit.

The lasting injury that had really done a number on him was the persistent vertigo. For most people, vertigo was a passing malady, a temporary but disorienting condition or inner ear infection that liked to set their world off its axis from time to time.

Central vertigo was a different story. It stems from issues within the brain.

The doctors kept telling him he might just wake up and be fine one day, but that day had yet to come. Until it did, he spent every waking moment alternating between spins and nausea, his eyes sometimes rolling in their sockets uncontrollably. Treatments like the Epley Maneuver didn't help, nor did drugs like Meclizine. When things got real bad, he had diazepam, a fancy word for Valium, to help take things down a notch. The stuff left him logy, this side of useless. He tried not to take it too often, as tempting as it was to down them like popcorn throughout the day.

Naturally, he couldn't work, and the long-term disability had dried up a long time ago. Matt had always been a laborer. He loved working construction. Even when the weather was boiling hot or cold enough to freeze the snot in your nose, he ended the day with a sense of complete satisfaction. Being outside, and building things with his hands, was what he was meant to do. Vertigo robbed him of that. Inactivity withered his muscles and made him weak. He could no sooner swing a hammer than erase the national debt.

No one understood his frustration. Empathy could only go so deep. On his best days, he hated himself.

SSI paid some bills, but not near enough. When Debi was laid off from her teaching gig last year, it had finally broken them.

Matt stepped into the living room, taking a moment to watch his father watching the game. He hadn't aged well. He looked like a crazy prospector from the gold rush days. When was the last time he'd had a shower, or washed his clothes? It was a little embarrassing. Would West now assume he'd degenerate the same way?

"What's the score?" Matt said.

His father scowled, a finger of booze sloshing around the glass in his hand. "Phillies are down by five. They need a cleanup hitter worse than that president of ours needs a set of balls."

*Sports and politics.* His father's favorite diatribes.

Matt settled into a loveseat next to his father's lounger. All told, there was one couch, three loveseats, and two lounge chairs in the room. None of them matched. They all looked like he'd taken them from someone's trash. None of this furniture had been here when he was growing up, but it all looked older.

A million motes of dust floated in the shafts of sunlight that dared to stab through the yellowed blinds.

"Have you ever been to the new stadium?" Matt asked, steering as hard as he could away from politics.

"Why would I spend all that money when I can watch them here?" He took a swig from his glass.

"I was there once. It was nice except for one thing."

His father's gaze moved to the corners of his eyes. "What's that?"

Matt smirked. "It was full of Phillies fans."

"You still in love with those pussy Yankees? Yeah, you would be. Anyone soft in the head can root for the front runner."

Matt struggled to keep from laughing. How much did the fates hate him to send him crawling back to the one place he swore he'd never return? And now there wasn't even his mother to break things up from time to time.

"What the hell's so funny?"

The crowd roared when the Braves centerfielder made a diving catch for the third Phillies out. Boos rained down on the Braves as they trotted off the field.

"I'm just happy to be back, pop," Matt said.

His father scowled at him as if he had a screw loose.

# CHAPTER THREE

West came down for dinner when his mother called up to him that there were grilled cheese sandwiches in the pan. He hoped the bread didn't have mold. He ate with her in the kitchen. She served his father and Grandpa Abraham in the living room. He'd stopped there long enough to see the Phillies were mounting a comeback. It was seven to five and the Phils had two on with one out in the eighth. Both men were engrossed in the game.

The plates she found were thin and cracked, the blue design on the circumference nearly worn off. He was afraid to touch it lest it shatter. Carefully, he picked up his grilled cheese. It was just the way he liked it, a little burnt on the edges, the cheese so hot it poured out like lava when he bit into it.

"Good job," he said, fanning his open mouth.

"I wish there was something I could give you on the side, but all I found was a can of sardines and hash. I didn't think you'd go for either."

"Maybe that's why old people smell that way," he said. "It's their diet."

She ruffled his hair. "Then I promise your father and I won't spend our golden years eating fish and hash in a can, offending your delicate senses."

He raked his hair back in place with his fingers, careful to first wipe the cheese off on his pants. Why did she insist on doing that? He wasn't five. It was an old habit she'd resurrected over the past year, as if pretending he was younger would make them forget how crappy the present had become.

"Sorry," she said, biting her lip. "And I promise better food tomorrow after I've had a chance to go food shopping.

"It's okay," he said, eyes on his plate. Shifting gears, because he could feel her sadness building, he said, "Hey, who had the room I'm in?"

She nibbled on the corner of her sandwich. There was no way she'd eat more than half. "I think that was your Aunt Stella's."

"Did I ever meet her? I've heard you and Dad mention her before."

"No. She passed away when she was a little girl. I think she was seven or eight at the time. She was older than your dad. He doesn't remember much about her."

A shiver sprinted down his back. "I'm sleeping in a dead girl's room?"

His mother rolled her eyes. "She didn't die *in* the room. I thought you wanted to live in a haunted house."

Recovering as quickly as he could, he shrugged her off. "I didn't say it like it was a bad thing. It's just… weird."

"You have nothing to worry about. Your father said she drowned in a pond between this property and the next. I always thought that might explain why things were so tough growing up for your dad. I'm not sure how I'd be if I lost you. As parents, you can't imagine living without your children. Your grandmother, the few times I met her, always seemed a little lost. It was like a part of her was somewhere else, which I suppose was to be expected."

Swallowing a huge bite, West asked, "How about Grandpa Abraham? What was he like back when you first met him?"

She pushed her plate away, most of the grilled cheese untouched and cool. "If your grandfather is one thing, it's consistent. You get me?"

*Oh, I get it. A consistent asshole*, West thought.

To his mother, he smiled and slowly nodded.

"But your grandmother once confided in me that he was a sweet, loving man who loved to dance and sing."

"Grandpa Abraham dancing and singing?"

"She neglected to tell me when this incarnation of Abraham Ridley existed. I have a hard time even picturing him as a carefree child."

"You hear any more squirrels in the basement?" he asked. He'd been waiting for their little thumps ever since he sat down.

"I think they went to their little nests in the trees for the night."

He asked her to make another grilled cheese, which she did, but she had to use the end of the loaf of bread, the piece he usually tossed or ignored. Starving because he'd skipped that horrid lunch,

41

he downed it anyway. When he looked in on his father and grandfather, they were both asleep, heads angled on their necks so they were leaning toward each other.

"Mom, check it out," he whispered, chuckling.

Grandpa Abraham was snoring like a wild boar. His empty glass was nestled in his crotch.

West guessed his father had taken one of those anxiety pills. The only time he slept this early was when he was on those meds. He couldn't blame him tonight. They all needed something to take the edge off.

Although with Grandpa Abraham asleep, the mood in the house made a definite, positive shift. It was like stepping out of the driving rain into a warm, dry shelter.

His mother found two old, crocheted blankets draped over the empty lounge chair, gaps in the weave large enough to stick your leg through. She gingerly placed them over the both of them, motioning for him to back out of the room.

"I almost want to take a picture. They look so cute," she said.

Unlike most of his friends, West didn't have a cell phone. That was one of the first 'luxuries' to go. His parents promised they would get him one soon, now that they had cut their expenses to the bone.

"They're all yours. I'm going upstairs to read," West said.

She pulled him in to kiss his forehead. "After we meet the movers at the storage place tomorrow, how about we grab some lunch out? There's a great diner a few miles away that serves huge plates that could feed an army for under five bucks."

"That sounds cool. Goodnight, Mom."

He knew she was trying to make this as easy on him as possible. It would be too cliché to play the pissed off teen, huffing and bemoaning their situation every time he opened his mouth. That phase had come and gone when the shit first hit the fan. Flashing her a smile, he headed up the stairs.

The shadows in the house had deepened. There was a light fixture in the ceiling of the upstairs hallway, but he couldn't find the switch.

Walking past his grandfather's room, he caught the spoiled scent of laundry way overdue for a trip to the washing machine. He wondered if the man ever changed his sheets. He looked like a dirty sheet kind of guy.

The nicked and scarred floorboards creaked mightily. Grandpa Abraham said he was in the bathroom a lot at night. West wondered how long it would take him to get used to the racket before he could sleep through it. Until then, he was sure each step would snatch him from his sleep.

The green paint on the walls was flaking in too many places to count. The floor was littered with broken bits of plaster from the ceiling.

He had to admit, it was kind of creepy up here alone. Was it the good, fun kind of creepy, or the crap your pants kind of creepy? The jury was still out.

Closing his door so he couldn't see down the hallway, he grabbed a random book from his shelf. It was Brian Keene's *Ghoul*, one of his favorites. He'd read it at least four times.

Settling into his bed that was more of a beanbag chair, minus most of the beans, he flipped the dog-eared pages to the first chapter. Laying the open book on his chest, he reached for his headphones and put them on, selecting New Year's Day from his playlist. The band described their music as haunted house rock, with lead singer Ash Costello belting out eerie melodies atop a hardcore, gothic beat. They were the perfect complement to this entire day.

Reading *Ghoul*, his eyes kept shifting to the words over the bed.

WE SEE YOU

Who the hell would write that on a ceiling? And who was the message for?

The storage facility was in a nearby town called Stroudsburg. It had a pretty cool Main Street lined with shops, Irish bars, and small restaurants. It wasn't much of a drive but it would be really hard for him to walk to it. It was a shame, because he could see himself wandering the place over the summer, finding the best spots to hang out, maybe even meet some kids his own age.

West spotted a small record store that sold vinyl. Vinyl! He'd heard that vinyl was the one true medium to listen to music the way it was supposed to be heard. A few of his friends had jumped on the record bandwagon last year when places like Barnes & Noble started selling reissues of classic like AC/DC's *Back in Black*, Led Zeppelin's *Led Zeppelin IV*, and *End of the Century* by The Ramones. It was a cool way to gain exposure to music they might have never caught on to. Anthony had a portable record player that he'd set up with wireless speakers.

Newer rock bands jumped on board, much to West's delight. He thought the old stuff from the 70s was cool, but he preferred his bands like Five Finger Death Punch, White Zombie, and Motionless in White. He wondered if the store carried their albums.

He also wondered if he'd ever get a record player.

Even though it was the first week of July, the weather was cool. The sun slipped in and out of the slow moving clouds. The street was pretty busy for late morning. West liked it. It felt more like home. Nothing like that old farmhouse in the middle of nowhere.

His mother's phone rang.

"Yeah. We're not far. Okay, we'll meet you there."

Dropping her phone in her pocketbook, she said, "The movers are five minutes away. We better hustle so we can make sure they don't break anything."

Because there was no room for all their stuff at Grandpa Abraham's, they had to rent the storage unit. He'd heard his father argue his case that they should have just sold all the furniture, but his mother wasn't having it.

West was glad his mother won out. It gave him hope that someday soon, maybe, he'd be back in his own bed.

The movers were muscular Hispanic guys with matching shaved heads and tattoos on their forearms. One had a warm smile, one of his top front teeth gleaming gold, and the other looked like he'd rather be anyplace but here. West felt a kinship with the scowling dude.

It only took a little over an hour. These guys were as fast as they were strong.

After they were done, his mother slipped the new padlock in place and they went out to lunch at the diner she'd told them about.

When their plates arrived, his father said, "It's good to see some old things remain the same. When I was a kid, you could eat until you burst for two bucks."

"You must have come here a lot, because you had a little more around the middle back then," his mother said, poking his stomach with her fork.

West had the cheeseburger deluxe, the burger so big, the bun could barely contain it. And there were enough fries to feed three. He slathered them in salt, pepper, and ketchup, letting it all marinate before he dove in.

No shock, his mom had a salad with no dressing. He did get her to eat two fries, which was a small victory.

"I know it's hard to think about more food, but we are stopping at a supermarket before we go back to… home, right?" West said.

"That's a necessity, unless we want to live off moldy liverwurst," his mother replied.

"Maybe Grandpa Abraham will loosen up if we make him our fresh sauce and meatballs," West said.

His mother smiled. "Spoken like a true man who thinks with his stomach. That's a very good idea."

They stopped at a ShopRite and filled a cart with essentials. His father waited in the car, holding his head. The spins had taken over. He'd definitely hit his limit for the day. West knew it frustrated him, not being able to do something as simple and mundane as food shopping. It frustrated all of them.

Driving away from Stroudsburg felt a little like leaving home all over again. West watched civilization fade away, stores and crowds and humanity replaced by flat farmland.

There was a surprise waiting for them when they pulled up to the farmhouse.

At least ten cats were on the porch, faces dipped into three bowls that had been laid out for them. He could tell they were outdoor cats because they were long and lean and a little on the raggedy side.

"Are those all Grandpa Abraham's?" West said.

His father squinted through his headache, taking in the mewling posse of felines.

"I've never known him to like cats before, or even dogs for that matter. I wasn't allowed to have pets. It looks like he's become the crazy old cat guy."

"How are we going to get past them, Matt? Some of them could be territorial."

West jumped out of the car. "I'll clear the way, Mom."

"West, be careful! We don't know if they have rabies."

Mothers were so exasperating. Every stray animal had rabies, every lawn had poison ivy lying in wait, and Halloween candy was full of razors and poison.

A black and white cat with pale, yellow eyes looked up from its feast when he stepped onto the small porch.

"Hey you, getting your lunch on?"

He stroked between its ears. It bumped its head against his leg, and then went back to eating. He petted tails and backs, most of the cats ignoring his presence. When the food was gone, they peeled off one-by-one.

He looked back to his mother, who stood by the car with a couple of shopping bags.

"That wasn't so scary, was it?" West said, wiping cat hair off his hands.

"I'm not a big cat fan."

"I know. You tell me that whenever you see a cat from fifty feet away."

"Okay, smarty, go grab some bags."

West nudged the bowls aside so they wouldn't trip over them. He found a folded piece of paper under one of them. He picked it up and unfolded it. It was a note. He read it out loud.

"*A gift for the new blood.*"

"What the heck are you talking about?" his father said. He leaned against the car, his cane a tripod between his legs.

"That's what the note says."

West handed it to his mother. Man, was it weird.

A tiny alarm chimed in the back of West's brain.

"Maybe your grandpa left it for the cats to read," she joked, dropping it in one of the bags. "I'll ask him."

As they stepped into the house, he thought he heard distant pounding, but it was hard to tell through the clatter of their own footsteps on the creaky floor.

"Wait, stop," West said.

His mother sighed irritably. "Why?"

Nothing.

*Okay, now I'm hearing things.*

"Never mind."

# CHAPTER FOUR

Grandpa Abraham was nowhere to be found. After they got all of the bags inside, they took turns calling for him.

"Guess he's out doing whatever the hell he does," West's father said. "I'd lay my money on him warming a stool at the Post, playing poker."

"Can he still drive?" West's mother asked, filling the refrigerator with milk, eggs, cheese, and yogurt. "I know he has that junker Dodge outside, but it looks like it hasn't been turned on for years."

"Lord only knows. Hey, he has his routine. I plan on keeping out of his business as much I can."

West found the pantry. It took some effort opening the door. The wood had warped, scraping against the floor. Inside the small room were empty shelves, brooms with frazzled bristles and lots of empty, dusty mason jars. An apron hung on a hook on the back of the door. It smelled old and musty, so much so that he had to step away and let it air out.

"When's the last time this was opened?" he said, waving at the air.

"That was my mother's domain." His father leaned forward in his chair enough to peek inside. "Looks like he cleared everything out when she passed away and just closed it up."

"When did Grandma die? Didn't she used to give me those little root beer flavored lollipops?"

His father nodded with a sad smile. "That was her. She bribed you with candy every chance she got. You had a way of making her laugh. Now mind you, my mother was a pretty serious woman. I always wondered what she was like before she met my dad. I have a feeling she just adapted to his personality, though the good and happy parts shined through every now and then. Man, when you were born, she shined more than I'd ever seen her. You had just turned six when she died."

"What did she die of?" He stopped himself from asking if she died in the house. Even if she did, he wasn't sure his father would admit it to him.

He tapped the center of his chest. "She had a bad heart. Smoked like a fiend until she was in her fifties. The doctor eventually convinced her to quit, but the damage was done. It's why your mother and I tell you all the time we'll beat your ass if you take up smoking."

West looked out the window over the ancient sink. A lone figure was walking in the field toward the house. Leaning on the lip of the sink, he teetered forward until his nose brushed against the screen. The sharp tang of metal and dust made him totter back to his feet.

"He's coming now. Looks like he went out for a walk or something."

His mother cast a quick glance.

"He's having a heck of a conversation with himself, too," she said.

He looked angry, hands balled into fists, lips moving furiously, occasionally breaking into a tight grimace. The breeze had blown his hair this way and that, an indignant Einstein on the prowl.

"I'm going to lie down," his father announced, pushing his chair away from the table. The legs screeched like frightened mice. He hobbled to the bedroom, closing the door.

His mother stopped unpacking, crossing her arms over her chest, looking back out the window. "Help me get these last few things put away."

Boxes of cereal and rice were stacked in a cabinet next to rusted cans of condensed milk and a jar of honey that looked to be older than the house. West remembered that honey was the only food that never went bad. Honey buried with Pharaohs was still edible.

He wondered who would be fool enough to test that theory and down a spoonful of three thousand year old honey.

When they were done, his mother said, "I have to get my stuff ready for tomorrow. You can hang in your room or go outside and explore a little."

"It's nice out. I think maybe I'll see what's around the house."

His mother made it out of the kitchen just as Grandpa Abraham came in the back door. West was trapped under his narrow gaze.

"What are you up to?" Grandpa Abraham huffed.

He steadied himself. His grandfather looked truly demented. Half his stained shirt was untucked from his pants. There were holes in the knees, and most of the belt loops had broken off. His hands were filthy, as if he'd been making mud pies in the field.

"We did some food shopping. I was helping put everything away."

"Did you get tuna fish? I asked your mother for tuna fish."

"I thought I saw some cans. I think we put them in there." He pointed to a cabinet behind his grandfather's left shoulder. The old man looked at it but didn't bother opening the door.

"You better not have moved my stuff," he grumbled, washing his hands.

*What stuff?* Talk about the cupboards being bare.

West decided it was probably best to head for the safety of the outdoors. This whole moving the family together was like introducing a new cat to the house. You had to keep the old and new cats separated for the first few days until they became acclimated to each other's presence.

And speaking of cats…

"Hey, are all those cats your pets?"

Grandpa Abraham whipped his head around. "What cats?"

West took an involuntary step back. "The ones you fed outside. I counted ten. I bet you get a lot of strays out here."

He stormed past West, bounding for the front door. "I don't feed any goddamn cats."

Despite every cell in his being urging him to walk away, West found himself following his grandfather. He slammed the screen door open and stood glaring at the empty bowls.

"You didn't put these here?" Grandpa Abraham said.

"No. They were there when we got home."

West's shoulders jerked back when his grandfather kicked the bowls off the porch. They shattered on the ground, shards of ceramic sprinkling the glass like hail. His eyes swept left and right, either looking for the cats or the person who dared to feed them.

"You see any cats again, don't go letting them in the damn house, you hear me?" he bellowed. "I'm allergic to the damn things."

"I… I won't. Who do you think was feeding them?"

He was too afraid to even bring up the note under the bowl.

"You see a cat, you have my permission to shoot it," was all he said before stomping back into the house.

✠

West wasn't afraid to admit, to himself at least, that his grandfather's outburst scared him just a little. He didn't just seem worried about the cats making him allergic. No, it went deeper than that. West really didn't know the man at all, but he knew what fear looked like. Grandpa Abraham had it in spades.

Of course, he wasn't the friendliest guy on the planet. It wasn't a stretch to consider that someone who had crossed his path had decided to have some fun at his expense. It could have been a neighbor or even kids like him, fucking with the weird old guy who lived on the farm that produced nothing but weeds and stray cats.

He went for a walk, hoping some fresh air would clear his head. A little walking would also help him digest that mongo burger. There was a moment back at the diner when he felt the meat sweats coming on. But it was so good, he'd powered through.

Shuffling until he came to the back of the farmhouse, he was amazed by how far he could see without spotting another house or road. Swaying fields of some kind of tall grass undulated like the wave pool at Splashdown Park.

There was a rotted picnic table and benches just before the overgrown greenery started. West tested his weight on a bench with one foot. When the wood didn't crack or give way, he dared to stand on it with both feet. Feeling bold, he did the same with the table until he was sure he could stand on it without demolishing the whole thing to splinters.

*Splinters that'll end up in my ass!*

Back home, their real home, his neighbor's houses were less than ten feet away. The street they lived on had twenty-three homes – eleven on his side of the street and twelve on the other. He knew because he'd counted them over and over again on walks to and from school or the corner store. Most of them were multi-family houses and he knew just about everyone who lived in them. People didn't move out very often, and when someone died, their kids usually moved back to continue a family tradition of ownership. There were always people outside, especially in the summer. Mrs. Hanrihan played cards with her friend Sister Martha in front of her house, two folding chairs set up on opposite sides of a portable aluminum table. Sister Martha was retired, living in the convent by their church two blocks away. West had heard that she and Mrs. Hanrihan were childhood friends. They'd taken their vows together, but sly Mrs. Hanrihan had fallen in love with the widowed father of a student when she taught at the same grammar school – St. Eugene's – that he went to. It must have been one hell of a scandal back in the day.

There were lots of kids on the block, most of them younger than West. They made pests of themselves, but at least they gave the neighborhood life.

Lawns were always being mowed by men in plaid shorts, black socks, and sandals. The Lawn Geeks, as West had named them. Cars rolled by every few minutes, traffic increasing after five p.m. on weekdays as everyone headed home.

The neighborhood was a breathing entity, a place of comforting familiarity. It was his home.

Out here, on the farm, there was nothing but a circling turkey vulture a hundred yards away. West wondered what it had its eye on. He hoped it wasn't a cat.

He spotted a giant pile of cracked and rotted lumber fifty yards out, close to the line of apple trees that looked to stretch on forever.

"At least we'll have fresh apples in the fall."

His foot crunched on a three-foot long stick. It was gnarled and thick, a perfect walking stick and weed slasher. Whisking it back and forth, he swatted at the wild vegetation, heading for the woodpile. It would make a great bonfire. He'd never been to one in person, but he'd seen plenty in movies, especially the flicks from the 80s with teen campers in peril. West loved those movies, especially the parts where girls took off their shirts and either went skinny-dipping or had sex in the woods or an empty cabin. Actresses took their clothes off a lot back then. He'd never even seen a naked boob until Anthony showed him this strange astronaut/vampire flick called *Lifeforce*. The girl vampire was totally naked, front and back, for half the movie. West's mind was blown. *Horror, sci-fi, and his first naked woman.* The constant flip-flopping between arousal and terror left him both exhausted and too tired to sleep that night.

Something crashed through the brush to his left. He stopped, the hairs on the back of his neck rising.

There was a garbled growl. The sounds of two cats tussling gave his nerves sweet relief. Not wanting to get in the middle of their fight, he veered to the right.

Closing in on the haphazard mound of wood, he realized what it was.

The farm would have had a barn at one time. It must have collapsed decades ago. The old walls and floorboards were blighted by the sun and elements. The stench of decay grew stronger with each step. Weeds grew through the gaps, some of them so thick, they hid whole sections of the former barn.

"I wonder what took you down," he said, lifting boards here and there with the tip of his sneaker. The ground beneath it was black as pitch and had an odd smell, like something scorched and long forgotten.

Could have been a fire. Or maybe it was a storm, some hurricane that sent people to their cellars.

That is, if hurricanes happened in this part of Pennsylvania.

Did Grandpa Abraham's place have a storm cellar?

And what about a fruit cellar? He heard about them all the time, especially when it came to places for crazed killers to hide bodies. What was the point of a fruit cellar? Why stick your fruit in some hole?

There was sudden movement in the brush behind him. He waited for one of the cats to slink into view.

The sound didn't repeat itself and no cats came out to play.

West felt the hairs stand up on the back of his neck. He had the very uncomfortable feeling that he was being watched. Out here, surrounded by the tall grass, anyone could be lurking.

He closed his eyes and saw the words on the ceiling over his bed.

WE SEE YOU

West was suddenly very uncomfortable. All of this was so alien to him, he felt as if he'd stepped into a place where he didn't belong.

"Time to go back inside."

He trudged away from the collapsed barn, unable to shake the feeling that there were eyes at his back.

# CHAPTER FIVE

Getting up at five in the morning hadn't been easy. Debi Ridley dragged herself out of bed, shuffling like a wounded zombie to the bathroom. She looked at her hollow-eyed reflection in the mirror, wincing at the deep pillow lines on her face. Just a few years ago, those lines would disappear by the time she got out of the shower. Now, it would take an hour or more, the youthful elasticity of her skin giving way to the doughy sag of middle age.

"Welcome to your dream commute," she said soft enough so Matt couldn't hear. He'd had a rough night − part of a long succession of rough nights − his vertigo making it difficult to keep his eyes closed.

When it got bad like that, his mood darkened, even more so than usual.

He used to be so much fun. They laughed all the time. Debi's friends envied the fact that she'd married a man who was more than her husband. He was her best friend, the kind that went out of his way to pick her up whenever she was down. And it was hard to be down around Matt.

*It's not his fault.*

It seemed to take forever for the shower to run hot, and when it did, it didn't last long. Debi jumped out of the tub the second the water turned to ice, conditioner still in her hair. She had to rinse the rest out in the sink.

It was pitch black when she got in the truck, her thermos filled with hot coffee. She'd been worried that she'd run into Abraham, but he was either asleep or keeping to his room to avoid her. Matt had said he'd always been an early riser, keeping farmer's hours while avoiding the actual labor needed to run the derelict farm.

She pulled into the lot in Marshall's Creek and waited for the bus to take her to Manhattan. With ten minutes to spare, she poured a cup of coffee, the caffeine helping to prop her eyes open.

When the bus pulled up, she and several dozen others emerged from their cars. The commute to the city was supposed to take just under two hours. She'd made sure to pack a book and several magazines.

Settling into a plush seat near the front, she leaned back and stared out the window as the bus merged onto Route 80. The same people must take this bus every weekday, but no one was talking. It was too damn early for idle chit-chat.

Four hours on a bus every day.

Debi didn't know whether it would be a blessing or a curse. It would be time to herself, hours away from her problems.

Getting up super early and arriving home late every day was a big con. When New Yorkers flocked to the Poconos for affordable houses twenty years ago, the early pioneers, as they liked to be called, said the commute was worth the money they saved and laid back lifestyle they enjoyed in the mountains and valleys of Pennsylvania.

Cut to five years later, and the lamenting began. Houses were sold or converted to summer homes.

It was a hell of a trip, five days a week.

More than anything, Debi worried about West. With her gone for so long each day, he was stuck with a father who could barely hold himself together and a grandfather who, on a good day, was as warm as an igloo.

*Please don't let this last long*, she thought, the rock and sway of the bus tempting her to fall back to sleep.

*Maybe I could find a job in PA. But then what happens when we rebuild our finances and it's time to get out of Dodge? I'll have to find another job in New York and who knows how long that'll take. We'll be right back where we started.*

As much as she disliked it, logically, she had to keep her job.

Sure, an administrative assistant position wasn't particularly lofty, but she did work for a private equity firm in midtown. The pay wasn't the best but the benefits were decent. God knows, that had become more important than ever.

Leaving teaching behind for this had seemed exciting a year ago, for more reasons that simply embarking on a new chapter in her life. The rewards of being with her second grade class of beautiful young minds were far outweighed by the burdens of teaching in the modern age.

Of her twenty-one students, fourteen were on prescription meds for ADHD, social anxiety, and other disorders. It broke her heart to see them shuffle into class, listless as the living dead – dull and silent, like the people in the seats around her. Children were supposed to be boisterous. How could you teach kids whose brains were dulled by pharmaceuticals?

And then there were the parents – helicopter moms and dads who questioned every poor grade, demanding she change it because their child was smarter than any other child in the world. She, and all of the schools in her district, was at their mercy. Threats of lawsuits or pulling their kids – and the tuition dollars – from the school left her and the other teachers little more than hostages.

When common core was introduced, Debi was almost relieved to be let go. It was one less hill of bureaucratic idiocy she had to climb. She pitied the teachers and students who had to wade through that mess.

Working in an office had taken some time getting used to. She no longer had little people looking up to her, hanging on her every word.

64

But there were other perks. Attention from people old enough to tie their shoes was a big one.

The sign for Denville whizzed by. Forcing herself to stay awake, she turned the small overhead light on and opened a magazine.

At least the bus was comfortable.

✠

The first time Matt tried to get out of bed, the ceiling slipped beneath his feet. He fell back, tangling himself in the sheets. He lay there for a while, fixating on the overhead light, trying to maintain some sort of focus. When his head felt steadier, he slowly sat up, grabbed his cane from beside the night table and stood.

Every little damn thing was a process. Some days, the process was more complex, the act of simply standing near impossible.

He hated his brain, his betrayer. Why couldn't it heal itself? Did it enjoy this existence? He couldn't count the number of times he fantasized about cracking his own skull open, dredging up the damaged bits with an ice cream scoop and tossing them in the toilet. Only then could he flush this waking nightmare away.

*Good riddance. I hope the fish eat you quick and shit you out.*

It was an insane image. Frustration gave him a lot of crazy thoughts. Standing in his childhood bedroom, the one place he never wanted to see again, was crazier than anything his seething mind could conjure.

The floor creaked overhead. West must be awake.

Day one of the three Ridley men at home, cooped up together. He couldn't tell if the knot in his stomach was from the usual nausea or the sinking reality of where life had dumped them. Swallowing hard, he resolved to make it a good day.

*Just think happy thoughts.*

Yeah, right.

The moment he opened the bedroom door, he smelled eggs and coffee. The kitchen was empty, but in the sink were the frying pan, one plate, one bowl, a coffee cup, fork and knife. His father must have already eaten. Debi ate breakfast at work and West hated eggs.

He wondered where the old codger was. Had to be outside.

Looking out the kitchen window, he saw a piece of paper fluttering in the early morning breeze. It was clipped to the clothesline.

"Give the kid a break," he said, heading for the door.

Growing up, Matt found notes all over the house daily, each one outlining a chore that needed to be done. His father never verbally told him to do anything; it was all communicated by notes, with scribbles of allowance to be earned. He always did the work, but rarely saw the allowance.

*Room and board. That's your allowance. You like to eat, don't you? I sure as shit don't see you thumbing our nose at your mother's cooking!*

*You like that bed? How about the roof and walls when it's raining or cold outside?*

*Now clean that shit up like I wrote down and stop talking nonsense about getting paid. You're not some Jew lawyer. This ain't a courtroom. You can plead your case to the walls if you like.*

It looked like his crazy old man was reviving that tradition.

"Not with my son," he rumbled, going out the back door. West wasn't here to be his step and fetch. Yes, he'd help out, but Matt would be damned if he'd let that note nonsense start up again.

His hand shook as he ripped the slip of paper from under the pinched clothespin. His rage was always boiling just under the surface lately. It didn't take much for it to spill over.

In a way, he was glad his father wasn't around. He wasn't sure he'd be able to control himself right about now.

Matt opened the note.

The shock set him on his ass. His cane rolled out of his grasp.

His eyes twitched; a vertigo precursor. He had to wait for them to settle down before he could read the note again.

WE WILL ALWAYS BE HERE. *WE* HAVE ALWAYS BEEN HERE. WE SEE THE BLOOD THAT RUNS THROUGH THE VEINS OF THIS HOUSE. KNOW THIS – WE HAVE NEVER STOPPED WATCHING. WE ARE STILL THE GUARDIANS.

"No."

Matt crumpled up the paper, stuffing it in the waistband of his pajama shorts. He crawled on his hands and knees for his cane. It was a supreme struggle getting to his feet. His head was full, as if someone had jammed a pneumatic air pump in his ears and gave it all it had. His legs quivered, knees threatening to give way at any moment. The cane became an oar. He planted it in the ground, pulling himself forward, the muscles in his arms and back straining. With a grunt he pulled it free, jamming it into the soil several feet forward. Once he was inside the house, he locked the door and leaned against it, panting.

WE ARE STILL THE GUARDIANS.

He balled his fists and punched the door. A splinter pierced his knuckle, his blood staining the wood.

What had he done?

West had spent the night tossing and turning, which was no easy feat in the slumping mattress. He was uncomfortable, but it was his mind that kept him up. He just couldn't seem to shut it down.

He almost wished summer vacation were over. Going to a new school, starting high school no less out here in Bumb Fuck, PA, had worried him at first. Now, he'd welcome the chance to get out of the house for seven hours a day.

Until then, he was trapped.

Putting on a sleeveless T-shirt emblazoned with the movie poster for *The Descent* and cargo shorts, he crept down the stairs, listening out for his grandfather. The house was quiet. He'd heard someone puttering around earlier and smelled breakfast. West thought it was best to wait them out, no matter how much his stomach rumbled.

Eyes darting to the kitchen, he saw the coast was clear.

*Thump!*

The sudden noise sounded as if it came from within the hallway wall. West froze, his heart pausing its steady rhythmic beat, every sense reaching out for the source of the sound.

*There's something behind me*, West thought. The flesh on the back of his neck chilled. It was the same feeling he used to get when he was little and had to go to the basement to get something for his mother or father. It was that dire sense that he wasn't alone, that something hungry and sinister was just a hand swipe away, waiting for the perfect moment.

*Ungh.*

*What the hell was that?*

It happened so fast, the quick release of a pent up breath somewhere near, but nowhere he could zero in on, that he wasn't sure he actually heard it.

It could have been a spasm of his own lungs, itching to exhale, which he now did.

*Just turn around. There won't be anything there, just like there was never a monster in the basement. It's all in your head.*

Except there had never been muffled sounds in the basement. It was all just his childhood imagination run wild.

He couldn't deny what he'd heard just now.

*Wait. Where's Grandpa Abraham? It's probably just him poking around the basement again.*

That first hard thwack hadn't come from below. He was certain of it.

*Turn... around... now!*

West steeled himself and spun, his hands balled into fists.

To his great relief, the hallway was empty. A square of sunlight peering through the glass pane in the front door was at his feet. The only thing trailing him was dust motes caught in the shaft of light.

*Idiot.*

For all his talk about wanting to be a paranormal investigator one day, he sure was jumpy. He was supposed to run *to* weird sounds, not *from* them.

Now all he wanted to do was grab something to eat and a bottle of water and get the hell out. He had a Jack Ketchum paperback in his back pocket and his iPod clipped to the collar of his shirt. That would be enough to keep him busy for most of the day. If he could somehow stay out of the house until his mother came home, he'd be happy.

Jamming the blueberry Pop Tarts under his arm, he yanked the refrigerator door open, plucking a bottle of store brand water from the top shelf. When he closed the door, his grandfather was standing beside him.

"Where the hell are you going in such a rush?"

The basement door was shut tight. He hadn't been down there.

But the pantry door was open. Grandpa Abraham held a can of coffee in both hands.

West jumped, dropping the water and Pop Tart. Bending down to pick them up, the book popped out of his pocket.

"I… I'm just going outside."

Grandpa Abraham wore a beige dress shirt that might have been white at one time. All of the buttons were undone, revealing pale flesh covered in coarse, white hair. He scratched at the coils between his saggy man boobs.

"You look like a jackrabbit in a fox den."

"A what?"

"Something scare you, short stuff?"

West's compulsion for flight veered toward the need to fight.

"I'm not scared," he said.

Grandpa Abraham huffed. "Well, you sure look it. That how you always look in the morning?" He started to laugh, then cocked his head and said, "I told you this house is never empty. I thought you said you liked the idea. Funny how thinking about something and actually experiencing it can change a man's perspective, isn't it?"

"I'm not afraid. I'm just hungry and want to get outside. I think my blood sugar is low."

West didn't care if his grandfather believed him or not. He just wanted out.

Grandpa Abraham's features softened, to the point where his eyes shined with a sort of paternal pity laced with sympathy.

"Nothing's gonna hurt you, unless you give yourself a heart attack."

"Thanks. I'll remember that."

Before West could head out the back door, he added, "I wouldn't go too far if I were you. You don't want to go wandering onto someone else's property. It's not the suburbs. You can't just walk on your neighbor's lawn. Out here, people get very particular about who steps over their boundaries. You know what I mean?"

Fuck no, West had no idea. Would they call the cops? Scream and holler like a madman? Take a shot at him with a rifle that had been passed down for generations? Or worse?

He shuddered thinking what worse could be.

"I'll just find a spot to read my book," he said, inwardly recoiling at the tremor in his voice.

The house suddenly felt like a living entity, closing in on him like a massive hand. And the only thing keeping him here, in danger, was his pain in the ass grandfather.

As he grabbed the door handle, Grandpa Abraham barked, "Hey! Remember what I said. You don't want to go losing your head or something. Outsiders have to be extra careful around here."

His mouth turned up in a cruel smile, but there was no mirth in his eyes. West shivered. He turned his back and left, not wanting to spend another moment in the decaying farmhouse.

West ran, hoping he remembered how to find the old barn. He was out of breath by the time it popped into view.

What had they gotten themselves into?

West thought they'd hit rock bottom before.

He was wrong.

There was another level to the shit pile their lives had sunken into.

Grandpa Abraham was weird. As weird as the house. Maybe visiting a haunted house seemed cool, but it was a far cry from actually living in one.

He fought back the urge to cry.

He thought about screaming.

Instead, he brooded.

They should never have come here.

# CHAPTER SIX

Hunger and thirst and a need to get out of the increasingly oppressive heat drove West back to the farmhouse hours earlier than he'd hoped. Plus, there was just so much nature he could take. He'd discovered that he wasn't a fan of the constant, grating cries of hawks. The damn things circled overhead ceaselessly. He waited outside the back door, listening for his grandfather.

It was just past four and already the crickets were out in force. Last night, they'd kept him company while he lay in bed, a lullaby that didn't quite work. Taking a quick peek to make sure the coast was clear, he opened the screen door, flinching as it creaked.

He stopped, one foot inside, ear cocked.

Nothing.

He had to slip in sideways to make it through the sliver of an opening without inviting more protestations from the ungreased hinges.

The TV was on, a commercial for catheters booming. His father never turned the sound up that loud. Good. At least he knew Grandpa Abraham's location.

Slowly opening the refrigerator, he pocketed two bottles of water. His mother said she wouldn't be home until seven. He felt as dehydrated as jerky. They would hold him over for the next couple of hours.

This time when he closed the fridge, there no one waiting on the other side of the door to scare the life out of him.

He wished he could recharge his iPod, but there was no way he was hanging around that long.

West took a sleeve of crackers, an apple, and a granola bar.

The squealing door bothered him less on the way out now that he was sure it couldn't be heard over the TV. He cracked open a bottle, tossing the cap away and chugging it all down. Crushing the plastic bottle and stuffing it in his pocket, he made his way to the front of the house. There were a lot of trees bunched up along the driveway. Maybe it would be cooler there.

West pulled up short when he came upon his father standing outside, staring at the house. Both hands gripped the cane propped in front of him. He looked like he was searching for something.

"Hey Dad."

His father blinked several times, then slowly looked his way. West saw his legs wobble a bit, but he was able to steady himself.

"Oh, hey, I was wondering where you've been all day."

West shrugged his shoulders. "I was just out back reading."

"Since this morning?"

"I was listening to music, too."

"Did you see anyone?"

That was a weird question to ask. As far as he was concerned, they were living on another planet, as far from civilization as a polar bear to the Amazon.

"No, why?"

His father's face darkened. "A simple no will do."

Uh oh, he was in one of his moods. They came as regularly as the traffic and weather reports on the news radio station.

Changing the subject, he asked, "You talk to Mom today?"

"No. She must be busy."

"I wonder how she liked the bus."

His father took a half-step toward him. "No one likes the bus, West. It's why the country is crowded with cars."

"But she said it had cushioned seats and folding tray tables and stuff. I thought it sounded cool."

"Yeah, well, when I was your age, I thought a lot of stupid shit was cool, too."

West knew where this was going. If love could be measured by restraint, his father would never question how he felt about him.

Waving his book, West said, "I have a few more chapters I want to get to. Do you need any help getting back inside?"

His father exploded, spittle dappling his lips. "Did I say I wanted to go inside? Did I ask for help? I'm not a goddamn cripple! I'm perfectly capable of being on my own!"

His initial shock at the severity of the outburst gave way to a trembling surge of tears that West fought to keep down. No way was he going to let him see him bawl like a baby. Tightening his fingers around the book until his knuckles hurt, he spun away, sprinting for the access road.

Fuck him! He *was* a goddamn cripple. How many times had he asked West to help him out of bed, onto the couch, to the bathroom, into the car? Not a day had gone by when he didn't need his help. Some people, when life kicked them in the balls, fought through the pain and got back on their feet. Watching his dad fold like a shirt, bit by bit of the man he knew drowning in self-pity, anger, and misery, was like standing vigil over a terminal patient. At what point was it morally okay to just pray for it all to end?

"Wait! West! Come back. I'm sorry."

West kept running. He wanted nothing to do with either of the men in that house. It was clear now that the apple didn't fall far from the rotten tree. Maybe this was why his father had stayed away all those years.

He couldn't stand to see his own reflection in Grandpa Abraham's face.

Debi was exhausted by the time she turned on to the long access road. She shouldn't have been, because she'd slept most of the ride back to PA. Just imagine how it would become in the fall and winter when the moon and stars were out at quitting time. She'd bet her right and left arms that the late nap would make it very hard to go to sleep later on.

Another adjustment to make.

*Add it to the list. Or you can find some way to keep awake. Just think about what you'll do when you win the lottery. Make it Power Ball.*

Turning into one of the many bends in the road, she smiled when she saw West leaning against a tree, waving to her. She stopped and rolled her window down.

"Boy, someone couldn't wait to see me," she said. He hopped inside and gave her a quick hug. Her heart stopped for the briefest of moments. She couldn't remember the last time West had willfully hugged her.

"I didn't want to be cooped up in the house all day," he said.

Something was off, but he looked so happy, and truth be told, she was basking in the show of affection. She didn't want to ruin the moment by asking him to spill the beans. She guessed at what could be eating him. It wasn't hard to fill the list of possibilities.

"How was work?"

"Same ol', same ol'. It feels strange getting home this late. Did your father or grandfather start anything for dinner?"

"I don't know."

She sighed. "Well, if they didn't, it's leftovers or PB&J sandwiches."

He turned to her and said, "I wish we never came here. I don't like Grandpa Abraham and I hate the house. Dad doesn't like it, either."

She tried her best to put a positive spin on things. "I know it's not the Ritz and your grandfather isn't exactly Santa Claus but we're together and safe and…"

She'd almost said healthy. That would have been a lie.

*Oh God, did we only make things worse coming here?*

When he didn't reply, all she could say was, "I'm sorry, honey."

Debi stopped the car, leaned over, and pulled him close.

He let her hold him for far longer than the teen two-second rule. It was hard to hate herself for putting him through all of this when having him so close felt so complete. Fathers could never understand what it was like to lose that easy affection, the years chipping away at the hugs and kisses until there were only head nods and the occasional high five.

She held his face in her hands. His scarlet cheeks were burning. She rested the back of her hand on his forehead to make sure he didn't have a fever.

"Do you think Grandpa Abraham's crazy?" he asked.

"Crazy? Why would you say that?"

He shrugged. "I don't know. He just seems… off. When was the last time you saw him? Maybe he lost it after Grandma died."

Oh, if he only knew.

Debi said, "The man in that house is the same man I met twenty years ago. He's a little dirtier, but underneath all that crust is the curmudgeonly center that's been there his entire adult life."

West's face lightened. "Curmudgeonly. Nice SAT word."

They both smiled. She dropped the car keys in her pocketbook. "I honestly thought I'd stump you on that one. I guess all those scary books are good for something."

She didn't add that she worried they were responsible for his imagination taking him to dark places like it did today. They had enough real life bad juju to deal with lately.

They walked to the house with her arm over his shoulder.

It was impossible to miss the blaring TV when they walked in the door. She shouted, "I survived my first day!"

She didn't get a reply.

She dropped her briefcase and took a moment to inspect West's face and neck. He'd gotten a nice little sunburn.

"Promise me you'll wear sunscreen tomorrow."

"Yeah, whatever."

"I'll see how you feel about that later when that burn settles in. I think I have some aloe vera gel somewhere. Hope it's not in a box in the storage unit."

Abraham was asleep in his chair. Where was Matt?

"I guess you haven't seen your father."

"Not for a while. He was out front last time I saw him."

Again, there was something he wasn't saying. Her mother's intuition was in overdrive tonight. Maybe the nap on the bus was a good thing. Sleep hadn't been easy for her, not as long as it had been an issue for Matt. They were both bleary-eyed most days.

"Well, I'm sure he'll turn up when he smells food."

Debi quietly worried that he had fallen somewhere outside. If she didn't see or hear him in a few minutes, she'd go outside to check.

She was just about to walk in the kitchen when something in the living room caught her eye. The early summer evening sun was making its last stab through the dusty blinds, illuminating the back wall. There was a large, rectangular mirror mounted on it. A hodgepodge of end tables, mismatched dining set chairs, and metal file cabinets kept the mirror out of reach, which would explain the ashy layer of dust.

What stopped her was the writing someone had made with their finger in the dust.

In huge block letters, it said: HELLO. HAVE A NICE NAP?

She looked to West. "That wasn't there yesterday, was it?"

His eyes were glued to the mirror. "No way. We all would have noticed *that*."

"Then who the heck... Abraham. Abraham!"

82

He lazily opened one eye. It seemed a great effort to roll his head to face them. "Whuu?"

"Did you see your mirror?" Debi said.

"My what? Why are you waking me up talking about mirrors?" He crossed his arms over his chest and shut his eyes.

"I'm talking about what's on the mirror. Did you write that?"

Both eyes snapped open. He slammed the leg rest down, the springs twanging like strings plucked on a warped harp. He waded through the junk furniture to get closer.

Debi saw the muscles in his back draw up. He scratched his head, then his ass.

"I never asked anyone to come here," he muttered so softly, she could just make out the words.

"What do you mean?" Debi asked.

Shrugging out of his threadbare shirt, Abraham used it to wipe the mirror clean, leaving behind rainbow arches of dust.

"Abraham, who wrote that? Was it Matt?"

He stormed out of the room without giving her so much as a parting glance. The sour pungency of his body odor lingered long after he was gone.

"Ooookay," West said. "Totally sane."

Debi ushered him into the kitchen. "I can't argue with you there. You want to help me get some semblance of a meal together?"

"Sure." West set the table while she popped the lids off of the Tupperware containers from the fridge.

*What the hell just happened here?* she thought. *Please don't tell me we've moved in just as Abraham is having dementia setting in. God, if you're testing us, please, we've been through enough.*

She smiled at West while he found glasses and silverware.

*All the more reason why I have to try to keep things as normal as possible for him.*

They looked up from their tasks when Matt appeared in the doorway. He held his cane in one hand and the back of a chair with the other. He looked terrible.

"Hey, I didn't hear you come home," he said. There was no warmth in his voice, no sense that he was happy to see her.

"I'm not surprised," Debi said. "Your father's TV could drown out a building demolition."

He turned back toward the living room. "Huh. I guess I'm already used to it."

She wanted to tell him about what West had been worried about, what they saw on the mirror and Abraham's bizarre reaction. But not now. Not in front of West. It would have to wait until later.

"Dinner will be ready before you know it."

She hoped Abraham would remain in his room.

If Matt had written on the mirror to get the old man's goat, in a way she was grateful. Abraham Ridley was an acquired taste, and after almost twenty years, even she still had a long way to go.

Dinner was mercifully quick and disturbingly weird. West's father kept shooting him glances over forkfuls of spaghetti, as if he wanted to talk about what had happened earlier. But he never did, so things were left in the air. West was still mad at him and not ready to accept an apology. Not this time.

"You want me to bring dinner up to Grandpa Abraham?" he asked when he'd practically licked his plate clean.

"I can ask him if he wants to come down," his mother said.

"It's fine. Hey, it's on my way. I want to bring my book and iPod back to my room."

He felt bad for being such a crybaby in the car with his mother. A blind man could see she was all torn up with guilt. He didn't need to pile on, but he was so pissed at his father, he needed to take it out on someone.

Maybe Grandpa Abraham wasn't all that bad. He'd never know unless he tried to get to know him better. He was his grandfather, after all.

"I think that would be nice," his father said, giving him a thumbs-up. "Maybe a little dinner in bed will help soften his stance on us interlopers invading his space."

His mother prepared a plate. When she went to pour a glass of milk, West said, "Wait. Maybe he'd like the stuff under the sink better." He pulled the curtain back to reveal several bottles of booze.

"How about something a little lighter, like a beer?" his father said, reaching over to fish a can out of the refrigerator. "He's still a Bud man." He handed the cold can to West.

"Are you sure that's a good idea?" his mom said.

"The man could drink varnish and wake up without a hangover. One beer won't hurt him."

The stairs popped and cracked as he carried the food and beer to his grandfather. He had to tap on his door with the toe of his sneaker.

"What?"

"I have dinner for you."

"Did I say I was hungry?"

"It's almost eight o'clock. I figured you would be. I have a beer, too."

The knob turned and the door opened. Grandpa Abraham was just sitting back down on the edge of the bed. He snatched the can from West's hand, popping the tab. After he took a long pull, he said, "You can put the plate over there." He motioned toward

86

the bedside table. On its surface were a couple of prescription bottles and a lamp. There was just enough room for the plate.

"Didn't we have that last night?" he grumbled.

"Mom didn't have time to make something new."

"Least I was hoping for out of this mess was some home cooked meals."

West went on the defensive. "That is a home cooked meal. We just made it last night. It's still good."

Grandpa Abraham's eyes rolled toward him, practically burning through him. West held his ground. His emotions had been all over the place today. He was too worn out to be afraid at this point.

"You're welcome," West said.

To his surprise, his grandfather chuckled. He drank the rest of the beer and crushed the can.

*Guess he doesn't get his cans redeemed.*

"You're not as much of a little fag as I thought you might be."

The *other* F-word was like a punch in the gut. It was just something that he and his friends never said. Like the C-word.

Was that supposed to be a compliment? The generation gap between them was wider than the Grand Canyon. West was only fourteen, but he understood that words changed their meaning from generation to generation. Like when he once said a girl in his class was ratchet in front of his parents and they looked at him as if he'd lost his command of the English language.

"She's a tool?" his father had said.

"No. Ratchet means ugly."

"I'll take you to my toolbox and show you what ratchet really means."

That was back when his father could easily walk down to the basement and grab his toolbox. Back when he still used those tools daily.

"What's the matter? Did you go mute on me?"

"No."

"Good. Wouldn't want to think I broke you. Why don't you get me another beer?"

He wanted to say, "Why don't you get it yourself? You're not crippled."

Instead, he said, "I could."

Grandpa Abraham ran his hand over his face. "Jesus Christ, you're not going to wait until I say please, are you? You're worse than a wife."

West couldn't resist a small smile. "You just said it. I'll be back."

He ran downstairs and grabbed another Budweiser.

Before West handed the beer over, he said, "I'll give you the beer if you can answer something honestly."

"It's my beer, so you don't have the option of keeping it from me."

The words sounded harsher than he looked when he said it. West held it out, but not close enough for him to grab it. His grandfather slouched back into a stack of grimy pillows by the headboard. He stared at the ceiling, heaving a couple of heavy sighs.

"You're one persistent little runt," he said. His stomach shook with a laugh. "You might not like hearing this, but I was the same way when I was your age."

West wasn't crazy about being called a runt, but Grandpa Abraham wasn't much taller. He wondered how much he'd been teased throughout his life. Maybe that's why he was so bulky, as a way to offset his small stature. God knows, West had considered downing protein shakes and lifting weights, if he had the money to purchase either.

"I've heard you say worse things," West replied. He stepped closer and handed the beer over.

Popping it open and slurping out the escaping foam, Grandpa Abraham said, "Okay, shoot."

"Were you serious when you told me the house is haunted?"

"Why you askin'?"

West played it close to the vest. "I just wanna know."

Grandpa Abraham studied him for an agonizing minute. "I knew something spooked you before." His blunt fingers got lost in the white tangle of his sprouting chest hair. "Look, this house has been around for a long time. It was built before Roosevelt was president. I mean Teddy, not that socialist FDR. Things happen in a house this old. Some of them good, some of them bad. The land itself has been in our family for two hundred years. Before that, it was all Unami Indian land. People have been living and dying here probably before that dago Columbus got his ass lost."

"What do you mean by bad things?" West wondered if he was going to regret opening this can of worms.

Grandpa Abraham stared wistfully out the window into the black blanket of night. "They say emotions can be left behind, just like spirits. These four walls have absorbed their fair share."

"Has… has anyone ever died in the house?" West's hands clenched in his pockets.

His grandfather nodded, eyes closed for a moment, as if he was recalling the names and faces of all those who has passed.

He drained the beer can dry and pointed at the floor by West's feet.

"Most recent was when I found your grandma right there. She'd been sick a while and stayed in bed all day and night. I'm not sure how she managed to get out on her own. I keep wondering if she knew the end was coming and was trying to get me. Everybody dies alone, but it's a comfort to have someone near. I was at the Post when it happened. If she wanted to haunt me, I guess it serves me right."

90

West didn't know what to say. For the first time since they'd arrived, his grandfather looked frail, vulnerable.

He was going to ask about his Aunt Stella, but decided against it. And there were all the questions he had about that strange writing on the mirror. Now wasn't the time.

"You want me to get another beer?"

"No, I'm done. I just want you to know this. You are never, ever alone in this house. Now I don't know if that'll keep you up nights excited or crapping yourself, but it's the truth. Even if we were all to walk out that door and drive far away, this old farmhouse will never be empty. Never."

West lingered in the doorway for a moment. The old man's voice was thick and raspy, sounding every bit the spent man. "Okay. Well, if I don't see you downstairs later, goodnight."

A head nod was all he got in reply.

Maybe Grandpa Abraham wasn't a total asshole. Just now, West couldn't help but feel the sadness and weariness that weighed the man down.

When it came to the crazy message on the mirror, it wasn't much of a stretch to consider his grandfather was the culprit, whether he was aware of his actions or not. Something wasn't quite right with him. Living out here alone all these years, surrounded by spirits and lingering bad energy, was enough to take a toll on anyone.

West lay on his bed, fiddling with his iPod. He kept glancing up at the words on his ceiling.

WE SEE YOU

What was with all the weird messages in this house?

*Maybe it really is haunted.*

West didn't know what to make of all of it, or how he felt. The possibility was as exciting as it was terrifying. If one of them was his grandmother, that should be a good thing, right? As for the other spirits, the remnants of bad energy, he wondered. Were they watching him now?

Of course they were. It said so on his ceiling.

# CHAPTER SEVEN

West awoke to the chaotic music of early birds chirping their fool heads off. The sun wasn't even up, but nature was ready to roll.

"I thought the country was supposed to be relaxing," he said, burying his ears in his pillow to no avail. He was on a damn farm, and the damn birds were making damn sure he didn't sleep like a normal teenager.

After quietly slipping into the bathroom to pee, he went back to his room and eyed the cardboard box of magazines they'd brought back from storage. He was up anyway. Might as well do something useful.

Using an X-acto knife, he peeled the flaps back. On top of the horror magazines were the carefully folded pictures that he had on his wall back home. A plastic tape dispenser and case of tacks had fallen to the side of the magazines. One-by-one, he took out the pictures, unfolded them, and placed them on the unmade bed.

If he was going to be here for a while, he needed to make this as much like home as possible. For West, home meant being surrounded by images from his favorite movies and stars.

There were stills from movies like *Paranormal Activity*, *It Follows*, *Hostel*, and the remake of *Dawn of the Dead*. He'd seen the original, but he preferred the fast zombies in the newer version. They were a lot scarier.

His favorite picture of Elvira in her black dress with the plunging neckline, reclining on a red velvet lounge chair, would be the centerpiece of the wall behind his bed. Bald and creepy Michael Berryman from *The Hills Have Eyes* and Nazi werewolves brandishing machine guns from *An American Werewolf in London* lay alongside 8 x 10 movie posters for *Halloween*, *Friday the 13th*, and *The Amityville Horror*. He wasn't alive when those movies came out – heck, his parents weren't even dating then – but he prided himself on knowing all the classics.

For the better part of an hour, he filled the walls with glossy and sometimes grizzly images. He'd had a poster of Scarlett Johansson but it ripped when he'd tried to take it down. He wondered if that record store in Stroudsburg had posters.

By the time he was finished, the sun was up and the soft breeze that had blown steadily through his window all night had given way to the insidious creep of humidity. The birdsong was overwhelmed by the incessant scratching of heat bugs.

And now he was hungry.

He went downstairs and made toast with cream cheese and grape jelly, washing it down with a mug of orange juice. Since coffee wasn't an option – his mother had forbidden it until he was older – he settled for an overload of sugar to get his ass in gear.

He got changed, made sure to put a bottle of sunscreen spray in his pocket, grabbed yesterday's book and a new one by Gord Rollo he'd found at a library book sale, and headed outside. The blackened, gnarly tree out front was there to greet him. From a distance, it looked as if it had once been on fire, but up close, he could see it was just some weird rot blackening the tree like an overripe banana.

"Good morning Halloween tree," he said, patting the trunk. Bits of bark flaked away in his hands. It looked like a good sneeze would uproot the crippled thing. Since it offered no shade, he had no intention of spending time beneath it.

It was going to be another long day, but he wouldn't be afraid to pop inside from time to time to get food and water.

West was still smarting from his father's outburst the day before. He'd had a chance to make it right last night but it never happened. When he was younger, his father wasn't just a dad, he was his best friend. They did everything together. "You two are as thick as thieves," his mother would say as they set out to create an elaborate scavenger hunt around the house or huddled in the basement putting models together. He should have treasured those moments more, taken more pains to sear them into his memory.

How was he to know it would all go away one day?

West could spend an entire day with his father now and miss him deeply.

*Enough.*

*You've played that song too many times.*

Walking around the house, he took time to absorb the creepy looking place his parents had consigned him to live in. Paint was flaking as bad as the bark on the tree. Most of the windowsills had been chipped away by time and rain and snow, splintered wood showing through garish green paint. The farmhouse had a wide, flat roof. West wondered what kind of stuff was up there, bleached by the sun. Would there be balls and Frisbees that his father had lost up there when he was a kid?

Along the side of the house was a pair of metal doors. A rusted chain was looped around the handles, fastened with a padlock. It had to lead to the cellar. West kicked at one of the doors. The metallic clang seemed to echo for miles.

The air smelled so sweet, so fresh and alive. He didn't want to plant his ass in some spot and read just yet. There was plenty of time to lose himself in another world.

He'd already been by the old barn. Time to head in another direction and hope he didn't cross into hostile redneck territory. He walked through the high grass with his arms outstretched, sharp and sometimes tacky stalks scraping against his palms and fingers.

A hawk circled high overhead. His shirt stuck to his back. He had to wipe a line of sweat off his forehead with the back of his hand. West took a quick peek back to make sure the house was still in sight.

*It'll be easy to get lost out here. That is not an option!*

The tall green and amber vegetation was getting to his shoulders and above. Something made a slithering noise by his feet. He stopped.

*Please don't let it be snakes.*

He may have loved horror books and movies, but he was still scared to death of snakes and rats. Anthony had a pet snake and no amount of cajoling would get West to even touch it with the tip of his finger.

He shuddered just thinking about it.

Once he felt the coast was clear, he resumed making his way through the least-tended field in history. He wondered what had once grown on all of these acres. An image of a young Grandpa Abraham hauling bales of hay, his squat, simian body lumbering from side to side, made him laugh out loud.

West breathed a sigh of relief when he emerged from the jungle into an immense clearing. On the other side, at least a hundred or more yards away, were tall, green rows of corn. He looked back, but couldn't see over the grass, much less the house.

Uh oh. How far had he come?

"Hey there."

The voice startled him so much, he actually jumped.

A beautiful girl lay on a blanket. Her long blond hair was the color of the afternoon sun, her eyes green as jade. Taking in her round, smiling face, West figured she had to be right around his age.

She wore a pink bikini, the small triangles barely able to contain her round, heavy breasts. She had the body of a woman, with curvy hips and long, shining legs.

In an instant, all of the saliva in his mouth had dried up.

She shaded her eyes from the sun. "Are you lost or something?"

*Stop standing there like a mute dork! Say something!*

"No… I'm, uh… I was just walking. I didn't know you were here."

She giggled. "How could you know? I didn't mean to scare you."

Jamming his hands in his pockets, he said, "I wasn't scared."

"You sure looked it."

"I just didn't expect to find anyone."

"Me neither. That's why I kinda made this my spot. How did you end up out here anyway?"

She didn't look the least bit nervous having some strange boy stumble upon her in nothing but a teeny bikini. Her total lack of concern had him a little off balance. Not that she had anything to be concerned about.

"I, uh, live back there… somewhere."

She pushed herself into a sitting position. West willed himself to look her in the eyes.

"You mean the old Ridley place?" she said.

He swallowed, feeling his heart throb in his throat. "Yeah. It's my grandfather's. Me and my parents just moved in."

"Wait, you mean your grandfather still lives there?"

"Uh-huh."

"Wow. I thought it was abandoned years ago."

Now he had to chuckle. "Trust me, I can see why. I guess he doesn't get out much."

"I guess not." Her smile blinded him. What were the chances of finding the hottest girl he'd ever seen out here in the middle of nowhere? He wished Anthony were here to see this. Scratch that, he'd rather tell him about it later. West wanted this moment all to himself. "What's your name?"

He had to stop and think for a moment. Finally, he blurted out, "West."

"West? That's different. I like it." She chewed on her bottom lip. "My name's Faith. Faith Simmons."

"You're the first Faith I've ever met."

She reached up to tie her hair back, her breasts swaying while she worked the knot.

*Her eyes, her eyes,* West shouted to himself. He couldn't help taking a quick glance at her chest.

"Everyone's gotta have a little," she said.

He said, "A little what?"

"Faith. You get it?"

He felt himself blush. "Oh. Yeah. I get it."

"Well, now that you've trespassed on my family's land, what do you plan to do?"

Oh Christ. He remembered what Grandpa Abraham had told him about going over the property line. Plus, he'd seen enough movies to know it never ended up well for the unwitting interloper.

"Hey, I'm sorry, I didn't know I was on your property. I could barely see where I was going."

She laughed so hard she had to hold her stomach. "You should see your face!"

That was the last thing he wanted to see. He was pretty sure he looked like a world class dumbass.

Seeing he wasn't joining in the joke, she settled down and said, "Look, I'm sorry. I was just kidding around. We're not all bumpkins with shotguns."

Trying to save some face, he said, "I knew that."

She narrowed her eyes at him, her smile widening. "Uh-huh." She stood and gathered up her blanket. "Well, it was nice meeting you, West. I dipped out for a little bit before I had to head off to school."

"School?"

"Yeah, I flunked earth science so I get to go to summer school. Yay. One more week to go. It really sucks because there's no air conditioning. Well, that and a whole bunch of other reasons."

West was disappointed when she draped the towel over her shoulder, covering the front of her insane body like a toga.

"Maybe I'll see you around?" she said.

He nodded. "Yeah, that would be cool. My days are pretty much free."

"Good. I hope you can find your way back here some day. I'm out of school by eleven. I like to come here to get away from things, you know?"

"I just hope I can find my way home," he joked.

"Make sure of it," she said with a wink. She gave him a little wave and walked into the corn rows. In seconds, it was as if she'd never been there.

West exhaled for what felt like the first time since he'd come here.

Faith Simmons.

Finally, a reason to not run away from this place.

✠

Matt Ridley started his morning just like every other – cursing his damaged brain and nauseous as hell. He gripped the puke bucket between his knees, choking back bile while the room spun slower and slower.

"Fuck me," he said, spitting into the bucket.

He'd taken a pill last night and it had knocked him out good.

*Guess old vertigo is just making up for lost time*, he thought.

He'd heard Debi getting ready for work hours ago. He could have woken up and kept her company while she got ready.

He chose to go back to sleep. It was the only place where there was order and sanity in his world. Truth be told, being awake pissed him off. It was a painful reminder of all his limitations.

Debi had been urging him to see someone, a shrink who'd helped one of her friends, but their insurance didn't cover it. When she volunteered to work extra hours or get a second part-time job, he'd lost it. He was enough of a burden. The last thing he'd do is let his wife work herself to death just so he could give lip service to a head shrinker. No goddamn way.

Coming back here was insult enough to the man he'd once been.

Now there was the Guardian note he found out back, not to mention the one slipped under the cat bowls and the writing on the mirror. Debi and West hadn't mentioned it to him, but he'd heard them question his father about it, sticking to the shadows to observe what the old man would say. He wasn't surprised when he simply wiped it off and stormed out of the room.

*It can't be happening again. This shit ended years ago.*

He'd talk to his father about it. That old son-of-a-bitch would do his best to give him the runaround. He just knew it. No matter. He couldn't bluster his way out of this one. Not this time. Matt was a grown man with a family of his own. He wasn't a scrawny kid easily pushed around, verbally and physically, by his father anymore.

When he was sure he could walk without dropping to the floor, he grabbed his cane and headed for the living room. As usual, the TV was on.

He hoped it was West. He still felt bad for the way he'd barked at him yesterday. There was no way he could apologize in front of Debi. Then she'd know something was wrong, and he wasn't in the mood for a discussion that would surely lead to a fight. She'd pleaded with him to be on his best behavior when they made the decision to move. If she knew he'd yelled at the kid over nothing their first day without her around as a buffer, it would be bad.

"West, is that you?"

He turned the corner into the living room. His father was in his chair, the fabric stained and faded just like his clothes. He was watching a rerun of a game show from the 80s.

"Well, if it isn't Nick Esasky," his father mumbled between slurps from a bowl of bitter-smelling soup.

"Who?" Matt just knew it was an insult. It was how the man dealt with most things, but especially something he didn't know much about or was uncomfortable with.

"You remember him. He used to play for the Reds. He got what you have when he was on the Braves and had to retire."

"No, I don't remember him."

"Good first baseman. Soft hands. He got that whaddyacallit…"

"Vertigo?"

"Yep. Last time I saw him on a field, he was stumbling like a drunk in the playoffs to celebrate with his team."

There was no mystery as to why Matt had worked his ass off in high school to get a full ride to a college a thousand miles away. He'd only come back here a handful of times since heading off to college – the last time being when his mother had passed away.

Matt swallowed the hundred replies he wanted to hurl. "Good to know I'm not alone."

His father grunted, tipping the bowl to his lips.

"What's with this Guardian crap again?" Matt blurted out. Sometimes the best way to get his attention was a sucker punch to the gut. His father raised an eyebrow, still guzzling from the bowl. If he wanted the element of surprise, it looked as if he'd lost that gamble.

The bowl clanked down on the table.

"What are you talking about?"

"You know exactly what I'm talking about. If you think you're going to start that just to get me out of your hair quicker, you needn't worry. I'm just as anxious to move on as you are."

His father wiped his mouth with the end of his shirt, settling back into the chair. "If you don't appreciate my hospitality, the door is right at the end of the hall." He glowered at Matt, dribbles of soup on his chin and chest. "That is, if you can walk it."

Matt's fingernails dug deep crescents in his palms. His teeth were clenched so hard, bolts of pain daggered down his jaw.

"You still didn't answer my question."

The old man waved him off. "You have an overactive imagination. Always did."

Was his father serious?

Did he forget Matt lived with him and this bullshit for two decades?

Matt huffed. "Not about this I don't. Just do me a favor and stop. I don't need West and Debi any more uncomfortable than they already are. Can you do that for me?"

His father bristled, gripping the chair's armrests. "Why don't you visit your mother and sister's graves while you're here? Maybe you can regain some perspective."

"Trust me, I have every intention."

And he did. Even though he barely remembered Stella, she had still been his only sibling. Any recollections he had were really just bits and pieces of things his parents had said about her. Poor

Stella. Life had never been easy for her. From what he'd gleaned from his mother, had she not drowned, her life was going to be one fraught with difficulties. He never knew specifics, just that she was considered *special*, both mentally and physically.

She was buried with his mother in the family plot, a plot he'd made sure he'd never spend eternity in. He'd bought his own in Woodlawn Cemetery in the Bronx five years ago. It was scary to think how close he'd been to making good use of it.

They stared at one another for a spell, his father breaking first and locking on the game show on the television.

There was no sense talking. They'd both hurt one another.

All those years away, and nothing had changed.

Absolutely nothing had changed.

✛

Dizzy or not, Matt had to get out of that house. He hoped to run into West lurking around, but his son was nowhere to be seen. It was warm but the air was fresh and sweet. He filled his lungs, feeling a little better, a little lighter with each breath.

"Think I'll go for a stroll."

His cane barely touched the ground as he made his way down the winding road, away from the house. He figured if things went bad and he fell, he could always wait for Debi to see him when she came home later.

He did have to watch his step. The ground looked like Normandy the day after the invasion.

Lost in the moment, happy to be doing something as simple as walking without falling, he was surprised when he stepped onto the main road. His feet hit the smooth blacktop. A crow cawed, swooping from a tree across from him and landing atop the telephone pole. It cocked its head, regarding him with onyx eyes.

Matt's surprise was doubled when he saw an SUV headed toward him. He took a step back, even though there was plenty of room for it to pass.

The blue Forester passed by, stopped, and backed up.

*If they need directions, I hope it's to someplace I actually remember.*

When the car pulled level with him, the driver's side window rolled down. A woman in her late fifties with long hair tied back in a braid smiled at him.

"Excuse me, but are you Matt Ridley?"

He couldn't help smiling back. "I am. Do I know you?"

"Don't tell me how, but I just knew it!" She slapped the steering wheel. "I used to babysit you about a hundred years ago."

"Babysit? Holy cow. Andrea?"

"The one and only. I haven't seen you since you were in high school."

"I really haven't been back much since I graduated."

She looked up the drive, as if she could see Abraham's farmhouse. Her face darkened for the briefest of moments. "Oh. Yes, that makes sense. So, what brings you back?"

He leaned forward on his cane. "Just an extended visit. I guess you're still in town."

"Yep. My husband and I live just up the road. It's the house with the old timey chuck wagon in the front yard. Bill likes to think he's a cowboy. I overindulge the man." She laughed. "You should come by some time. We can finally share a happy hour."

Matt chuckled. "Sounds good. Well, I better head back. It was good seeing you."

"Good seeing you, too. Wow, Matt Ridley. My little man turned out to be a tall drink of water. Don't be a stranger." She flashed him a cougar smile and sped off.

*Wow. Andrea Lender. The babysitter from hell.*

The happy hour line was what made him want to end their reunion. He remembered how much she used to drink when she watched him, threatening him if he told on her. She was smart enough to bring her own booze, knowing his father kept a sharp eye on his own stores.

The more Andrea drank, the stranger she acted, calling him her little man, making him sit close to her, kissing his face, sometimes grazing his lips. Yeah, all men had fantasies about being seduced by the babysitter, but when you were ten and nowhere near puberty, your idea of a good time was playing with your Star Wars figures, so the advances of an inebriated woman fifteen years your senior were unsettling.

To make him feel even more trapped, she babysat him for next to nothing, an offer his father couldn't refuse, no matter how much he hinted to his parents that he didn't like her. He wished he could tell them why, but he was afraid of what she'd do.

*How did she recognize me? I don't look even remotely the way I did in high school. Before the accident, yes. But not now.*

It was as if she already knew he was back, and had been waiting for a chance to 'run in' to him.

He walked slowly back to the house.

*It's the house with the old timey chuck wagon in the front yard.*

Now he knew which house to avoid.

Debi stopped at the Sam's Food Mart on the way home to get fresh ground turkey. It had been a long, trying day and she needed the familiar comfort of making dinner for her family.

To her relief, West wasn't a burned lobster waiting outside. He was at the kitchen table, reading a magazine with a blood-drenched woman on the cover.

"That looks just lovely," she said. "Promise me you'll put that upstairs before we eat."

"Okay," he said, flipping through the pages. He had a faraway look tonight. Wherever his mind was, he at least looked happy.

Abraham was in the basement puttering around, banging and thumping under their feet. She heard him curse a few times, and then settle down.

Matt came into the kitchen just as she was browning the turkey and adding salt, pepper, and cumin to start.

"Tacos?" Matt said. He looked his usual less-than-chipper self.

"With all the fixings," she said, bracing herself. He never asked how her day went. The fact that he didn't now, when she was dealing with the commute from hell, irked her.

"I got sick so bad this afternoon, I think I strained my ribs," he said instead. "And this damn headache won't leave."

*Please, not now. I'm not in the mood to hear about your litany of ailments. I just want to make dinner, eat, and go to sleep.*

"Uh-huh," she said, her back to him, adding more spices while breaking up the meat with a wooden spatula.

"I'd hoped the fresh air out here would make things a little better. Jesus, the spins have been worse than ever."

There was a time when Debi felt like a monster for not giving a damn about Matt's repetitive complaining. It was always the same thing, day in and day out. But it wasn't his fault he was this way. He didn't ask for that accident. She was his wife. She was supposed to give him comfort, even if it was just hearing him out.

There were days, though, when saying something positive or just suffering in silence wouldn't have killed him. Times like this, she just didn't want to hear it. She wanted to shout, "I know, Matt, I know! You're dizzy. You're nauseous! It's hard to get around! You're sick and tired of not being able to do things! I know. I know, goddammit, I know! Anyone who's been around you for more than five minutes over the past few years knows!"

Just thinking about saying it released some of the pressure she'd felt settling in between her shoulders.

"You guys want hard or soft shells?" she asked.

"Soft for me, with lots of refried beans," West answered, his nose deep in the magazine.

"Did you hear what I said?" Matt asked.

She rounded on him, the spatula pointing at his chest like a greasy gun. "I did, Matt. I'm sorry you had a bad day. What can I do to help?"

There was no softness to her words. They came out as a dare, asking him if he had the balls to drone on about his vomit after she'd been out of the house for twelve hours and was now standing over a stove making dinner.

He stared into her eyes, then headed out of the kitchen. "Nothing. Call me when dinner's ready."

His legs went wobbly and he had to reach out, his palm flat on the wall. Debi watched him hobble away, wondering what had happened to her. Why couldn't she bring herself to have even an ounce of sympathy for her disabled husband?

*Maybe because you're exhausted and it would be nice to not have to do everything.*

West saved the day by saying, "You want me to chop up the tomatoes and lettuce?"

She wondered if West knew how she truly felt at this moment, her patience worn too thin to show simple empathy. If he did, she guessed he understood.

"Make the lettuce into long shreds," she said. "Use that chopping block and the butcher knife."

"I know what I'm doing. I watch the Food Network."

He opened the drawer and instead of a knife, he removed a single sheet of paper.

"What is that, one of grandma's old recipes?" she asked.

He shook his head. "No." West handed it over to her.

HAVE YOU CHECKED THE BASEMENT YET? – YOUR GUARDIANS.

"What the hell is this?" she said, the paper fluttering in her shaking hand.

"It's kinda like what was on the mirror," West said.

"Matt, can you come here a second?"

"What?" He sounded very irritated.

"I need you to come here," she shot back, using the same tone she had on West when he was five and liked to run off in department stores.

"I know dinner can't be ready this fast," Matt said, his cane thumping into one of the kitchen table legs.

She held out the paper for him to see. "West found it in the knife drawer. Should we be worried about your father?"

His eyes flicked to the basement for a split-second.

"Have you ever heard him talk about being a Guardian? This is some weird, crazy stuff, Matt."

"I agree," he said, nodding. "And yes, I am worried about him a little."

She studied the paper, the strong capital letters in precise alignment.

"Is this his handwriting?" she asked.

West tried to take it from her but she jerked it back. It was bad enough he saw it already.

"I have no idea," Matt said. "The last time I saw his handwriting was on a check he handed over to me when I left for college. I can look around and find stuff he's written recently."

He looked pale, but then again, his face was often pasty. Recurring nausea and his reluctance to go outside for fear of falling was turning her husband into a ghost.

But the bleeding of what little color was in his flesh seemed different this time. He knew something and wasn't telling her.

Debi crossed her arms over her chest, crumpling the paper. "You need to talk to him about this."

She followed it with a look that said *we need to talk about this later, when West isn't in the room.*

"I will. I will."

Something crashed in the basement, causing them all to jump. It was followed by a muffled, "Damn son of a bitch!"

"Maybe he wants us to check on him in the basement?" West said. "He does spend a lot of time down there."

Matt said, "He always did. It was his man cave before there were man caves."

Debi almost shot West's theory down, stopping herself short. If thinking that made him feel easier, she couldn't take that away.

She glared at her husband. Matt stared at the floor, as if he could see through tile and wood at his possibly unhinged father.

Matt took a deep breath. "I promise, I'll talk to him. If he's losing it, I don't know what we'll do."

# CHAPTER EIGHT

The strange noises in the house kept West awake until well past the witching hour. There was a steady wind that caused the usual pops and creaks in an old house. It was unseasonably cold. He'd had to shut the window, the thick pane of glass threatening to break with each gust.

Under the whistling cacophony were other noises – scuttling sounds, the dull whack of something hitting the floor, and most chilling, what sounded like a girl crying – those are what prevented him from closing his eyes.

At one point, he'd turned on his light and started recording the various sounds in a notebook, along with the time. It's what they did on some of those ghost hunting shows. He hoped that methodically cataloging things would ease his growing fear.

The crying is what bothered him the most. It had only lasted a few seconds, but it was enough to make every hair on his body stand on end. Slipping out of bed, he got down on all fours, pressing his ear to the dusty floor.

No, it hadn't been his mother.

When the breeze died down, so did the other sounds. It would be easy to chalk it all up to a rotting house protesting the intrusion of the weather.

If it wasn't for that crying.

Maybe it was an animal. West was no wildlife expert. He wouldn't know the difference between a bleating deer and a whistling bat.

Was Grandpa Abraham's house haunted?

That was the question that wouldn't go away. He knew what his grandfather would say. And what his father would say. Somewhere in the middle lay the truth.

It was hard to hear the soft sobs and not think about his long dead Aunt Stella. She was young when she died.

So, maybe he wasn't as brave as he thought, living in the suburbs, surrounded by neighbors and normalcy.

The total silence that ensued didn't make matters better.

*Just stop thinking about it. Take your mind off this effed up house.*

Now, what to direct his thoughts to?

*Faith.*

✠

He got so worked up thinking about Faith Simmons in her bikini, her sunkissed skin, the way she smiled at him, that sleep retreated even further. It took masturbating twice to finally shut down, his brain and body so exhausted, he barely had time to clean up before passing out.

He woke up still thinking about her, a million questions flitting around his brain.

Would she be there today? Would he be able to find his way to her special spot?

Should he play it cool? Would he look like a stalker if he showed up today at the same time? Or maybe he should wait until the afternoon, when her summer school was over. Maybe then she'd have more time to hang out.

He was a mess.

Sure, he'd had crushes before, especially Gina Michaels in seventh grade, but nothing like this. The most Gina had ever done was tell him to get out of her way in the school halls. She barely knew he existed, and on one level, he was fine with that. Unrequited lust had a kind of simplicity.

No girl had ever talked to him like Faith. Or looked at him the way she did. Just thinking about her eyes and dazzling white teeth sent his heart galloping.

"Where are you off to today, Mr. Explorer?"

Grandpa Abraham came out of his bedroom door as West headed downstairs. He was dressed in a pair of jeans so old and worn, they were barely blue anymore. At least his white shirt was clean. West's mother had done a load of laundry the other night after dinner.

"I don't know," West said, stopping on the top step, hand wrapped around the newel post.

"I need you to help me with something."

West didn't try to bother hiding his disappointment. Whatever help Grandpa Abraham needed, he hoped it wasn't something gross or time consuming. West's prime directive was to get back out to the field and find where Faith did her sunbathing. He even had his swim trunks on under his shorts, just so he wouldn't weird her out standing in his regular clothes while she lounged in her bikini.

"Okaaaay," West said. His legs wanted to keep on moving, right out of the house and deep into the wild field.

Grandpa Abraham brushed past him. "It's about time you sang for your supper anyway."

West followed him, the stairs making an unholy racket. "What does that mean?"

"It means you need to earn your keep."

'Hi, Dad,' he said, giving his father a nod as they walked past the living room. His cane was across his lap. The newspaper was in a heap. Sometimes, it was really hard for him to read, the words swimming all over the page like drunken goldfish, as his father might say. The state of the paper always bespoke the level of the spins. The lump of paper said it was an average day, at least so far.

"Hey, where you two headed off to?"

"He said he needs my help."

The back door slammed shut.

"Looks like he's starting without you," his father said.

West jogged to catch up. For an old guy, Grandpa Abraham could move fast when he wanted to.

There wasn't a cloud in the sky. Whatever chill the night had brought was long gone. Grandpa Abraham stood under the kitchen window holding a dented, metal toolbox.

"See that hose?" he said, pointing to a coiled up garden hose on the ground.

Did he think he was blind?

"Yeah, I see it."

"See all that water leaking from it?"

It was sitting in a sizeable puddle of mud. Steady drips of water squeezed out of the connector to the house.

"It's leaking pretty bad," West said.

"You're going to change the washer for me." He dropped the toolbox onto the ground. The tools inside rattled and clanged loud enough they might be heard in New Jersey.

West looked at the toolbox. "I don't know how to change a washer."

Dragging an aluminum chair over, his grandfather settled into it and said, "I figured as much. That's why I'm here. I can't bend down that low. You just do exactly what I tell you and we'll be fine."

In another family, at another time, this might be considered a tender moment between grandfather and grandson.

"Capice, short stuff?"

This wasn't that family or time.

"I don't like being called that," West said, opening the toolbox. All of the tools inside were either covered in grease, rust, or a combination of both. Grabbing a wrench, his palm turned orange.

"Well, neither did I. Taking in a little ribbing puts hair on your balls."

West reddened. Did old people say stuff like that, especially in front of kids? He couldn't remember his friends' grandparents ever saying such a thing. Just thinking about Grandpa Abraham's balls made him want to puke.

"Now, first thing you gotta do is take the hose off. Just unscrew it counter-clockwise. Good rule of thumb – lefty loosey, righty tighty. You got that?"

On his knees in the muck, all West could think was that he'd need to shower and change before he even thought of looking for Faith. It took a lot of effort, but the hose finally started to unscrew. Warm, putrid water poured out of the end onto his hands. It smelled like low tide at the beach and something dead.

*I wonder what diseases are in this nasty water!*

He tossed the hose aside in disgust.

"Good. That was the easy part," Grandpa Abraham said. He rummaged around the toolbox and tossed a can of household oil.

"Just squirt that all over the faucet there and we'll give it time to loosen up. I'll bet that mother is rusted tighter than a gook's eyes."

"What's a gook?"

"Never you mind."

West may have never heard the word before, but he knew it had to be some kind of awful slur. They flowed from his grandfather as easily as the funk water running from the hose.

The smell was making West sick.

"Can I get rid of this?" he asked.

"That's a perfectly good hose. You're not throwing it out." He swatted at a fly.

"Well, can I at least move it somewhere else? It stinks real bad."

With a roll of his eyes, Grandpa Abraham said, "Fine. Just drop it by the side of the house. But you have to hook it back up when you're done."

West looked up to see his father watching through the kitchen window. He had a glass of water in his hand. West raised his eyebrows and smirked, as if to say *Gee, I'm having a great time out here with grandpa of the year!* His father shook his head, probably happy it was West doing this and not him. Not that he could.

Traipsing through fat bumblebees dancing through the wild flowers that sprouted everywhere around the house, West held the hose at arm's length. He noticed that the remaining water dripping out was red, like diluted blood.

He dropped the hose unceremoniously on a brown patch of grass. Wiping his hands on his shorts, a pungent odor, different from the ichor in the hose, caused him to look up at the side of the house.

"What the heck?"

Someone had written on the house in big swaths of shit. The smell and preponderance of flies were the only clues he needed to know about what had been used to scrawl the words.

"Grandpa Abraham! You gotta see this!"

Between the first and second floor windows it said :

THIS IS OUR HOUSE. WE HAVE GUARDED IT FOR 4 GENERATIONS. YOU MAY NOT HAVE OUR BLOOD.

"What happened, you see a spider?" Grandpa Abraham grumbled. Following West's stare, he stopped, his mouth dropping open.

It looked like the words were alive with so many flies devouring the message of festering shit.

Whoever did it would have to have been on a ladder. The words were painted between his and his parent's bedroom.

It wasn't here yesterday. He'd walked by this side of the house. There was no way he could have missed it. The stench alone would have stopped him and made him look.

This meant someone had done it last night, while they were sleeping.

Had he been awake when it happened, tossing off, thinking about Faith? Did whoever wrote it see him?

He felt sick to his stomach.

"What happened?"

West's father joined them, using two canes this time. He only did that when he was in a rush and wanted to make sure he didn't face plant in the process.

"Look," West, pointing. "What does it mean?"

Grandpa Abraham cleared his throat. "It means we have to fix that hose and clean that shit off the house."

He stormed off, hands thrust deep in his pockets.

"Dad?"

His father looked down fast, hissing with pain. His body swayed. West was quick to put a hand on his arm.

"Dad, who would do something like this?"

His father turned to him, the flesh of his face like freshly poured wax. He opened his mouth and vomited, chunks of last night's tacos splashing on West's bare shins.

First West had to help his father inside and get him on the bed with a new shirt. Then he had to clean himself off, putting his sneakers in a plastic bag. He hoped his mother knew some mom-alchemy to save them. They were his only pair.

"You okay?" he asked his father. He was sitting up in bed with a cold washcloth on his face.

He nodded, his voice muffled by the hand towel. "I'll be all right. I'm sorry, buddy. I know that was beyond disgusting. Looking up and then back down so fast really sent me for a loop."

"Now I know what you and Mom went through when I was little," West joked.

"Hey, Stretch, where'd you go?" Grandpa Abraham shouted from outside.

His father, face covered like a wet mummy, said, "Stretch?"

"I told him I didn't like it when he called me short stuff."

West jogged outside.

"Hope you didn't take a quick shower. There's bound to be some blowback from that shit when we hose it off," Grandpa Abraham said with a grimace.

He hadn't thought of that. As much as he'd like to run upstairs and grab a bandana to cover his mouth and nose, he knew his grandfather would kick up a huge fuss if they waited any longer.

They took turns powering the strange words off the house. Water and flecks of shit filled the air as well as their hair and

124

clothes. A couple of times, West felt like puking himself. It was a miracle he didn't automatically barf when his father lost it.

*I wonder if it's animal or human shit.*

*Why would it matter?*

Well, a *human definitely put it there.*

Now that the madness of the past fifteen minutes had died down, the reality of the vandalism hit West hard. He suddenly felt like there were sets of eyes all around, hidden, waiting.

"Has something like this ever happened before?" West asked, arcing the spray to wipe out the word GENERATIONS.

"Oh sure, my house getting crapped on is an everyday occurrence."

West eased off the hose's trigger, the water reducing to a trickle. "It is?"

The old man looked like he wanted to slap him. "I thought all New Yorkers understood sarcasm. Guess I was wrong. Come on, let's get it off before the sun bakes it in."

"Do you know who would do it?"

Grandpa Abraham took the hose from him, getting closer to the house to concentrate the stream more. "It's nothing you need to worry about."

That was less than comforting. How could he not worry about someone writing strange ass stuff like that all over the house? Did this same person write on the mirror, *in* the house?

"Tell that to Mom when she finds out," he said. "This is freaky, like scary freaky."

When Grandpa Abraham turned to him, his faced was speckled with brown spots. Flies zipped in and out of the halo of tainted water around him.

"This here is nothing new. It's been going on for longer than even I've been on this side of the dirt. Out here in the country, you get some strange folks who carry grudges all down family lines. This fool likes to call himself the Guardian, but I call him Fuckhead Faulkner. Whoever it is hasn't learned his words don't mean shit. Including this shit. I can't say I'm not upset with this mess, though."

He turned back to his work.

West said, "But do you know who it is?"

"I have my suspicions. I beat a fella up over it when I was younger. Spent a week in the county jail for it. Turned out I was wrong. I've kept my temper since then. Won't give that jackhole the satisfaction of seeing me brought down again."

"But what does it mean by 'you may not have my blood'?"

He shrugged. "How the hell should I know? None of it ever made any sense."

"Shouldn't we call the police or something? If they're writing notes on the mirror and putting them in drawers, that's breaking and entering."

Grandpa Abraham slammed the hose down, his chest puffing up like an angry gorilla. "I told you it's nothing to get your panties in a twist about! Now quit pissing in my ear and get lost! I have work to do and I don't need you bawling like a baby over some nonsense words."

West's stomach trembled, the shiver reaching down to his knees. Grandpa Abraham wiped a smear of shit across his upper lip, spat, and went back to hosing down the house.

*You fucking asshole!*

He didn't have the courage to say what he felt. Not to this strange man whose house they now shared; a house that was under the watchful eye of some lunatics who called themselves the Guardians.

Instead, he ran into the house, slamming the shower door. He stripped off his filthy clothes and let the hot water nearly scald his flesh. After he changed and grabbed a book, he headed for the front door. Pausing with his hand on the knob, he considered going in to his father and venting.

If this had been going on for as long as Grandpa Abraham said, his father had to know about it.

So why didn't he say anything when they found the other notes?

Was he hiding something, too?

Was he so wrapped up in his pity party that he couldn't see past it enough to fully grasp the potential danger of the situation?

This wasn't normal, no matter what Grandpa Abraham said. This was psycho-stalker shit.

West slammed the door, circling around the other side of the house, relieved to see no bizarre messages scrawled in blood, puke, or piss.

With the field in his sights, he walked into the wild brush, wanting to get as far away from the house of secrets as he could.

☨

West found a clearing after walking in what felt like circles for the better part of an hour. He just wasn't sure it was *the* clearing. There was no sign of Faith anywhere.

*You gotta have faith.*

Boy was that the truth right now. He wanted to go back in time and make sure his father never got in the car that day. Then they wouldn't be living with that bastard in a house watched by another crazy bastard – or bastards. Who knew?

*I'll bet Dad knows. Probably better to wait for Mom to come home so we can both ask him to spill the beans.*

He liked the odds of two against one, especially when his mom was angry. Then it would be more like five against one.

Good. He was pissed off, and had every right to be. Shouldn't this have been something his father warned them about before they came here?

West's ruminations stopped cold.

*What if Mom knew all along?*

"Hey you."

He looked over to see Faith emerge from the corn like some kind of fairy tale wood nymph.

"Bet you didn't think I'd find my way back," he said, sounding more confident than he felt. He was so wrapped up with anger and confusion that he simply didn't have room for being nervous.

She smiled, turning his insides to jelly.

"Oh, I knew you would. Anyone named after a point on a compass couldn't get lost."

There was a sliver of disappointment that she wasn't wearing her bikini today. Instead, she wore shorts that were cut high on her shapely thighs, a sleeveless shirt with Tweety Bird's head on her chest and old work boots.

She looked down at his feet.

"Ouch. Does that hurt?"

He checked out his feet. He'd had to wear his flip-flops since his sneakers smelled like a baby's diaper. Stomping his way here, he must have been too wrapped up in his own head to notice the beating his practically bare feet took. They were sliced with red lines, as if he'd been given twenty lashes.

"I didn't even notice it."

"City boys," she said, giggling. "That's rough terrain out here. You have to protect your feet. See?"

She wiggled a booted foot at him.

"We gotta get you cleaned up and find some socks."

He shuffled closer to Faith, feeling his heart beat in his throat. "I'll be fine."

"Not out here you won't. You can all kinds of infections walking through these fields with open wounds. Nope, you're coming with me."

Faith grabbed his hand, tugging him into the corn.

*Holy crap! We're holding hands!*

He willed his hand not to get cold and clammy, which only made his sweat glands open up even more. Her hand was so soft, yet strong. Trailing behind her, he could smell her floral perfume. It was the sweetest, most intoxicating scent he'd ever inhaled.

The stalks and ears of corn crinkled as they weaved their way between the rows. She must be out here a lot to be able to find her way through the monotony. The tips of the stalks were well above their heads.

"You want an ear?" she said, pausing for a moment.

"I guess I could bring one home for later."

"Not later." She plucked two green-sleeved ears, handing him one. "You do know how to shuck corn, right?"

"Yes. We have corn in New York." He chucked some silk at her. She tossed hers right back. "Don't we need to cook it?"

She shook her head. "Not fresh corn. You can eat it just like this." Faith took a loud bite, kernels settling in the corners of her mouth. "Try it. I'll bet you've never tasted corn this good."

West normally considered corn a perfect delivery vessel for butter and salt. Faith could have asked him to eat his flip-flop and he would have done it without question. He took a bite, then another. She was right. It was amazing. Tender and sweet. How could it be so perfect without being cooked, naked of all the necessary condiments?

It was backwoods magic.

"Come on, this is take-out food," Faith said, intertwining her fingers with his. They ate while they walked. When she tossed her finished ear overhead, he did the same.

They emerged from the cornfield, the air outside the neat rows markedly hotter. Ahead of them was a long, sloping yard with a pair of picnic tables and benches at the top of the rise. Her house was a three story bright yellow Colonial with an enormous front porch that wrapped around three quarters of the structure. Unlike Grandpa Abraham's, it was clean and warm and inviting.

"Nice place," he said.

"I'd rather live in an apartment in San Francisco or Chicago," she said. "The grass is always greener."

As she opened the unlocked front door, West hesitated. "Is it okay that I'm here? Your parents won't be mad with you bringing a boy in the house, will they? Even if it's a wounded one?"

Faith laughed. "No, they wouldn't mind. I take in stray, hurt animals all the time." She pulled at his arm. "Plus, they're not even home. They went to Marshall's Creek for lunch. And my brother and sister are in camp for the summer. *They* got passing grades."

Wow, this house could have come out of a magazine. All of the furniture was new and plush, the walls were painted bright colors, sun shone in streams through windows that had been shined until they were as clear as the sky, and snug scents of vanilla and cinnamon lingered in every room.

"Your house is amazing," he said as she led him upstairs. A narrow carpet ran down the row of steps, muting their footsteps.

"My mother is a clean freak addicted to all those home and garden mags. Sometimes it's like living in one of those fake model homes. I'd love to just mess it all up some day, but I think my mom would have a stroke… after she killed me."

The bathroom had one of those claw foot tubs, the porcelain buffed to a blinding shine. Racks of expensive shampoos and body washes were lined up on the walls surrounding the tub. It smelled like one of those stores that sold scented candles. West normally hated those places, but he was willing to make an exception here.

Faith opened the medicine cabinet and took out a bottle of peroxide and some bandages. "First, we gotta clean those busted feet."

He was about to protest when she giggled, removing his flip-flops. She let some water in the tub, sprinkling soap powder on the surface.

"You don't expect me to take a bath, do you?" West said, wondering if she did, would she join him? He was pretty sure he wouldn't survive it if she did.

*That's not something you need to worry about. You didn't fall into a PornHub video.*

"It's for your feet. You better not expect a sponge bath, mister."

*Lord, can she see how red my face is?* West thought. It felt like he was sitting close to a roaring fire.

"No way!" he said a little too fast, a little too loud. She didn't seem to notice.

"Just soak those suckers for a minute or so," she ordered, pointing at the tub.

The water stung his cuts, but no more than the peroxide she poured on them next. After covering his wounds with several bandages, she got a pair of white socks from her father's drawer. He put them on as ordered.

"You wanna listen to some music before my parents get home?

"Yeah, that sounds cool."

Maybe he should leave. What if her parents got home and found them in her room together. Would her father shoot him with a rifle he was sure all farmers had close at hand?

"Welcome to my crib," she said, nudging her bedroom door open with the toe of her boot.

If the rest of the house was planned perfection, Faith's room was barely controlled chaos. West loved it.

"What do you think?"

West took it all in. The walls were covered with posters and cut-outs from rock magazines, all of them tacked on at odd angles. Clothes were piled in corners, a dresser and desk littered with knick-knacks, books, jewelry, and perfume bottles. She had a king sized bed – a king sized bed! – that was unmade, the bikini he'd wanted her to be wearing lying atop the rumpled sheets. It was a glorious mess.

But like the rest of the house, it smelled wonderful, like a riot of flowers.

"I think I have room envy," he said.

She slapped his arm with the back of her hand. "Are you making fun of me?"

"No way. It's awesome."

"It's a little bit messy," Faith said, rummaging under a stack of jeans.

That was an understatement.

West said, "I like messy."

All of his favorite bands were on her walls. Pierce the Veil. Bring Me The Horizon. Lana Del Rey, Rob Zombie. And his favorite, New Year's Day.

"Here it is," Faith said, a Bose iPod speaker in her hands. She plugged it in, and settled her iPod in the cradle. "What do you wanna listen to?"

He stood in the center of the room, unsure what to do. Did he just sit on her bed? It looked like there was a chair under that mountain of shirts, shorts, and bras.

*Oh Jeez, don't stare at her bras!*

"Anything's good. You pick," he said.

The industrial metal edge of Marilyn Manson blasted from the Bose speaker. It practically made the walls quake.

"Sorry!" Faith shouted, turning the volume down so they could listen without their ears bleeding. "You can sit, you know."

"Yeah, I know. Just taking in the sights."

West gazed at a poster of New Year's Day hung over her bra pile. He felt it was safer staring at lead singer Ash Costello's half red, half black hair and goth makeup.

"You like her?" she asked.

"She's an awesome singer," West said. "I saw them in the city once. They opened for some LA band at Irving Plaza." He didn't add that because he was thirteen at the time, his father had come along, standing at the rear of the venue by the bar, keeping a watchful eye on him, especially when the mosh pits started to break out.

"I'm sure that's all you like about her." Faith smiled, laying across her bed, fishing for something on the floor. She reemerged holding a mini-poster of Ash. "For you."

"Thanks," West said, hoping she didn't think he was some kind of letch, leering at the singer. *Better that than ogling her bras. She'd probably kick me out for that.*

Faith patted the bed. "Come on, get off those professionally treated feet and chill."

It felt wonderful and terrifying all at the same time as they lay back, listening to music together. West couldn't remember ever feeling this happy and excited. Her arm was so close to his, he could feel her body heat.

They lay there listening to music, not saying much, which was surprisingly comforting. It was like he'd known her for years, not minutes.

At 2:00, Faith sat up and said, "My parents should be home soon."

West's heart whaled in his chest, but he did his damnedest to stay calm. "Yeah, I should get going anyway."

She walked him to the edge of the cornfield. The cuts on his feet stung but he refused to let her see him limp.

"It was nice seeing you again, West. Don't worry about the socks. You can keep them. My father will never notice they're missing." She gave him a quick peck on the cheek. "I'll see you around."

She turned to walk back to the house.

"Um, I'm not sure I can make my way through there," West said, knowing he absolutely couldn't. He'd be lost for good. No doubt.

Faith spun on her heels. She tried to hold a straight face but busted out laughing. "I was just kidding! Come on, I'll take you to my spot."

Again, she took his hand and blazed a trail through the corn. When they got to the clearing, this time she really did smile, turn, and walk away.

West somehow made it home despite tumbling into a daze. He didn't even notice if his father or grandfather were around as he walked up to his room, his body lighter than air.

Plopping down on the bed, he stared at the WE SEE YOU scrawled on the ceiling. He thought about the other things written around the house, his senses recalling the fecal smell from this morning.

"Screw that!" he blurted.

Propping a chair precariously on the bed, he taped the poster of Ash over the words.

Now they couldn't glare back at him, ruining the moment.

It was very hot in the room, but he didn't pay it any mind. He didn't care about the weird notes or crazy words of shit that had been outside his window.

He just stared at the poster, thinking of Faith.

# CHAPTER NINE

"Please tell me you're joking."

Matt sat on the bed with his head in his hands.

"I wish I was."

Debi had spent the better part of her day avoiding her old boss who had come to the office on business. He was going to be there for the next week or more. Frank Daniels was a pig with outdated, misguided conceptions of proper workplace relationships. To him, women in the office were there to either do his bidding or to be ogled and groped.

Monika Olson, Debi's closest friend at the office, helped Debi by giving her a heads up whenever Daniels was in her vicinity. Monika was the office manager, possessing an almost prescient ability to know everything that went on between the four walls and three floors.

"He just got out of a meeting, doll, and he's headed your way," she'd said on the phone at ten this morning. She'd been the little bird in Debi's ear all day. She had to repay Monika with something really nice once the storm passed.

"You're a life saver," she'd whispered.

"Hurry, get off the phone. He's almost there," Monika said.

It was the first of three warning calls. Monika had taken her out to lunch, her treat, at a little sushi place around the corner.

She'd always regarded Debi as a daughter, even though she was only ten years older. Debi appreciated her more than she could express in words.

"You know what?" Monika said when they were finished. "I think I'm going to expense this. Call it hazard pay."

Debi sagged in her seat. The sushi was excellent. The thought of going back to work wiped away all that goodness.

"Can sushi make you invisible?" Debi joked.

Monika reached out to hold her hand. "I've got your back."

"It's my front I'm worried about."

The stress of the day had exhausted her. She didn't have the strength to deal with this now. She turned away from Matt, motioning for him to be silent, if even for a minute.

Frank Daniels was rich and so tied into the New York political scene, he was practically untouchable. Women who complained about his boorish advances just disappeared, either paid off or threatened. No one knew for sure.

What he did to Debi six months ago still made her blood boil. She'd kept her mouth shut because they couldn't afford for her to lose the job. They would literally be living in a shelter, waiting on lines at soup kitchens. At least that's what Debi told herself. It made the sacrifice of her silence seem noble, rather than cowardly.

She certainly hadn't told Matt about it.

Daniels had grabbed her from behind one day, pressing his hardness (probably aided by a dose of Viagra) against her ass.

Debi was dumbfounded; shocked by his brazen and clumsy pass. She couldn't recall exactly how she'd extricated herself from the situation. Her mind went on autopilot. Whatever she'd said, it wasn't enough to send the message home loud and clear that she was not fair game.

In the mind of Frank Daniels, that just made her more appealing. His comments and sly glances over the following weeks made her skin crawl.

She almost whooped out loud with joy the day she'd heard he was setting up shop in the Chicago office to be closer to his wife and kids, who lived in Oak Park.

Good riddance.

But her joy was short lived and the bastard was back.

And now there was this to deal with.

"How could you have not told me?"

Matt sighed, refusing to look up at her. "I honestly thought this shit was over."

"Even after West and I found those notes and what was on the mirror? Christ! Are you and your father insane? Whoever is doing this was *in the house*. Were you not the least bit concerned about the welfare of your child?"

"They never did anything to us before."

"They?"

"They. Him. Her. We don't know. They're just words, Deb. They want to scare us. It didn't work when I was a kid, and it won't now."

Debi wrung her hands together. She felt betrayed. This was crazy. How could Matt not bring up the fact that some psychos had been writing strange, possibly threatening messages in his father's house for decades? She had the sudden urge to slap her husband as hard as she could.

*Hold it together.*

She snatched her work skirt from the floor, flinging it into the open closet.

"Goddamn you!" she hissed. "We're getting the hell out of here."

"And where will we go? A hotel? I know what's in our account. We have enough to last four, five days tops. Then what?"

She rounded on him.

"I don't need you to tell me what's in our bank account. I'm the only one putting money in it!"

She knew it would hurt him, even throw him into a rage, but she could care less. Right now, she wanted her words to burn him like a branding iron.

"Go screw yourself," he spat.

"Don't you dare turn this on me, Matthew. I'm not the one who put us in a dangerous situation."

Matt practically leapt off the bed, shouting, "Dangerous? Dangerous? I lived through it. So did my parents. You think I'd expose West to something that could hurt him?"

Debi clawed at the underside of her hair. She felt like pulling her scalp away to relieve the pressure in her head. "Honestly? I don't know anymore. You're so wrapped up in your own world of misery, I don't think you're even aware he and I are around most of the time."

Matt staggered, flopping back onto the bed. He slammed his eyes shut, pinching the bridge of his nose.

"Jesus, Deb, I can't do this."

"Of course you can't," she spat. "Anything more than tip-toeing around you is too much. Well, too fucking bad. I'm not backing down this time. You better figure out a way to get us out of here, fast."

He blindly lashed out, wrapping his hand around the alarm clock. Yanking it out of the wall, he threw it across the room, cracking the glass display in half.

"You think I want any of this? Huh? You think I chose to be this way? When I left here, I promised myself I'd never, ever come back. Yet here I am, more helpless than I was when I was a kid. This isn't easy for me, either."

There were tears in his eyes. He clutched his stomach, rolling onto his side.

As mad as she was, Debi also wanted to reach out to him. Normally, that's how their arguments ended. Matt's condition would trump all. He was a victim after all.

But he was wrong about one thing. He could choose the way he handled his life after the accident. He didn't have to be the victim forever. Oh, how she'd tried and tried to help him rise above his condition, to control it instead of the other way around. She wept in quiet corners of the house for years, praying to God to give her husband the strength he needed to remake himself.

Debi lowered her voice, stopping herself from lying next to him. "What hurts me, Matt, is the fact that you never told me. And now I'm wondering what else you're not saying. We should call the police. I don't care how long this has been going on. It needs to end now. Your father let it go on, but you're not him. These Guardian psychos need to be caught."

Matt opened his eyes, filmy with tears. "It's not that simple."

The knock on West's door startled him. He'd been listening to his parents argue for the better part of half an hour. Only over the last couple of minutes had they grown silent. He wondered if his mother was about to come in, ordering him to pack a bag because they were leaving, like a family fleeing a haunted house in the middle of the night. He thought of that scene in *The Amityville Horror*, when the father finally snapped out of his possessed fugue and dragged the family out of the house, running back inside to rescue their dog.

West didn't have a dog. Less to worry about if, and when, they fled.

"Come in."

To his surprise, Grandpa Abraham opened the door. He was peeling the skin off an apple with what looked to be a military knife. The blade was wide and deadly, curving to a pointed tip, perfect for skewering the enemy.

"They always fight like this?" he said, standing in the open doorway.

West closed the book that had been propped on his chest since the arguing started.

"Sometimes."

His grandfather let the end of the peel drop to the floor. He carved a slice, bringing it to his mouth on the edge of the knife. "Used to be, a wife knew her place."

West was about to say something to defend his mother when his grandfather pointed the knife toward him. "Don't go getting your shorts up your crack. Your mother is different. She's tough. A real fighter. You may think I'm some old fool, but I respect that. I'd tell her what I told you, that there's nothing to worry about. You and I both know, she's not going to believe a word I say."

145

"Can you blame her?"

An odd smile played on Grandpa Abraham's lips.

"I guess I can't. Do *you* believe me?"

"I don't know," West said, not backing down from his sharp gaze. He felt as if his grandfather was measuring him up, looking for signs of weakness. Not telling an obvious truth would be a weakness. So why not let the man know he didn't fully trust his assessment of the Guardian's intentions?

"Well, that's only because you don't know me. You're my kin. I protect my own, just like my father protected me. It's what men do, son."

Grandpa Abraham hammered his point home by driving the knife into the wall, letting it hang there, the handle vibrating slightly. It went through a picture from *The Texas Chainsaw Massacre*.

He ate the rest of his apple, studying the pictures on the walls. "Fuckhead Faulkner might shit himself if he saw this room. You really like all this blood and guts stuff, huh?"

"Yeah."

"Maybe you're the one we should all be afraid of, not the Guardians."

The smile died on his face. He stared at West for an interminable minute, not moving, not blinking.

West's bowels protested, begging for release. He felt like a specimen in a petri dish, a diseased cell being scrutinized by a scientist intent on wiping it out. All he wanted to do was run past the man to the bathroom, but that was not going to happen.

Grandpa Abraham broke the tension when he burst out laughing. "You should have seen your face, short stuff! I know this old mug isn't much to look at, especially when I give the evil eye."

"That was a pretty convincing evil eye." The knot of tension unfolded in West's gut. His grandfather's smile was a mile wide.

"Years of practice. If you can stop someone with a look, it saves wear and tear on your fists. But there's one thing you should know. You don't need to be scared of me. Ever. I'll never be your favorite person in the world, but I won't be your enemy. And Fuckhead Guardian Faulkner is a lot like that little guy." He pointed to the corner of the ceiling over the dresser where a lone fly buzzed, bouncing against the wall as if it could zip through wood and plaster.

"A pest is just that, a nuisance. Don't give it nonevermind. You got that?"

West gave an almost imperceptible nod.

"Good."

His grandfather clutched the knife handle, pulling it free from the wall, leaving a gaping slash mark across Leatherface's neck. He chuckled all the way down the hall to his room. West finally exhaled when he heard his bedroom door close.

✠

His parents continued arguing in fits and starts until sometime before midnight. At one point, he'd heard Grandpa Abraham pound on the floor and shout, "Give it a rest, already!"

They'd settled down not long after that.

Even though West hadn't been involved in the fight himself, he felt as exhausted as a boxer after ten rounds. Sleep grabbed him by the shoulders, dragging him to the dark without the slightest protest.

The belching of a battered engine woke him up. He shuffled to the window, opening the screen so he could see around to the front of the house. A quick inspection revealed that there were no new notes scrawled in shit under his window. Grandpa Abraham was behind the wheel of a Dodge pickup truck. When West had first spotted the truck, hulking next to bales of diseased hay, he'd assumed it was a rusted wreck.

*Guess it's not as dead as I thought.*

The wheels spun, kicking up tufts of grass and dirt, spattering against the house.

West was relieved he was gone. He couldn't shake the image of his grandfather jamming that knife into his wall.

*"You're my kin. I protect my own, just like my father protected me. It's what men do, son."*

Who the heck called their family kin? It was weird, just like everything else here.

148

Showering and changing – he had to look and smell his best if he was going to see Faith – he padded downstairs. His mother had cleaned his sneakers, leaving them by the front door.

"Thanks, Mom." He slipped his feet into the black and red hightops.

"What are you up to today?" his father called out from the kitchen. He leaned in his chair so West could see him. "I made bacon if you want some."

Ah, the day after a blowup. His father was usually at his nicest then. Or maybe this was his way of making up for the way he'd yelled at him a couple of days ago. It didn't matter. West was starving and just hearing the word *bacon* was enough to start his stomach growling.

"Cool," he said as casually as he could muster.

"I left out the butter so it melts easier on your toast."

West dropped two pieces of bread in the toaster and poured a glass of orange juice. He couldn't remember the last time his father had made bacon. The man was a master – crispy and perfect every time. His roommates in college had even nicknamed him Mr. Bacon. He was in charge of making it on a hotplate for his dorm's floor for a whole year.

"Sleep well?"

"Okay, I guess," West said, downing the first glass of juice. It had been a sticky night. He woke up dehydrated.

"Look, I'm sorry about all the… you know… last night," his father said. "Your mother was right. I should have told you both about this house."

West looked down at his clean sneakers. "So was Grandpa Abraham trying to tell me in his own weird way about those messages when he said the place was haunted?"

"I honestly have no idea what goes on in that man's head." His father sipped at his coffee. He looked clear today. It was the only way to describe it. The usual fog that enveloped him was missing, at least for now.

The toast popped up. West snatched them in mid air, slabbed butter on them, and folded each slice over two pieces of bacon.

"So you grew up with all that Guardian stuff?"

"Unfortunately, yes." He looked ashamed to admit it.

*At least he doesn't seem scared.*

West had to ask him something that had been loitering around the back of his mind. "You never found out who did it, right?"

"No. We tried for a while, but when we did, things would stop, only to pick back up again when we let our guard down, so to speak. The silver lining in all of it was that we were never physically approached by anyone. It was just a bunch of messages, nothing more. There are some… eccentric types living out here. Your grandfather being one of them. I always suspected he did

150

someone wrong a long time ago. Maybe cheated them in cards or screwed them on a land deal. I know there were a lot of people interested in buying sections of this property, before it got to this sorry state. This town isn't exactly Hatfield and McCoy territory, though." He smiled, the crow's feet crinkling in the corners of his eyes.

"Who are they?"

"Never mind. Before your time."

"Did you ever think that Grandpa Abraham's been the one doing it all along? I mean, was he different when you were a kid? Or was he always this way?"

His father's eyes flitted for a moment. It was usually a precursor to a bad case of the spins, but he took a breath and that seemed to settle things down.

"As I got older, I thought so. When you're a kid, you think your father is a hero, no matter what he does. After my sister passed away, my mother fell apart for a couple of years and your grandfather was the only thing holding us together. When she got back on her feet, it was as if he'd decided it was his turn to go into a funk. Except his funk never went away. Maybe he's a little odder and grumpier than he used to be, but not by much. He's never been an easy person to get along with. Could he be the one behind all of this? I don't know. I can't say I'd put it past him. He says this Guardian person has been writing these messages since he was a

151

kid, but I've never had a way to verify that. My grandparents passed away before I was born."

"How did they die?"

West wondered if there was yet another mystery in the family, some dark secret that no one dared speak about. He knew his father's tells. If he lied, it would be as plain as the quick scratch he'd give under his chin.

"Well, my grandmother got cancer – your grandfather told me she smoked like a chimney, and grandpa had a heart attack not long after when he was working in the field. So when it comes to the Guardians, all I have is the word of my father and mother. I'll leave it to you to decide which one I put more faith in."

West downed his breakfast while his father spoke. It had been a long time since they'd had a serious, grown up conversation. He had to admit, it felt nice.

He said, "You know, while you and Mom were fighting, he came to my room to tell me that nothing bad would happen to us."

"That was actually pretty nice of him," his father said, looking surprised.

"And then he stuck his knife in my wall, I guess to show me what he'd do to someone that tried to hurt me."

His father shook his head. "And there's the Abraham Ridley I know. No yin without a yang from him."

West thought about telling him that WE SEE YOU was carved in his ceiling, but then he'd probably ask to see it. He didn't want to risk tearing the Ash Costello poster Faith had given him.

"So, got another day of excitement planned?"

West fought with himself. If he told him he was going to meet a girl from the nearby farm, it would turn into a whole production. Questions would be asked he either couldn't or wouldn't want to answer.

"I don't know. Do some more exploring, read a little, listen to music."

"I'm sorry we dropped you in the middle of nowhere, kiddo. I know you'd rather be back in New York with Anthony, doing whatever it is the two of you did all day."

"It's all right."

"I might take a little walk myself. Better than being cooped up in here. I keep hoping I'll wake up one day and everything will be better. You and I can hop in the car and go to a movie, do some horseback riding, just go out and do whatever we want."

"Horseback riding would be cool. They have that here?"

"There are stables and trails everywhere. If you want, your mother and I can take you one weekend."

"Cool. I'll hold you to that."

West cleared the table, leaving the dishes for later. He had a rolled up *Horrorhound Magazine* in his back pocket, something to keep him busy until Faith got back from summer school.

"I'll see you at lunch, Dad."

He watched his father get up without the cane, though he did wobble a bit once he was fully upright. "Have fun, or whatever passes for fun out here."

West opened the door, took a step and tumbled. He came to a rolling stop in the yard, covered in dirt. His knee barked from slamming into the one patch of the yard that wasn't cushioned by grass.

"You okay?" His father stood at the screen door.

"I think so," West said, massaging his knee with one hand while dusting himself off with the other.

"Did that step come loose?"

West looked.

It wasn't the lone step from the house to the yard.

There was a large stone on the step, with a piece of paper wrapped around it, secured by a thick rubber band.

His heart racing, he picked up the rock, despite assurances from his father and grandfather that there was nothing to be concerned about, but he knew who it was from without even needing to unwrap the band and flatten out the note..

"Let me take a look at it."His father took the note, casting the rock aside. It hit the ground with a loud thump. West sidled next to his father to read it.

WATCH YOUR STEP. THE WORLD IS FRAUGHT WITH DANGER.

154

West felt ice spiders prancing around his gut, skittering up and down his back.

"You sure we shouldn't call the cops or something?" he asked, feeling a chill despite the cloying heat.

His father stuffed the note in his pocket.

"Fucking assholes. Maybe I should stake out a spot one night and finally catch them in the act."

*If you did, then what?* West thought. His father had the balance of a newborn foal. If he managed to grab one of the Guardians in the act of leaving another note, he'd be shaken off as easily as flicking dandruff from your shoulder.

But he would see who did it.

"Isn't that what the police should be doing?" West asked.

"I doubt they'll come out here for a welcome home note." He stared into the distance, hand reaching for West's shoulder to keep steady.

West was pretty sure the notes constituted a threat. Didn't cops give restraining orders for this kind of stuff?

"We can at least show them the notes."

Hard swallowing sounds told West that his father's breakfast was in danger of making a reappearance. His fingers dug into West's collarbone.

"You want me to help you inside?"

He hoped he didn't barf on his sneakers again.

"Yes. Please."

The next five minutes were spent getting his father to the couch and settled in with a warm ginger ale, a waste bucket with a new plastic bag just in case, and one of his pills.

"You go out," his father said, squeezing his eyes shut. "No need to babysit me."

"Will you at least think about calling the cops later?"

He shook his head. "Yeah. Sure. I just need to settle my head down first."

West left him in the living room, turning on the TV so he had some company. On the way outside, he stopped to stare at the brick that'd held the note.

Where were the Guardians now?

Were they out there in the tall grass, watching… guarding?

WE SEE YOU

Maybe they were night owls. It was easier to do sneaky things under the cover of darkness.

Or, was this something Grandpa Abraham left before taking off in his truck this morning?

West shivered. None of the possibilities made him feel any better.

With each step in the field, he wondered if the Guardians were close by, taking note of his every move.

Only the irrefutable magnetism of Faith could get him back out there in the middle of an overgrown nowhere, alone and exposed.

156

# CHAPTER TEN

West's disappointment at not seeing Faith clung to him for the rest of the day. He waited in her spot for hours, reading and re-reading his magazine until he couldn't take the punishing sun anymore.

Several times he stared at the cornrows, feeling like he should give it a shot and try to find her house.

Thankfully, he never got up the nerve to do it.

With his luck, he'd end up hopelessly lost, wandering into the night, hollering for someone to save him.

Jesus, he missed her, the lone bright spot in his very dark existence.

And missing her made Anthony's absence in his life that much heavier. They'd been inseparable. The divide between them never seemed larger. Shit, he didn't even have a cell phone he could use to call or text him.

Every fucking thing sucked out here.

West headed back to Grandpa Abraham's home. It would never be *his* home. Ever.

His father was asleep, zonked by the pill he'd taken earlier. Grandpa Abraham was still out.

There were no new Guardian notes, thank God. He wished he could go back to just thinking the house was haunted. Sure, he'd acted like a pussy when push came to shove, but ghosts couldn't hurt you.

Or maybe this place was a double whammy – a refuge for the souls of departed Ridleys and living lunatics.

West was too hot and tired to get worked up right now.

"Now what do I do?"

At least back home in New York, he'd had his own TV. It was now in storage, since Grandpa Abraham wasn't going to extend cable to the upstairs.

In his room, he looked at all the books that he'd read and decided he wasn't in the mood. Sweat dripped from his hairline. Crescent moons bloomed under his armpits.

His mother had the only computer, so he couldn't go down a YouTube rabbit hole right now.

His frustrated eyes settled on the old steamer trunk by his bed.

Now there was something to do. Yippee.

Taking off his sneakers, he quietly went downstairs, finding a pair of scissors and a thick butter knife. One of them should be enough to pry the trunk open. He also grabbed a cold bottle of Pepsi from the fridge, rubbing it against his forehead.

His father snored with his mouth wide open, one hand on his chest, the other dangling over the edge of the grungy couch. There was a time he wouldn't hesitate to wake him up so they could do a little treasure hunting together. West wasn't too old to remember that bond and the warm comfort it brought him.

Now, just getting his father upstairs would cast a pall over the whole thing.

*I'll wake him up if I find anything cool. Maybe the trunk is locked because it contains all the good memories in this place. God knows, Grandpa Abraham wouldn't want that to get around.*

The locks on the trunk were old. He could feel how fragile they were just by running his hands over the cool metal. Opening the scissors, he wedged one of the blades in the lock's gap. Pressing down, it snapped open with a slight pop. The second one was a little more stubborn, but it was no match for modern tempered steel.

*There could be anything in here.*

He'd watched enough *Antiques Roadshow* and *Storage Wars* with his mother to know that valuable stuff – things that looked like junk to him - were often found in trunks just like this.

Maybe, just maybe, there was something in there that could get them the hell out of this place.

That is, if Grandpa Abraham didn't snatch it back and stuff it in the trunk again.

*Okay… whatever I find, I won't tell him about it. If it looks like something worth money, I'll hide it and find one of those antique stores in Stroudsburg when I get a chance. That town looks like it would eat up collectible stuff.*

And if he did come into a landslide of money – how would he explain how he'd gotten it?

*Fuck it*, West thought. *I can figure that out later.*

He took a swig of the Pepsi.

It felt like the temperature in the room had risen ten degrees. The cicadas stepped up their racket outside. He looked at the pictures on his wall, then at Ash Costello on his ceiling, his mind superimposing Faith's face over hers.

*All right, enough tension building.*

The hinges on the lid made a perfect, haunted house creak as he lifted it oh-so-carefully. A heavy, moldy odor puffed from the open chest like a long-held breath. He cringed, coughing into his hand.

Peering inside the chest, the first thing he noticed was a neatly folded square of white linen and lace. At least it must have been white at one time. Now, it was the color of old bones.

He reached inside, picking up the fabric. It unfolded as he lifted it from the chest.

"It's a dress."

It looked like one of those special white dresses little girls wore to their First Communion. A mothball the size of a marble fell from the folds, rolling across the floor.

West laid the dress on his bed.

*I'm not gonna get rich with a dress. Hope there's something better under it.*

160

There were two boxes of puzzles, both with images of flitting butterflies. The corners of the boxes were worn. He opened one, saw that many of the puzzle edges were ragged or torn. This was a puzzle that saw a lot of playtime. He didn't bother opening the other, just shook it to confirm that it was full.

Next was a laminated placemat. On one side was a map of the world. West turned it over. The other had a list of all the presidents, ending with Jimmy Carter.

There was a tin box of hair barrettes, bows, and other stuff West couldn't name but knew they belonged in a girl's hair.

"This must be Stella's stuff."

Now that he said it out loud, he felt a little ghoulish. Here he was looking for lost treasure and he was actually up to his elbows in a dead girl's things. He plucked his arms out for a moment and considered closing the lid.

*Maybe I should just put it all back. Grandpa or Grandma locked this up for a reason. If he found out I was going through it, he'll lose his shit.*

He hoped there was a way to fit the locks back together, if not securely, at least in appearance.

He was about to put the placemat back when curiosity nudged him further.

*It's open now. There isn't much left anyway. Might as well see what else they stored away. This is probably the closest I'll ever come to knowing about Stella. Dad was so young when she died. I wonder if he's ever even seen this stuff.*

He set a couple of Judy Blume books aside, revealing a small stack of report cards, bound with a red string.

*Mrs. Ketih – Buttermilk Creek Elementary – Grade 2 Final Report Card*

He slipped the heavy card stock reports from under the string, looking at her grades – all Bs and Cs – and comments from her teachers.

'Stella showed improvement this year. Keep working hard.'

'Work on those addition and subtraction tables over the summer.'

'Very good effort, despite numerous absences.'

He scanned down to the absentee line. She'd missed school twenty-seven times! West would have killed to have missed that much school, especially in second grade. He hated Ms. Kaplan, an old crone who embarrassed him at the chalkboard at least twice a week.

A special note from Principal Martle caught his attention.

'Stella's social skills improved this year, but there is still much work to be done. She must learn to control her anger and keep her hands to herself when agitated. I highly suggest further evaluation over the summer. We should meet before the start of the new year to determine a course of action.'

# WE ARE ALWAYS WATCHING

There weren't many report cards. Unfortunately, she hadn't lived long enough to amass the stack he was sure his mother kept of his own somewhere. But there was a noticeable trend – she was an average student, obviously sickly, with a temper that warranted the school asking for her to be evaluated, most likely by some psychiatrist.

West wondered if she had a bit of autism. Did people understand autism back then? His school had several kids with varying degrees of diagnosed autism. Scholastically, some of them were brilliant. In almost all, there were very clear signs of socialization issues, some more obvious than others.

The rest of the chest held a box of crayons, the 64 box with the crayon sharpener on the side. He'd always wanted that, but his parents wouldn't pass the 24 mark.

He found an instruction book for a Holly Hobbie Oven and other loose papers.

Oh well, nothing very exciting, or of monetary value, but he did get a little insight to the relative he'd never get a chance to meet.

He was careful to put things back in the same order they'd been. Plucking the Judy Blume books, several papers slipped out from the well-thumbed pages. One of them opened on the trunk's bottom. The handwriting was eerily familiar.

WE WATCHED YOU, MONSTER. WE KNOW. AND WE ARE ANGRY.

West jumped back from the chest as if a cobra had sprung from the weathered trunk.

"Oh no, no…"

He pushed himself to open the other slip of paper. It was fragile and faded, with the folds dull as a spoon's edge, the blue ink paling from time.

Reading it made him queasy.

I WATCHED HER DIE, GUARDING HER SOUL, USHERING HER ON TO THE NEXT RESTFUL PLANE. SHE WAS EVEN MORE BEAUTIFUL IN DEATH THAN SHE WAS IN LIFE. YOU WERE TRULY BLESSED AND TOO BLIND TO REALIZE IT.

He ran downstairs, holding the papers with his thumb and forefinger as if they were made of toxic material. Stumbling on the last step, he caromed into the wall, shouting for his father.

✠

"Where did you find this?"

For a moment, Matt thought maybe his father wasn't kidding and there was a ghost in the house. West sure looked as if he'd seen one.

"In that old trunk in my room. It was in this kid's book underneath toys and a dress." West's throat was so dry, it clicked when he tried to swallow. Matt had never seen him so scared.

"A dress?"

"Yeah, a small white one."

*That must be one of the places they put Stella's stuff,* Matt thought. *I know Mom stashed as much as she could all over the house before Dad could throw it out after that first year.*

His father said one year of grieving was enough, and thought getting Stella's things out of the house would help her overcome her grief. Would it have hurt to let his mother keep the parts of Stella she wanted? How could he erase her like that? If only he knew how much she cried before he came home from work. Matt knew she had boxes of Stella's effects tucked away in the attic and basement. He'd seen her weeping over those open boxes.

"Were there any others?" he asked West. His son paced around the room, chewing at his nails.

"I don't think so. I didn't see any more. Dad, are the Guardians talking about your sister?"

"I don't know," Matt said, running his hands through his unruly hair. West's cries had woken him from a deep, narcotized sleep. Now he was sitting up on the couch, still dazed, the room wavering on the periphery of his vision.

The truth was, he *did* know. He may have never seen these particular notes before, but even West, who hadn't been here back then, knew. The only question was, why did his mother save them? She'd been terrified of the Guardians, throwing away notes as soon as she found them, sometimes even burning them on the stovetop. Did she hold on to these particular notes to show the police? Something like this would have gotten them out in force. Or did his father stuff them in one of Stella's books?

He patted the couch, motioning for West to sit beside him.

"Look, I need you to settle down. These notes are almost forty years old. There's nothing you need to worry yourself about."

West slumped onto the couch, an explosion of dust and skin flakes swirling in a corona around him. "Yeah, those are old, but there are new notes. If they're about Stella, they say the Guardians were there when she died. If they didn't kill her, they at least didn't do anything to help her. That's sick. Like, psycho killer sick."

"Nobody killed Stella."

He sighed. There was so much he wished he knew about his sister. His mother had always been reluctant to talk, but that didn't stop him from pestering her with questions.

What he did know was that she wasn't like other kids her age. She had some kind of glandular issue that caused her to grow quickly. Even in first grade, his mother said she was taller than the biggest fourth grader. But there were other problems. Behavioral issues that his parents were ill equipped to deal with. Even the school had a hard time knowing how to help her.

Matt stared at the open notes on his lap.

166

He felt so small, so helpless.

West was scared, and he had every right to be. If Matt were a whole man, he'd be able to comfort him, save him from their predicament. He could take West and Debi and storm the hell out of here and never look back.

No matter how much he wanted to do just that, he simply couldn't. It was because of him they were here. Because he was a crippled fuck, his family had to go through the same bullshit he'd had to endure.

The spins. Always the spins. And when they weren't twisting his head around, they were close, waiting to pounce. He couldn't save a cat from a low-hanging branch, much less his family. He was a dependent, even to his son who had to help him get around and clean up his vomit and fetch his meds.

*We all would have been better off if that drunk bitch had just finished the job.*

It wasn't the first time he'd had the thought. Hell, it wasn't even close to being the thousandth. He had a pretty good life insurance policy back then, when he was able to make the payments. What good was it, and he, to them now?

"I'll talk to your grandfather about it when he gets home."

*God that sounds lame.*

"Where is he?"

"Probably at the Post."

"What's the Post?"

"It's a place where military veterans hang out, usually to have a few drinks, play cards, watch TV. It's where he's always spent most of his time."

West tapped the notes. "Maybe we can show these to the police. There's no statute of limitations for murder, right?"

"Where did you learn that?"

"I watch those real crime shows sometimes. Since the Guardians are still around, if we show the cops these notes, that could give them probable cause to catch them and prosecute them for Stella's murder."

Matt's stomach went sideways. He burped into his hand, biting his lip until things settled down.

"You're forgetting one thing," he said. "Your Aunt Stella wasn't murdered. She drowned. My mother was hanging up the laundry outside and she wandered off. Stella had never been taught how to swim because there wasn't any call for it. Not out here."

West looked puzzled. "So where did she drown?"

"There was a little watering hole we called a pond, but it was more like a deep puddle. It was in a depression in the field. At most, it was two feet deep. After the accident, my father drained it completely. My mother had asked him to do it a hundred times before, and when he finally did, it was too late."

West collapsed onto one of the loveseats.

"How long do you think we'll have to stay here?"

Matt gripped West's shoulders, those same narrow shoulders he'd leaned on to get in and out of bed, chairs, and the car. "Not one more minute than we have to. I promise you that. Let me hang onto these notes and I'll have a talk with your grandfather the moment he gets home."

West left without saying another word. He went upstairs, then came back down, Matt assumed with one of those horror books in hand, and went out the front door.

He stared at the open notes in his lap, fighting the gorge roiling in his gut, burning his esophagus.

Maybe, just maybe, his anger could overshadow his inadequacy.

The Guardians had hung over his childhood like a gray cloud, always threatening rain but never unleashing its horrid potential. It had worn him down, as it had his mother. This fear, and Stella's death, had taken her life decades before she drew her last breath.

Deep down, when he and Debi had decided moving back to the farmhouse was the last option, he'd hoped the Guardians had died of old age or moved on.

Matt should have known better than to cling to hope. What was the point when it always let you down?

He couldn't let that cycle repeat itself.

Even if it killed him.

✠

West didn't stray far from the house, settling behind the diseased tree in the front yard where he would be able to see Grandpa Abraham when he came home. At the angle he'd situated himself, he was pretty sure his grandfather wouldn't be able to spot him, as long as he parked that shambling wreck in the same spot. And he would. There were four deep depressions where the tires had settled into the earth.

The tree's onyx bark was jagged, stabbing his back in a dozen places. All he had to do was shift his back against the tree for the bark to crumble, flakes falling like devilish snow until it was relatively smooth.

There wasn't a chance in hell he would venture out back. He needed to be outside, but not out of sight of the house that was rapidly degenerating into a prison.

Nor did he want to be in his room. The chest was a benign enough object, but the secret it had held came with its own psychic emanations. It tainted everything, and at least for now, he wanted nothing to do with it.

So he'd blindly grabbed a book from his shelf. It was a poor choice – a Richard Laymon collectible edition about, of all things, a home invasion. He tried to read the first page but couldn't go further.

Who the hell were the Guardians? What would compel someone to harass a family for generations? It had to be something major. Crazy could only account for so much. Sooner or later, crazy either burned itself out or took one step too far.

The Guardians had been patiently pestering Grandpa Abraham's family forever, using creepy words to make them uneasy.

Or had they taken that fatal step when Stella died?

West's arms were riddled with gooseflesh. He looked like a freshly plucked chicken.

One thing was for sure. He had to find a weapon, something he could conceal and keep with him at all times, even in the house.

They weren't safe out here, where a person's screams would never be heard.

✛

Grandpa Abraham didn't get back until the late afternoon. He slowly pulled the sputtering Dodge right into the grooves. Hocking up a lungful of phlegm, he opened his door, stepping in the gelatinous goo. Weaving slightly, just like West's father, he worked his way to the front door.

West was pretty sure he could have been sitting in the middle of the road and the old man wouldn't have seen him.

Grandpa Abraham was crocked. He even left the keys in the ignition, the door wide open.

It would be hours before West's mother came home. She'd been looking more and more exhausted with each passing day. He wished more than ever that she worked closer. Her presence was sorely needed right now.

Creeping up to the living room window, West spied his father sitting up in one of the loveseats, his cane across his lap.

Grandpa Abraham stumbled into the doorway. Even his eyebrows were askew. West smelled the sharp tang of whiskey coming off the man as it curled through the window screen.

He ducked under the window, lest he be seen. All he needed to do was listen.

It didn't take long for the fireworks to begin.

✠

"Hey there, Esasky. How's the head?"

Matt had made a pact with himself that he would address the notes West had found as calmly as possible. When he got upset, everything had a tendency to slide out from under his feet, cutting him short. He needed to see this through.

The immediate insult set his teeth on edge.

"I see you and your Post buddies still haven't learned moderation," he shot back.

It didn't faze his father in the least. The squat man settled into his favorite, filthy chair, grabbing the remote off the table and changing the movie Matt was watching to a cooking show.

"You fight a war and tell me what the point of moderation is," he said dismissively. "Look at the caboose on her. I'd eat whatever she cooked... and then some."

Matt was disgusted.

*How are we from the same gene pool?*

He flicked the notes onto his father's lap. "Here. You might want to read those."

"What the hell are they, love letters?" he said, a deep laugh culling the sludge from his lungs, rattling his chest until he spit a yellow wad between the pages of yesterday's newspaper.

"Just read them."

Matt fingers tensed around the cane, his knuckles whitening.

*Stay calm. Don't let him throw you off.*

His father dared to take his eyes off the pretty TV chef long enough to read the notes. A measure of sobriety seemed to wash over him. He narrowed his eyes at Matt.

"Where did you find them?"

"Does it matter?"

"Where the hell did you find them?"

"The trunk in West's room."

"That couldn't be easy, seeing as how it's locked."

"It's old. Maybe the locks broke. That's not the point. You knew about those Guardian notes, didn't you?"

He crumpled them in a ball, tucking it between his leg and the chair's cushion.

"First your fool son, and now you. I'll tell you what I told him. You don't need to worry about old Fuckhead. You hear me? You need to stop worrying like a couple of Marys. You know better than that. I ought to take the belt to that kid for snooping in locked places."

Matt's blood went to an instant boil.

"You touch him and it'll be the last thing you do!"

A sly smile crept onto the old man's face. "You still have some of that fire. I'm just not sure you have the stability to back it up."

Matt's brain sizzled. He pictured beating his father with the cane—*whack, whack, whack*— blow after blow on his thick skull until it turned the consistency of tapioca pudding, leaking reds and grays and yellows, forever ruining that horrid dumpster chair.

"You got something else you want to say to me?"

*Oh no! Stop! Stop!*

The living room walls shifted, the floor moving back and forth like a funhouse walkway. Matt's father split into two nasty drunks, both scowling at him.

He closed his eyes, but it never did any good. It felt as if he were falling through dark matter, tumbling end over end.

"I didn't think so," he heard his father grumble within the deepening pitch. Matt willed himself to stop falling while a woman droned on about making a tuna casserole.

*You can't even do this right.*

He spun and spun, loathing every molecule that comprised his broken mind and body.

# Chapter Eleven

The next two weeks were uneventful… at least in terms of the Guardians. After witnessing the confrontation between his father and Grandpa Abraham, West had made it a point to keep anything Guardian related to himself. As much as those notes, especially the one in Stella's books, freaked him out, he rationalized that they were only words. Nothing physical had happened to any of them.

Except, maybe, Stella. But that was a long time ago.

The Guardians, if they were the same ones from back then, had to be old by now. And old people didn't run around killing people. Well, except for those news stories where some eighty-year-old who'd had enough of his or her spouse offed them over tea and toast one morning.

The truth was, it had frightened him, seeing his father wither like that. He'd been tempted to run into the room and defend his hobbled father. One look at his grandfather's cold eyes told him it would only make things worse.

And above all, he didn't want his father to know he'd seen everything. He may not have been the man and father he was before the accident, but he still had pride. When life stripped you of everything, pride was usually the last to go.

West had moved the trunk into the closet so he couldn't see it. It seemed babyish and a little ridiculous, but so what? He had to sleep in the damn room. It wasn't like living in Grandpa Abraham's moldy house of horrors was the seat of comfort and relaxation. If getting that chest out of his sightline made him feel even one iota better, so be it. He was just glad that his grandfather never spoke of the chest or the contents West had unearthed.

The night sounds of the house still bothered him. *It's an old house with unsettled bones,* Grandpa Abraham had told him one day when he said it sounded like someone had been walking around the downstairs hall all night. West hadn't been able to muster the courage to investigate for himself. What if he came face to face with one of the Guardians? What would happen then?

There was the other possibility – that his grandmother or aunt's ghost was still there, pacing the halls, letting them know they were still around. Maybe if Anthony had been here, they could have checked it out together. But alone? No freaking way.

So West did what he knew best. He downloaded a recording program on his mother's laptop and asked if he could keep it running after they went to bed. She didn't object. Things between her and his father had been chilly. It was sadly the one thing that made it seem like they were back home. She was just as nervous living in a place watched over by some weirdo as he was, though she, like the rest of them, hadn't said a word about it lately. He

178

could have asked for a pet ostrich and she would have said yes. Anything to take his mind off their living situation.

But he had no need for an ostrich…or any pet for that matter. Except a tarantula. That would be one fucking awesome pet.

All he wanted was a night to record the audio of the house, the 'settling' of the wood heated by day and cooled by night.

When he played it back, he heard a lot of pops and creaks, wood groaning as if weary with sleep.

And then there was the scream.

He hadn't heard it while he slept.

It had happened, all right. Just after two in the morning. One short-lived shout. He couldn't tell what was behind it. Frustration, fear, pain, mourning? It sounded as if it came from *within* the house and at the same time somewhere distant.

He let his parents listen to it.

"Could be an owl, or a deer," his father said, handing the headphones back to him. "Believe it or not, deer can make some strange noises. They almost sound human, especially when they're spooked or hurt. I wouldn't put it past someone taking an off-season shot at one, wounding it, and then being too lazy to track it down and finish the job."

His mother listened, pressing the headphones tight against the sides of her head.

"Play it again," she said.

179

He did, four more times to be exact.

"Creepy. It probably is an animal. If it was a person, they'd have to scream really loud to be heard out here."

"Yeah, I bet that's it," West said, shutting the laptop down. "I could check YouTube for any deer recordings and stuff like that, try to compare it."

"Or it could be that ghost your grandfather warned us about," his father said.

"Really? Cut the crap, Matt."

His mother shook her head, turning away from him as she went back to cleaning the dishes.

"That's all right, Mom. I wouldn't care if it was," West said, keeping the fallacy alive that he'd love to live in a haunted house.

Deep down, he knew it wasn't a ghost. There was a weight to the scream, something organic about it. Which made his father's animal explanation all the more plausible. He wasn't sure whether that was a disappointment or not.

"Remember, we're going to that big outdoor flea market after lunch," his mother said. "A woman I ride the bus with said it has everything. There's even a used bookseller. I'll give you ten bucks so you can stock up. That'll probably buy you fifteen or more books."

"Thanks. That sounds cool." He knew the horror pickings would be slim, but he was willing to branch out to thrillers or even a mystery or two. Maybe they would give him some pointers how to solve the Ridley farm's conundrum.

"You have your watch with you?" his father asked when he was mid-way out the door.

He flashed his wrist. The old Timex with the cracked black leather band had been his father's, back when he needed to keep track of time.

"Good. Make sure you're back by noon. You know how your mother gets if she has to wait."

It had been meant as a joke, but West saw that his mother wasn't in on it. She shot a dagger at his father before tromping from the kitchen.

Grandpa Abraham sat by the weathered picnic table, smoking a cigarette. It was the first time West had seen him smoke. The cigarette just looked right, dangling from the side of his wizened mouth.

"Where you off to?" he said.

"Just gonna walk around."

The old man grinned, the cigarette tipping up towards his eye. "Sneaking off to see that girl?"

West went on the defensive. "I'm not sneaking."

*Wait, how does he know about Faith?* He'd never told anyone about her.

"I see where you go." He gestured over his shoulder, to the path that led to Faith's private place. "Think I don't know what's over there? She's a pretty one."

West's stomach fluttered. Did Grandpa Abraham skulk around like the Guardians, watching him?

There hadn't been much to see the past few days. Faith told him she was going to visit her aunt in West Virginia for a week. Today would be her first day back. He wasn't ashamed to admit he was anxious to see her again.

"Have you been following me?" West asked.

His grandfather burst out laughing, degenerating into a hacking cough, the cigarette falling to the floor. "I was just taking a stab at it. You crack like a soft egg, short stuff." Plucking the coffin nail from the grass, he added, "I got no need to spy on young lovers."

West's skin felt as if it was consumed by a flash fire. "We're not lovers."

"No, I suspect you aren't. But I am happy to see you're not… you know." He let his hands hang limply in front of him.

"Why would that matter?"

West had gone to a couple of meetings for the Gay-Straight Alliance club in his school to support his friend Mario who had come out to his parents when he was twelve. They took it very well. In fact, they hadn't seemed surprised at all. Not many of Mario's friends or family were.

People like Grandpa Abraham were dinosaurs, banner wavers for a dying mindset.

"Oh, it matters," he said, shifting on the bench so he turned away from West.

*Guess I'm dismissed. Good.*

West stormed around the table and Grandpa Abraham.

"Just be careful, little man. The good looking ones are always trouble."

"Good talk, Grandpa," he said, not holding back his disdain for the words of advice. Nor did he look back to see if his sarcasm hit home. The way forward was sanity.

He heard Faith crying before he saw her.

She was sitting cross-legged, shoulders heaving, her face in her hands. Her golden hair hung around her like a curtain drawn to afford her privacy. West stopped short of emerging from the high grass.

What should he do? He was no expert when it came to weeping girls. Jesus, he was the furthest thing from it.

Should he wait her out? Would she be mad if he saw her like this?

He'd waited a week to see her. He didn't want to start things off by getting her even more upset.

He didn't realize he'd been holding his breath until his lungs cramped.

"You can come out," she said, wiping the tears from her cheeks with her knuckles.

"I… I'm sorry," he said, stepping into the clearing.

"For what?"

She looked up at him, her eyes so red they looked painful. A line of clear snot dripped from one nostril. Normally, it would be gross to look at, but on Faith, it seemed just short of adorable.

*Oh, you've got it bad.*

Yeah, and so what?

He didn't exactly know what he was sorry for. He let her question hang there. Daring himself, he settled beside her, draping an arm over her shoulder. It's what you were supposed to do, right?

*I hope she doesn't think I'm taking advantage and hitting on her.*

At first, he was as tense as a suspension line, waiting to see how she'd react.

He practically swooned when she leaned into him, nuzzling her face into his chest. West brought his other arm around her, feeling her every stuttering breath.

"What happened?"

Faith's sobs settled down some.

"When my mother and I came home last night, my father was waiting for us on the porch. I'd never seen him so mad."

As much as West wanted to be the good guy, he couldn't stop himself from taking a deep whiff of her hair, scents of coconut and peaches lingering in his brain. He relished every second she was in his arms, in spite of the circumstance.

"How could he be mad at you? You were away all week. Did everything go all right with summer school?"

"No. I didn't pass. I… I thought I did good on the last test. Turns out, I bombed. Now I have to take earth science *and* chemistry next year. I'm not even supposed to be out of the house. I'm grounded for the rest of the summer."

West's heart sunk.

"But that's a month from now!"

"I know." Fresh tears spilled from her eyes. Her fists pounded the ground. "I tried. I really tried. I don't know why I keep drawing blanks when I take the tests. It's not like I failed on purpose."

"I passed earth science this year. Maybe I could tutor you."

Faith collapsed within herself. "I can't even tell him I met you, much less have you over to tutor me. That would mean I left the house when I wasn't supposed to."

"You could tell your parents I'm one of the kids from your summer school class."

His mind whirred with possibilities. He'd try anything, so long as she didn't end up locked in the proverbial tower for the rest of the summer. If he wasn't careful, he'd be crying next.

"Thank you, West, but there's really nothing I can do. Not now, anyway. I came out here to tell you goodbye. I guess I'll see you when school starts."

One of the silver linings was when he learned they'd be attending the same public school in the fall. A week without Faith had been hard. A month would kill him.

She stood up, swiping grass from her denim shorts. West jumped to his feet. He wanted to grab her hand, lock her in a bear hug, sling her over his shoulder and carry her to someplace where angry parents could never find them.

*This can't be happening.*

Biting her top lip, Faith sniffled. "I'm the one who's sorry, West."

She took a quick breath, and pulled him close. Her lips, so soft and salty with her tears, pressed against his. West didn't even have the time or sense to close his eyes. He stared at this impossibly beautiful girl kissing him, his first real kiss.

Faith pulled away both too soon and an eon later. She'd done something to him, robbed him of his mass, or suspended the laws of gravity. He felt as if he'd simply float away.

"I really like you, West. You're nice, for a city boy."

Before he could babble all of the things he felt for her, and he knew it would come out a clumsy mess, she ran into the cornfield.

And just like that, she was gone.

Debi had been looking forward to the flea market. They used to have one in her town in upstate Connecticut back when she was a kid. Her mother would take her there every week. They'd load up on socks and underwear, kitchen gadgets and spices, cards and toys when birthdays rolled around. There were stands that sold sausage and peppers, the sweet aroma never failing to make her stomach rumble. Her mother always treated her to fried dough, powdered sugar piled on so thick, it became a paste when it mixed with the oily epidermis of the dough.

More importantly, she needed time with West. Thanks to her insane commute and work schedule, she barely saw him. She could tell he was feeling the strain of living out here. How could he not? With no one to hang out with and all the bizarre Guardian crap, she worried about his mental state. The moment she left for work before the ass crack of dawn, he was trapped here. She may as well have thrown him in solitary.

Matt couldn't drive him to town, even to see a movie or grab a bite to eat.

And there was no way in hell she would allow him to get in that truck with Abraham. If the man wasn't soused, he was on his way to tie one on at the Post.

Speaking of Abraham and the Guardians, she was beginning to suspect that West was right and they were one and the same. Abraham liked to control people, put them in their place, and assert his dominance. What better way than using fictitious Guardians to keep everyone around him afraid and looking to him for strength and courage?

Debi had taken her share of psychology courses as she prepared for her teaching degree. To her, Abraham's motivations and actions were as thin as onion skin paper. In truth, he was just a sad old man, clinging to a last shred of masculinity.

But it was scaring West, no matter how stoic he tried to be, and it had to stop. A deep confrontation with her father-in-law was coming… soon. He'd been making himself scarce lately, even taking his meals at the Post. Funny how with his absence came the cessation of the Guardian notes. Coincidence?

Debi massaged her temples, kicking the bathroom door open with her foot. The pipes rattled when she turned the faucets, the hot water slow to come.

Giving it a few minutes, she stepped into the shower, piling liquid lotion onto a soft bath sponge.

*I have to take West to see Anthony next week. With or without Matt.*

It would be without. No sense kidding herself. If he'd been in a blue funk in New York, Pennsylvania had turned it black as tarpaper. Guilt and self-pity were eating him away, and out here, she was just too damn tired to pull him out of it. He'd been taking more of the pills, which was why he'd been sleeping a lot. When she asked him about it, he swore he hadn't. But he'd hidden his pill bottle so she couldn't count them. She didn't know whether to be angry or sad. She was so tired of being both, it left her numb most days.

Work was no picnic either. Her lecherous old boss was making her life a living hell. She'd been looking for other jobs, even a way to get back into teaching, but there just wasn't anything out there right now.

She may hop on a bus every day, but she was just as trapped as West.

"Maybe I should take some of Matt's pills." Her voice echoed around the tiled walls.

*Just for now, try to think about nothing. Clear you head, Deb. Enjoy the shower, at least until the hot water runs out.*

Soaping her chest and collarbone, she tilted her face into the spray. Steaming water sluiced between her breasts, cascading between her legs like a waterfall.

For the briefest of moments, she touched herself there, felt the water trickle between her fingers.

It had been so long.

*When was the last time Matt and I had spontaneous shower sex? Three years?*

She was about to turn around to soak her hair when a cool breeze wafted over the shower curtain. Her nipples hardened instantly. The bathroom door creaked.

"Is that you Matt?"

Just as suddenly as it had come, the breeze was gone, tamped down by the insistent steam of the shower.

"Matt, are you okay?"

When there was no answer, she pulled the curtain aside, careful to keep her body behind it. She wouldn't put it past Abraham to just waltz right in, looking for a stool softener or nail clipper.

The door was slightly open, but Matt wasn't in there with her.

"Thanks for not closing the door."

She washed her hair quickly. She couldn't even get peace in the shower.

Stepping out of the tub, Debi grabbed a towel for her hair, wrapping it around like a turban. Slipping another under her armpits, she went to shut the door.

Her eyes caught something on the mirror.

Someone had used their finger to write in the vaporous fog.

WE ARE ALWAYS WATCHING

Debi's scream came roaring from the pit of her stomach, a primal jolt of terror that burned like battery acid.

✠

Matt jumped from bed when he heard Debi shouting. He ran to the bathroom, his shoulder banging off the hallway wall. The door was open. He almost slipped on the slick tile. Grabbing onto Debi was the only thing that kept him upright.

She stared at the mirror, one shaking hand covering her mouth.

"Matt, look!"

He saw what had been written on the mirror. The escaping steam was slowly erasing the words, the menacing message fading like a departing apparition.

"They're in the house! Call the police!"

"Stay in here and lock the door," Matt said, shutting it tight, then remembering there were no locks on any of the doors. His father had forbidden them. If a door was closed, that meant don't come in. Any infraction was cause to bring out the belt.

Matt stumbled back to the bedroom, grabbing his sturdiest cane. If someone was still here, he needed some way to defend himself. No, forget defense. The cane was an offensive weapon. If he got the chance, he wasn't going to wait to use it to fend off a blow. He meant to impart some serious pain to whoever had been in the bathroom with his wife.

Barging back into the hall, he stopped to listen for the sounds of an intruder moving about the house. He could only hear Debi's sobs.

The edges of his vision danced a mad jitterbug.

He could taste the spins coming on in the back of his throat, like the metallic foreshadowing of an approaching storm.

*No! Nonononononononono! Not now! You can't do this to me now!*

He shouted, "Where are you? Come out, you piece of shit!"

"Matt!"

"Stay in there, Debi."

The house was utterly silent. In this old place, the pattering of a mouse would cause a ruckus. Either the pervert who had written on the mirror had fled, or he was waiting in some dark corner, not daring to even take a deep breath.

The rage buzzing through Matt surprised even him. He wanted this bastard more than a return to his normal life.

*Just give me a chance to smash you until there's nothing left. You want to creep into the bathroom while my wife is in the shower? I'll fucking kill you. I'll kill you and your family if I find them.*

With the surge of adrenaline came a bright flash of pain. Even when he shut his eyes, he saw flickering bolts, each static burst unseating his balance just a little bit more until he fell to his knees.

*The phone. Get to the phone. Call the police.*

When Matt opened his eyes, the hallway expanded and contracted, tilting at odd angles. He had to fight through it somehow. Find the phone. Just find the damn phone.

Using the cane as a paddle like an inebriated gondola driver, he pulled himself across the hardwood floor. The living room was just a few feet away. The corded phone was right there on the little table beside the TV.

His breath came in ragged gasps. His fingers were ice cold. Torn between helplessness and blind fury, he'd never been so disoriented.

"Matt? Matt? Are you okay?"

"I'm fine. I'm calling the cops."

He saw the phone. Or actually, two of them. There was two of everything.

*Go for the one on the right.*

Whenever his vision split like this, he always went for the right. He was never sure why and his doctors had no answers. Maybe he was right brained. Or was that just human nature – your *right* hand man, stand up for what is *right*, the *right* hand of God. Didn't the angel stand on your right shoulder, the devil your left?

His hand lashed out, fingers closing on empty space.

A door slammed. There were footsteps. Matt lifted the cane as if it were a baseball bat. He would swing it as hard as he could. Right or left, he was bound to hit whoever had invaded the house.

His heart beat wildly, the organ seeming to have traveled up his throat, kicking his Adam's apple. If he had even the slightest drop of spittle, he was sure he'd choke to death on it.

"What the hell is going on?"

His father tramped into the room, fists clenched.

"It's them," Matt said. He knew he looked pathetic, on his knees, cane raised like he was waiting for a 2 and 1 pitch. "The Guardians. They're in the house! They were just in the bathroom with Debi."

"What?"

Before Matt could open his mouth, his father was off and running. He charged through the house with all the grace of a bear wearing tap shoes, knocking things over, throwing doors open, clomping up the stairs.

Matt fought to regain control.

The phone. He still had to get the phone.

"Matt, who's in the house?" Debi shouted through the thick door.

"It's just my father. Are you all right?"

What he wanted to ask was, *are you alone?* It was ridiculous. Now that she was out of the shower and his father was checking every room, there was no place left for the Guardians to hide.

*If they're flesh and blood.*

It was ridiculous, but when he was a kid, he used to wonder if the Guardians were actually spirits, more tricksters than guardian angels. How else could they enter their lives soundlessly, leaving trails of breadcrumbs that led nowhere?

*Get to the damn phone, Matt!*

This was a humdinger of the old spin cycle. His quivering eyes managed to lock on the phone, then watched it turn round and round, speeding away down a long, tapering tunnel.

*I know you're right there. You're not moving. Just my brain. All I need to do is move a little closer.*

The cane slipped from his hand, clattering on the floor. Matt's face dipped hard, his nose crunching. He sucked in a great, slurping breath, the pain stabbing between his eyes, years of dust capering into his lungs. He went into an immediate coughing fit, the pressure shifting the cartilage of his broken nose, the tang of old pennies sluicing down his throat.

A thick veil of tears clouded his wavering double vision. On the other side of the watery curtain were vague shapes resembling nothing he'd ever seen.

Matt lashed out, this time grabbing hold of something tangible – cold, plastic – a small victory!

He pulled until the whole phone dropped next to him on the gritty floor.

*I'm gonna throw up.*

Swallowing hard, tamping the bile down, his jittery fingers danced over the tiny squares, searching for where he knew the 9 button to be.

*Just three numbers. You can do it. Hell, two of them are in the same spot.*

It was impossible to take a breath through his nose. Debi was saying something, but he couldn't answer her and dial the phone at the same time.

He pressed what he hoped was 9, the tiny chime sounding as if to say, *well, you definitely hit something, Mr. Esasky. Was it 9? Your guess is as good as mine. I only make the little noises.*

Tracing his finger to the top of the number pads, he moved three buttons to the left.

The phone was ripped away from him.

"What the hell do you think you're doing?"

He hadn't even detected his father coming back down the stairs. The pain and spinning were so bad, he felt as if his senses had been completely obliterated. If this kept up much longer, he worried he'd completely short circuit.

"I... I have to call the police," he chuffed, the words sounding so alien, his broken nose snuffing his consonants.

"Like hell you do."

A pair of hands, the rough mitts of his crazed father, shoved under his armpits, lifting him onto the couch.

Three, four, five Abrahams leaned close to him. Matt could smell the sour milk stench of his morning breath.

"You do that and we're all done for."

# CHAPTER TWELVE

West came home to bedlam.

He'd been in a deep funk. The thought of not seeing Faith again had left him numb, in a state that scuttled below depression, a sub-level of hopelessness.

The leaden feeling that rode on his shoulders, deep in the pit of his soul, vanished the second he walked in the door.

He came in just as his mother, wrapped in a towel, burst from the bathroom. She'd been crying, her wet hair sticking like spaghetti to her beaded back.

He followed her into the living room where his father was on the couch, bleeding profusely from his nose. Grandpa Abraham was leaning close to him, as if he were telling him a secret.

What the hell?

"Matt, oh my God, what happened?"

As his mother leaned down to inspect his father's nose, West noticed the cinch at her robe loosen. He quickly turned away. God knows he didn't need to see that!

"He fell and busted his nose pretty good," Grandpa Abraham said. "He'll be all right. I've broken my nose twice. It doesn't get prettier but it'll work just fine."

"Did you find anyone?" his mother asked, looking like a mouse that had just missed being scooped up by an alley cat.

Grandpa Abraham replied, "No. The place is empty."

"What place?" West asked.

"Nothing for you to worry about, short stuff." His grandfather left to go upstairs.

"Dad, what happened?"

His father kept swallowing – *gulp, gulp, gulp, gulp, gulp* – like a hamster drawing in tiny drops from a water bottle. There was so much blood.

*He's trying not to puke.* West knew that frenetic swallow well.

"West, honey, can you please get me a towel? I have to clean your father up."

"Yeah, right!" West darted to the bathroom, grabbing a fresh hand towel from the stack in the small linen closet. It went from yellow to red in an instant as his mother gingerly dabbed at the blood running onto his father's chest. A translucent blood bubble blew out from his lips when he exhaled sharply, his mother brushing the bridge of his crooked nose.

When it popped, West's stomach clinched. He surrounded himself with stories and images soaked with blood – make believe blood – but this he couldn't handle.

Grandpa Abraham came back down with his keys jingling around a finger. "I'll take him to the hospital."

"I can take him," his mother said.

"It's better I do it. I know everyone. Spent too much time there with my Violet towards the end."

"Let me get changed. We're all going. West and I aren't staying here alone. West, can you finish up while I get some clothes on?" She held the bloody hand towel out to him.

West wanted to shout *no way am I touching that!* He'd done a lot to help out his father the past couple of years, getting intimate with the contents of his stomach more than he'd ever want to.

But this was different.

He hesitated. His mother shook the towel at him. "Come on. We have to get him to the hospital."

West found an unstained corner of the towel and pinched his thumb and forefinger around it. His mother dashed off.

"Thanks, bud," his father said, taking the towel and pressing it to his nostrils. "I'll hold back the tide."

He tried to smile, tears leaking from the corners of his eyes.

"Your nose looks like a lightning bolt," West said, focusing on the jagged point of the break. *A few inches higher and he could be Harry Potter.*

"Then it looks a lot better than it feels."

Minutes later, they were in Grandpa Abraham's truck, jouncing over the rutted road to the hospital. His parents said very little on the ride, but West knew there was more to everything than his father simply cracking his nose. He felt it the way he sensed them watching over him when they thought he was asleep at night when he was younger. He'd perfected the art of fake sleep, waiting his parents out so he could read comics or magazines.

They were scared.

And he knew exactly who they were scared of.

What had the Guardians done?

*Did they attack Dad? Mom was very insistent about not being left behind.*

West was very glad she had.

✛

The hospital was actually a medical center, a small box of a building that had been refurbished so recently, you could smell the fresh coat of sterile white paint everywhere. West was expecting something far more… *rednecky*.

It showed that he still had a lot to learn about this area. He couldn't judge all of Pennsylvania by Grandpa Abraham's crumbling old farm.

*Just look at Faith's place.*

Thinking of Faith tied his stomach up in knots.

"I've got a broken nose for you, Brenda," Grandpa Abraham said to the woman at the admitting desk.

The woman sat upright when she saw the bloody towel. Her mousy blond hair was wound up in a tight bun, the features of her face sharp and severe, looking every bit the part of the angry librarian. Her face softened when she looked to his grandfather.

"You been getting into fights?" she said playfully.

"This here's my son," Grandpa Abraham said, leaning an arm on her desk. "He had an accident."

"I'll bump him right up for you," she said softly so no one else in the waiting room could hear. West was surprised by the connection she shared with his grandfather. He could tell she really liked him. Not in a romantic way. More in the way a person would act in the presence of a close acquaintance who'd been nothing but kind.

Was there another side to Grandpa Abraham? West wondered how things would be if they could keep Brenda around the house.

After his mother answered a bunch of questions and handed her insurance card over, a nurse took his father right in. His mother stayed at his side, holding him by his elbow. Grandpa Abraham nodded toward a stack of magazines.

"Have at it," he said. "A reading junkie like you, this should be hog heaven."

West shuffled the magazines. They were either women's or sports mags. He had no interest in either.

He plucked an *Entertainment Weekly* from the pile. There was an article about the new slate of superhero movies for next year. He was halfway through the second paragraph when his grandfather said, "They did a nice job with the place. My money paid for a good part of it, I can tell you that. Hell, this visit should be free, like a buy back at a bar."

West looked over at him.

"What's a buy back?"

"That's a bartender's way of saying 'thanks for all the tips, you rummy.' For every few drinks you buy, they give you one on the house. It's a lost art. By the time you're legal, it'll be gone. They'll charge you triple for crap beer and you'll be none the wiser."

He folded his arms across his chest. He had to slump down in his seat a bit so his feet were flat on the floor.

West said, "What happened to Dad?"

An eyebrow went up. "I told you. He fell. You must see it all the time, the way he stumbles around the house."

A flare-up of anger pulsed at the hinges of West's jaw.

"That's not cool, the way you make fun of him all the time. He's your son. He can't help what happened to him."

Whatever daggers West was throwing at the old man bounced off harmlessly. "There are some things you can't help, and some you can. It's what you do with the shit life deals you that matters. How you ended up in the shitter is out of your hands."

*Thanks for the tough guy philosophy,* West thought, simmering. *He's only doing that to throw you off. He still didn't answer your question. Not honestly.*

204

"How did he fall?"

Now the other eyebrow went up. Two bushy, gray caterpillars inching toward his hairline.

"How the hell should I know? I was outside when it happened. Ask him yourself later."

He said that last line as if it were a dare.

"Was it something to do with the Guardians?"

Grandpa Abraham visibly stiffened. He looked away from West. "You've got an overactive imagination."

"Mom and Dad will tell me anyway."

His grandfather got up from his chair and walked away. "Don't be so sure," he said as he left the waiting room.

West looked around the room. There were a few middle-aged couples, a guy who looked like a biker holding his elbow in the cup of his hand, and a mother with two little kids enchanted by whatever was on her phone. The TV was tuned to the local news channel.

"Asshole," he muttered, dropping the magazine onto the seat next to him.

An hour and a repeat of the news later, his mother and father came out of the single door that led to the treatment area. His father's nose was criss-crossed with bandages, the flesh under his eyes a deep, angry purple. Wads of bloody cotton were stuffed in each nostril.

"You were supposed to wait for a chair," someone called out from the treatment room.

"I'll be fine," his father said without turning around. He looked determined to get out.

"You look like half a mummy," West said.

"That's funny, because they gave me nine tana leaves to fix my nose." He draped an arm over West's shoulder. "Where's your grandfather?"

"I don't know. He walked away a while ago."

"He must be grabbing a bite to eat," his mother said. "I think I saw a sign for vending machines. I'll go check. You both have a seat for a sec."

West scrutinized the bandaging. "Does it hurt?"

"They gave me a shot of something, so it feels fine for now. They also gave me this." He reached into a plastic drawstring bag that his mother had carried out. He showed West a clear plastic mask. "I have to wear it at night, especially, to make sure I don't do any more damage."

"That's like those guards basketball players wear."

"Yep. They get their noses broken all the time. Too many long arms and flying elbows."

A harried looking woman with deep, dark bags under her eyes came in with an older woman, presumably her mother. They went to the admitting station. West thought he heard one of them mention chest pains. Two nurses came right out, ushering them inside.

"How did you fall, Dad? Was it something to do with the Guardians? You and Mom seemed pretty freaked out."

He wanted... no, needed to ask it now, just to prove Grandpa Abraham wrong.

His father patted his knee. "It was just me being clumsy. Something like this was bound to happen sooner or later."

West's heart sank.

"But Mom looked like she was crying."

His father's face was unreadable under all the gauze and tape.

"She didn't look that way to me. I think she was just worried I'd done something worse to myself."

His mother came back with Grandpa Abraham in tow.

"Perfect timing. He was just walking in when I turned the corner."

The old man smelled like beer. West remembered seeing a tavern a block away from the medical center.

"Now your face has some character," Grandpa Abraham said. No one laughed or cracked a smile. Even his grandfather seemed to regret the flippant remark.

West's mother helped his father to his feet. "Come on, let's get you home and in bed."

West stayed several feet behind the adults on the walk to the truck.

*They're all hiding something.*

It made him angry.

And a little scared.

✠

Debi's father-in-law dropped them off and headed for the Post.

*He's probably getting soused right now with his vet buddies, laughing about his clumsy son, cheating at poker.*

The painkiller they'd given Matt at the medical center had him snoring like a band saw within moments of getting home. It sounded painful, like a metal spatula being scraped over pebbled cement.

"He's gonna have a real bad sore throat when he wakes up," West said. They were in the living room, watching a ghost hunting show. West loved anything filmed with a lot of night vision that involved people trying to scare up some monster or apparition. She was surprised he wanted to watch it, considering their current situation.

But, whatever gave him comfort was fine with her.

"I think I'm going to sleep out here… with ear muffs on," she said. They each had a bowl of Italian wedding soup on their laps, an ice cube floating in the center to cool it down enough for them to dig in. Soup in the summer wasn't her preferred choice, but it was quick and they were starving.

"I bet the couch has bed bugs," West said, eyes glued to the people on TV. They were in the basement of an abandoned factory, calling out to the restless spirit of a worker who had accidentally fallen into a vat of acid eighty years ago.

"Gee, thanks for putting that in my head. I guess I'll bunk with you then."

He flashed a brief, crooked smile, slurping soup from the oversized spoon she'd found in the utensil drawer. "Good luck. That bed can barely support me."

Through everything, Debi hadn't forgotten about the message on the bathroom mirror.

WE ARE ALWAYS WATCHING

She'd locked all of the doors and windows, save the one at their backs. The air inside was stifling. No matter. There was no way she was leaving anything to chance. She'd turned on an old table fan but it only spread the tacky warmth around.

Debi could call the police, but West had been through enough. He seemed on edge, drawn into himself. Normally, he was a human question machine. She and Matt used to refer to him as Lil' Clark Kent. He'd been unnaturally quiet since they'd gotten back.

*What must he be thinking?* she wondered. *It can't be good. When kids are left to fill in the blanks, they usually come up with the worst possible scenario.*

But if he did this time, would he be right?

No matter, she and Matt had decided not to tell him what had happened earlier. He was already exposed to too much. At some point, they had to be parents, real parents, and protect him.

Debi couldn't help but feel as if they were being watched right now, despite sitting in a room with the curtains drawn, whatever breeze there was barely moving the shade.

WE ARE ALWAYS WATCHING.

The four words made her shiver, despite the sickly heat of the room and hot soup in her belly.

They needed to get out of this place.

What if they were attacked? Who would hear them cry for help out here amidst the whispering cattails?

It always came down to money. Sure, they could pick up and get in the car this instant, but their freedom would be short-lived. The money would run out before they knew it and they'd be forced to come crawling back. She missed her parents so much right now. They would have taken them in with open hearts and arms. Things would have been so much better. She and West would have been happy. So happy, they might have even turned Matt's funk around.

But they'd been gone almost seven years now, their dream trip to St. Thomas spiraling into a nightmare when a category five hurricane tore the island apart. Over fifty people had died that day, Debi's parents among the victims.

For the first time in a long while, thinking of them filled her with an urgent need to cry.

She willed her tears to stay put.

*Think of West and what you can do to make this better. Mom and Dad aren't going to be able to help you.*

*I should take him to the city with me next week. There's always a free office, especially during the summer with people taking vacation.*

Would he go? He wasn't a little kid anymore, fascinated by trips to mom and dad's workplace. She didn't want to use fear to get him to go with her. Then he'd be terrified coming back each night.

What kind of mother would leave her son behind in a house guarded over by maniacs who could come and go as they pleased?

*One thing I'm sure of, it wasn't Abraham this time. No wonder Matt left and never looked back.*

Debi still seethed over Matt's intentional omission of the Guardians. Even if he thought they were no longer in the picture, he should have told her about the house's past. Matt's duty as her husband was to be honest with her.

*Thwack!*

West nearly levitated off the couch, soup sloshing over the bowl's rim. "What was that?"

Debi's heart rocketed up her throat.

The noise came from the open window behind them.

Slamming her soup bowl on the coffee table, she leapt off the couch, hands balled into fists.

A black and white cat pawed at the screen. It was a big alley cat, probably pushing twenty pounds. It was so strong; it had pushed the screen off the track.

It took her a minute to catch her breath.

"I'm losing it," she said, forcing a laugh. "Was I just about to punch a cat?"

West looked to be having a tough time settling down as well.

"If you did, I bet Grandpa Abraham would give you a reward."

# CHAPTER THIRTEEN

The doorbell rang for the first time since they'd moved in. Matt had just taken off his face guard and made the bed. He'd slept late, thanks to the painkillers. It was the best night's sleep he'd had in as long as he could remember.

*See, there is a silver lining in a broken nose.*

Debi had left for work hours ago. The house was silent, save for the ringing of the bell. God knows where his father was. West was probably outside reading.

"I'm coming, I'm coming," Matt said. Before he knew it, he'd made it to the front door without his cane. He really was feeling good.

When he opened the door, he thought he might need his cane to stay on his pegs.

"Oh man, you look like you head butted a wall."

The heavily bearded man looked at him as if he could feel the pain himself.

Matt said, "Better that than looking like a Mennonite."

"Beards are in now, buddy. It's a total babe magnet."

Throwing the door open, Matt grabbed the man, pulling him in for a hug. "Holy crap, how long has it been?

"Long enough to go through two divorces, three businesses, and come down with ulcerative colitis."

Matt stared at his old friend as if he were a ghost – a welcome ghost. James Adams had been Matt's best friend from kindergarten all the way through eleventh grade, until James's family moved to Kentucky. Matt had been devastated. They'd stayed in touch for a year, writing the occasional letter, calling once a month. But senior year brought a boatload of distractions and both boys settled into their new worlds without one another.

James had changed a lot, but those mischievous eyes and easy smile, even though it was surrounded by a year or more's worth of wiry growth, gave him away.

"How… how did you know I was even here?" Matt said.

"My dad ran into yours at the Post."

"Of course. The local grapevine all starts there."

They walked to the kitchen, Matt stumbling for just a step. James was quick to grab his elbow.

"I heard about what happened," he said. "You okay?"

"Actually, today I'm better than usual." In the echo of the kitchen, he could hear how nasally his voice sounded. One of his nostrils was packed with fresh gauze. "I'm sure you know why I'm here, or at least my father's version. What the hell brought *you* back?"

James took a seat and laughed, that same hearty guffaw that got them thrown out of libraries and assemblies. "Did you not hear the part about my divorces and businesses that went up in smoke? Kentucky sucked. So did West Virginia, Vermont, and New

Mexico. My parents moved back here to a smaller place about three years ago. They got one of those Pocono Mountain homes for practically nothing. I could have stayed in New Mexico, but dad hasn't been doing too well and my mom needed the help. So, here I am, down, but not entirely out."

Matt sat across from him. He couldn't believe James was here. It lightened the dark mood he'd been under for months.

"I've got down *and out* covered," Matt said, though with a laugh.

"Yeah, to hear it, you came crawling back so your old man can take care of you."

"As you can probably guess, he's still an asshole."

"And would we have it any other way? I mean, come on. A kinder, gentler Abraham Ridley is an actual sign of the Apocalypse. I literally just read it in Bible study class."

Matt laughed, the sound and the feeling so alien to him.

*My God, how long has it been since the stick was removed from my ass?*

That old, easy rapport with James came so easily, naturally, it was as if they hadn't been apart for almost twenty-five years.

James leaned as far back in his chair as he could, looking in the living room. "I love what your father's done to the place. It's got a very retro-Sanford and Son vibe."

"Yeah, without my mother around, the place kinda went to shit. But I guess I shouldn't complain. At least there's room for me and my family – rent free, just like the good old days."

Slapping Matt's arm, James said, "Rent free? You dog. I'm paying big time over at the moms and pops. Speaking of big spending, you remember that time we stole from our father's wallets so we could buy the Playboy with Raquel Welch in it from Jerry MacKenzie?"

Matt slapped a hand on the table. "And she wasn't even nude in it!"

"We didn't know that before we risked our lives. Now, we could just Google it and get it for free. If I was a kid today, I don't think I'd ever leave my room, as long as the door was padlocked."

They hurtled down memory lane for an hour, recalling every major gaffe, goof, and victory in their young lives together. Matt hadn't thought of most of the things James brought up since college, when things got a little hazy, thanks to a fraternity that grew their own weed behind the off-campus frat house. The conversation eventually steered toward what they had done since their parting in high school and how vastly different their experiences had been.

"Yet, here we both are," James said.

"Back at the scene of the crime."

James went to the refrigerator to grab a can of soda. He'd always been like that, able to make himself right at home. It used to drive Matt's parents up a tree.

"You know who I ran into?" Matt said. "Andrea Lender."

James wiggled his bushy eyebrows. "The hot babysitter who was warm for your form?"

"I didn't have a form when I was ten."

James chuckled. "True. You were always a late bloomer. How's she looking?"

"Old. Older. Just like the rest of us. She invited me to her house for cocktails."

"Don't go without a chaperone. You remember all about stranger danger, right?"

Matt swatted his arm. "She doesn't live too far from here. Hope I can avoid her." And he hoped she was avoiding him. Something in the way she looked at him screamed *stalker*!

"So, where's your son? You say his name was North?"

"West," Matt corrected him. "Kim Kardashian is not his mother. Thank God. He's outside somewhere. Kid's a bookworm. He reads horror, the more twisted the better. Debi used to worry that exposure to all that craziness would turn him into a serial killer. He's way better adjusted than we were at his age. The most horror we saw was Ms. Jullian's underpants that day her skirt fell down when she was at the blackboard."

James wagged a finger at him. "That's right! Now I remember." He shivered. "I divorced Annie, my first wife, because she wore granny panties."

The soda later became a beer, and even though it was pressing ninety degrees, Matt didn't feel the encroaching heat in the kitchen. Thanks to James, he was a kid again, at least in memory.

Matt hadn't had a beer in well over a year. It was the last thing he needed. At the moment, he didn't give a frog's fat ass if it brought on the spins.

At one point, James grew serious and said, "I'm real sorry about your mom. Man, she was a saint."

Matt was taken aback. "All she ever did was roll her eyes at you."

"Saints are not the most fun to be around. But she tolerated me, and she didn't pull a Lorena Bobbit on your dad. To me, that makes her a saint. I kind of looked at her as a second mom, albeit one of very few words."

"She really liked you. She said as much the day you left. She said, 'You know, I'm going to miss Jimmy. He was a good kid. A little brash, but you evened each other out.'"

James put his hand over his heart. "That really means a lot. No joking. Is she over at Oakland Cemetery?"

Nodding, Matt said, "Yep, right with all the other Ridleys. My dad will be the last to go there. I've already got a sweet land deal in the Bronx. Got a great view of a nice pond and Duke Ellington's grave."

"You shitting me?" James said, sucking foam caught in his mustache.

"Nope. I tried for Miles Davis, but all of the real estate was taken."

They drank in silence for a bit. James went to the window. "Maybe it's the beer talking, but how about we visit your mom? I'd like to pay my respects properly."

At first, Matt thought it was just about the strangest thing his old friend could think of. On the other hand, he'd been hoping to do the same thing himself ever since they'd gotten here.

"You okay to drive?"

James patted his ample belly. "It'll take more than three beers to throw me off my game. I know it's weird, what with us having fun and all, but after what you said about her, I just want to see her, metaphorically. As I get older, I realize I have to do things while they're fresh in my mind or else I'll never remember or get off my ass to do them."

"I think that's a good idea. Let me call West inside." He tried to stand, but ended up plopping back down in his chair. "Three beers is more than I've had in total since my accident. You're going to have to help a brother out."

"Sweet. Now I get to drag your drunk ass around, just like we had planned to do when we were in college."

219

James brought him to the back door, a beefy arm around his waist. Matt called out for West as loud as he could.

His son replied, "I'm right here, Dad. I can hear you."

Right here was under the shade of the picnic table. Sure enough, he had a book in his hand.

✠

James seemed like a nice guy. He was pretty funny.

And he provided a perfect distraction, taking West's mind off of Faith for a while and getting them away from that creepy ass house.

On the way to the cemetery, he shared a slew of stories about him and West's dad when they were teens. His father cringed during a couple of them, especially the one about dropping a cherry bomb in the school toilet, but there was always a smile close behind.

"You used to cut class?" West said.

"Only gym, and only when it was the last period of the day. We were both on the baseball team. We didn't need gym to get us in shape."

"That's not what Mr. P thought," James said. "A month of Saturday detention got our asses back in the gym, I can tell you that. Oops, sorry."

"West is fourteen. He's heard far worse." His father turned back in his seat, tugging on an earlobe. "I've heard you and Anthony when you think no one is around."

West felt himself redden. He and Anthony cursed like guests on *The Jerry Springer Show* when they were together, minus the bleeps. They were careful never to let the f-bombs fly in the presence of their parents or other adults. At least they thought they'd been.

"It's perfectly normal," his father added to lessen his embarrassment. "You should have heard me and this guy when we were your age."

James chuckled. "Everything we learned we got from watching Eddie Murphy and George Carlin on HBO." He flicked the blinker on. "There it is."

Oakland Cemetery wasn't anything like the sprawling graveyards back in New York. The iron entranceway was devoid of rust, but it looked like it had seen its share of years. The entirety of the cemetery lay right before them. West figured there had to be less than a couple of hundred graves in all. The grass was lush and green, so someone was watering it. But it was a little overgrown.

"Is this all there is?" he asked, moving up in the seat, wedged between his father and James in the front.

"Yep," his father replied. "Oakland is for the old families in Buttermilk Creek. I'm talking the ones that really reined in the farmland in the late 1800s. Each parcel holds a family plot, with main stones in the center showing the last name and the surrounding smaller stones for each person buried there."

There were no trees in Oakland Cemetery, or rolling hills or fancy statues. It was, in a word, utilitarian. The sun was directly overhead, so there weren't even spooky shadows reaching from the old tombstones. In West's limited experience, it was the least scary cemetery he'd ever seen.

"Where's Grandma buried?"

His father pointed it out to James. "It's to the right, in the back. That one with the brown sandstone."

James pulled as close to the Ridley plot as he could, helping West's father out of the car and walking with him. West had smelled the beer on their breath and knew his father was a little looped. He decided he liked his father buzzed. He'd have to ask James to come over more often.

A hawk cawed high overhead. West hoped it wasn't feasting on something that had popped up from the century old graves.

The Ridley marker stood over four feet high. The edges were chipped, the chiseled writing faded a bit, but they could still make out the big RIDLEY in the center of the stone. Surrounding it were very small stones, simple markers with first names and dates.

"What the hell?"

West froze. His fathered wavered a moment in James's grasp.

"What's wrong," West asked, moving around his father.

Two of the headstones were covered in spray paint. He could still make out the names underneath the looping, red scrawl. One was for Violet, his grandmother.

The other was Stella's.

On his grandmother's had been written – FOREVER UNDER OUR

On Stella's – WATCHFUL GAZE

"Those motherfuckers," his father literally spit out, seething. "Those goddamn motherfuckers."

"Jesus, I'm so sorry, man. Holy crap," James said. None of them could take their eyes off the desecrated graves.

West's hands and feet went cold. It felt as if his heart had dropped into his stomach.

No one was safe from the Guardians. Not even the dead.

He heard James whisper, "They're still around?"

# CHAPTER FOURTEEN

After hanging up with Matt, all Debi wanted to do was grab a car and race home. She'd never heard him so angry before, and that was after two years of enduring his simmering rage.

She wanted to be there with him. With West.

*God, he must be so scared.*

Even though Monika lived in a studio apartment in Pelham, last week she'd asked Debi to bring the family and stay with her after hearing about the Guardian insanity. Logistically, it would have been impossible.

But right now, Debi didn't care. Even if they had to sleep under Monika's bed, it would have been preferable to spending another day in that farmhouse.

She checked her watch. It was only 2:15. The bus wouldn't be here for another couple of hours. Until then, she was trapped with an overflowing tide of emotions. The first tears spilled down her cheeks. She looked around to make sure no one saw, wiping them quickly with a tissue.

Debi ran to the bathroom, locking herself in a stall.

Her hands shook so bad, she almost dropped her cell phone on the unsanitary floor.

She barely heard the door open and the clicking of heels. Covering her face in her hands, she let the tears run freely, struggling to keep as quiet as possible. Debi couldn't stand women who cried in the office or back in school. She'd been around her share of steady weepers. She never saw men break down and cry when their days went sideways.

Now she was one of those women – and she didn't give a damn.

There was a light knock on her stall door.

"Debi. You alright?"

She sucked in a big breath, tasting the salt of her tears. "I'll be fine, Monika."

"That's not the way you looked when you came in here, hon."

Sniffling, Debi said, "You really are everywhere."

"It's a gift."

Debi turned the silver lock on the door. When Monika saw her sitting there, irregular lines of mascara on her cheeks, she rushed in to wrap her in a hug.

That did it. Debi bawled into Monika's shoulder, soaking the fabric of her cream blouse. She couldn't help herself. It felt as if all of the stress and fear of the past year was pouring out of her.

"What happened that's got you so upset?"

It took a couple of minutes to compose herself enough to speak without hiccupping in starts and stops.

"It's getting worse," was all she was able to sputter.

Monika smoothed her hair. "Is it Matt?"

Debi shook her head. "The... the Guardians. They desecrated the graves of Matt's mother and sister."

"Jesus, Mary, and Joseph. Are Matt and West okay?"

"Yes. They're with one of Matt's old friends. He took them to his house. I just want to be there with them. Matt's flying off the handle and I can only imagine how terrified West is right now. But I have to wait for the damn bus!"

Unrolling the spool of toilet paper, Monika placed a wad in her hands. "Here, dry yourself up. I'll be back in a few minutes. Just stay right here. I'll lock the door behind me so no one comes in."

Monika hurried away, the lock engaging with an echoing click. Debi got up and stood by the sink.

*You're a mess. Pull it together.*

She ran some water, using the toilet paper to wipe off her makeup. Her eyes were red rimmed and glassy. No way to cover that up. At least the well had run dry... for the moment.

Monika was back five minutes later. She had a key ring on her index finger. "Here, take these."

"You're giving me the bathroom key? I'm better. I'll wait it out at my desk. Not sure how much actual work I'll get done."

Monika gave a half-smile. "These are the keys to one of the company cars. Take it and get to your family."

She dropped the keys in Debi's hands. "But those cars are only for the executives. I could get fired."

Resting a hand on her shoulder, Monika said, "Hon, who do you think controls who gets to drive those cars? Now, go to your desk, grab your purse and get out of here. And call me when things settle down."

Debi was at a loss for words. She hugged her friend, fighting back a new wave of tears, these of gratitude, and opened the bathroom door. Behind her, Monika said, "You're all clear from here to the garage. Frank Daniels already left for the day. And remember my offer."

If Debi ever needed proof that guardian angels existed, she had it now.

Matt had had the phone in his hand, just to drop it on the couch at least a dozen times in the past hour. James's parent's place was a comfortable faux cabin. His parents were retired psychologists. The living room was lined with stocked bookshelves. It screamed *intellectuals reside here!* The central air ran cold, but it was comfortable. James told him they were visiting some old colleagues and wouldn't be back until after dinner.

"I'm telling you, man, just call the cops." James sat next to him on the couch. West was across from them in one of those rocking chairs you buy at Cracker Barrel.

"Believe me, I want to." He picked up the phone again, running his fingers over the 9 and 1 buttons. "They're just going to tell me to contact the caretaker and take my statement. It's not an emergency."

West spoke up. "It is if we tell them everything. Stalking is a crime. They've even been in the house!"

Matt shook his head. "We both know that, but where's the proof?"

"The notes! What they wrote on the mirror in the living room and bathroom."

Matt cringed. He'd forgotten that he and Debi had spared West the details about what had happened in the bathroom. So when he explained it to James, West naturally heard every word.

"West, what was on the mirrors is gone and we can't definitively show the police that the notes we found were in the house."

James took a long swallow from a can of soda. "Maybe if those assholes see some cop cars around, they'll get the hint that you're not like your old man. You're serious about putting a stop to all this. That could be enough to scare them off."

The lump of dread in Matt's stomach burned like battery acid. He was dizzy, but his anger refused to let it take center stage like it usually did.

How many times had he been in West's shoes, begging his father to alert the police? He'd even threatened to run away if they didn't. His mother always sat there stoically, cold fear visible on her face but refusing to say anything that would be counter to his father's demand that they ignore the messages and move on with their lives.

*"No Fuckhead Faulkner is gonna run me out of my home!"*

*"But I'm not saying we should run! We need the police to find them and arrest them."*

*"I said no goddamit! This doesn't leave the farm."*

Oh, how Matt had hated his father. Sometimes, he lumped him right in with the Guardians. Both existed to make his life miserable.

Staring at his lap, Matt said, "It won't make them stop. But it will make things worse."

"Worse than defacing your family's graves?" James said. He'd been the only person Matt had confided to when he was a kid about the Guardians. That's what you did with best friends, even when your parents made you swear never to tell anyone under penalty of unimaginable punishment. Matt needed someone to share his family's dark secret. To his credit, James had kept it to himself. They'd even plotted ways to catch the Guardians, culling ideas and contraptions from Road Runner cartoons. The only problem at the time was that there was no ACME store to supply them with gadgets, anvils, and dynamite.

Matt had told James almost everything, which really just amounted to ominous notes found outside the house. The intrusions into the house were a new twist.

Maybe if he'd told his friend everything, he'd understand why Matt was conflicted about calling the police. He sure as hell couldn't clue him in now, not with West a few feet away.

Swallowing hard, Matt looked to his son, then his childhood friend. "There is a chance. Yes."

When his cellphone rang, all three of them stiffened.

"We're not too jumpy," James joked, shaking his head.

It was Debi.

"We're fine, Deb. Really. No, we're staying at James's place for now. He's okay. You're in a car? Whose car? Oh. That was really cool of her. Yeah. Yeah. We'll sit tight until you get here." He cupped a hand over the phone. "James, what's the address?" Matt repeated it to his wife, who was crossing the George Washington Bridge.

"See you soon." He paused. "I love you, too."

"Mom's driving?" West said, going to the window.

"Her friend Monika got her a company loaner car. She should be here in a little over an hour. Maybe less, knowing her."

"And then what?" West asked. He fingered the blinds, flipping the slats so they opened wider.

"I don't know. Your mother and I will talk about it and decide together."

James rose from the couch, motioning for Matt to walk with him.

"I'll be back in a sec, West. You okay?"

West nodded. "Can I turn on the TV?"

"Absolutely," James said, handing him the remote. "We've got satellite, so you only have about a thousand channels to choose from."

"You have Chiller?"

"I'm pretty sure we do. You have to check the guide to find it, though. The ones I know are all the sports channels."

While West flipped around the guide on the big screen, Matt followed James to his room in the back of the house. It was a tidy guestroom with a tightly made bed and spotless wood floor.

Matt whistled. "Your room used to look like a cyclone hit it."

"I also used to swear I'd never see a naked titty and wrote terrible songs I'd send to Journey, hoping they'd record one and take me on tour." He laughed for the first time since the cemetery. "Gotta respect my mother, the spawn of Felix Unger. She let things slide when I was young and dumb. Old and dumb means you keep your room clean."

Matt sat on the bed. "I know you didn't bring me here to show me you can make your bed well enough to bounce a quarter off it."

"That I didn't." James opened a walk-in closet, rummaging around the shelf over the clothes rack. It was crammed with boxes

232

and luggage. He unzipped a suitcase, along with an inner compartment. "Here it is."

He pulled out a black handgun.

"You have a gun?"

"For years. I had to get one to protect myself when I owned a Laundromat in West Virginny. People don't realize how dangerous that job is, especially when it's time to take the money out of the machines. You'd be surprised by how many owners and worker bees get rolled, stabbed, or shot."

Matt stared at the gun. "You ever use it?"

"Nope. But I had to flash it a few times to stop some bad shit from going down."

"Can I hold it?"

"Try it on for size."

Matt hadn't had a gun in his hand since before West was born. Going to a gun range when he was in his twenties was just something he did a couple of times a year with his buddies. It was either that or a driving range. Matt always preferred shooting targets to smashing little white balls.

"Smith & Wesson .38 Special. They get the job done at close range." Matt checked the cylinder, shocked to find it fully loaded. "You been expecting trouble here?"

James leaned against his dresser. "What's the point of having a gun if it's not loaded? You think if someone broke in here, he'd give me time to find my bullets and load the gun?"

"If he meant to do you harm, you'd be dropped before you got it out of that suitcase."

Cocking an eyebrow, James wagged his finger at him. "You've got a point there. Anyway, that one's my spare. Serial number has been scraped off. Totally untraceable. I have a .44, but that one's legal. I got the .38 from a guy I met at a Coin Laundry Association convention. And before you ask, yes, they have conventions for people who own Laundromats. They're good for the booze and a chance to see a new city, though they're usually held in places like Cincinnati and Provo. Anyway, I want you to have it."

Matt liked the heft of the gun, the cool steel and palm-sized grip. "Hey, man, thanks and all, but I can't take it. Debi will shit if she sees a gun. I married a pacifist."

"Then don't let her see it. If you're not going to call the cops, you need a way to protect your family. For all you know, those Guardians are getting old and want to make one last splash. That shit back there crossed a line. And you know they've been in the house. You shoot them once they've crossed that threshold, you're within your rights."

A part of him desperately wanted to accept the gun. James was right. Spray painting his mother and sister's graves was taking things too far.

*No, too far was slipping into the bathroom when Debi was showering,* Matt thought, feeling his blood pressure rise even further. *This is just sick.*

The Guardians were getting bolder. What the hell was their endgame? After all these years, they had to have something in mind, a final straw they'd been meaning to break.

"I'd be arrested for possession of an unlicensed firearm. Not to mention, with my vertigo, I can barely see straight most days, much less shoot straight."

He held it out for James to take it back. His friend refused.

"Then just keep it as a last resort. Like I told you, I only had to let dudes *see* the gun to put the fear of God in them. These Guardian pussies will turn tail just the same."

Matt saw there was no returning the gun. And to be honest, he *wanted* it. The hard part would be the guilt of keeping it from Debi. But that guilt would be wiped clean if the .38 was all that stood between him and his family's safety.

He emptied the bullets and put them in his pocket, then tucked the gun at his back.

"Man, that's uncomfortable. They make it look so natural in movies." Turning his back toward James, he asked, "Can you see it?"

"No, you're good."

"Thanks."

James closed his closet doors. "On another note, you guys are welcome to stay here for the night. You and your wife can take my room. I have a sleeping bag somewhere for West. I'll be happy on the couch. It's actually where I sleep most nights anyway. I tend to pass out while I'm watching TV like the old man I'm becoming."

"We couldn't put you out. You've already done enough. What a way for us to reconnect, huh?"

"It has been exciting, I'll give you that."

There was a shrill scream in the living room, followed by the sound of gunfire. Matt reached for the gun, stopping himself when he realized it was just the movie West was watching.

"That's one tough kid," James said. "After everything, he's still watching a scary flick."

Matt scratched the stubble of his five o'clock shadow. "He doesn't look at horror stuff like you or me. That's his security blanket."

"Like I said: tough kid."

He was right. West was strong. Every day, Matt saw more glimpses of the man he'd soon become. He was both proud and sad; proud of what he and Debi had created together, and sad that he was rapidly losing the little boy who had been his shadow and his greatest joy.

And now, he was more determined than ever not to let any harm come to him.

236

# CHAPTER FIFTEEN

West leapt from the chair to answer the door when the bell rang. It wasn't his house and anyone could have been on the other side, but he just knew it was his mother. There was a slight hesitation when she saw him, but he opened his arms to let her know this was one of those times it was all right to hug, and hug hard.

"Matt," she said. She pulled Matt close to her as well. West knew they looked corny as hell, but for the moment, he didn't care.

"I'm surprised I didn't get pulled over getting here," she said.

"Jersey cops like to take naps in the afternoon," James said.

"Sorry, Debi, this is James, my friend from the bad old days, at least until he left me."

He shook her hand. "It's nice to meet you, James, though I wish it was under better circumstances. Thank you for keeping my boys here."

"Hey, it's like nothing's changed. Matt always spent more time over here when we were kids… for obvious reasons."

West's mother exchanged a strange look with James, as if she were looking for some kind of hint to the full meaning of *it's like nothing changed*. Instead of elaborating, he said, "I'll go forage in the kitchen and give you guys some privacy. I told your hubby that you all can stay here. It's a small place, but we can manage."

"Thank you again. That's very sweet of you."

When James left the room, West's mother and father sat on the couch. West turned the TV off, preferring to stand.

"Okay, first things first, are you okay, Matt? I know that must have been a shock. You sounded so angry on the phone, I was worried about what you might do."

He put a hand on her thigh and gave a gentle squeeze. "Trust me, if the person that did it was in the cemetery, I'd either be hiding out or in central booking for murder."

"He was so red, I thought his head was gonna explode," West said, pacing.

"And how about you?" his mother asked.

It would be easy to tell her that the idea of being under the secretive, watchful eyes of people who didn't think twice about desecrating a grave scared the living crap out of him. But as angry as his father was, his mother looked equally as worried. What was the point in adding to her concern?

"I'm fine. It's kinda weird, but so is everything about Buttermilk Creek. It's like living in one of those small towns in Goosebumps."

She turned to his father. "Have you called the house and spoken to your father?"

"I tried once but he didn't pick up. He either can't hear the phone or he's still out at the Post."

"Maybe we should check the Post and tell him what happened. We're sure as hell not going back to that house."

Matt's father looked down at his lap, shaking his head. "I know James said it's no big deal, but I wouldn't feel comfortable staying here, even for the short term. This is his parent's house. I can't see six people sharing one bathroom. Plus, James's father isn't in the best of health." That was obvious by the small table filled with pills by the rocking chair. West had glanced at the bottles earlier, unable to recognize any of the names of the medication. They didn't give him any clues as to what was wrong with the man.

"That's fine. I agree with you. We can splurge for a hotel tonight. Maybe we need a little separation from the place to figure things out. After we find your father, we really should call the police, if not today, then tomorrow."

Just the mention of the word *police* seemed to pain West's father.

But why?

West's curiosity wasn't going to let that one go. No way.

For now, though, it was best he keep out of it.

"We'll see," he said. "We passed by a Super 8 before. We could check in there. It's at the same exit as the Post. Rates should be cheap at least."

"That sounds good."

West hadn't seen his mother and father look at one another with such affection in a long time. It was weird how fear and anger were what was bringing them together.

"Don't we need clothes and stuff?" West asked.

"That we do," his father said. "So, we'll get a room and you can hang there with Mom. James and I will swing by the house and pack some stuff up. After we check the Post."

His mother was about to protest but stopped herself.

It had been a long time since his dad took charge of things.

He faltered getting up from the couch, but was able to right himself. "James, I have one more favor to ask," he said as he walked into the kitchen, keeping a hand on the wall.

"I can't remember the last time we were in a hotel," West said. Despite everything the day had brought, he couldn't deny a small thrill at something that seemed so extravagant.

His mother flashed a tired smile. "Don't set your sights too high. There's no room service at the Super 8. We'll be lucky to get clean sheets."

It didn't matter.

Sleeping in a new bed without those creepy words hanging over him, even though they were hidden behind the Ash Costello poster, was a vast improvement.

✠

After James's parents returned home, his mother tearing up at seeing Matt and being concerned about his nose, they ordered pizza while James explained what had happened.

"That's horrible," his mother said. "Your poor mother and sister."

"Animals," his father said. He was shorter than Matt remembered, with loose, sallow skin and bulbous bags under his eyes. "I hope the cops find them and rough them up before they throw them before a judge."

As much as Matt wanted to get going after dinner, he had to be polite and catch up with Mr. and Mrs. Adams. They had been surrogate parents to him, after all.

The sun was setting when they finally left. Debi tookWest in the loaner car to the hotel.

Matt asked James to stop at the house first. If he could avoid the boozy geezers at the Post, all the better. The farmhouse loomed dark and silent. Matt got out of the car and looked around, wondering who was out there watching them at this very moment.

Did the Guardians take shifts, a pair of eyes always trained on his family?

*Fuckers.*

"Hold up a sec," Matt said. He took the gun out from his waistband, keeping it in his right hand, his index finger crooked over the trigger guard. "Just in case."

James pulled out his .44. "I'm with you on that."

Together, they entered the still house, the front door unlocked, just the way Matt had left it. What was the sense of locks when the Guardians seemed to have total and free access?

He flicked the hall light on. His father wasn't home. It was too early for him to be in bed, even if he was sleeping it off. Plus, his omnipresent pungent odor, the smell of booze sweating out of old pores, was missing.

"I can sweep the house," James said.

"Don't bother. I just want to pack a bag and get the hell out."

He packed a couple of days of clothes for Debi and himself, making sure he got work outfits out of the closet for her. They went to West's room next, the stairs cracking like gunshots. Climbing them with a cane in one hand and a gun in the other was no easy feat. He worried about slipping and the gun accidentally going off.

He was glad James was with him. Everything about the place felt tainted now.

What they were going to do from here on out was anyone's guess. They had a rock on one side and a hard place on the other and he was feeling crushed by them.

James carried the suitcase to West's room, plopping it on the bed. It sank several inches. "What's the mattress made of, quicksand?"

Matt looked at the awful condition of the bed, adding a fresh wave of disappointment with himself. It was the first time he'd been upstairs since they'd moved in. He couldn't even provide a decent bed for his son to sleep in.

He threw some clothes into the suitcase, along with a couple of books and magazines. West needed them more than the clothes.

"I like your kid's style," James said, looking at the horror pictures on the walls. "Especially that." He pointed at the ceiling. Matt looked up and into the face of a goth girl with hair that was strikingly red on one side and black on the other.

"All horror and no honeys," Matt joked. The mood needed lightening. "Okay, I'm all set. Let's get the hell out of here."

They just stepped into the hallway when a dull thump they could feel through the bottom of their feet froze them in their tracks.

"Front door?" James asked.

"No," Matt whispered. "It would have been louder."

The day's heat felt as if it was all trapped on the second floor. Sweat trickled down the back of his neck.

After a minute of not hearing anything else, they proceeded cautiously. No matter how quiet they wanted to be, the stairs gave them away. One of the steps protested mightily under James's weight. It was during that creak of distressed wood that Matt thought he heard someone groan.

It sounded as if it came from right behind them.

He looked back so fast, he almost lost his balance.

"You hear that?" Matt said, still not daring to raise his voice above a strangled sigh.

"No. What'd you hear?"

Matt pointed to the upstairs hallway, just outside his father's room. "It sounded like a person."

James rushed back up the stairs, the massive .44 leading the charge. He ran into Abraham's room and pulled the chain on the ceiling light. Matt waited on the stairs, dizzy, flexing his hand on the gun's grip. This was crazy. If his father was home drunk, they'd end up shooting him for sure.

"All clear," James said, turning the light out.

"It might have just been my imagination."

"Well, since I'm already in room sweep mode, I might as well check downstairs."

"Just don't shoot first and ask questions later," Matt warned him as he passed him on the stairs.

It took him a little longer to make his own way down.

The spins wanted to set him on his ass. His stomach acids gurgled, looking for a way out. Matt refused to give in.

"Nothing down here, either," James said. "Something could have fallen in that packed living room."

Matt nodded through gritted teeth. "Probably what it was. The place is a mess, and that's after we did some straightening up."

"Post next?"

"Post next."

Before they left, Matt took another look up the stairs.

The earlier noise distinctly sounded like a woman, the start of a suppressed sob before it was quickly cut off. He couldn't see the top landing in the gloom.

*That's right where Mom died.*

*Dad keeps telling West the place is haunted.*

*Maybe he's not a total lying sack of shit.*

They weren't surprised to find his father at the bar. He had a half-full highball glass of whiskey in front of him and a bottle of beaded Budweiser, playing solitaire. The smoke in the Post was thick as cheesecake. The veterans didn't give a fiddler's fart about the new no-smoking laws. As well they shouldn't. They'd done enough to earn the right to smoke at the bar.

All eyes turned to Matt and James. The Post was a protective enclave of regulars. They were not one of them, in addition to being the youngest people in the bar by a couple of decades.

"Well, if it isn't Esasky," his father said, taking a swig from the beer. "I don't remember calling for a driver, but you'll do. Though I hope the hairy fella is the one behind the wheel." He looked to the bartender. "Hey Johnny, that's my prodigal son. Get him a beer, will ya? You can have a beer, right?"

245

Matt leaned heavily on the cane, waving the bartender off. "Dad, we need to talk."

James said, "I'll take his beer." He settled down between a couple of gray- haired men that looked old enough to have served in Korea. They started at him as if he were a stone gargoyle come to life.

Abraham patted a stool next to him. "You want to talk? Park it and start yapping."

*Jesus, this isn't going to be easy. He's crocked.*

There was a dim hope that the booze had dulled his father's usually caustic personality, though his calling him Esasky didn't bring much encouragement.

"I think it would be better if we go outside," he said.

"Here is just fine. Everyone here is my family. You don't have to keep secrets from them."

He raised his glass to the dozen old men sitting around the U-shaped bar. A couple of them raised their drinks in return. Most of the others had turned their attention back to the television mounted on the wall. The Phillies were on and already down five runs in the third.

"I think it would be better if we had a little privacy."

His father smirked at him. "That's how I feel about my home. You can't always get what you want. What was the name of that nigger-lipped white guy that sang that song?"

246

"You can talk in the back if you want," Johnny, the bartender, offered. He was a big man in his early sixties with a severe buzz cut and deep cleft in his chin. He stared at Matt's busted nose, his black eyes, obviously taking pity on him.

"Or right here," his father insisted.

Matt sighed. He pictured punching his father square in the face. It helped to ease the tension that had his insides in a death grip. "Fine. I went to the cemetery this afternoon."

His father knocked back the whiskey. "It's about time you saw your mother and sister."

*I wonder when was the last time you dragged your sorry ass to see them,* Matt thought.

"Someone spray painted over their graves."

"What the hell are you talking about?" His bloated tongue had a tough time getting the words out.

"It said, 'Forever under our watchful gaze.' I think you know who wrote it."

Something behind his father's eyes flared, like the blue flame of a blowtorch.

"Show me," he said, standing up so fast, the barstool went flying out behind him.

Heads turned from the TV back to them.

"I can't. The cemetery's closed."

"That don't mean jack." He stumbled and this time it was Matt keeping the old man on his pegs.

"Actually, it does. Debi, West, and I are staying at the Super 8 tonight. I thought you should know. You know what I want to do and I know what you're going to say, so there's no sense wasting time."

Matt flinched when his father grabbed the beer bottle, flinging it against the wall. Johnny didn't admonish him for it.

"They think they can do that to Violet and Stella," he mumbled, leaning on the bar.

"You can come to the Super 8 with me," Matt said, surprising himself. All of his father's racist, mean bluster had melted away. He looked old and pitiful and lost.

His father pulled away from him. "I'm not leaving my house. Never. I need another beer."

Johnny said to Matt, "I can take him home. Wouldn't be the first time."

Matt looked at his father, the tight set of his lips and the wild look in his eyes. There was no sense trying to change his mind. He looked rattled. Maybe, once he sobered up, he'd finally come to his senses.

"Thanks," Matt said. His father ignored him, chugging his beer. "Come on James."

As they left, Matt sensed everyone in the bar staring at their backs.

It felt the exact same way as when they left the farmhouse earlier that night.

# Chapter Sixteen

Abraham sat on the bench behind his home. The moonlight bathed the swaying stalks of cattails. Scents of mint and cinnamon coasted on the pre-dawn breeze. He eyed the open bottle of Jack Daniels on the picnic table.

No.

The rifle felt heavy on his lap, as if gravity were trying to claim it for its own and drag it down to the center of the Earth. His vision blurred. He rubbed at his eyes with the back of his knuckles, but it only made things worse.

"You there?" he whispered. If they were, they would be close enough to hear him.

Something rustled in the grass to his right. He turned and fired. The rifle's report was louder than a hydrogen bomb in the cold, dead field.

Abraham's heart banged so hard in his chest, his breath came out in sharp whistles. Staggering from the bench, he spotted a still shadow just fifteen yards from his position. Swallowing dryly, the alcohol having bled all the moisture from his body, he stepped toward the gray lump.

As he got closer, a chuckle forced its way up his constricted throat.

*Fucking cat.*

The turn to go back to the bench sent his brain for a loop. He dug the barrel of the rifle into the dirt, using it as a crutch, to keep from falling over.

"Got one of your damn cats," he said, laughing so hard, he burped acid.

He stared into the open field, knowing that somewhere, eyes were looking back at him.

*Let them. I'm not afraid of you. Never was. Not even when you did…*

"You know I'm not going anywhere, you sons of bitches," he said, his voice escalating until it degenerated into a wet cough.

That was the cold, hard truth. Those fucking Guardians could kiss his hairy, wrinkled ass. There was nothing they could do to him that would make him lose one minute of sleep. Nothing.

But he was no longer alone.

*Goddammit, Matt, why did everything have to go tits up and shoot you right back here?*

Matt and Debi and West desperately wanted to leave, but there was no money to go anywhere. And it's not like he had any to give. All he had was this crap house and decayed farm. Like him, they were stuck here.

Escaping was an option that was off the table.

The Guardians, when they had their dander up, meant it when they said you couldn't leave. No, those assholes held true to their promises.

250

He remembered the Toons who used to live on the tract of land across the way. They left, picking up stakes one night when Mel Toon had had enough. He took his wife and three kids, loaded them in his truck, and left with nothing but a couple of suitcases and his rifle.

Abraham's father went white when he read the paper a week later. The entire family had been found in Lake George, New York, dead from carbon monoxide poisoning in their cramped motel room.

They all knew that hadn't happened by chance.

Abraham sure as hell didn't wish that on Matt and his family. That's why he'd taken precautions.

The Guardians were pushing his buttons, seeing how far they could drive him before he cracked.

"Tough shit, Fuckhead Faulkner," he spat.

He wished he knew what it was that drove them; what compelled them to lord over this Podunktown and do all of those horrible things. He didn't believe the old superstitions. They weren't supernatural. They didn't come from rent doorway to hell. Oh, he'd tried to find out, but some things were meant to be a mystery.

They were degenerates and psychopaths, their twisted genes passing down from generation to generation because of...

He thought he heard something moving in the grass. He tensed, finger on the trigger. The crickets hadn't stopped chirping, so it couldn't have been one of them.

He took another swig of Jack.

Besides, Abraham didn't care squat about mysteries. He lived in reality, not speculation. And the reality was that generations of Guardians had made life a living hell for the citizens of Buttermilk Creek.

Equally true was that the Ridleys didn't cow tow to the Guardians. No sir. It wasn't going to happen. With Matt gone, Abraham was happy to say he'd fought them to the end. Once he was gone, there would be no one left for them to torture…at least on Ridley ground. He'd willed the house and land to a charity, leaving Matt nothing.

It was the best thing he could ever give him. Total freedom from this cursed land.

"Why couldn't you at least give me that?" he asked the dark sky.

His thoughts devolved to static, fading to black.

Abraham didn't feel a thing when he passed out, the back of his head bouncing off the hard packed dirt.

"You going to work, Mom?"

It was 6 a.m. The room was pitch-black thanks to the heavy drapes, save the subdued light coming from the bathroom. West had a double bed to himself. Even though he'd been jazzed up last night, he'd slept better than he had since they came to Pennsylvania.

His mother, dressed in a maroon skirt and white blouse, spoke softly so as not to wake his father in the next bed. "As much as I don't want to, I have to bring the car back. Other people might need it. Why don't you go back to sleep?"

West slipped out from under the covers, scratching his head. "I'm wide awake. I must be turning into a farmer."

She smiled. It was good to see she still could. She'd been so frightened last night. It felt as if a month had passed while they waited for his father to return, even though it had been less than an hour. They'd passed the time in silence, watching TV. West kept stealing glances at his mother, alarmed by the worry lines at the corners of her eyes and forehead.

"You hungry?" she asked.

"Always."

"Get dressed. I'll take you for some breakfast before I leave. If I'm late today, I'm late."

He ordered hot cakes, sausage, scrambled eggs, and a hash brown from McDonald's. His mother had a coffee. They watched the sunrise, pink rays painting the asphalt of the parking lot.

"You can come to work with me," she said as they left.

He rolled his eyes. "Only little kids go to work with their mommies. People at your job would think I was slow or something."

She took his baseball cap off and ruffled his hair. "No they wouldn't. It's summer. A lot of the big cheeses are on vacation. I can find an empty office and you can pretend you're the boss."

He knew she wanted him close by today. And yes, it would be nice to hang out in an air-conditioned office, maybe see some sights at lunch.

But that would leave his father alone. At least at work, his mother would be surrounded by people. And she would have her friend, Monika.

After everything that had happened, West wondered if James would bother coming back. He couldn't blame him if he didn't. That would leave his father all alone, trapped in the room with his thoughts.

"I think I'll stick around here. Maybe I can talk Dad into reporting everything to the police."

A strange look passed over his mother's face. She'd wanted to say something, but thought better of it.

"Okay," she said. "But you make sure to call me at least twice."

"I will."

"We're going to figure a way out of this mess. I promise."

She started the car, the leather interior smelling new and expensive and this side of decadent.

Driving back to the Super 8, West wasn't convinced they could get out of this. Not without doing something drastic.

The Ridleys were not drastic people. At least not the trio from New York. They were the true middle-class, sticking to the middle of the road, the one much traveled.

Which meant, and it was disturbing to realize this, that everything might come down to Grandpa Abraham.

"I don't think that's such a good idea, West."

His father sat up in bed, his hair matted to one side. Even though he'd just woken up, he looked exhausted.

"What if something happened to Grandpa Abraham?" West couldn't believe the words coming out of his mouth, but it was true. For some reason, he was worried about the cantankerous old man. Sure, he'd lived with the Guardians all his life, or so he said, but West had the feeling what had happened at the cemetery had changed the age old game. His grandfather may have been a prick, but he was also the only other family they had left. And there were times, fleeting moments, when he was almost nice, just shy of normal.

"He can take care of himself. He's made that abundantly clear for decades."

"But what if he can't this time?"

His father swiveled his feet out from under the covers. "I can't get us there anyway. A cab would be too expensive."

"James could take us."

He swayed a moment when he stood, pinched the bridge of his nose and shuffled into the bathroom. "James did enough for us yesterday."

The splash of urine echoed in the small bathroom.

"He said he'd call in the morning," West reminded him.

"Yeah, well, he and I made similar promises twenty-five years ago."

"Now is different. You're old men with responsibility."

He popped his head out of the bathroom. "Old men?"

West smirked. "Well, not *old* old, but old enough."

Before his father could answer, his cell phone rang. West checked the screen and saw it was James. "See. Old guys like you stick to your word."

Sighing, his father asked, "You really want to go? After all the time you bitched about getting away from that place."

"I do."

He answered the phone, saying, "Hey James, you free to chauffeur me and West one more time?"

Grandpa Abraham's truck wasn't in its usual spot. The front door was wide open.

"You think he left in a hurry or something?" West asked.

"His truck is back at the Post," James said. "I drove by before I picked you up. Maybe the bartender forgot to close the door on the way out."

James wore a green trucker hat with a picture of a coiled snake with DON'T TREAD ON ME stenciled above it in gold. He most likely wasn't aware that there were two Cheerios in his beard.

"I'm sure he's sleeping it off on the couch," West's father said.

He noticed both men stuffing their hands in their pants pockets when they got out of the car. Even though it was a hot start to the day, James wore a long windbreaker. They exchanged a knowing look with one another and approached the house. His father was having a good day so far. He wasn't leaning on his cane so much.

"You stay back while we check the house," he said. "Trust me, you don't want to see your grandfather in a compromised position."

West leaned against the car, watching them cautiously step into the house. They looked more like cops entering a suspect's lair than two men expecting to find a hungover old man, perhaps covered in vomit or with his pants halfway down.

"Dad?" his father's voice floated out the front door.

West tentatively walked toward the poor excuse for a front porch. He heard his father and James walking around the house, the creak of the stairs. "He's not up here," James reported.

*I'll bet he's in the basement,* West thought. That was Grandpa Abraham's little hideaway, the place where he went when he'd had a few drinks in him. When they'd first moved in, West had been curious as to what could be in the dingy cellar. Knowing it was his grandfather's special place dulled his desire to see it. He imagined it as a filthy dungeon, with moldy furniture, empty bottles of booze, urine in mason jars, and generally smelling like impending death.

"Dad?"

West wasn't about to go inside until his father gave him the all clear. Despite everything, or maybe because of what had happened, a little of his old father had returned. And they were getting along, comrades in arms in a difficult situation. He didn't want to screw that up, which is why he hadn't brought up calling the police… yet.

The sun beat down on his head. *Thank God we'll be going back to an air-conditioned room,* he thought. It was going to be a scorcher.

He had to get out of the concentrated rays or he'd fry like an ant under a magnifying glass.

He walked along the side of the house and saw the long shadow of the decaying structure stretch all the way to the untended wild growth in back.

*Ahh, shade.*

He'd just knock on the back door to let his father know where he was.

Scanning the high grass, his heart clenched, knowing that Faith was across the field, locked in her room for the summer like a princess in a tower. If he wanted to be her prince, he'd need to ditch his frog persona, but things like that are never easy when you're fourteen and in love with the first girl to give you the time of day.

"*But you gotta have Faith,*" he sang to himself, kicking a rock out of his way.

The rock skittered ahead of him, hitting a divot and making the turn around the corner of the house. It made a hard ping as it hit something. It sounded like it banged into something metallic.

Rounding the corner, West pulled back in horror.

Grandpa Abraham lay on his back, a halo of blood circling his head. His arms were stretched out, as were his legs. His wrists and ankles were held in place with pitchforks, each joint wedged between the rusted tines.

He tried to call for his father but nothing came out. His mouth opened and closed like a fish bobbing for food. It felt like his heart was at the back of his tongue, clamoring away.

There was a note pinned to his chest. A chest that he was relieved to see was moving up and down with each shallow breath.

The note said:

DON'T YOU LEAVE AGAIN. YOU DO THAT, HE DIES, AND WE TEAR DOWN THAT WHICH WE'VE GUARDED FOR SO LONG.

# Chapter Seventeen

Matt was beyond frustrated, both with the situation he'd gotten them into and himself. He mentally kicked himself for not finding his father first, practically crucified into the ground like that. The shock at seeing him, and the wild look on West's face, sent his vertigo into overdrive. The ground swelled, sending him to his knees, his cane skittering away from him.

With James's help, they pulled the pitchforks free. His father reeked of booze, but he was alive. Lifting up his head, he found a quarter-sized ding that accounted for all the blood. Matt had to pluck a jagged rock from the wound. It looked as if he had fallen down drunk. The bottle of Jack on the picnic table supported the theory.

Was that really the case? Did the Guardians seize the moment to ramp up their campaign of terror? Or was he attacked by them?

"West, you able to give me a hand?" James asked. Matt, on his knees, could barely keep his vision straight, much less get his father in the house.

West, who had been staring at his grandfather with horror, stammered, "Uh, y... yeah, yeah."

James did most of the lifting, with West being his spotter. Abraham snorted, mumbled something, but otherwise didn't awake. Once they got him inside, they came back for Matt.

"You okay, man?" James asked, hooking his hand under his armpit and lifting him up. His old friend had multiplied. Matt concentrated on the James to his right.

"It's just my vertigo. It'll settle down."

*At least I hope.*

His father was on the couch, a ratty blanket draped over him. He snored, oblivious to everything. Matt had a sudden urge to throttle him.

"*Now* can we call the police?" West asked, pacing in the hallway.

Matt reached out, motioning for his son to come close so he could lay a reassuring hand on his shoulder. "We're not just sitting by anymore. That I can promise you."

"Maybe we should just pack everything up and go. If they want to watch over the house, let them," West said. "Once Grandpa Abraham sees that note, I don't think he'll even want to stay."

*I wouldn't be so sure of that*, Matt thought. *If their threat is real, the house will turn into a bonfire, and there's no way my father will let that happen.*

"Once your grandfather wakes up, I'm going to have a very serious talk with him. And I think it's best we wait until your

262

mother gets home to tell her about this. If we call her now, she's just going to panic, and she's two states away. You understand?"

West nodded without hesitation. Good, they were on the same page. A rare occurrence lately.

"I'll grab the note and pitchforks," James said. He had plastic bags over his hands. When Matt looked at him, he replied, "I don't want to ruin any prints."

Every molecule in Matt's being screamed to be sensible and alert every authority in a ten-mile radius. It was the only sane thing to do.

So why had Abraham insisted they never do so? He had made that very clear to him the day he broke his nose. *"I can't guarantee everyone's safety if you go for outside help."* The thinly veiled threat had chilled him.

DON'T YOU LEAVE AGAIN. YOU DO THAT, HE DIES, AND WE TEAR DOWN THAT WHICH WE'VE GUARDED FOR SO LONG.

Now he knew, this wasn't the first time the Guardians had been so outright menacing. There was more to this than even he, who had lived with it for eighteen years, had ever realized.

He planned to get every last detail out of his father when he woke up from his drunken slumber.

✛

West sat at the kitchen table, the sweat on his flesh craving the stray breezes that flitted through the window and open door. His father and James were out back, talking too low for him to hear. They kept looking over the field, no doubt searching for any sign that someone was nearby, watching them.

When James stretched his arms over his head, his windbreaker lifted just enough for West to spot the holster and gun clipped to his belt. Seeing the weapon didn't frighten him. Quite the opposite. It gave him comfort. The big, bearded man looked like he could take on a bear. With a gun, he could surely handle the Guardian freaks if they dared show themselves.

But they wouldn't. They were shadow people. Decades of stealthily stalking the family gave them a kind of superpower. Intangible as ghosts, they were imbued with a sick compulsion to alter the Ridley family's reality, traipsing into the physical world just long enough to leave their stain.

Not that he believed they were ghosts. Not in the traditional sense, anyway.

He heard coughing in the living room. Looking out the screen door, he noticed his father hadn't heard. West got up and went to his grandfather. The old man looked like hell refried, warmed over and left to coagulate in the sun.

"Grab me a beer, will you, short stuff," he rasped, resting on an elbow and rubbing his head.

264

"A beer?" It was morning and Grandpa Abraham stunk like a barroom floor. Why on Earth would he want a beer? "Wouldn't you rather have coffee or water?"

He closed his eyes, shaking his head. "Not if I want to feel better, no. Just one. That's all I ask."

His head flopped back down on a stack of stained, flat throw pillows.

Getting the beer from the refrigerator, West considered letting his father know he was awake.

Not yet.

Ever since he found his grandfather and read the note, something had been brewing in his mind – a dark, potentially dangerous question that only Grandpa Abraham could answer. Maybe now, when he was in a delicate condition, his defenses down, he would provide an answer, or at least the hint of one.

"Here you go."

Grandpa Abraham sat up with a deep groan. The hair on the back of his head was crusted with dried blood. He drank half the can in one long gulp.

"Christ, my head is pounding. Where's your father?"

"Outside. You fell last night and cracked your head."

He raised a gray, bushy eyebrow, then reached for the source of the pain, wincing.

"I really did a number on myself." He finished the rest of the beer, dropping the can on the floor where it rolled under the couch.

"Did someone attack you?" West decided it was best to just be straight with the man. His grandfather was not one for hemming and hawing.

Laying back down, he said, "Not that I recall, unless you mean Jack."

West's heart fluttered. "Jack? Jack who?"

The corner of Grandpa Abraham's lip curled in a weak smile. "Daniels. He's a guy I know from Tennessee."

West recalled the bottle of whiskey with the black label on the picnic table. How could he make jokes?

*Because he doesn't know what happened after he passed out.*

West went to the kitchen, slipped his hand in a grocery bag, picked up the note, and one of the pitchforks.

"The Guardians did something to you."

That got his eyes to open all the way.

"I found you in the yard. They had your arms and legs pinned to the ground with pitchforks. And there was this note."

He held it close enough for his grandfather to see, but was careful not to let him touch it and spoil any evidence. Grandpa Abraham squinted, his lips moving as he read.

His face, the pallor of fresh milk, paled even further. He looked at the pitchfork, then his hands, checking for wounds.

266

"Dad wants to talk to you about it. I think this time he's going to call the cops. Before he does, I wanted to ask you something."

West paused, holding his breath, waiting for his grandfather to tell him to hit the road.

When he didn't, he pressed on, feeling like a bombardier. "Did... did the Guardians drown Stella?"

The hands slid down his face.

"What did you say?"

West tried to swallow but his mouth and throat were dry as wool.

"Did Stella drown by accident, or did they do it?"

He was terrified of the answer. He'd had a niggling suspicion ever since he learned of the Guardians, but part of him couldn't fathom his grandfather keeping the family in harm's way after such a thing.

Now, with the threats spelled out in this morning's note, he was filled with a sickening surety that the Guardians had spilled Ridley blood in the past. That and the threat of more violence would be the only reason his grandfather had refused to make the stalking public.

Grandpa Abraham's face contorted with an overwhelming sadness.

"I loved my girl more than you could ever imagine. I hope you never know what it's like to lose a child. Especially a daughter."

*I was right! Does Dad know? If he doesn't, he's going to flip out.*

He was beginning to regret asking, but it was too late now.

"Stella, as beautiful as she was... she was different from other kids. We had a hard time keeping her under control. She'd be smiling one moment, then burst into these... these fits. Plus, she grew so fast. She was so strong. I was a young, grown man and I could hardly control her when she got like that. The doctors urged us to see these specialists, but we couldn't afford it. So, your grandmother and I did the best we could." He sat up, motioning for West to take a seat in his lounger. "When she got angry, most of the time for no reason, she'd lash out, break things, and run away. For those moments, as long as they lasted, she was another person – reckless, violent, wild. That day... that day, she'd had one of her fits and ran from the house. We knew it was best to let her be. We had to give her space and time to let it all out. Sometimes, we could hear her shouting in the field. The words that would come out of her mouth. Your grandmother blamed me for teaching them to her. She wasn't wrong."

His eyes glassed over, one fat tear teetering on the edge of his lid.

"Her fits wouldn't last long. Five, ten minutes. They wore her out, and she could never remember what got her going to

268

begin with. The day she... passed... she didn't come back. Your grandmother and I ran in opposite directions, calling for her, searching all of her hiding places. She especially liked to be in the barn. But she wasn't there that day. I prayed she was, but God never hears me."

West said, "Is that the barn out on the edge of the field?"

"What's left of it."

"What happened to it?"

"Collapsed in a storm a few years after Stella passed. Your grandmother asked me to leave it, not to rebuild it or have the wood carted away. To her, it all contained some part of Stella."

He took a deep breath, coughed, and licked his dry lips. The tear snaked through the grooves of his face. "Thank God I was the one who found her. She was face down in the water. I turned her over, tried to get her to breathe. But I was too late. She was gone. I covered her with my shirt and carried her to the house. Your grandmother heard me open the door and came running. The sight of Stella nearly broke her for good right there. It nearly broke both of us."

Grandpa Abraham was silent for a long moment, as if reliving every agonizing second of that day.

West's chest felt full, his nerves raw. He wanted to hear the rest, and he wanted to run from the house, getting as far from the story as possible.

"Like I said, when she got angry like that, she was reckless. I think she must have tripped and fallen into the water, face down, knocking herself out. There were no signs of a struggle, no marks on her body."

"But what about the note I found?" West asked.

He hadn't seen the note hidden in the children's book in the trunk since he'd shown it to his father. Something about it had felt like hazardous waste. He'd spent many nights wondering if it had been put back in the trunk... in his room, fouling the atmosphere with its implied horror.

WE WATCHED YOU, MONSTER. WE KNOW AND WE ARE ANGRY.

His grandfather shook his head. "No, that was just Fuckhead Faulkner trying to ruin your mother. In the end, I guess those bastards did."

"So, the Guardians didn't do anything to Stella?"

"They didn't."

He stood up, the bones in his back and knees popping. Picking up the pitchfork, he examined the handle.

"But they did murder your grandmother."

# CHAPTER EIGHTEEN

Debi had been shocked to get the call from Matt telling her to come to the farmhouse and not the Super 8 after work. He'd sounded angry, but not with her. "I need you here," he'd said. There was a hint of desperation in his voice. He was holding something back. She was glad he'd called her when she was on the bus. If he'd done so earlier while she was in the office, she wasn't sure what she would have done.

*I never want to see that farmhouse again, unless it's to pack our stuff,* she thought, watching a state trooper blow past the bus in the left lane, lights flashing. The Delaware Water Gap Bridge was coming up soon, the twisting river to her left. She spotted a red and green tour bus in the distance. She and Matt had taken the Water Gap trolley tour on a vacation to the Poconos before West was born. They hadn't visited his parents then, even though they'd been close by. She never questioned his decision to separate from them. He wasn't the first person to have a shitty childhood. She loved him and respected his feelings on the subject.

Now she knew firsthand how bad it was, and she didn't blame him one bit.

And for the first time since the accident, it seemed as if they were on the same side. It felt good to be in synch, despite the horrid circumstances. Maybe, when they were finally out of here and back on solid ground, they could rekindle what they'd lost.

God, she hoped so.

She got off the bus three exits past Buttermilk Creek to get her car, which had been parked close to the Super 8. Traffic was light and she made good time getting to the farmhouse. If there had been an accident or roadwork, she might have lost it, being so close.

West and Matt sat in folding chairs outside the front of the house. She stomped on the brakes, running out of the car without turning the engine off.

Matt held her close. His body was coiled tight as a tripwire.

"Are you both okay?" she asked.

West didn't look to be in the hugging mood. No, he looked… haunted. Her chest tightened at the sight of his sunken eyes.

"Yeah, we're good. Well, maybe good is stretching it. I thought it would be better if we talked outside."

"Where's James?"

"I told him to go home."

"What happened?" She could feel her blood pressure cresting. Any suspense just might kill her.

"The Guardians left a note on Grandpa Abraham last night," West said. "They had him pinned to the ground with pitchforks."

Debi couldn't believe what she was hearing.

Why the hell wasn't the house swarming with police?

Matt held her hand. They sat down.

He said, "My father had passed out drunk. West was with him when he woke up later in the house. He... he asked some very delicate questions. Questions my father answered, probably aloud for the first time."

"Were you with West?"

"I didn't call Dad in because I thought maybe he'd talk to me," West said.

Matt told her about how they'd found his father, showed her the note. Her stomach dropped. "West asked him if the Guardians murdered my sister. Truth be told, when I got older, I wondered the same thing, but I knew asking him wouldn't get me anything but a beating."

"Oh my God, did they?"

Matt shook his head. "No. According to him, she drowned. She had... issues. I think if she were alive today, they'd probably diagnose her with a form of autism or something like it, coupled with a thyroid or glandular disease. It mustn't have been easy for them. My mother used to hint at it, but I never picked up on it. When I'd throw a temper tantrum, she'd say, 'You have noting on your dear sister, young man.' She could be pretty wild."

"So, if they didn't hurt your sister, what *did* they do?"

West sauntered away, giving them a little space. He picked a blackened stick from the diseased tree and poked at the ground.

Matt took a deep breath, his eyes reddening.

"He said they killed my mother."

Debi's heart stopped.

"But... but she'd been so sick. That doesn't make any sense. Did your father lie about her illness?"

"No, she was sick. Remember I stopped to visit her a month before she... there wasn't much left of her then. It was only a matter of time." He wiped a tear from his eye. "She knew the end was coming. She told my father it was time to break their silence about the Guardians. He wouldn't hear of it. She said she'd call the authorities. She was worried that the harassment wouldn't stop with them. That whoever lived in the house would suffer the way we all did. My father wouldn't give her a dying wish. He even went so far as to remove the phone from their bedroom. The only other phone was downstairs, and by that point, she was bedridden."

Matt was trembling, and for once, Debi knew it wasn't from the vertigo. It's as if the revelation had thrust it into remission, at least until he could get everything out. West kept his eyes to the ground, but she knew he was listening.

"If she couldn't tell anyone, why would the Guardians kill her?" she asked, rubbing Matt's arm.

"A few neighbors came to visit. Women she'd known at church. They wanted to say their goodbyes. My father thinks she told one of them, and somehow word got around. This is a small town after all. Once it filtered to the goddamn Guardians, they snuck into the house when my father was out. She'd been on oxygen. It looks like they simply removed her from her bed and her oxygen, leaving her on the floor to die."

She saw his knuckles whiten as he gripped the aluminum arms of the chair.

"But if he wasn't there, how did he know it was the Guardians?"

"They so much as told him it was them. A lesson to be taught for not following the rules."

"Matt, this can't stay within the family anymore. You know that."

He sagged into the seat. "That's the problem. The moment we make a move, they're going to kill my father." He leaned so close, she could feel his lips on her ear. "And I'm worried it won't stop there."

She took a quick look at West. He pretended he wasn't interested to know they were saying. "Then we all get in the truck and drive the hell away from here. Right now."

Matt grabbed her hand and they got up from the chairs. She followed him to the car, out of West's earshot.

"Right now, I don't think we can take a chance," he said, looking nervously over her shoulder. The deepening sense of paranoia clouded his gaze.

"But why? We can leave right this minute and never look back."

"You don't understand, Debi. They're watching us. Even now. We can't see them or hear them, but they're out there."

Goosebumps dotted Debi's spine. Somewhere in the overgrown field, the eyes of sick demented men were on them, imprisoning them. A pair of crows perched in the dead tree cawed to one another.

Or were they sentries for the Guardians? Black spies with free access to their every movement.

*You're losing it, Deb. The Guardians aren't supernatural. Don't give them any more power than they already have.*

Matt was resolute about their not leaving, so there was no point pressing him… for the moment.

"Where's your father?"

"Sleeping in his room. West came to get me after he told him about my mother, and that's when it all came out. He's got a hangover to beat all hangovers, and he gave himself a big blow to the head when he passed out. He kept saying, *nothing's gonna happen. Nothing can happen, not to me, not to you, West, or Debi. Trust me.* He won't tell me what the hell that means. I guess I can't expect everything, can I?"

Debi put her arms around him, laying her head on his chest.

"You should when it comes to family. You really should." Dusk would be coming soon, followed by darkness out here on the farm that was unlike any she'd ever experienced. She wasn't sure she'd be able to sleep a single wink tonight. Not here. Maybe not

276

anywhere. Matt felt so solid in her embrace, steady and fuller than he had in years.

*Silver linings.*

"So what do we do now?" she asked.

He couldn't stop looking around. Out here, they were completely exposed.

"We go inside and we make dinner. We'll just have to take it moment by moment."

Her hand fell to his lower back. She felt a solid bulge tucked beneath his belt. He stiffened.

She didn't say anything. Instead, they walked hand in hand, got West, and entered the house.

She'd had a sudden change of heart when it came to guns.

✠

West didn't sleep much and neither did his parents. He heard them moving about all night. Grandpa Abraham, however, slept like a man who'd been anesthetized. His snoring never ceased, growing louder and deeper as the night went on. West found it oddly comforting.

"Maybe it's a good idea to stay in the house," his father said. He was surprised to see his mother home. She made him a waffle.

"It's going to be like a hundred degrees in here," West said. It was only eight o'clock and it didn't feel that far off.

"We could all go for a drive," his mother said. "I haven't gotten out and about much since we moved here."

"I think it's best we all stay here. At least for today." His father pulled himself up from his chair with the help of his cane, walking unsteadily to the living room. West knew the spins were in control today. That happened a lot when he didn't get enough sleep.

"Are you going to get in trouble for not going to work?"

His mother smiled. "It's an office, not a penal colony. I do get sick and vacation days."

He took a bite of the dry waffle. "Which one is this?"

She gave a few fake coughs into her hand. "I think I'm coming down with one of those summer colds."

Not wanting to upset his father, West spent the day in the house, mostly in his room. He gave the appearance of lazing around, but all of his senses were on high alert.

Grandpa Abraham got up around noon, spoke to no one, and left. West heard his mother and father debating something in earnest.

By that time, the house was a hot box. He opened every window on the upper floor, even venturing into his grandfather's bedroom so there was a cross breeze. The sheets stunk like sweat and something gone sour.

278

There was nothing to do but read and stare at the picture of Ash above his bed.

He wondered what Faith was doing now. She was punished and probably in her room, just like him.

Or maybe she'd snuck out and was now sunbathing in her spot in that pink bikini. Once he started, he couldn't stop thinking of her full breasts barely contained in the two small triangles of fabric. He had to close his door and masturbate, the ending coming quickly. In that small amount of time, the temperature had seemed to double.

His mother called in sick again the next day, Friday, and Grandpa Abraham continued his vow of silence. Maybe he thought he'd said too much. He left the house early, returning late, though he didn't quite stink like the inside of an old keg.

West and his father and mother stayed in the stifling house. Windows were opened, but doors were locked. The wind never seemed to make it as far as the farmhouse.

They played a couple of board games his mother had found in a closet – Parcheesi and Trivial Pursuit. They watched TV, but West knew none of them were paying much attention. The tension in the house was thicker than the heat.

Again, he heard some strange noises at night, bolted up in bed, worried that the Guardians were trying to break in. His parents must have heard it too. The floor downstairs cracked as they walked around. Whatever it was, it didn't repeat itself.

By Saturday, their seclusion had become routine.

He went so far as to sit on the back step for a while, when the sun's glare was shaded by the house. He and his mother had a blessed break when he went with her to get some groceries. She plunked down two dollars at the service desk for lottery tickets.

"We can use all the help we can get," she'd said to him, stuffing the tickets in her purse.

The drive back felt like a walk down executioner's row, the trees on either side of the winding driveway their jailers, making sure they made it to the gas chamber. West knew it was a dramatic way of looking at things, but he was going stir crazy, and perhaps a little nuts from the oppressive heat.

James stopped by and they had sandwiches for dinner with cold potato salad because turning on the stove or oven was simply out of the question. He stayed late, West's father and him talking in hushed tones in the kitchen. West went upstairs while James was still there. Tossing and turning in his damp sheets that night, he decided Sunday was going to be different.

There hadn't been any notes from the Guardians, either inside (not that they could get in undetected at this point) or out. His mother and father did a sweep of the grounds twice a day.

Sure, they weren't being harassed or threatened by the Guardians, but at what cost? Was this how it was always going to be? He kept waiting for his mother and father to make an announcement and order him to pack his bags, but they never did.

The funniest thing happened over those long days and nights. All of his fear had bled away, sweated out like poison, replenished with a burning desire to make a break and a maddening streak of disappointment with his parents. It was if they had given up.

Sneaking out of the house was going to be a problem. There was no way to stealthily move about within the old bones of that house. The drop from his window was just enough to hold the threat of breaking an ankle or leg. His parents, bags under their eyes growing puffier each day, were on perpetual guard duty. Only Grandpa Abraham was living his life as usual – including pretending he was still living alone.

The plan came to him as he was getting ready for breakfast.

He'd have to dash out of the house right when his grandfather made his morning exit. The man made enough noise to mask the clatter of a cow traipsing through the house.

"I'm not feeling so good," he said to his mother. She put a hand to his forehead.

"You feel a little warm."

Of course he did. They all did. He didn't look so good, either. It was an easy lie to pull off.

"I think I'm gonna just lay down and go back to sleep."

"You must be sick," his father said. "You never take naps."

A weak smile played on West's face. "Maybe I caught Mom's summer cold."

"Very funny," his mother said.

He nibbled on some toast, despite being starving, then went back to his room and closed the door. Grandpa Abraham, who'd taken to sleeping later each day, was up an hour later.

As he clomped down the stairs, West followed, careful to avoid being detected. He slipped out the front door while his grandfather went to the kitchen to get his morning coffee.

The bakery sweet air kissed his face.

He was free!

Now for the hard part.

# Chapter Nineteen

Getting to the clearing that separated the property lines was simple. West had literally carved a path in the overgrowth from his trips to steal even a few minutes with Faith. Thorny weeds sliced up his legs. He didn't bother inspecting the damage. A little blood might actually make him look cool.

Some of the air went out of his sails when he saw the clearing - Faith's special spot – was empty. That meant he'd have to navigate the cornfield and hope to God he didn't end up lost for the day. He'd only been to her house that one time. The chances of coming out the other side right where he wanted to be were slim, but it wasn't as if he had anything else to do, aside from thinking how furious his parents would be if they found out he'd escaped.

By all rights, he should have been terrified to be out here alone. The Guardians, as they'd come to feel, were everywhere. But even they were no match for teen boredom, rebellion, and raging hormones.

Making his way among the rows of corn, he stopped every now and then to listen for any signs of human activity. If he heard a tractor or a man's voice, he'd head back. West was pretty sure Faith's father wouldn't take kindly to a kid sneaking around his farm to spend some time with his daughter, no matter how innocent his intentions (no one needed to know what kept him up at nights).

Right now, coming upon her father by accident held more dread for him than stumbling into one of the Guardians.

Half an hour in, he felt no closer to getting out. His shirt was pasted to his skin by sweat. His sneakers and lower calves were crusted with dirt and it looked like a cat had gone to town on him. It wasn't quite the picture he wanted to present, but he was desperate.

At one point, he tripped on a huge rock, spilling out of the cornfield and onto his back. The sun burned a fiery globe onto his retinas.

Eyes tearing, he sat up and looked around.

No house. Nothing but another cornfield about twenty feet away.

He stuck to the edge of the cornfield. Sooner or later it had to lead somewhere other than more damn corn.

Cresting a small rise, he was rewarded for his determination.

Faith's house looked like something from a postcard.

West approached cautiously, wary of being spotted by her parents. He made it to the side of her house, just under Faith's window. He knew it was her window by the music emanating from it – classic White Zombie.

There weren't any cars around.

*Good. Maybe her parents are in town or deep out in one of the fields.*

Scanning the ground, he scooped up a handful of pebbles. The first one hit the side of the house with a tiny plink. The second came up short of the second story window.

The third was a success.

Nothing happened.

"She probably can't hear it over the music."

He found a bigger rock, throwing it harder. It bounced off the screen, making a hard twang.

Faith's face pressed to the screen.

"Hey," he half-whispered, waving.

Her eyes lit up, teeth peeking out from her smile.

"West, what are you doing here?"

He'd prepared himself for that question.

"I had to see you. Waiting until school starts isn't an option." He tried his best to not look like his knees were about to buckle. Seeing her got his heart galloping.

"I'll be right down."

He waited for her to disappear before giving a fist pump. The sounds of her sandals slapping against the bottom of her feet as she went down the stairs was music to his ears.

She surprised him by running out the door and throwing her arms around him. West shifted his pelvis away slightly so as not to embarrass himself.

"You're crazy," she laughed. "How did you find my house?"

"It wasn't that hard," he lied.

"You've got perfect timing. Everyone left about ten minutes ago."

Maybe it was a good thing he'd gotten lost for a bit.

"So, what have you been up to?" West asked.

She tucked a strand of hair behind her ear. "You want to hear the definition of pathetic? I'm actually counting down the days until school starts. I'll trade this prison for that one any day. How about you? At least you're not punished. Tell me what the world is like. Do they have hover cars and world peace yet? Is pot legal?"

*I just might be punished before the day is through,* West thought.

"Nothing much. Just hanging around. Not being able to drive or catch a bus somewhere sucks."

She led him to the back of the house, next to a shed that was big enough to house a family of four.

Faith said, "The day I get my license, I'm driving to New York. I want to get a sundae at Serendipity, walk around Central Park, go up the Empire State Building, and shop. You ever been there?"

"I went to Ellis Island on a school trip. My mom works in the city. She keeps asking me to go with her, but I'd feel like a dork."

286

She playfully slapped his arm. "You're crazy! Next time she asks, go! Find a way to take me with you! We can be dorks together."

They fell into easy conversation, Faith reminding him several times that he was the first person she'd spoken to that wasn't an immediate family member in what felt like forever. Her father had even taken her phone and computer away. Sitting in the grass, facing one another, West felt alive for the first time since the last time they'd been together. Whenever she touched his arm or bit her lower lip or laughed, his stomach did somersaults.

"It sounds like you've been just as bored as I have," Faith said.

He hesitated. She looked at him quizzically.

"Or maybe not," she said.

"Can I be honest with you?"

"If you don't know that by now."

West snickered. "We've had… some crazy stuff going on at my grandfather's place."

"Crazy how? Like is your grandfather getting old timer's disease? I hear that's no fun."

"No, it's not that. He's got his mind together still, at least I think he does."

"I've heard he's kind of a loner." She plucked some clover from the soil, twirling it in her fingers.

"He kinda is, unless he's at the Post with his drinking buddies."

"So what's going on?"

Faith rested her hand on his knee.

*Do I really tell her? She'll think we're all insane. Or worse, that I'm a liar, trying to get some sympathy.*

*Fuck it. Just do it.*

"We're being stalked."

Faith snorted, chucking the clover at his face. "Yeah, right."

"I'm serious. The house, me, my family, we're being watched all the time by these people who call themselves the Guardians."

The words came out in a rush. He felt lightheaded.

No longer playful, Faith stared at him with such deep concern, he worried that she thought he was full of crap.

*You should've kept your mouth shut!*

And maybe he would have, if he'd had Anthony around to talk to. As it stood, Faith was the only person his age that he knew in the entire state. He prayed he didn't blow it.

Faith said, "Did you say the Guardians?"

"Yeah. They leave notes all over the place, even in the house. My grandfather says they've been stalking the family for as long as he can remember. I know this sounds insane, because it is! But I swear it's the truth. I'm not even supposed to be outside the house because my parents are completely freaked AF."

Faith didn't say anything. She looked… scared.

"Look, I'm sorry. I shouldn't have unloaded on you. I keep thinking I should just call the cops, since my parents or grandfather won't."

"Don't!" she blurted.

"What do you mean?"

She leaned closer, so close, he could smell the yogurt she'd had for breakfast on her breath.

"I mean you can't. I know the Guardians, West."

West's body went numb, the thump of his heartbeat pounding in his ears.

He rocked on his haunches.

"You... you know the Guardians?"

A shadow fell over them.

A deep voice answered behind him, "She does, and who the hell are you?"

"You know you're going to have to go back to work tomorrow."

Matt patted the couch for Debi to sit next to him. A box fan on the floor pushed the hot air full blast at them. It gave the illusion of being cool.

"I'm sick just thinking about it. I know West thinks it's babyish to come to work with me, but I'm putting my foot down."

He patted her leg. A tide of vertigo had planted him on the couch an hour ago and he still wasn't up to moving about. For once, there were more important things on his mind than his own suffering.

"I'm with you on that," he said. "He has no choice in the matter. Will you get in trouble, having him there every day for the rest of the summer?"

"No. Monika has her ways. No one will even know he's there." She rested her head on his chest. He ran his fingers through her hair. "That still leaves me worried about you. Thinking about you in the house, alone most of the day, is going to give me an ulcer."

"You forget I have a gun now." He tried to sound macho, despite the nausea that had been roiling his gut.

"That's not reassuring to me. And I know it's not rational to expect James to be with you every day."

"He's between careers and he said he'll be around a lot, take me out of here as much as possible. I'll be fine."

She laced her fingers within his own.

Debi asked, "How are we going to get out of this?"

Matt sighed. "Every time I think about it and run different scenarios in my head, it's not pretty. As long as you and West are all right, that's all that matters."

290

"No, that's not all that matters," she protested, squeezing his hand. "We all have to walk away from here, without those assholes following us or doing something,"

He wanted to look at her face, but knew moving his head would make things worse. "Even my father?"

"Even your father. He's all the family we have left. And he's as much a victim as we are."

"And that's it right there."

"What's it?"

"Victims. We're letting the Guardians keep us on our heels. And by identifying ourselves as victims, we're just helping them along. That's what I keep thinking about. And when I imagine how we turn the tables, that's when things get dicey."

Matt wasn't sure if he ever loved his wife and son more than he did now, or at least appreciated his love for them. Every time he thought about something happening to them, his love and need to protect them grew.

He was prepared to do anything to keep them safe, to free them from this place.

They both flinched at the sound of something heavy thumping on the floor somewhere in the house.

"What was that?" Debi asked, rising from the couch, her hand still in his.

Matt reached for his cane, his stomach doing backflips as he pulled himself up.

*Fump!*

Matt angled himself so his wife was behind him.

He whispered, "I think it's coming from the kitchen."

# CHAPTER TWENTY

They sat at the big kitchen table, the wood top so thick, West wasn't sure if he could get his hand around the edge. A glass of iced lemonade dripped condensation. He nervously took a sip, the ice cubes jangling against the glass.

Faith's father sat on the other side of the table, along with his daughter. West was able to sum him up in one word – mountain. The man was a mountain of flesh and thick bones, with a black beard and low hairline that almost met his eyebrows. His hands were massive and scarred from years of working the farm.

Those hands rested on the table, inches from his own. There was a faint smile under the beard, but West felt it was pasted on simply to calm him down.

"I apologize if I startled you back there," he said with a baritone that would have been soothing if the situation were any different. "You'll understand someday when you have a daughter of your own."

"Dad, stop," Faith said. She looked just as nervous as West felt.

West swallowed hard, the lemonade far from refreshing. The acid tang of the lemons burned his vocal cords, made it difficult to talk. "I understand," he managed to croak.

Her father narrowed his eyes at him, letting an uncomfortable silence fill the space between them. He scratched at his beard and said, "You don't, but like I said, you will one day. So you're related to Abraham Ridley, huh?"

"Yes."

*Should I have said Yes, sir?*

"And how do you and Faith know one another?"

He was going to lie and said they'd met at school, but he knew he'd fold like laundry under the man's icy gaze.

Faith saved him by saying, "We ran into each other in the field. West was doing some exploring and I was just hanging around."

"Exploring."

West didn't like that he'd fixed himself on that word. It implied way too much.

He tried to save himself. "I don't have much to do, so I spend most of my time outside, just walking around or reading. Faith is the first and only person I've met since I moved here."

"You come to my house often?"

*Be very careful what you say next!*

Again, Faith interjected, "He came looking for me because I haven't been around. I told him where we lived."

He looked at Faith and she held her ground. That seemed to satisfy him.

His next question was like a punch to the solar plexus. "How do you know about the Guardians?"

Taking another sip, he replied, "Because they've been leaving notes around the house. I asked my grandfather about them, too."

Faith's father sat back, looking grave.

"Tell me what your grandfather said."

Both Faith and her father locked onto him, absorbing everything as it spilled from his mouth. West found that once he started, he couldn't stop, touching on the words scrawled in shit on the house, the time the Guardians were in the bathroom when his mother was in the shower, and the pitchforks around Grandpa Abraham. The only things he kept to himself were Stella and the admission that the Guardians had murdered his grandmother. Was it fear that prevented him? He wasn't sure.

He was pretty scared now, his voice trembling and cracking constantly.

When he was finished, her father flexed his hands, exhaling mightily. "I'll be goddamned. We're not the only ones."

Faith looked like she wanted to cry.

Her father surprised him by extending his hand. "Sorry, my name is Gregory Simmons. But you can call me Mr. Simmons. I'm not going to lie to you. I'm not happy that I found you sneaking around with my daughter. But I am appreciative that you told your story. That takes courage."

"Th-thank you."

Gregory Simmons got up and poured a fresh glass of lemonade for himself. He drank it in one large gulp. "So, those bastards are everywhere," he said to no one in particular.

"They leave notes around your house, too?" West asked.

"Every now and then," Faith said. "Although it's never been as crazy as what's been happening to you."

"I've met your grandfather only a couple of times. My father knew him a little better, though you'd never call them friends. We pretty much keep to ourselves around here. Guess that's why neither was aware what the other was going through."

*The Guardians are the dirty secret of Buttermilk Creek that no one will talk about*, West thought.

"Did you know my father growing up?"

"Is his name Mark?"

"Matt."

"Right, right. I think we were in first and second grade together. That's right when my parents split up. I went to live with my mother in West Virginia. I didn't come back to Buttermilk Creek until I was in my twenties. I don't remember much of my childhood here. You said he'd known about the Guardians all his life?"

"Yes." West felt a glimmer of hope. He dared to ask, "So, have you ever called the cops on them?"

Gregory Simmons shook his head. "Never seemed to be much point. A few notes don't scare me. I actually used to think

296

the Guardians were your grandfather. You live with him, so you know he's not the most amicable guy. When I was younger, I thought he left the notes just to mess with us. But he must be pretty old now. I can't see him trekking out here just to be a wise guy."

"Were any of the notes every threatening?"

"I don't get to read them, but I don't think so," Faith said.

"Not at all," Gregory Simmons said. "Just strange. Nothing like the things you just said."

"Maybe they're doing it to a bunch of people in town," West said.

Were these farmers so insulated that they really never talked to one another? Looking at Faith's father, his bulk taking up most of the doorway to the dining room, and thinking about his grandfather, West believed it. These were men who relied on themselves. It reminded him how far removed he was from New York, by environment if not my sheer mileage.

"I never thought much about it, to be honest," Gregory Simmons said. "Some pranks go on longer than they should, but it's no reason to run around like a chicken without a head."

"Well, I think someone should call the police. If my parents won't, I will. I'm tired of being cooped up in that house, afraid of every sound."

Gregory Simmons leaned close to him.

"You'd really do that, even though your parents told you not to?"

Sensing a test – he probably wanted to see if his daughter was getting mixed up with some kid who didn't mind his parents – West hesitated, the answer clogging in his throat.

The front door opened and closed and a pretty woman with short, chestnut hair and a warm smile walked into the kitchen.

"And who do we have here?"

When Faith saw her mother, she visibly relaxed. "Mom, this is my friend West."

"So nice to meet you," she said, putting a couple of shopping bags on the counter.

"He came here to break our daughter free from her punishment."

West felt an urgent need to shit. He thought they'd already turned that corner.

Her mother waved him away. "I think it's high time we did that anyway. Do I know you? You look familiar."

"I... I don't think so. I just moved here with my parents. We live with my grandfather."

"He's Abraham Ridley's grandson," Gregory Simmons interjected.

Was that a look of pity that washed over her face? She recovered, putting a light hand on his shoulder. "Well, it's nice to meet a neighbor. You and Faith must be around the same age."

298

Before he or Faith could answer, her father said, "West here says that they have a problem with the Guardians, too. A big problem."

Her mother's hand fluttered around her mouth. "Oh my."

Gregory Simmons leaned against the refrigerator, running his hand through his beard. "That's right. Oh my."

Debi was not thrilled to see that Matt had the gun on him. He pulled it from his pocket, but he was so unsteady on his legs, she worried he'd shoot them both before an actual intruder.

"Put that away," she hissed.

"What good will it do me then?"

They kept their voices low.

"More than if you accidentally do something you'll regret."

Silence had descended on the house again. But those sounds were too prominent to ignore. Debi stared Matt down until he put the gun back in his pocket, shaking his head ruefully.

*We'll have to talk about that later*, she thought.

He took the lead creeping to the kitchen, mindful to keep her at his back, unexposed should someone be lurking.

Debi's heart thrummed. Could they actually be about to catch the Guardians in the act? Or were they too late? What did they leave behind this time?

And if they weren't too late, just what would they do? Ask them to stand still long enough for Matt to shoot them?

The ancient floorboards gave them away. How could the Guardians skulk about when they couldn't take two steps without it sounding like the house was coming down?

Matt picked up the pace, the rubber tip of his cane thumping with each hobbled step.

The kitchen was empty.

The door was still locked, the window open just a slit, exactly the way they left it. Debi took a quick look around. Mercifully, there weren't any fresh notes, at least in plain sight.

"We're getting too jumpy," she exhaled, head leaning forward until her nose touched the back of Matt's shoulder.

"I could have told you that."

Debi and Matt flinched.

Abraham scooted past them, heading for the refrigerator.

"How... where did you come from?" Debi asked. She'd been so spooked, she was dizzy.

"The front door," he replied, drinking milk straight from the carton.

"We didn't hear you," Matt said, aiming for the chair. He slumped into it so hard, the old metal whined.

Abraham pointed down the hallway. "See that board there? The one that's lighter than the others? I put that there about five years ago. The old one rotted out. You walk on that, it doesn't sound like my bones."

Now Debi was angry. "So you intentionally snuck up on us?"

He wiped milk from his upper lip. "Not on you. On whatever had your hackles up, which it appears was nothing."

"I could have shot you," Matt said, taking out the gun and dropping it on the table.

Abraham eyed the pistol. "Well, let's be glad you didn't."

Debi said, "Now that you're here, maybe we should talk."

The old man shook her off. "What for?"

"If what you said about Violet was true – "

"It is true. I may be a bastard but I'm no liar."

"Okay, so the Guardians killed Violet and have threatened all of us. We're living in here like we're under house arrest."

"*You're* living like you're under house arrest. I'm not."

"That's not the point, Dad," Matt said, his head in his hands.

"Actually, Esasky, that is the point. I don't let them win."

"You call what they did to Mom, and now you, *not letting them win?*" Matt looked like he wanted to leap from his chair and pin his father to the wall. Debi wasn't so sure she wouldn't be right alongside him.

"Abraham, enough is enough. This has to end," Debi said.

"You gonna let my son shoot them and probably go to jail? I guess that's one way to do it, if they stick around long enough for him to do it. Which they won't." He slammed his fist against the refrigerator. "I told you before, it's not going any further than it did last week! Why can't you just trust me?"

Matt huffed. Debi stared at her father-in-law incredulously.

"You can't be serious?" she said.

"As cancer," Abraham said. "Stop moping around the house, go to work, make your money, and move on out. I'll be just fine here. I was before."

"Unlike Mom," Matt said, seething.

Abraham rushed him, both of them nearly spilling onto the floor.

"Don't!" Abraham shouted. "Don't you dare!"

Debi tried to pull them apart. Abraham had a death grip on Matt.

"What?" Matt spat. "Tell the truth? Try to talk sense into you? How could you let this carry on after what they did to Mom?"

Abraham shook him. Matt's face paled. "I don't need you telling me what to do. You hear me? This is my house, not yours. You want to play the hero? Be my guest. Pick up the phone and call the police. Get them out here right now. I won't be responsible for what happens."

"Get… off… of… him!" Debi said, struggling.

Abraham let go, chest heaving.

302

Matt regained his seating, but looked ready to throw up. "Is that what you tell yourself? That you're not responsible? Is that how you sleep at night? Or do you know how full of shit you sound? You must. It explains the drinking."

Abraham looked ready to explode again. Debi tensed.

He balled his fists and said, "You feel so sure, like I said, get on that phone. I'm tired of fighting you. Or you do things my way, and you and your family can walk away from here and not have to spend a lifetime looking over your shoulders." Abraham ran his hands through his wild hair. He grabbed a liquor bottle from under the sink. "It's your call, son." His face softened, his eyes saddening. "One thing you've never understood about me. I love my family. Maybe I don't show it the way you think I should, but I can't help that."

Debi moved closer to Matt, laying a hand on his rising and falling chest, feeling the wild beat of his heart.

"Just remember that," Abraham said as he turned and left, slamming the back door behind him.

They stared at one another, speechless.

# Chapter Twenty-One

West stayed with the Simmons family for most of the day. Conversation moved away from the Guardians and onto much safer topics, but the heavy undercurrent was there.

He learned that Faith's mother was Sarah. She kept giving him funny looks when she thought he wasn't looking. He wasn't sure what to make of them. They weren't the knee-buckling glares her father locked him under before the talk of the Guardians.

If he didn't know better, he'd almost think it was sorrow, though for whom, he wasn't entirely sure. Did they know something he didn't? They'd been under the Guardians watchful gaze as well. Was it possible that she knew what was in store for him and his family?

Coming up with the courage to outright ask her had proven impossible. Noting the time on the wall clock – it was late afternoon already! – he told them he had to get back to his house, leaving out the part that he'd snuck out in the first place.

"You take care of yourself," Sarah Simmons said. She handed him a bottle of water. "It's a scorcher out there. Just in case you get thirsty on the walk back."

Gregory Simmons walked him to the door alongside Faith. "You be careful. Don't let your guard down."

On the one hand, West was relieved that the Guardians weren't just his problem. If the Simmons family was living with them without any visible problems, that was a good thing. Right?

*Don't let your guard down.*

It made perfect sense, but there was something in the way he said it that implied a much, much deeper meaning.

"Can I walk him halfway?" Faith asked her mom.

"Sure."

Her mother was right. It was a scorcher. The sun felt as if it had descended to a hundred feet over their heads. In the walk from the house to the edge of the cornfield, West's hair felt hot enough to burn.

As soon as they stepped within the corn, Faith grabbed his hand.

*Great, she can feel how sweaty I am!*

"That's so crazy that the Guardians have been watching your house, too," she said.

"It's way crazy. I'm just glad they're getting weird with us and not you," he said, trying his best to sound brave.

"I'm not. I just wish they'd go away. Or we'd find out who they are and... and... I don't know."

He knew exactly what she was saying.

"It's bizarre that no one's caught them all this time," West said.

She stopped, sweeping her hand around the high stalks of corn. "It's kinda easy to hide and get lost out here. That's why I want to go to New York. Less places for bad people to take cover."

West stopped himself from reminding her that the crime rate in New York was a thousand times larger than out here in Pennsylvania.

When they reached Faith's spot, she asked him for his phone number, taking her cell phone out of her back pocket.

"I don't have one," he replied with a flush of shame. What teenager didn't have a phone? "I thought your father took yours away."

She smiled. "My mother slipped it to me before I left. I was hoping we could text each other, you know, at least until you come over again."

His heart soared. It was amazing, this ability of Faith to trump the growing dread of the Guardians.

"I can?"

"My father didn't kill you on the spot, so I take that as a good sign."

She leaned in and gave him a quick kiss on the lips.

Faith said, "You better be careful. We have a lot of hanging out in our future. Why don't you come by in a couple of days?"

He almost couldn't get the words out. "I will."

*If I'm not grounded for life.*

Once he could no longer see her, he started running.

There was no way he'd be able to sneak back into the house without being caught. Once he gave up that hope, he was able to think clearer.

A whole other family was being harassed by the Guardians.

He had to tell his parents.

Maybe it would make them forget he wasn't supposed to leave the house in the first place.

✠

Matt stared at the pill in the palm of his hand.

He felt like shit. Even his daydreams were tilted by vertigo. The tussle with his father had really set things off.

The man was such a bastard.

But for the first time, Matt could see the pain he lived with. And that pain had been dredged up by Matt's words.

*He said he loved his family! I don't think I ever heard him say the word love, in any context.*

Trying to wrap his head around everything only made things worse.

He could take the pill and float away to a calmer place where the floor stayed under your feet and the sky didn't do a jig. But he'd be so out of it, he couldn't help Debi or West if they needed him.

*They need you, man. And they need you all the time. You've got to stay out of your own head. It's a bad place. Been there way too long.*

Debi was loading up the washing machine in the small washroom off the kitchen. The radio was tuned to a local station playing scratchy bluegrass records. Listening to the music, out here on a farm on a sweltering day, made him feel as if he'd tumbled back in time.

"Need any help?" he asked, pocketing the pill… for now.

She turned to him, wiping great drops of sweat from her brow. "'I'm good, but I'll hold you to it when it's time to fold later."

Her smile made him realize how much he'd missed her, missed this, this easy comfort.

There was a knock at the back door that startled them both. Matt swiveled in his chair and was shocked to see West outside.

"What the hell is he doing out there?" he said while Debi opened the door.

"I thought you were sick," she said, concern, not anger, in her voice.

West came inside. His hair was matted to his head, the collar and underarms of his shirt soaked with sweat. He was breathing heavy. Matt went on instant high alert, wondering if he should get the gun that he'd stashed in his night table drawer.

"West, what happened?" he asked, the fog in his head dissipating like an alcohol daze the moment one sees police lights in the rearview mirror.

"I'm okay," he said, turning on the faucet and lapping water straight from the tap. "I just… ran back."

Debi said, "Was someone chasing you?"

He shook his head. "No. I wanted to get back here to tell you."

"Tell us what?" Matt asked.

"That we're not the only ones. The Guardians, they've been watching another family and leaving notes for them, too."

"How could you know this?" Debi asked. She swiped a lock of sweaty hair from his forehead.

"Because they told me."

"Who told you?" Matt asked, wanting West to speak in complete sentences. If he had to fish for every piece of information, his patience was going to wear thin mighty fast.

Taking the seat next to him, West said, "The people who live on the next farm. Did you know them, Dad? I met the father, Gregory. He says you guys went to school together when you were little."

Gregory Simmons. Matt vaguely recalled him. He ate peanut butter and cream cheese sandwiches every day. He'd been his neighbor only in the sense that he lived in the next house over – way, way over. It was nothing like West and his best friend and

310

neighbor Anthony. He couldn't remember ever having a conversation with him.

"We did," he said. "So my question is, how did you run into him when you were supposedly sick and sleeping? And when I expressly told you to stay in the house?"

His son nervously looked between him and Debi, biting his lip.

*This is where the lies typically start flowing with teens*, Matt thought. *He looks ready to pop.*

To ease West's nerves, Matt added, "Just tell us the truth. I promise we won't be mad."

*Please don't say something that will make me mad.*

"Well, I met this girl a few weeks ago. Her name is Faith."

*Ah, that's it. There's a girl. Of course.*

"Where did you meet this girl?" Debi didn't seem as relieved as Matt.

"One day when I was walking in the field." He didn't appear to want to linger on Faith, so he changed gears, telling them how her father, Gregory, had asked him to come in the house when he found West talking to his daughter. He'd overheard West telling Faith about the Guardians, and had his own story to tell.

Matt sat in rapt attention, asking West to repeat himself when he spoke about the Simmons's experiences with the Guardians.

"Holy crap," Matt said when West was done. "Holy mother freaking crap."

Debi looked as if she were about to jump out of her skin. She paced the kitchen, grabbing a bottle of beer from the refrigerator and rubbing the cool glass on her face and neck.

She said, "If they've been harassed by these animals, maybe other people are going through the same thing. Is that even possible? Wouldn't someone say something?"

Matt breathed deep. "Not out here, honey. When it comes to little things, they gossip just as much as the next person. But big stuff like this? Pride or fear gets in the way."

*Just like they have in this very house.*

"Maybe we should go over there and talk to them. Just the adults.If they're being watched, too, how many Guardians are there? Just between the two farms, there's a ton of ground to cover," Debi said.

Matt was still trying to process the revelation.

"You're right. We should go over there," he said. "Maybe between the two of us, we can find a way to put a stop to everything."

West said, "Faith's father is huge, like a football player. He looks like he could crush a man with one hand if he got a hold of him."

Matt couldn't help feeling a twinge of inadequacy. West was obviously impressed by his old classmate.

312

"I don't think we'll need him to crush people," Matt said. "But I do want to talk to him. What do you think, Debi? Want to take a ride over now?"

"I do, but we're not leaving West here."

Matt smiled. "I'm sure he wouldn't mind seeing Faith again. Would you?"

West couldn't hide the blush that bloomed on his cheeks.

"I mean, I could stay here with Grandpa Abraham when he gets home," he said half-heartedly.

"I think it's better if you come with us. You can make the introductions," Matt said, letting him off the hook.

"I'll get my pocketbook," Debi said. "Oh, should we bring something over? I don't have time to bake a pie. Isn't that what people do out here?"

"We only bring pies on nights when *Hee Haw* is on. Or if it's square dance Friday. I don't think what we're going there to talk about qualifies as a light social call."

Debi rolled her eyes and dashed to their bedroom.

West got up. Matt touched his arm. "Hey, don't think you're not getting punished for what you did."

"I know," West said.

At least he was going to take it like a man.

Matt asked, "This girl, Faith. Is she pretty?"

West tried to hold a smile back and lost. "She's amazing."

Matt gripped his cane and walked to the front door.

*Amazing is definitely worth the consequences.*

Things out here just never seemed to work as planned. The moment West and his parents walked outside, Grandpa Abraham's truck came barreling down the long drive, weaving from side to side.

"West, get back," his mother screeched, grabbing hold of the back of his collar and yanking him onto the small porch.

They watched with mouths wide open as his grandfather hit the brakes, the truck sliding sideways along the dirt and grass, miraculously settling into the deep grooves the wheels had made over time.

"How the hell did he do that?" West's father said, clearly impressed as much as he was distressed.

Grandpa Abraham spilled out of the truck. He gripped the sideview mirror to keep from falling.

"Didn't know I had an audience. I would have made a dramatic entrance," he slurred.

West couldn't imagine what something more dramatic would have entailed.

"You're smashed," his father said.

"And you're observant." Only it came out *obshervent*. He bobbed and weaved, brushing past them into the house.

"He's going to kill someone if we don't put a stop to this," West's mother said.

"One thing at a time."

They were about to go to their car when West smelled something. "Is that fire?"

"Huh?" his father said, pausing and having to lean heavily on his cane.

His mother went to the screen door and peered inside. "Your father just lit up a cigar."

"A cigar? I didn't know he smoked cigars."

"He does now."

"Christ. He'll burn the house down if we let him."

West knew what was coming next. He just knew it. Faith was so close!

His father looked at him and said, "West, would you mind staying with your grandfather? I'm sure he's just going to pass out. Lock the door and windows and we'll be back in a half hour, tops."

He knew his mother and father were jumping out of their skin to talk to Gregory and Sarah Simmons. As much as he wanted to say no way, there was a chance that their meeting tonight could lead to more permissible visits with Faith in the very near future.

West decided to sacrifice the needs of the now for the promise of the future.

"Sure, Dad."

His mother's forehead creased with worry. "Matt, maybe I should stay with him, too."

"He'll be fine. It'll be like babysitting a kid who passes out five minutes in. Right, West?"

"Yeah, I guess."

"We'll be back before you know we're gone. I promise," his mother said.

West watched them drive away and headed back into the house, snapping the lock shut on the door.

Grandpa Abraham leaned against the kitchen counter, a smoky cigar between his fingers. His eyes were at half-mast.

"Where'd Esasky and Skinny go?" he asked.

"Over to the Simmons farm." He double checked to make sure the back door was locked as well. After that, he looked in the cabinets for an ashtray, though his grandfather was doing just fine dropping the ashes in the sink.

"What the hell for?"

*Do I tell him? Will he even understand me?*

West went for broke, retelling the day's events and revelations. Grandpa Abraham's eyes opened wider, his posture getting straighter. He stunk like whiskey and cigar smoke, but he appeared to be sobering up before his eyes.

"Why didn't you tell me this before?"

West was confused. "Before when? You just got home."

"Jesus. They shouldn't have done that. You should never have gone there."

"Why? At least now we know we're not the only ones."

He pulled a chair out, holding onto the back and leaning on it. The cigar smoldered, a blue fog obscuring his face.

"Because *they're* the Guardians."

# CHAPTER TWENTY-TWO

"That doesn't make any sense," West said. "If you know they're the Guardians, why wouldn't you have had them arrested or worse?" He knew Grandpa Abraham understood what he implied by the word *worse*. If someone from the Simmons farm was the Guardian and had not only harassed the family for generations but murdered his wife, Grandpa Abraham surely would have killed them. West was sure his grandfather could do it in cold blood and never feel an ounce or remorse. He'd probably celebrate by going down to the Post.

"I just know. And now your mother and father are going to wreck everything."

"Wreck everything? Nothing's been normal since we got here."

"I made sure you'd be safe the moment I knew you were coming, short stack. I handled it. That's what I do, goddammit. I keep telling you people to trust me. Why don't any of you listen?"

He turned away from West and started opening and slamming drawers. West had no idea what the hell he was looking for.

One of the drawers slid out too fast. Grandpa Abraham back peddled into the table, knocking the salt and pepper shakers to the floor. West realized he was dealing with a man who wasn't in his right mind.

It scared him.

Between what he was saying and his condition, West didn't know what to do.

"I want to show you something," Grandpa Abraham said. He had a can opener in one hand and a can of tuna fish in the other.

"Maybe you should sit down, Grandpa." West positioned a chair so all he had to do was relax his knees and he'd be safely on his ass.

"Nope. You need to see this so maybe you'll believe me." He put the tuna on the counter and fumbled in his pocket, his hand reemerging in a tight fist.

West's hands and feet went cold. *What the heck is he talking about? What's in his hand? What's he going to do with the tuna fish?*

"Come on. Follow me."

West followed him to the basement door. Ever since they'd moved in, West was curious about the basement, Grandpa Abraham's dank haven. He'd wanted to sneak a peek many times.

Now, he wanted nothing to do with it. At least not without his parents around.

The wood of the door appeared to have been painted over numerous times, different colors showing through the chips, nicks and gouges. Grandpa Abraham used a rusted key to open it.

He turned to West on the top step. "Are you coming?"

"Maybe… maybe we should wait."

"Waiting shit the bed five minutes ago." He grabbed West's wrist and pulled. "I should have shown you this earlier. You're more like me than you think. You'll understand."

West was forced to follow him down the splintering stairs. The stench of wet cardboard and rust was overpowering. This was no man cave. Not unless the man was part earthworm.

Grandpa Abraham pulled on a chain at the bottom of the steps. A bare bulb snapped to life.

The basement was an unfinished crap hole. Old junk, bundles of newspapers, and rotting boxes were everywhere. There was no paint on the stone walls. The floor was gritty with years of dust and dirt.

"I keep this key on me at all times," his grandfather said, waving the key to the basement door in front of West's face. "It's a skeleton key. Opens up all kinds of things. You ever hear of a skeleton key?"

"Yes." West had read and watched enough horror to know. And this basement was right up there when it came to a derelict, haunted setting.

His grandfather winked at him. "You are smart. I'll give you that. Now, this is what you need to see."

There was an old steamer trunk like the one in his room leaning against the wall. West saw where the dust had been swiped away recently.

*What has he kept in there?*

West felt his stomach tighten, cramping so hard, it hurt.

But Grandpa Abraham didn't go to the trunk.

West didn't see the other door in the gloom.

His grandfather inserted the key, turning the lock. The door was surprisingly thick, with sheets of tin nailed inside and out.

"What's in there?" West asked, his heart somewhere around his tonsils.

"What you need to see."

He flicked on the light, and West saw with soul rending clarity what he needed to see.

"Are you sure this is the right farm?" Debi asked, pulling up to a beautiful Colonial home.

"We took a left and turned up the first road we saw. Has to be it," Matt replied. He compared the house and sprawling, neat farmland to the run down disaster his father had cultivated. If he'd been a Guardian, he'd rather train his eyes here than at the Ridley disaster.

"I hope they don't mind us coming over," Debi said, killing the engine.

"We'll find that out soon enough."

Stepping out of the car, Matt had to take a second to get his sea legs. Debi held his hand as they walked up the whitewashed steps onto the sprawling, wraparound porch. Wind chimes tinkled softly in the barely-there breeze.

There was no bell, just a polished brass knocker in the center of the door. Matt took a deep breath and gave it a couple of knocks.

"I can't believe how pretty it is," Debi said, admiring the uniform rows of corn unfolding in every direction.

"It's a hell of a lot of work," Matt said, remembering how hard his friends toiled away on their family farms. They all envied Matt, who lived a relative life of leisure in comparison, while he would have given anything to be in their mud caked boots.

When no one answered, Matt knocked again. The door swung open before he could take his hand off the knocker, almost dragging him inside. Debi grabbed him by the back of his shirt and belt loop.

"Whoa, sorry there," the burly man, Gregory Simmons, said, stepping back. "Didn't realize you were still attached."

The near face-plant set Matt's vertigo into a free fall. He couldn't speak, desperate to stop the world from canting.

"Hi, I'm Debi Ridley. West's mom. This is my husband, Matt. I hear you two went to school together."

Matt regained his senses, having to crane his neck back to take in all of Gregory Simmons. He looked like every depiction of Paul Bunyon in the kid books. Matt could imagine him using logs as toothpicks. He'd come a long way from the pipsqueak in grammar school with his odd lunches.

"For a little while," Matt said, extending his hand. "At least as far as Mrs. Joyce's class."

Gregory's grip was firm but not crushing.

Matt couldn't tell if he was smiling under his beard. "She was the one who kept the pet turtle in the classroom, right?" Gregory asked.

"That's the one. It's been a long time."

"It has."

Gregory didn't invite them in. In fact, it seemed as if he were blocking the doorway, which was easy to do for a man his size.

Debi said, "We wanted to thank you for how you handled everything with West and we apologize for him coming out here when he shouldn't have. Once they get to their teens, you start to wish for the nighttime feedings and crying again. It's easier when you have perspective."

The big man exhaled through his nose, the air whistling.

"I think I put a pretty big scare into him when he saw me. Thought it best to have him come inside and talk a while. He's a

324

good kid. Faith likes him. I knew this day would come, boys sniffing around. Makes it a little easier when the boy isn't someone you want to kick in the pants."

He emitted a low chuckle, which was cue enough for Matt and Debi to laugh along. He was being nice, saying the right things, but Matt sensed something brewing beneath the surface.

"I don't blame you. I always worried how I'd be if we'd had a girl," Matt said.

Matt wasn't sure how long he could keep standing out on the porch. He had to cut to the chase.

"Look, I know we're basically strangers, but I was wondering if I could talk to you about the whole Guardian thing. I'm sure West told you some of what we've been going through. I wasn't aware your family had been experiencing the same thing all this time."

Gregory tucked his thumbs in his pockets. "It hasn't exactly been the same, but I understand."

"Have the Guardians been… watching your family for long?"

"Long enough. Too long for my taste."

"I thought we could compare notes, maybe get to the bottom of things." Matt felt Debi's hand press against his sweaty back. He finally noticed the cicadas as they serenaded the bleak humidity.

In an instant, everything changed. Despite being outside in the cloying heat, Matt swore he could see his breath turn to vapor, the air between them and his neighbor plummeting to sub-zero, all pretenses at neighborly cordiality evaporating like good will at the tipping point of a hostage negotiation.

Gregory leveled his gaze at him with small, flinty eyes. "You knew about them. You should never have come back. You got away once. I don't know if they're big on second chances."

Matt stiffened. He opened his mouth, but nothing came out. Gregory's hand went to the doorknob.

"Only reason I spoke about the Guardians to your son was because *he* was talking about them to my daughter. I don't have any notes to compare. I've learned to live with it. Maybe you should too."

Before he or Debi could say anything, the door was slammed in their faces. They heard the click of the lock, and Gregory's heavy steps retreating into the house.

Debi looked to him. "What the hell was that?"

"You asked if they'd mind us coming over. I think we got your answer.

# CHAPTER TWENTY-THREE

Every cell in West's body screamed, *run! Get out of here as fast as you can, find your parents and never come back!*

Instead, he stood there, paralyzed, his mouth gone drier than desert winds, limbs numb as a corpse.

The crackling reek of ammonia kept him from passing out. It came from everywhere, was pouring from the stone and soil.

A cobweb so dense it obliterated whatever was on the other side hung in a two-foot span across the boarded window. It looked to be the work of a team of spiders given years to complete their thick, complex masterwork.

There was an ancient coal chute in the corner of the room, with a few lumps of coal scattered around. The opening looked like a dark, bottomless mouth, a swallower of souls from a Stephen King novel.

*That's where all the strange noises were coming from!* West thought, remembering hearing the moving about and crying, sometimes seemingly from the walls. Because they had been in the walls. There were probably all kinds of ducts throughout the farmhouse, transferring the sound of the girl to the upstairs, making it sound like the place was truly haunted.

But that wasn't what rooted him to the dank floor.

"You don't have to come inside if you don't want to," Grandpa Abraham said, shuffling into one of the bleak corners of the room. "But there's no sense keeping this from you anymore. Not now. Everything's about to change. I can smell it as good as I can feel it." His feet scuffled on the filthy floor, his breath heaving in wet rasps. West couldn't see what he was doing in the dark.

West felt himself slipping free from his body. If not for his unwavering perspective, he would swear he *had* stepped from his mortal constraints, the tether to this world fraying with each agonizing second.

Grandpa Abraham emerged carrying a metal serving tray, a bent and rusted spoon sitting atop an indescribable goop of mush that more resembled a watery termite mound than food. He bent close and took a sniff, crinkling his nose.

"Thought it had gone bad when I opened the can. Guess I was right."

He bumped into West as he left the room, mumbling to himself.

West couldn't take his eyes off the sleeping girl.

She lay on a thin mattress, the sheet and bottom of her feet stained black. One wrist and one ankle were wrapped in iron manacles, chained to a massive plate in the wall. She was dressed in a long pink shirt, the kind his mother would sleep in. It was almost as filthy as the sheet.

Despite all the commotion they'd made, she hadn't so much as twitched.

"Is… is she dead?"

He didn't feel the sensation of the words as his mouth formed them, his breath expelling from his lungs up through his nonexistent throat. Hearing them, it didn't even sound like his voice. It was too high, a pre-pubescent squeak with nary a hint of testosterone.

Had someone else asked the question?

Were they alone?

Was this the ghost his grandfather had warned him about? Or was it his grandmother, her soul trapped in the farmhouse where she'd been murdered, unable to move on, choosing to stand vigil over this strange, ragged girl?

"No, she's not dead, though she has gotten quieter lately," Grandpa Abraham replied, going back into the room with a white, plastic pail. He put it next to the mattress, grabbing a tin watering can and inspecting it. "I just wish she'd use what I give her for pissing and shitting and stop decorating the room with it. Fucking kids. Always gotta rail at something."

Breaking his faraway gaze from the girl, West stared at his grandfather. He was no longer a flesh and blood man.

He was every monster West had read about or watched in the plethora of horror movies he and Anthony devoured like buttered popcorn. Grandpa Abraham was the beast in the basement that sent children scurrying to the safety of well-lit rooms and the comforting press of family and friends.

"Who is she?"

Grandpa Abraham cocked his head. "Not able to put two and two together? I understand. This is a shock. I get it. Hopefully you'll understand the why of it when you settle down. That girl Faith you've been talking to, she ever tell you she has a sister?"

West could barely hear him over the *swoosh* of his thrumming heartbeat.

A sister.

A sister.

Yes! Faith did say she had a sister.

But she was away at camp.

This couldn't be her, then. Why would Faith tell him her sister was at camp if she were actually here?

Unless she didn't know.

"Y-yes," West answered, trying to swallow and nearly choking on his own Adam's apple.

"Her name's Rayna. You know what that means?"

"No."

*Why are you talking to him? Get the hell out of the house! Run down the driveway and keep running until you find Mom and Dad!*

"I looked it up. It means, *one who is pure.* That family doesn't just pick names out of a hat. They always have to mean something. Crazy Bible thumpers." He squatted down and almost tenderly

330

shifted her stringy auburn hair from her face. She looked older than Faith, but not by much. Then again, she could be younger, her imprisonment in this hellish cell prematurely aging her.

"Well, she's not as pure as they'd like to think."

West felt like he was about to throw up.

His grandfather saw the expression on his face and scowled. "I haven't done anything to her, idiot. She's just a damn kid. But word travels, and I heard she's got a wild streak in her. Her parents were going to send her to some Christian camp. School principal comes down to the Post every now and then. Told me all about her. She was quite the handful in school. Well, at the very least, I got her to settle down. She can't get in much trouble down here."

"You kidnapped her?"

There was a tingling feeling in his hands and feet, as if his spirit were returning to its home, nerves flaring from the invading pressure.

"I killed two birds with one stone. I've kept her out of trouble, and her family from going too far, from doing what they did to your grandmother."

The girl moaned softly, her mouth opening and closing. It was the first real confirmation that she was alive.

"But the Guardians watch them, too," West said.

His grandfather snorted derisively. "That's what they want you to think."

"You can't keep her like this. You have to let her go."

*Even if it means you have to go to jail, which is exactly where you belong.*

"Trust me, son, you don't want me to let her walk away. Not yet."

West considered rushing his grandfather. If he could somehow take him by surprise, find a way to overpower him, he could free the girl and call the police. Grandpa Abraham may have been thick as a Clydesdale, but he was also old, and drunk.

But how would he get those manacles off? He couldn't just leave her down here with him.

"It's not time for her to go," Grandpa Abraham said. "For now, she's serving a purpose. If they so much as touch a hair on your head, well, things won't end well for their model of purity. And they know it. Same goes if they try to break her out. The room is rigged. She'd live long enough for them to see her die."

West cast nervous glances around the dim room, but could see nothing. That didn't mean the crazy bastard didn't have a booby trap somewhere.

Or he could be full of shit.

West's brain fired off neurons, sparkling tendrils of thought, of possibilities, of fight or flight. His head ached.

"You understand, don't you?" his grandfather asked, and in his face was true concern. He really wanted West to believe him. Because he believed that what he did was right.

All to keep the family safe.

"Help me."

They looked to the girl. Her eyes were closed, but her chapped lips parted, repeating 'help me' over and over again.

West turned and ran, hitting the basement steps hard, the wood cracking under his weight.

"Come back here!" Grandpa Abraham wailed.

West didn't turn back, didn't slow down.

Rayna's frail *help me* looped like an ear wig spinning round his eardrum, propelling him forward, into the kitchen, crashing into the back door, fumbling with the lock until he hit the humid air, as desperate and crazed as any horror movie final girl had ever been, only this time, the terror was real.

# CHAPTER TWENTY-FOUR

Debi pulled up to the farmhouse, feeling more apprehensive than before they'd set off for the Simmons farm.

The way he'd looked at them.

He was frightened.

And angry.

But why was he angry? What had they done? Weren't they both being victimized by the same sick people?

Every time she thought Buttermilk Creek was as strange and threatening as it could possibly be, it sunk down to even creepier levels.

"We're going back to the motel," she said to Matt. He needed her help getting out of the car.

"We can't afford it."

"I don't give a damn if we lose every penny we have in our bank account. We're getting West and leaving."

Matt reached out for her and missed. He staggered, planting the cane deep to keep from falling. "Then we have to take my father, too. You read the note."

Debi thought about it. Would Abraham even come with them? She doubted it.

Then there was the bigger question: would the Guardians hold true to their promise and follow them? She couldn't take that chance. The Motel 8 wasn't far enough.

She grabbed her cell phone from her purse.

"Who are you calling?"

"Monika. I know she'll let us crash at her place tonight. We can look for something else tomorrow."

"My father isn't going to go all the way to New York to cram into a studio apartment."

Debi's temper flared. "Then the hell with him! I don't care anymore! All that matters is that our son is safe… with his parents! If you so much as try to stop me, I'll punch your fucking lights out."

Matt stared at her, jaw open far enough for birds to settle in and build a nest.

They'd fought plenty of times. More times than she could count. But she'd never, ever threatened physical violence.

What scared her even more – she meant every word of it.

In her anger, she accidentally disconnected the call.

She stormed to the house, fumbling with the keys to get the front door open.

"West! Honey, I need you to pack a bag." She ran through the living room, then trotted upstairs. "West? Where are you?"

*Answer me, dammit!*

She made it back downstairs just as Matt came stumbling in. "I can't find West," she said, frantic.

"He can't be far. West!"

Debi bolted for the kitchen. The back door was wide open. She ran out back, calling his name until her throat was raw. There was no sign of him. Or Abraham.

"Matt, he's not here."

He was at the back door, both hands wrapped around the cane's handle. He looked as dreadful as she felt.

"Where could he have gone?" she asked, shoving Matt aside.

"I don't know. My father's truck is still outside, so he didn't take off with him anywhere."

Debi thanked God for that.

She was about to go back outside when the basement door opened. Abraham emerged from the darkness, looking the worse for wear.

"He left," he said matter-of-factly.

"What do you mean, he left?" Matt said, his shoulder's stiffening.

"He just took off out the back. I thought for sure you'd run into him. You didn't just pass him?"

"I'll get in the car and check," Debi said, sprinting through the house.

Why would West do such a thing? Was he that desperate to see that girl?

337

Or had something scared him so much, he couldn't stay in the house one second longer.

Debi cursed herself for letting him stay behind with Abraham. If anything happened to West, she'd never be able to live with herself, much less Matt.

✢

West ran heedless of direction or endgame.

Now in the middle of the field, the scorched sky giving way to the moon and pink prelude to night, he had no idea how he'd ended up here.

Panting, sweat pouring down his face and into his mouth, the salt tang turning his stomach, he dared to glance behind him.

The farmhouse was long out of sight.

When he'd hit the ground, he had a burning need to just run straight and fast. That would get him furthest away from the house, and his insane grandfather. He should have taken the driveway, hoping to catch his parents coming in the opposite direction.

That would have been the logical thing to do.

But logic had pointed its thumb out and hitched a ride to a place called Anywhere But Here.

And just like in his horror movies and books, people did stupid things when faced with overwhelming stress and fear.

Standing here in the middle of nowhere was plain evidence of that.

"You are one dumb asshole."

His breath was returning, but he couldn't stop his heart from pounding away.

*Help me.*

Even if that wasn't Rayna Simmons back there, she was still a girl that needed help desperately.

The high, steady screech of crickets was all around him, so loud, he could barely hear himself think.

Maybe he was right to come this way.

If that was Rayna, he had to tell Faith and her parents. And maybe there was a chance his parents were still at their house.

He took off running, hoping to beat the dying light. He'd never traversed this way in the dark, and he was less than confident he'd find his way if he wasted one more second.

He pumped his legs as hard as he could.

*I wish Anthony was here.*

He needed his best friend to share his burden. Maybe that was a selfish way for him to think, but to hell with it. He was scared as hell. Anthony would stick by him, no matter what.

But he was a hundred miles away.

West was on his own. At least for the moment.

He hit the corn stalks at a full gallop, fat ears thumping him like wild dancers at a nightclub. His hacking and slashing made a hell of a racket, scaring the crickets into silence.

*Please be there, Mom and Dad.*

Tiny paper-thin cuts opened on his arms as he batted away the stalks.

Was this the right way? He'd passed by Faith's spot, taking what he was sure was the same route to her house she took.

The moment he doubted himself, he stumbled into the Simmons's front yard. A few lights were on downstairs. His parent's truck wasn't there.

He didn't slow down, taking the porch steps two at a time. His chest bumped into the door. West pounded on it with his fists.

Faith opened the door, her face waxen.

"West, what's wrong?"

Now that he was here, he couldn't find his voice. His lungs burned like lava. He wheezed and gasped, motioning with his hands that he'd be able to speak in a minute... if he was lucky.

She led him to a wicker chair. "Sit down and catch your breath."

"Where... where's your father?"

Faith fidgeted with her hands. "He and my mom left for your place. I got the feeling my father was kind of a butthole to your parents. My mother said they were going over there to make things right."

340

*Jesus*, West thought. *If I'd just stayed there…*

He was here with Faith now, which was good, but he desperately needed adults.

"I need to tell you something," he said.

She leaned on the porch rail opposite him. "What? West, you're scaring me."

"I know this is going to sound crazy, so I'll just say it. Is your sister's name, Rayna?"

She looked at him suspiciously. "Yes. Why?"

He took a stuttering breath. "My grandfather has her locked in his basement."

Faith stared at him, studied him, biting her lip. "But that's impossible. She's at camp."

"Do you know that for sure?"

She didn't hesitate, saying, "Yes. I've gotten texts and emails from her. At least when I had my phone. She's supposed to come back next week. She wanted to take me to Stroudsburg when she got back, but I told her I was punished. I was hoping my father would give me a get out of jail card."

West collapsed in the chair, feeling his bones turn to putty.

How was that possible?

Then who was the girl Grandpa Abraham said was Rayna?

"I… I saw a girl in the basement. My grandfather showed her to me. He said her name was Rayna Simmons and he was keeping her there to keep me and my family safe."

Faith started pacing. "You're not making any sense."

"I know! But I know what I saw. There's a girl, chained up and barely alive down there."

"This is insane. Are you sure?"

"I was standing next to her, just as close as I am to you right now. At first I thought she was dead, but she moved a little and asked me to help her. I totally freaked out and just ran." He got a lump in his throat as he admitted his childish cowardice.

Faith looked ready to cry. "We have to tell our parents."

"That's why I ran over here."

She dashed inside, returning with sneakers on her feet and a pair of flashlights. Plucking him from the chair by his hand, she said, "Come on!"

# Chapter Twenty-Five

Matt was sick with worry.

But his father seemed indifferent. He'd even go so far as to say cold as a well digger's ass.

Why?

Did he really not care that much about his own grandson? Was he so oblivious to everything going on that he couldn't grasp the severity of the situation? Maybe it was all the drinking. It not only chewed away at the liver, but brain cells withered and died right along with it. Matt was well acquainted with the process of watching a brain deteriorate.

No matter the reason, Matt wanted to throttle the man.

Debi was close to hyperventilating. He tried to take her hand, but she pulled away, going back upstairs to look for West, even though they both knew he wasn't there.

When he was three, West had fallen into the habit of hiding in the house and refusing to reveal his location, no matter how frantically they shouted his name. They'd eventually find him in the toybox, a living doll lying atop trucks, balls, and game boxes, or under the bed, and once, somehow crammed in the tight space where they kept their pots and pans. It was a big game for him, and no matter how severely they admonished him for hiding, their raw panic and anger never sunk in. They were exceedingly grateful when he simply grew out of the game by the time he was four.

He was a long way from three now. Matt knew he wasn't hiding in the house, chuckling as he heard them desperately searching for him.

He turned to his father. "What happened while we were gone?"

"How the hell should I know? That kid is always off in his own world." He grabbed a bottle from under the sink, twisted the cap off, and took a hearty swig.

"That's the last thing you need," Matt said.

His father scowled at him. "I'll take that under consideration, Esasky."

*He knows something*, Matt thought. *What the hell did he say to West?*

The man held on to secrets as if his life depended on them. Matt knew he wouldn't reveal anything he didn't want to divulge, no matter what he threatened.

For the thousandth time, he cursed that damn drunk woman for bringing them back to this madhouse.

Debi rushed down the stairs. Now she was crying.

"Where can he be, Matt? It's getting dark."

The Guardians seemed to be most active in the night, like vampires. The thought of West out there, unprotected, chilled Matt to his soul.

344

"I don't know, but he can't be far. You think he went to Faith's house? Maybe he was upset we told him to stay here."

"I... I guess. Let's go back there. I didn't like her father one bit and I don't want West anywhere near that man."

"You and me both. Look, you stay here in case he comes back. Dad, you're driving us to the Simmons farm."

"I thought I was too drunk," he said mockingly.

"You are, but I'll have to take my chances. I'm not asking you to do it."

His father put the bottle down, glaring at him like one would a rabid raccoon. Matt waited for a flurry of insults, or at the very least, a derisive dismissal.

The old man surprised him by taking his keys from his pocket.

"I drive just as good drunk as I do sober."

Matt thought back to the way he'd swerved the truck perfectly into its resting spot earlier tonight and wasn't able to argue.

Debi looked horrified, but there was no other way.

"Matt, be careful."

He sighed. "It's pretty much out of my hands. I'm sure West will be back as soon as we leave. Try not to yell at him too much." He kissed her wet cheek, feeling her soften just the slightest bit.

It was a struggle, hurrying after his father. He tried to concentrate on the mechanics of walking rather than the spinning of the house or gyrations of the moon when he stepped outside. He dry heaved, collapsing into the truck. The engine sputtered to life.

"I'd tell you to buckle up, but the seatbelt on that side broke years ago."

His father gunned the accelerator and they tore across the front yard, spewing dirt and grass and gravel. They sped past the gnarled, dead tree, nearly clipping its withered, flaking trunk.

Matt couldn't help feeling his father, the farmhouse, and now them, were all infected by whatever blight had withered that nightmare tree.

✛

Debi scurried from one end of the house to the other, peering out of every window, waiting to see West come strolling back home.

Home.

This was no home.

She hated this place. Hated her father-in-law.

Most of all, she hated the Guardians as much as she feared them.

And West could be out there with them.

The thought of it burned like acid in her gut.

"West! West!" she shouted out the back door. Flashes of swirling yellow dotted the rapidly decaying dusk. West used to love collecting fireflies when he was little, keeping them in a sealed mustard jar on his nightstand. They poked holes in the lid and placed bits of grass and leaves on the bottom of the jar. Debi was never sure what fireflies ate, but West was the one to suggest making the jar look as much like the outdoors as possible. He'd catch ten, fifteen, or even more fireflies, or as he called them, lightning bugs, a night.

If he was lucky, a couple would still be alive by morning, the daylight robbing them of their ethereal beauty. Debi would unscrew the lid and release the living while pouring the hard, dead bodies under one of the rose bushes in the back corner of the yard.

Where had the time gone? What cruel trick had life played on them?

She made a promise to go back to church if West came back any minute now.

"Please God, no more games. Haven't we been through enough?"

Debi barely noticed the half-moon dents her fingernails made in the palms of her hands as she went from window to window. She'd made sure to turn on all the lights, opening every blind and shade, creating a beacon he couldn't miss.

It left her wide open to be watched by the Guardians, but she didn't care one bit.

A brief pinprick of light, bigger than a lightning bug's, caught her eye. She squinted, waiting to see it again.

It snapped into focus for another moment, trailing away like a thin searchlight.

"West!"

Debi sprinted out the front, the screen door slamming behind her.

"West, honey!"

Heading around the corner of the house, something snagged her foot. Debi sprawled forward, her face smacking hard against the ground. Her head bounced up, then back down for a second blow that knocked her out instantly.

Matt grimaced as his father narrowly avoided sending the truck into a ditch. He didn't say a word. The last thing the man needed was a distraction, and getting him mad by criticizing his drunk driving would surely lead to a heated argument.

"The entrance to their farm should be coming up," Matt said, gripping the dashboard.

"I've lived next to the damn place all my life. I think I know where it is."

A pair of bright headlights approached them.

His father shielded his eyes, the truck swerving into the oncoming lane and whatever vehicle was behind those lights.

Matt reached over to steady the wheel. "Look out!"

The car or truck, he couldn't tell, sped past with inches to spare between them.

Matt expelled the breath he felt he'd been holding for a lifetime. "Jesus, that was close."

"What the hell was that asshole doing driving with his brights on?"

"Just concentrate on the road."

"Fucking moron," his father muttered.

They almost missed the entrance to the Simmons farm. His father pumped the brakes and jerked the wheel. Matt felt half the tires rise from the safety of the road. The truck bounced crazily, heading up the driveway like a runaway train.

Faith turned to West when they reached her special spot.

"You're going to have to take the lead from here. I never went to your grandfather's property before."

Night had fallen suddenly and fast. West had never been anywhere near as dark as the field. Even with the flashlights, it was disorienting and oppressive.

But he wasn't going to let her know that. She had enough to worry about, wondering if her sister Rayna was actually chained up in his grandfather's basement.

Just thinking it made West feel as if he'd stepped into the pages of one of his books, a book he desperately wanted to escape *from*, not to.

"Just stick close to me," he said, navigating by memory. There were no markers, especially in the pitch, to tell him if he was headed in the right direction. The stars and half moon were bright, but they were also millions of miles away.

Faith kept a death grip on his hand. They ran through the wild growth of the Ridley farm, nearly tripping more times than he could count.

He checked himself from crying out with relief when he spotted the blazing farmhouse up ahead. It looked like every light on both floors was on.

That was odd.

"That's it," he said, a flush of renewed energy picking up his pace.

As they got closer, Faith pulled back. "You live there?"

He stopped to look at the dilapidated house. It was a disturbing sight at night, especially knowing the secret hidden beneath it.

"I don't think I will after tonight."

The back door was unlocked, adding to the strangeness. Faith kept stepping on the heels of his sneakers as they walked through the house.

"Mom? Dad?"

The front door was open as well.

"Grandpa Abraham?"

Faith clutched his arm when he mentioned his grandfather.

"Don't worry, I don't think he's here. His truck is missing."

But his parents' truck was right there. Where the hell could they be? And why were all the blinds open? Nothing was making any sense.

"You don't think he's hiding in the basement?" Faith asked. "Maybe he's having second thoughts about showing you and wants to lock you up, too."

She was trembling with fright, her eyes as big as silver dollars. West wondered if he looked the same to her.

"I don't think he would," he reassured her. "He's got this whole thing about protecting the family. And as much as I wish I wasn't, I am his family. We better go to the basement now, before he gets home."

Faith hesitated. "Maybe we should just call the police."

"We can't. My grandfather wrecked the phone a while back and hasn't gotten it fixed."

"And I left my cellphone home."

He led her to the kitchen, and down the basement steps. It still smelled like his grandfather – alcohol infused sweat and body odor. He hadn't been gone long.

Or maybe he was still down here? What would Grandpa Abraham do if he saw Faith? Would he try to lock her up, too?

West would hurt him, hurt him real bad, if he even tried.

"I don't see anything," Faith said when they reached the bottom, the meager light casting strange shadows among the piles of junk and boxes.

"She's in there," he said, pointing to the door, immediately cursing himself.

Grandpa Abraham had the key. The door looked like a poor man's bank vault, but impenetrable just the same.

Plus there was the added threat of it truly being booby trapped.

"We have to be careful," he whispered, even though he knew they were alone. They were in the presence of evil, its essences as cloying as the humidity outside. "My grandfather said he rigged it so if anyone tried to get it, Rayna would be hurt."

*Or worse*, he thought.

"Then how will I know if my sister, or anyone for that matter, is inside?" Faith looked terrified, a glimmer of hope shining in her eyes that he was pulling a prank on her.

West took a deep breath of the musty air. "Well, she wasn't moving much, but she did talk a little. Maybe if we let her know we're here, she'll answer. If the girl in there is really Rayna, you'd know her voice, right?"

Faith swallowed hard. She kept stealing glances at the stairs, and toward escape.

He held her hand, as much to soothe her as keep her down here until he proved he wasn't crazy.

"Of... of course I would," she replied, a hint of a tremor in her voice.

He knocked on the door hard enough to make his knuckles burn.

"Hello! Can you hear me? My grandfather isn't here. I'm going to find a way to get you out of there. Please, say something so I know you're all right."

They waited and heard nothing. Not even the shuffling clink of the chain.

"She was really out of it," he said, this time kicking on the door.

"Maybe you shouldn't be so loud," Faith warned him. "What if your grandfather comes home and hears?"

Her fingernails dug into the flesh of his bicep.

"I have to do something to wake her up."

He didn't confide that he was worried she might be dead. She looked as if she were knocking on its door earlier.

"Why don't you try saying something?" he said. "If Rayna's the one in there, I'll bet hearing your voice will wake her up."

353

"Maybe we should go. If there is a girl in there, we can call the police from my house."

"Just try. I promise, we'll call the police whether she answers or not."

Faith stepped up to the door, her fingertips trembling against the cool metal. She cocked her ear to the door, listening.

"Hello?" she said softly.

"The door is real thick. You're going to have to be louder."

She shook her head, biting her lip until it turned white where her top teeth pressed.

"Is, is anyone in there?" she said, louder. "We're here to help you. Can you hear us?" She took a trembling breath, then said, "Rayna, it's Faith. Please, Rayna, let me know you're okay."

She went rigid as tent pole at the sound of movement on the other side of the door.

A small, raspy voice replied, "Faith? Faith, is that you?"

Faith covered her open mouth with both hands, her eyes wildly looking back at him. "Oh my God!"

West's heart sank a little lower.

Grandpa Abraham hadn't lied.

Faith pulled on the door's handle, crying out, "I'm going to get you out, Rayna! I swear!"

"Help me, Faith. Please."

Desperate, Faith grabbed an old shovel and hammered the door, sending blue sparks everywhere.

354

West grabbed the handle as she reared back for another blow.

"Stop!" he said. "I don't think my grandfather was lying when he said the room was rigged in case someone tried to get in without the key."

She wouldn't let go, her chest heaving. Faith glowered at him with half-moon eyes. "Did he tell you what would happen?"

"He didn't say exactly how he rigged the room, but it didn't sound good."

"Do you know where the key is then?"

"He keeps it on him."

The steel shovel head hit the floor with a deafening *ke-rang*. West stepped back, giving her space. She looked like a feral child trapped in a corner.

She said flatly, "That's what I thought."

Faith pulled the shovel from his loosened grip. West didn't have time to register what happened next. She went into a batter's stance, the shovel high over one shoulder.

When it slammed into his ear, a high-pitched whine exploded in his brain.

He was unconscious before he realized he'd gone permanently deaf in that ear.

# CHAPTER TWENTY-SIX

No one was home at the Simmons house. Abraham had refused to get out of the idling truck. Matt hammered on the door to no avail.

"West? Are you in there?"

*He'd have come to the door by now,* Matt thought. *Dammit, where is everyone?*

Stepping off the porch, a quick glance at the truck's headlights set him off balance. He dropped to a knee.

"You need help?" his father asked, much to his surprise.

Matt waved him off. "I'll be fine." He got up slowly, taking small, measured steps to the truck. "We might as well go back home. If West isn't there, I'll have to call the cops."

"You need to be missing twenty-four hours before they'll do anything."

"West is fourteen. I seriously doubt they'll sit on their asses for an entire day."

Matt hoped to holy hell it wouldn't come to that.

One thought kept flooding his brain, unbidden and unwanted.

*What if the Guardians took him?*

He could have set off from the house for Faith and been intercepted by one of them.

*Please God, you can't do that to us. You hear me! You just can't do that.*

After an awkward three-point turn, they sped back to the farmhouse. Matt fished his cellphone out and called James. His friend answered on the first ring.

"What's wrong?"

"I need you to come over," Matt said. "West is missing."

"I'll be right there," James said, hanging up.

They almost missed the entrance to their property, the truck fishtailing and clipping a hedge.

"Try to get us back in one piece," Matt said, gripping the door's handle to keep from sliding into his father.

"If you can drive any better you're free to do it."

The front door to the house was wide open.

*Debi must have found him and forgotten to close it.*

Which made sense. Her relief would have overridden everything.

The truck came to a rough stop. Matt's forehead hit the windshield hard enough to bloom a whopper of a headache.

"Jesus," he hissed, rubbing his head.

"You'll be fine," his father said, getting out.

"I need you to help me inside," Matt said, despite every cell in his body crying out for him to crawl on his hands and knees rather than accept a hand from his old man.

But that would take too long to get in the house.

"Aren't you glad I'm around?" his father said with a sloppy smirk. "What would you do without me?"

As he helped him from the car, draping Matt's arm over one shoulder, Matt replied, "There's not enough time in the day to list everything."

His father chuckled. It sounded so odd, considering the backdrop. And it made Matt uneasy. "You know, I gave you a master course in being a smartass. I'm sure it helped you up there in New York."

They walked inside, Matt trying to extricate himself from his father's grasp, but his legs deciding otherwise. "Deb? West?"

No answer.

"What the hell is going on?" Matt said. He called out again, louder and more urgent.

His father plopped him down in a chair in the foyer.

"I need to get to my bedroom," Matt said.

"And I have to look outside."

"Outside? Why?"

"Just stay put."

His father stomped through the house and out the back door. Matt lurched from the chair, reaching for the banister. The walk down the hall was like traipsing through a funhouse. He wanted to vomit. He thought he would pass out.

Neither happened. Stumbling into his room, he collapsed on the bed, rolled to his side, and pulled his night table's drawer open.

Concentrating through his double vision, he fumbled for the gun and shoved it in his pocket.

Where was everybody?

Now even his father was gone.

✛

Debi awoke with a gasp.

Her ankle throbbed.

Something was in her mouth. It felt like a wet rag. When she tried to pull it out, she found her hands were bound.

Her heart went into overdrive.

*Where am I?*

She looked around, realizing she was seeing the field through a pair of slits in something that covered her head. The fabric felt rough against her nose.

In fact, her entire body was tied up, her arms splayed out as if she were crucified.

Pure, unfiltered panic flowed in an acidic burst of bile that singed her throat.

*How did I get here?*

*West!*

*I thought West was outside.*

*Then I... then I tripped or something.*

*No, I didn't trip. It was like someone grabbed me.*

The more she woke up, the greater the pain flared in her ankle.

Then the unimaginable hit her.

She was tied to a stake in the middle of the untended field. The sack over her face was burlap and old, judging by the smell.

Someone had turned her into a scarecrow!

Debi tried to scream through the wad of bitter cotton in her mouth, tears and snot streaking down her face.

The Guardians had tricked her.

Did that mean they had West, too?

What were they going to do to them? Why make her a living scarecrow?

She shrieked and shrieked, her lamentations so soft, they didn't even disturb the crickets.

Abraham went back to his truck, grabbing the sawed off shotgun he kept behind the driver's seat. Adrenaline had overpowered the alcohol in his bloodstream. He was straighter than six o'clock now.

Fishing keys from his pocket, he slowly and quietly undid the lock on the storm doors leading to the cellar.

Those sons of bitches weren't playing by the rules.

He'd warned them what would happen, hadn't he?

He shouldn't have shown the kid. But he had to know. Abraham saw a lot of himself in the boy, underneath all the bookworm nonsense. It went beyond their similarities in appearance. If West only knew how much his grandfather looked like him when he was his age. It was like looking in a mirror.

He'd grown up soft in the suburbs, but Abraham sensed something special in his grandson. He'd thought, in his boozy haze, that they could share a private moment, form a bond that had never materialized between him and Matt. West had a darkness in him. Shit, it just took one look at his walls, at the books and magazines that he obsessed over, to see it.

But the boy was so skittish, he probably took off like a jackrabbit with no clue about where he was going.

That was the best case scenario.

It was the one he clung to, at least until they got back to find Debi missing.

Shit was hitting the fan all right.

He winced when one of the doors made a sharp squeal.

*Fuck it. So much for the element of surprise.*

He ran down the concrete steps, his finger on the trigger, happy to show them what happened when you went too damn far.

✠

*Something bad must have happened*, James thought when he pulled up to the house. It was lit up like the Fourth of July.

"They're probably inside scared shitless," he muttered to himself, running to the front door.

It was open, which was surprising.

"Hey, Matt, you in there?" he called from the safety of the porch. He'd given his old friend a gun but he didn't know if Matt really knew how to use it. If he was on high alert, James had no desire to have the words 'friendly fire' in his obituary.

"In here," Matt answered.

James found him in the bedroom. "Where is everybody?"

"I don't fucking know. Every time I turn around, someone else goes missing."

James took out his own peacekeeper.

"What do you mean, missing?"

Matt's eyes were wild, literally swimming in their sockets, rimmed red as raw steak. "First West, then Deb, now my father. I have to find them." He got up, swooned, and collapsed back onto the bed.

"I'm calling the cops," James said, reaching for his cell phone.

"You can't! They might hurt them."

"You mean the Guardians?"

Matt nodded, his body caving in on itself.

"You know they have them?" James asked, feeling as if eyes were at his back.

"I don't for sure, but what else could it be? My family wouldn't just run off into the night."

A rusty screech of metal gave James a start. "What the hell was that?"

"I don't know. Think you can help me?" Matt said, reaching out.

James pulled him to his feet, one beefy hand around his friend's waist.

"Sounds like it came from the front yard," James said.

They hobbled down the hallway. James halted at the sight of a sheet of paper tacked to the screen door. He pulled it free with the hand that held his gun and showed it to Matt.

NO MORE WATCHING

James felt Matt's body freeze up, his own blood chilling as if he'd been transfused with liquid nitrogen.

"Shit," Matt said, trying to keep on his own two feet.

"Murderers!"

They turned to face the voice.

James saw the butt end of a rifle a nanosecond before it hit him between the eyes.

# CHAPTER TWENTY-SEVEN

West unsteadily rose out of the fog, feeling like he was going to puke his guts out.

His hands pushed into something soft and crumbly.

He was outside.

When he touched the side of his head that was throbbing to the beat of a manic samba, it was like feeling a body part that was somehow disconnected from the whole. The entire side of his head felt numb… was numb.

But there was more to it.

His hand brushed past his ear.

He couldn't hear a single thing.

Tugging on the ear that may or may not have been attached to his head only elicited more pain, not sound.

Deaf and disoriented, he struggled to stand.

He looked around, saw that he was in a sunken depression in the field. Very little weeds or vegetation grew in the oblong clearing.

"Faith?"

She'd been with him, down in the basement. Yes, he was sure of that.

He'd wanted to see if the girl in the room was her sister.

And it was!

Yes, Faith's voice got the girl to speak.

Then... nothing.

"Faith? I need help."

The agony ripping his brain in two assisted his stomach in emptying its contents with a meaty splash.

One word kept repeating itself: *concussion.*

After laying the contents of his stomach bare, all he wanted to do was lie down and sleep. He was so tired. Maybe if he closed his eyes for a little while, he'd wake up able to hear out of his left ear. It could all be just a symptom of the concussion.

Had he hit his head in a fall? And what made him fall?

Dropping so his knees, he swayed, trying to focus on the stars, but they were too bright, blinking too fast. It hurt.

"This is where he killed her."

West turned fast, lost his balance. He didn't see anyone.

"I'll bet she took her last breath right where you're kneeling. Of course, this was all filled with water then."

Something... someone, rustled in the tall grass.

West inhaled sharply when Faith materialized like a specter.

"I think I need a doctor," he croaked.

"I hear she struggled. She was strong. Stronger than any other girl. Even most boys. It wasn't easy. But he did it."

He tilted his head to the right so he could hear her. Why didn't she care that he was hurt?

"He didn't just kill her that day. Everyone died. And everyone since has been born dead."

"I don't know what you're talking about. I'm hurt real bad. Please, can you help me get back to the house?"

Faith squatted just out of his reach. Her face was fuzzy in the dark, in the pain and confusion.

"You know about Stella, don't you?"

West struggled to keep his eyes open.

"Stella?"

Faith's hand lashed out, slapping him hard across the face, snapping him fully alert.

The slap opened up the dark partition in his brain.

*Faith hit me with the shovel in the basement!*

*Why? And why is she talking about Stella?*

"Do you know why he killed her?" She sneered at him, the beautiful girl he'd fallen head over heels for replaced by a grinning lunatic.

He struggled to speak. His teeth hurt, his tongue seeping copper from the blow. "Sh... she... she drowned."

"She did. But she had a little help."

He sat back on his rump, trembling. He suddenly felt so cold. "You mean, the Guardians killed her, too?"

Faith loomed over him, hands on her hips.

"No, West. The Guardians didn't drown your late aunt. They saw, but by then it was too late."

The effect of the slap was wearing off. Sleep, wonderful, painless sleep, was crying out. "I don't understand."

"But you will. Before the night is over, you will."

✠

Debi heard voices – distant, words indecipherable.

One of them sounded like West.

She struggled against the ropes binding her to the post, swaying her body back and forth.

Scarecrows were light and still, sentinels over the fields.

Unless they cemented the post she was tied to, it might give way if she could get enough momentum going. The gag in her mouth was bitter, vile juices slipping down her throat.

But she kept silent. It was best to let them think she'd passed out, or worse.

She rocked, barely moving at first, tensing her back, arms, and legs.

There was a faint popping sound from the wooden pole.

*Don't stop! Don't stop! Come on, give way!*

She felt her body dip to the left, then stop. Her struggling attempts to shift to the right met by total inertia.

Which meant there was only one way to go.

Sagging like dead weight, Debi willed gravity to claim her body, to pull her back to Mother Earth.

The wood gave a sharp crack, tiny splinters ripping like uncooked spaghetti.

Debi braced herself.

The pole snapped in two.

The board supporting her right arm broke on contact with the fall, nearly separating her shoulder. The pain was unlike anything she'd ever experienced outside of childbirth. She hit the ground face first.

Biting hard on the rag in her mouth, she managed to pull her damaged arm free, using it to untie her other arm and legs.

She pulled off the hood, tugging on the gag. So much had been stuffed down her throat! She looked like a magician pulling colored scarves from her mouth.

Debi got to her knees, panting.

*They didn't kill you. Was this a message? What kind of game are the Guardians playing?*

More importantly, where was West?

Was that his voice she'd heard?

It hurt to stand, pins and needles stabbing her feet and hands. At least her ankle wasn't broken. It was a slight sprain at best. She trudged as quietly as she could through the field, hoping against hope that she'd find her son before them.

Abraham was surprised to find the basement empty and the door to Rayna's room locked. After a careful sweep, he felt the coast was clear enough for him to open the door and check on his insurance policy.

The girl was pretty much where he'd left her – unconscious on the bed, the stench of urine overpowering, the tray of uneaten food on the floor.

Little thing was willing herself to die. He gave her food and water every day. It wasn't his fault if she didn't make it.

No matter.

He locked the door, keeping the shotgun at his waist, ready to empty both barrels into anything, or anyone, that moved.

No more fucking around.

The chickens were coming home to roost.

Well, might as well make chicken salad out of chicken shit.

Rayna was where she needed to be. They'd have to kill him to get the key.

*I'll bet they want that more than anything.*

They didn't realize they'd already taken all the good parts of him decades ago. Personally, he had nothing left to give. And they knew it, which is why they'd left him alone those years after they'd murdered his wife. They wanted him to die a long, slow, lonely death.

And he was fine with that. He even helped it along with his drinking.

He'd finally be free. If there was a next world, it had to be better than this stinking pile of shit he'd been saddled with.

Matt had fucked it all up.

So here they were, shit hitting every fan.

Good.

Maybe lying down and dying was never in the cards.

This way, he'd take his pound of flesh with him before he settled in for his long dirt nap.

Someone was making a hell of a racket upstairs. Couldn't have been Matt. The footsteps sounded too sure, too steady.

Abraham smiled, heading for the door that led to the kitchen.

✠

Matt was barely able to make out James leaning unconscious in the love seat next to him. He only had one working eye, the other swollen shut.

A shadow passed over him. He tried to lift his head from the cushion and failed. The bones of his neck and spine had been replaced by tapioca. He smelled the stinging tang of vomit, sure it was his own.

"This is the shitbox you came back to?" a rumbling voice said. Matt couldn't locate the source. He could barely keep his one eye open and semi-focused. "Seems we'll be doing you all a favor tonight."

Matt ran his tongue over his sandpaper lips, croaking, "Just leave my wife and son alone."

Heavy footsteps. Something nudged the chair he was in.

"It's a little too late for that. But I didn't invent this game."

The Guardians were finally here, in the flesh, out of the shadows, and Matt still couldn't make out who they were. He willed his mind to focus, attempting to restore order to a tumbling overload of thoughts and deranged sensory input.

"This isn't a game," Matt said, sounding weaker than he'd intended.

The man drew in a heavy breath, whistling through his nose. "I tend to agree with you there. You're right. It's not a game...anymore. I actually thought the game ended some time ago, but what the hell do I know?"

# Chapter Twenty-Eight

The fog in West's brain was lifting, but that didn't help him make any sense of what the hell was going on. Faith paced before him like some kind of caged animal. Could this crazy person possibly even be the same girl he'd been mooning over for weeks?

West was by no means a brawler, but he felt confident he could take her on, now that she didn't have a shovel and the element of surprise. Not rushing her and pummeling her to the ground went deeper than the rule that boys weren't supposed to hit girls.

Despite everything, he didn't want to hurt her.

Maybe there'd been a mistake, some kind of misunderstanding. The things she said were flat out crazy. Someone had poisoned her mind, turned her against him and his family.

"Faith, you're not making any sense. The Guardians have been stalking both our families. How can you know that my grandfather killed Stella? Did they tell you that in one of their weird notes? Why would you believe them?"

She curled her lip at him. "For a New York kid, you're awfully dumb. We *are* the Guardians!"

West felt as if a horse had kicked him in the gut. He fumbled for words, anything to get her to admit that she was lying.

"But… but you can't be."

"I'm just part of a long line, West. And we know everything that happens here."

"I don't understand."

"My family has always watched over this land. We are one with the soil. Just like your family has watched us. Sometimes, lines get crossed. I'm not trying to say that we're angels, but we're certainly not the devil. That's Abraham, right down to his tainted black soul."

The moment West made to stand, Faith pulled a butcher knife out of her back pocket. Threat taken, he settled back on his ass. The night critters were quiet tonight, as if they were too afraid to be in the presence of madness.

"Why would he kill his daughter? That just doesn't make any sense. If this feud or whatever you want to call it has been going on between our two families, why would he take it out on his own child? Don't you see how crazy that sounds?"

He saw the briefest flicker of doubt pass over her moonlit face.

She quickly recovered, waving the knife at him.

"Because he's crazy and evil."

"So if he's so bad, why did your family keep on harassing him? Weren't you worried he'd do even worse to you?"

"He took my sister!" Spittle foamed at the corners of her mouth. West tensed, waiting for her to attack, wondering what he'd do to avoid having that blade plunge into his chest. So many scenarios played out in his head, most of them ending horribly for one of them, or both.

West stammered, "Because he was worried you would do something to me and my family. I'm not saying his locking Rayna up is right. He should go to jail for what he did. I'm the last person who will defend him. Not after everything." He had to tread carefully, but he was also being honest. What Grandpa Abraham did to Rayna alone was unconscionable. "We can help put him away. We can free your sister. I just don't understand why you attacked me, and why you feel you need to have that knife."

Faith's lips parted in a worrisome grin.

"You're not going to talk circles around me. I'm not some country mouse. I know exactly what I have to do."

West's diaphragm hitched, his heart going into overdrive.

"What do you have to do?" he asked, terrified of the answer. This was no horror movie starring Bruce Campbell and a host of demons. There was no director to shout, "Cut!" No special effects team laden with crimson corn syrup.

This was real life and death, with death's hot breath bearing down on him. He readied himself. There was no way around it. If Faith came at him, he'd have to give everything he had to bring her down and get that blade out of her hands.

"For the moment, I'm going to keep you right here. My mother and father are setting things right now."

"Faith, what are they doing?"

"The less you know, the better. I've already told you more than I should."

"Are they going to hurt my mother and father?"

He couldn't stop the trickle of burning tears from coming. Not that it mattered. What was the point in trying to look tough and brave before a deranged person?

She remained eerily silent.

"Once we tell them about Rayna, they'll feel the same way I do. They'll get her out and turn my grandfather over to the police."

Faith plucked a piece of grass free and sucked on the end.

"My father says it's too late for that. Too many bad things have happened. Your grandfather needs to be stopped for good. No police. Ever. My father says tonight is the night we set right what was done to poor Stella."

Did she think they could kill his grandfather and they wouldn't tell the cops?

And what did Stella, who was murdered over thirty years ago, have to do with everything?

Then it hit him.

They knew exactly how things would play out.

And they had no intention of leaving loose ends.

"Wait, Faith. It doesn't have to go down like this. If everything you said is true, I'm on your side. We're all on your side."

376

Her features softened for the first time since he'd awoken in the field, and he saw the Faith that had stolen his heart.

"I'm sorry, West. You may not believe me, but I really am. You're nothing like that man. But you share his name, and your being here is what brought this all about."

"Please, let us go. Please."

With one hand behind his back, he scooped up as much dirt as he could without her noticing. He hoped throwing it in her face would blind and disorient her enough for him to get the upper hand. It had worked in more movies than he could count. This wasn't a movie, but the logic was sound.

Right?

"You know I can't. Now just sit tight and no more talking."

"I don't wanna die."

"Find me someone who does. But in the end, we all have to do it anyway."

West launched a fistful of dirt at Faith's eyes, rising to his feet.

She flinched just enough for it all to miss her completely.

West realized in mid-leap that his plan had failed. And now he was heading straight for the blade in her hand.

A dark shape burst from the high reeds. Faith turned to face it.

There was a scream, then Faith tumbled end over end, grappling with the pouncing shadow.

He tripped over their intertwined bodies, somehow somersaulting back onto his feet.

"Mom!"

Faith was writhing on the ground, keening that her stomach was on fire.

West's mother backpedaled from the girl.

"Oh my God. Oh my God," she said, finding West's shocked face.

"I need help. Please. I need help," Faith moaned, clutching her stomach.

West felt his mother's hand slip around his. "I didn't mean to. I didn't even see the knife."

He helped her to her feet. They stood over Faith, blood blossoming under her T-shirt.

"We need to call an ambulance," West said. Even though she had been ready to kill him a moment ago, seeing her in abject agony, her life force flowing from the deep wound in her belly, he couldn't just sit here and watch her die.

"My cell phone is in the house," his mother said. "Are you okay?"

"Huh?"

She stood on the side where he had taken the blow from the shovel. When she touched his cauliflower ear, he winced.

"This looks bad."

"I can't hear at all out of that ear. Should we take the knife out?"

"No. That'll only make it worse. Come with me to the house and we'll call for help."

"And leave her out here alone?"

Faith caught his eye, her own streaming with pained tears. "West, I'm sorry. Please, don't let me die here. I need a doctor."

He knelt by her side, careful not to touch her. He wasn't sure whether he kept his distance because he worried she'd rally and attack him or if he simply didn't want to hurt her any more than she already was.

"We'll get one," he said.

"I can't leave you out here," his mother said. She was holding her shoulder and walking with a noticeable limp.

"Then I'll go to the house."

"Not alone you won't."

"Maybe we could take her with us."

She looked at the wounded girl. Mostly the whites of her eyes were showing now.

"I don't think that's going to be a good idea. Here, give me your shirt."

She wadded it into a ball, waking Faith from her delirium with light taps to her cheek. "You need to press this tight to your stomach." She put the shirt just under the jutting blade. "Can you do that?"

Faith nodded, her breath coming in wet rasps.

"Just hold on. We're going to get you help as fast as we can."

She grabbed West's hand, dragging him toward the house.

"I don't think she really wanted to hurt me," West said, more to himself than his mother.

She gave him a look that frightened him.

"Yes… she did. And she's not alone out here. Now come on!"

✢

Abraham burst through the basement door to an empty kitchen. The back door was open. He looked down the hallway. So was the front.

"Matt?"

His hands gripped the shotgun so tight, every knuckle was jellyfish white.

"Simmons? I know you're here. You touch one fucking hair on any of my family's head and you'll never see your daughter alive."

His footsteps on the scratched floorboards sounded like cannon fire.

"In here," Matt said.

He and his friend were tied to chairs in the living room, both looking like they'd head butted a brick wall.

Matt said, "He just headed out the front."

"He dead?" Abraham asked, pointing the shotgun's barrels at James. The man's face looked like spoiled chopmeat.

"Just knocked out. Untie me, quick!"

Abraham considered leaving him there. The more time he wasted freeing Matt, the further Gregory Simmons got away.

Or would he?

They had closed ranks on his farmhouse. They wanted Rayna.

No, Simmons wouldn't go far.

"He took our guns," Matt said.

"Shit. Where's Deb and the kid? They didn't come back?"

"I don't know."

"What a goddamn clusterfuck."

*And the old man is the only one with a weapon and not fucked up. The Simmons have the odds stacked in their favor... to a point.*

He got Matt free, and they undid the binding on James, who began to stir.

"You gotta get his ass out of the clouds," Abraham said. He filled a glass with water, dousing James's face. Blood and water cascaded down his shirt. He came to, sputtering and confused.

"I can't do everything by myself," Abraham said. "The two of you together might equal one person. We're going to find Greg Simmons."

James dabbed at his ruined nose. "Who's Greg Simmons?"

"He's the Guardian," Matt said. "My neighbor. Christ, we went to school together. Remember him?"

"We don't have time to shoot the shit. Get up, if you can," Abraham barked.

He handed them each a bat he found in the hallway closet. "It's better than nothing."

James helped Matt up, but he looked like he needed a mighty hand himself.

They made their way to the front door, a sad posse indeed.

Abraham said, "Look, when we get – "

"Aaaaaaaeeeeeiiiiiiii!!"

A shape as big as a razorback gorilla filled the doorway, tearing the screen door from its hinges. Abraham was folded in half as the charging beast laid a shoulder of granite into his midsection. He flew backwards, sweeping Matt and James off their feet like a struck bowling pin.

He regained his senses just enough to see a fist the size of a Christmas ham come rocketing toward his face.

Abraham had time for one thought before it was lights out.

*Fuck me sideways. Not another one!*

# CHAPTER TWENTY-NINE

The mad dash to Abraham's farmhouse was not without its pitfalls. Debi and West, guided only by the moon, faltered time and again, feet snagging on overgrown weeds, gopher and snake holes, and other obstacles seemingly thrown up by Mother Nature herself.

It was hard to miss the house.

As they got closer, Debi slowed them down.

*Be smart, Debi! God knows who's lurking around... or even inside!*

She placed her hand on her son's chest. "Wait here."

They were back by the old picnic table, out of the arc of luminescence emanating from the blazing kitchen lights.

"I'm coming with you," he whispered.

"Just give me a second," she said, cupping his face in her hands. "I need to make sure it's safe."

West cast a wary glance back at the gloomy field.

Faith was out there, maybe clinging to life, maybe not. He wanted to help her, despite everything. She loved his heart, his capacity for kindness.

She didn't mean to stab the girl. In fact, Faith probably stabbed herself. If she'd only let go of the damn knife.

But she hadn't.

*Because she wanted to kill you. And West.*

Getting Faith medical attention wasn't high on her list.

Finding Matt was.

Abraham could go fuck himself.

She crept to the kitchen door, careful not to make a sound.

The sounds of shuffling footsteps bled into the warm night. Someone was in the house. She daren't call Matt's name.

The kitchen was empty. She bent low, hugging the side of the house so she could peek into the living room window.

Again, there was no one she could see. But there were ropes bunched by two of the chairs and blood on the carpet and the old love seat.

She clasped her hand over her mouth to stifle a cry. Something bad had happened in there. She prayed Matt was all right.

A twig snapped behind her. She whirled, fists lifted as if she were a boxer. For a brief flash, she wished she had plucked the knife from Faith's belly. At least she'd have a weapon.

Once she realized there was no one behind her, or at least no one she could detect, she snuck around to the front of the house. It being so wide open, she felt exposed and vulnerable.

Abraham's crappy truck was there. So was James's. Which meant they all had to be near.

Debi dared to approach the front door.

*What the hell happened?*

It looked as if a wild animal had stomped its way into the farmhouse. The door was in shattered bits, the screen torn in half. She stepped on a hinge, freezing from the slight noise it made as it scratched across the diminutive porch.

There was more blood on the floor of the foyer.

The chair was tipped over and the runner bunched up, a sanguine trail leading toward the kitchen.

*I can't go there alone*, she thought. *If the Guardians are there, and they have Matt and Abraham, what can I do? I need to find my cell.*

*They're not the Guardians. They're the insane Simmons family!*

She was pretty sure she'd left it in her room. Getting there would be no easy feat. The damn house moaned and groaned with every step they took. The short walk to the bedroom would be enough to announce her presence.

And then what?

She sure as hell couldn't box her way out of this.

Debi looked around for a weapon. Anything would do.

She found an umbrella, picked it up, and realized it was useless, unless she was going to fight some raindrops.

She remembered a little junk drawer in the table Abraham used to dump mail and keys. After a quick, but silent rummage, she found a screwdriver.

It was sharp and pointy and would have to do. Sometimes, wishing for hammers or nail guns was wasted time.

Now was the big question: to run or creep?

*Screw it,* Debi thought, sprinting for her bedroom. If someone was in the house they were going to hear her anyway. Might as well get from point A to point B as quickly as possible. She did her best to stick to the new floorboard that Abraham had put down and used to sneak up on her and Matt.

She closed the door behind her with just the slightest click.

Last time she saw her phone, it was on the bedside table, plugged in because the charge was low.

It was gone.

The charger was still plugged into the wall socket, the empty connector lying atop the Mary Higgins Clark book she'd been reading.

"Shit, shit, shit."

She checked the drawer, just in case. No dice.

Someone had taken the phone.

Along with her husband, his friend, and her father-in-law.

Her purse was also missing, which was a double fucked sandwich.

The keys to their truck were in her purse.

The Simmons wanted to make sure they were good and stranded out here. Just like sitting ducks, lined up in a nice row at a traveling carnival. *Pay your buck and try your luck!*

What the hell was the prize here?

Total annihilation?

West!

She couldn't leave him alone out there any longer.

Shrugging all pretense of stealth, she ran out the front, wary of the more direct route out the back door. She sensed something ominous in that area of the house. Sometimes, a mother's intuition had to be heeded.

West was crouched behind the picnic table, rising the second he saw her.

"Did you find Dad?"

She shook her head, motioning for him to keep his voice down.

"Where can he be?"

"I don't know."

"Did you call for an ambulance?"

"I couldn't. My phone is gone. So are the keys to the truck."

"Fuck."

For the first time ever, she had no desire to correct his language.

He was right.

*Fuck!*

"Do you think Faith is gonna die?"

"I don't know, honey. If the wound seals around the knife, she could be fine for hours."

"We have to find Dad."

Debi knew what Matt would say if he were here.

*You have to get the hell out of here. Don't worry about me.*

A muffled shout rooted them to the spot.

"Was that Dad?" West whispered.

"No, I don't think it was."

"It came from inside the house."

She squeezed his hand harder than she'd intended.

He was right. A man had just barked something. He sounded angry. It most definitely wasn't Matt or Abraham.

And she knew exactly where it was coming from.

The basement.

"Come with me," she said softly.

There was a half-window set low to the ground on the side of the house. The glass was painted over, but she hoped to God, who had apparently abandoned them, that it was thin enough for them to hear what was going on inside.

Matt couldn't believe what he was seeing.

For the moment, his vision was clear. No double vision. No blurriness. Not even a hint of a headache.

For the first time since the accident, he wished he couldn't witness what was before him with such soul-deadening clarity.

He was on his back on the unfinished basement floor. The smell of the dank cellar was exactly what he'd expect it to be, but with an undercurrent of a ripe, sickly odor that made his stomach clench.

Matt knew where that odor was coming from.

The man's bulk seemed to fill the entire basement, though Matt knew that was an exaggeration. His pale flesh glistened under the dim light, rings of sweat spotting his denim overalls like Minnesota's lakes. Drops of sweat dripped off the tips of his long, black hair. His face was all square angles, with a wide nose set between narrow eyes as dark and bottomless as the ass end of a black hole.

It was his eyes that terrified Matt the most.

The flat gaze reflected at him seemed as detached from humanity as a freshly cut blade of grass from the sloping lawn it once called home.

"Everyone wake up!"

Gregory Simmons stepped out from behind the behemoth. His old classmate was massive as well, but seemed puny in comparison to the other man. He carried a rusty sickle in one hand, the flaking blade resting against his thigh. "You don't have any more old pals stopping by, do you? Because it sounds like someone's upstairs to me." He turned to the enormous man. "Go check it out."

The man's footfalls sounded like thunder as he ran up the stairs. He clomped about for a couple of minutes and came back, breathing heavily.

"Nothing?" Gregory said.

He shook his head.

"Well, we'll have to keep an ear out, then. We've got important business to attend to."

Matt heard a groan, turning to see his father on one side, James on the other. Both were trying to sit up, hands massaging their heads.

When Abraham came to, he stared at the man beside his neighbor, grimacing. "I should have known."

"You play cards down at the Post, don't you old man?" Gregory said. "You know you've always got to have your ace in the hole."

"More like another goddamn monster."

"Dad, what's going on?"

Matt sat up. When he tried to stand, the hulk took a deliberate step toward him, his hands flexing into fists. Matt took the cue to remain seated.

James coughed. He looked like he was having a hard time focusing. After taking two heavy blows to the head, it was a wonder he was even alive.

"You're going to give me back what's mine," Gregory said. "I've waited long enough."

"Go fuck yourself," Abraham spat. He fumbled inside his shirt.

Gregory grinned. He dangled a key in the air. "Looking for this?"

Matt's father heaved a gargled chuckle. "Go ahead then, open the door. You know how to work a lock, don't you?"

"You must really think I'm stupid, Abraham."

"You really don't want to know what I think of you."

Matt felt helpless. He had no idea what the two men were talking about, or why his father didn't appear the least bit surprised that a man the size of a wrestler crossed with a grizzly bear was standing guard over them.

"Where are my wife and son?" Matt asked.

"Well taken care of... I suspect," Gregory replied. "My boy here got a little creative and has your wife trundled up all nice. I have something special in mind for her. Sometimes, I have to let him do things his way. Keeps him focused. As for your son, nice kid, last I saw, my daughter was with him, though not in the way I'm sure he wet himself over when he jacked away in that sagging bed of his every night. But hey, thanks to him, we had to step things up a bit. Seems your boy had intentions on calling the police. Now that's something we couldn't let happen. Ain't that right, Abraham?"

"Let Debi and West go," Matt said. "They have nothing to do with any of this."

"Don't waste your breath," his father said, staring at the ground.

"It's a little too late to separate the wheat from the chaff," Gregory said. "No, we're just going to take our child back and finally set things right. Why couldn't you just let go and die, old man? See what pain your stubbornness has caused?"

Abraham spat, a gob of his phlegm landing on the big man's boot.

"You could have sent your mongoloid over any time to finish me off," he said.

The big man's chest puffed up. Gregory gave his son a reassuring pat on the arm.

"I don't like the way you insinuate that my boy is a killer. Now, you and I, we're of a different breed. Aren't we?"

James retched, his vomit reeking of blood and bile. "Matt, where the hell are we? What's going on?"

"I did what was necessary," Abraham said.

"You murdered part of my bloodline!" Gregory swung the sickle close to Abraham's face. It was only meant as a threat. He could easily have sliced his nose off if he'd wanted to.

"Your bloodline is poison," Abraham said.

"What's he talking about?" Matt said, staring at his father. The squat man refused to look him in the eye. "Who did you murder?"

Gregory snickered. "I'm not surprised he didn't tell you. It's some real bad business. Not the kind of thing you discuss over dinner. 'Can you please pass the rolls? Thank you. So, did anyone else take a life today? No? Oooh, those green beans look wonderful.' Am I right, Abraham?"

Matt grabbed his father's arm. "Dad, what the hell did you do?"

Abraham's rheumy eyes rose to meet his, the lines around his mouth deeper than ever.

"It was your… your sister."

Time seemed to stop. Matt's stomach gave an urgent signal to empty his bowels.

"Stella?"

"She was a monster. She would have ended up like him." He motioned his head at the huge man beside Gregory.

"What does that mean? I don't understand. You killed my sister?"

"She wasn't your sister."

Gregory seemed to be taking great joy in the baring of the skeleton in their family closet. "Go on, Abraham. In for a penny, in for a pound."

Matt stared at his father with utter incomprehension.

"She was your half-sister. Your mother was raped by Isaac Simmons, Gregory's father."

Gregory interrupted him, shouting, "Does saying it was rape make you feel better? I hear young Violet Ridley practically begged for it."

Abraham shot him a withering look, but didn't take the bait. He continued, "He impregnated her. When Stella came out, she nearly tore your mother to pieces. We tried to raise her. Tried to deny what had been done to your mother, what would become of Stella. But as she got older, it became impossible to deny."

Matt inched away from his father. "Deny what? Because she was the product of a rape that gave you the right to kill her?"

Abraham shook his head.

"It was her blood. There was something wrong with her. It comes from them." He glowered at Gregory Simmons and his towering son. "When they mate with someone outside their bloodline, something goes wrong. Very wrong."

It took every ounce of effort not to punch his father square in the mouth – anything to stop the spewing of this madness.

"Do you realize how insane this sounds?" Matt said.

When his father didn't reply, he said, "I saw Gregory's daughter. She's as normal as West. Why would you assume Stella would turn out like… like him?"

The sickle thunked into Matt's calf. The pain was immediate and exquisite. Matt's mouth opened in a silent scream.

"I'm getting tired of everyone insulting my son!" Gregory roared.

394

Abraham jumped to his feet but was easily swatted back by Gregory's son.

"It only happens when they don't mate with their own kin," Abraham said, breathing heavily and in obvious pain.

Matt's vertigo came rushing back like a tsunami. He felt the back of his skull bounce off the ground, but barely registered the pain.

Sinking into oblivion, he was consumed by one thought: *Dad killed Stella. Dad killed Stella. DAD KILLED STELLA!*

# CHAPTER THIRTY

West's heart was somewhere in his throat.

He couldn't swallow. Could barely breathe.

His mother was crouched beside him, hearing the same unspeakable things.

A quick look to her to confirm that he wasn't losing his mind gave little comfort. His mother was pale with dread.

"Mom, Grandpa Abraham has a girl locked up in a room down there."

Her eyes were wet with tears.

"What?"

"He showed me earlier. That's why I ran to Faith's house. To tell her. The girl is her sister."

"Why the hell would he lock her sister up in the basement?"

"To keep the Guardians... the Simmons family... from hurting any of us."

She craned forward, pressing her ear to the glass.

"This can't be happening."

"We have to do something."

"Shhh."

West crab-walked away from the window. He'd heard and seen all he wanted tonight. His mind burned with sensory overload. And there was still Faith out in the field, bleeding to death.

She was just a pawn in a long standing game. She didn't want to kill him. Not deep down.

*Bullshit. You never know what goes on in someone's head,* West thought. *Why else would such a hot girl even talk to you? She was keeping a close eye on you.*

"Mom, how far would it be to get to a main road?"

She chewed on a thumbnail, listening to what was happening in the basement. "Too far. By the time someone found us and we got the authorities out here, it might be too late."

West felt a strange feeling of calm wash over his body.

When your choices were limited, there was less to confound your brain. You either did one thing, or another. Simple as that.

It sounded as if running for help was out of the mix.

So he and his mother would have to somehow get in the basement and free his family.

Just how the hell they would do it was a mystery, but knowing this was the only viable road to take, he was ready to think of ways to salvage their dire situation.

"They don't know we're free," he said. "We could take them totally by surprise."

His mother exhaled, shoulders sagging. "There's no *we* in this, West. You're going to hide away someplace safe. Or better yet, you go get help. I'll find a way to get your father out."

"You can't do it alone. There are at least two of them down there, and they were able to overpower dad, Grandpa Abraham, and James. You're going to need my help."

"What I need is to know that you're safe."

A chilling thought crossed his mind. "It sounds like there's just Mr. Simmons down in the basement and his son. Faith is in the field. Her sister Rayna is locked in the room. Where's her mother?"

And better yet, *what's* her mother? Grandpa Abraham said that when the Simmons men mixed with women outside their kin, they gave birth to abnormal children. If Faith and Rayna were what everyone considered normal, did that make Mrs. Simmons a relative? Was she Gregory's cousin? Or worse, his sister?

But then where did the son come from?

It was almost too much to think about. His brain felt as if it were on fire.

His mother looked around, scanning the moonlit field. "Crap, I hadn't thought of that. I didn't hear her down there."

"Which could mean she's somewhere out here," West said.

"I can only hope she found her daughter and is taking caring of her as we speak."

"But what if she didn't?"

His mother grabbed his hand and stood up.

"Okay, we need to arm ourselves. We could grab some knives in the kitchen."

West thought about it. "We need something bigger."

"You sound like you have something in mind."

West wasn't sure if his plan was the best, but it was the only one he could think of. After years of immersion in horror stories, he knew a thing or two about ways to defend oneself or take proactive action. He was also pretty confident in understanding the mindset of a psychopath.

Maybe all that time *wasted*, wasn't wasted at all.

"I'll need that screwdriver," he said.

Shehanded it over to him.

"We need to drive out to the old barn," West whispered, making his way around the house, keeping a watchful eye out for Faith's mother.

"There's a barn out there? Where?"

"Not far. I can show you."

"How are we supposed to drive the truck with no keys?"

"I saw people break into cars in a movie using a screwdriver. I didn't know it would really work, so I watched a bunch of videos on YouTube. It wasn't just something made up for the movies. I'm pretty sure I can do it. First, we need to get inside Grandpa Abraham's truck."

His mother said, "If we have any bit of luck tonight, his keys will be in the ignition."

During his long afternoons just walking around, West had peered inside his grandfather's truck several times. There was a

400

storage area behind the front seats that was filled with tools and hard plastic cases. He'd even gone so far as to rummage through it all one day, wondering if the old man had stolen all of the tools, because he sure as hell didn't use them to fix the farmhouse. Some of them were new, a lot old, and what he came to realize was that they were probably the spoils of victory from playing cards. The men around here were sure to have plenty of power tools on hand.

"No luck," he said when he opened the door and looked to the ignition.

"Of course not."

He bent over the front seat and found the drill case. He opened it and heaved a sigh of relief. It was a battery powered drill, not electric. He pulled the orange trigger, the drill whirring to life.

Luck hadn't totally abandoned them yet.

They slipped into their second hand truck, hackles raised when the hinges on the driver's side door groaned. He closed his eyes, recalling the videos he'd watched, trying to work out the steps in his mind. Again, this wouldn't work with a new car that used those key fobs. It was the first time he'd ever been happy they'd traded their nice car for this shit box.

He found a drill bit that looked to be about the size of a key.

"I hope you know what you're doing," his mother said, watching their backs.

"You and me both."

He inserted the drill bit into the ignition and pulled the trigger. The drill met some resistance, then started to spin, destroying all of the lock pins. He pulled the drill out and dropped it on the floor. Jamming the screwdriver into the ignition, he gave it a sharp twist. He and his mother recoiled at the sound of the motor rumbling to life.

His mother looked at him with complete shock and pride.

"Have you been stealing cars when I'm not around?"

"No, but it's good to know I have a career to fall back on."

She slipped behind the wheel while he moved to the passenger seat. She didn't turn on the headlights until they were behind the house.

"It's just over that way," West said, pointing to the opposite direction where Faith had dragged him.

The truck dipped and bounced, finding mini-sinkholes that had been hidden by the choking weeds. A couple of times, the suspension sounded as it if were going to break in half.

"West, honey, what are we looking for when we get to the barn? Are there old tools like axes and stuff?"

"No. The whole thing is collapsed. But I know what we can do with the remains."

She reached over to caress his face. The truck took a severe dip to the right, and her nails scratched his skin.

"I'm so sorry."

"It's all right. We're almost there."

They were blinded by an explosion of harsh, white light.

His mother slammed on the brakes. The truck skidded, the rear fishtailing across trampled grass.

He heard the roar of an engine.

"Mom, look out!"

The light raced toward them, aiming for a head-on collision.

His mother hit the gas, turning the wheel as fast as she could, trying to angle out of the way.

They spun in mad circles as the bed of the truck took the full brunt of the impact. The sound of crumpling metal and exploding glass pierced his one working ear.

West slid across the seat. He smashed into his mother, both their knees coming up and crashing into the dashboard. The breath was knocked out of him.

The engine sputtered and died.

It hurt like hell to turn around to face the lights, which were now right behind them.

He knew who was in the other truck.

Sarah Simmons revved the engine, gearing up to deliver a fatal blow to their stalled beater that had taken its very last beating.

# Chapter Thirty-One

Abraham didn't know how Simmons had managed to hide that bear of a kid for so long.

Kid. He was the size of two men, but appeared as simple as a gerbil.

He should have known.

The Simmons men strayed. Whether out of a lack of morality or a need to create monsters, he didn't know. And Ridley women had bore them monsters for generations. But they weren't the only ones.

There were stories of the Simmons clan being birthed from the soil itself, put here by a demonic force to hold sway over the land and torture all those who had the misfortune of trying to make a living off it. Abraham knew that was superstitious bullshit, but he also knew that there had been a Simmons in Buttermilk Creek for as long as anyone could remember. They were a blight that even an exorcist couldn't eradicate.

Everyone knew of their penchant to lure other women, but they were powerless to stop it. There was always the hope that the current generation would be the one where it stopped. It was all wishful thinking.

Like vampiric marauders, they took what they wanted.

Gregory's sick father had wanted Violet. And now Gregory, from the sound of things, wanted Debi.

"Women don't tend to stray," his father had told him on his wedding night. "But when it comes to the Simmons men, they'll go against their nature. Keep an eye out for that. And if it does happen, don't blame her. There's something bigger than we'll ever understand going on out here. I don't pretend to be smart enough to figure it out. Maybe you'll be the one."

In that conversation was his father's confession that his own mother had had her an affair with one of the Simmons men.

*And if it does happen, don't blame her.*

Abraham was never able to look at his mother the same, even though his father doted on her until he passed on. How could he?

He knew it would never happen with Violet. She was so chaste, they couldn't even make love with the lights on. With Violet, whatever was going on between the two families would end.

He was so wrong. And Violet, she'd been destroyed by the indiscretion. Abraham had not been able to take his father's advice. He blamed her. And he blamed whatever curse was on this land. That's why he left it to rot.

So he watched and harassed them, just as they had done to his family. He suspected his father had as well, though he'd never come out and said it. There was something very wrong with the Simmons family that went beyond incest and their proclivity for

406

creating beasts with other women. What did it say about the Ridleys and the handful of other families who had called Buttermilk Creek home for centuries, who stubbornly refused to vacate the town, living with the unspeakable consequences? Was it more than just family ties to a parcel of land that had been passed down for generations? Did Abraham, and his father, and all the Ridley men before them, derive some sort of twisted pleasure from the bizarre game?

Questions like this, and the memories of what he had done, and what had been done to him, were what made him drink. If he could just soak it all too deep to reach, there was a chance he could die not a happy man, but not a tortured one either.

It's why he'd been glad to see Matt leave for college, never giving him a reason to return. When Abraham died, the Ridley line would finally be free from this cursed place. It made people do terrible things, left them with constant reminders of their fall from grace.

One of those reminders was blocking their escape as surely as the door on a bank vault. Abraham didn't know where this particular monster came from, but it was just further proof that his family wasn't the only one damned to their watchful eye and hateful machinations.

Gregory and his tainted progeny had the upper hand in every way.

But there was one thing they didn't have – Rayna.

And they were smart enough to be worried about what he'd done to make sure she couldn't be easily rescued. He'd counted on that to keep them clear of his family until they got back on their feet and moved out.

This attack was a total surprise.

If West had only kept his mouth shut.

*Don't go blaming him. He's not from here. He isn't tainted. He's a good kid. And he's been scared. He had no way of knowing that the Simmons family was behind everything. He probably just wanted someone to help them. Calling the police was what normal people did.*

But there was nothing normal about the town of Buttermilk Creek.

Gregory Simmons and his diseased kin were like rats, happy to be in the shadows. Most of the time.

No matter.

Abraham still had Rayna, and even the big dumb one was too scared to rush headlong into that room to get her.

Matt looked like he was about to pass out. His eyes twitched and rolled. It was as if they were trying to fall right out of their sockets.

"Did I ruin your family dynamic, Abraham?" Gregory Simmons asked with unmasked glee.

"There wasn't a dynamic to ruin."

He looked toward the door where his daughter lay locked up.

"I'd say different. Now, why don't you get my girl out of there or I start taking my anger out on Matt. Shit, looks like anything I do to him would actually be a mercy."

Abraham curled his lip. "Be my guest. That won't get you any closer to your daughter – alive, of course."

Gregory motioned to his behemoth son who strode over and picked Matthew up with one hand grasped around his throat. Matt started choking, his limbs feebly twisting, hands bouncing off the kid's chest like acorns off a dirt floor.

"Kill him, and I kill Rayna right now."

Matt took two sharp jabs to his face. He was dropped to the ground like a used tissue. The mongoloid kid gave him a kick to his kidney for good measure.

Abraham wanted to rush over to him, but he couldn't give Gregory the satisfaction.

"It's only going to get worse if you don't cooperate," Gregory said, grabbing a gun that had been tucked at his back. He pointed the gun at the seeping wound on Matt's leg. "A bullet tearing through a knife wound will hurt like hell."

Abraham shrugged.

"What I have in store for your daughter will be much, much worse."

Gregory cocked the hammer back, but paused.

He waved the gun toward Abraham. "You know, a part of me keeps screaming that you're bluffing."

"That part must be as small as your dick, because I haven't seen you try to get her out since I took her. Not even now when you have the key."

They stared at one another, neither wanting to break the other's hard gaze.

Abraham didn't see James clamber to his feet, but he sure as hell watched him square his shoulders and lay into Gregory's beastly son, driving him into the concrete wall as if he were a tackling dummy. The two wrestled each other to the floor.

Gregory shouted, "Get him boy! Get him!"

Abraham lunged at Gregory, hoping the distraction was all he needed to knock the gun out of his hand.

The younger man turned when he was just a step away. He didn't have time to bring the pistol all the way up to Abraham's chest or face. Abraham would debate whether that was a blessing or a curse.

Instead, he settled for shooting him in the thigh.

The bullet was a hot poker, burrowing into the meat and ricocheting off bone, exploding out of his leg in the opposite angle it went in. Abraham dropped to a knee, yowling in pain.

"Music to my ears, old man." Gregory kept the gun trained on him. "Music to my ears."

There was a lot of blood. Abraham wondered if the bullet had nicked an artery.

Gregory must have been wondering the same thing, because the smug look quickly melted from his cheering face.

To make matters worse, James was thrown on top of his legs. The burst of agony was beyond words, beyond screaming. The edges of Abraham's vision went blurry, then darkening like the skies of an approaching hurricane.

"Get him off!" Gregory Simmons shouted.

There was a dull, distant relief of pressure. Hands on his leg. The tearing of fabric. Matt's voice. Then Gregory's.

*What are they saying?*

*Can't die. Not yet. Please, not yet. Not until...*

"Mom?"

West shook his mother's shoulder. She was out cold. A bright, red gash bisected her forehead, the point of a triangular flap of skin covering part of her eyebrow.

Smoke billowed out from under the truck's hood. West looked at his bare chest, saw the beads of broken glass embedded in his skin, little droplets of blood making it look like he had a new strain of seeping chicken pox.

The headlights of the other truck swung toward them, blinding him for a moment. When the truck changed position, he saw Sarah Simmons, her hands at ten and two on the wheel.

"Mom, get up. We have to get out of here."

West had never been so scared in his life. Any second now, Mrs. Simmons was going to ram into them. He couldn't leave his mother. But he was terrified to stay in the truck. He didn't want to die. Not here, and certainly not now.

He unclipped their seatbelts and tried to open his door. It felt as if it had been welded shut.

The other truck roared. West felt panic trying to take hold, telling him to just run, run as far and fast as he could.

"W... West?"

His mother's eyes fluttered open. They jittered the way his father's did when the vertigo got real bad.

Could he carry her?

He couldn't even get out of the truck. It may be a moot point.

West leaned over his mother and tried her door. It clicked and popped open.

"Oh, it hurts," she moaned as he scrabbled between her battered body and the steering wheel. Being squished like that, only for a moment, drove the pebbled glass deeper into his flesh.

"I know, I know. I'm going to pull you out. It's going to hurt even more."

412

Her gaze fixed on the truck opposite them. "No. Go. Leave me here."

"I'm not doing that." Tears choked him as he tugged on her arm. She started to slip free.

She fell to the ground just as he heard the tires start to spin.

"You have to get up!"

The truck raced toward them. West hoped Mrs. Simmons couldn't see them behind the open door. It was going to be like a matador hiding behind his cape. He'd have to time it just right to move out of the truck's deadly path.

He tugged on his mother's arm. She rose, but it was as if gravity was tripling its pressure on her, urging her to stay down. West shoved his forearms under her armpits, taking on as much of her dead weight as he could.

The headlights sped closer, closer, closer.

A second before impact, he threw them as hard as he could to his left. The trucks collided with a chest-rattling crunch of steel and glass. The back end of their truck swung toward West and his mother. He was helpless to do anything but watch in wide-eyed horror. The rear cab swung above them, the back tires just missing crushing their lower legs. He felt a great whoosh of air as it blew over them.

In a flash, the entire truck pin wheeled away, and flipped over.

The front end of Mrs. Simmons's truck was crumpled, but the engine was still running. The horn blared in a steady hum.

West approached the passenger side door.

"Honey, don't." His mother was on her knees, reaching out to him. "We need to go."

He didn't answer her. She was right. But if Mrs. Simmons was okay, she'd just run them down in the field. He had to check.

And what would he do if she *was* conscious, putting the truck in gear for another run? He had no clue. Anything seemed possible tonight. He had no weapons, but he had his hands. How much good that would do against a crazy person was anyone's guess.

He peered inside the broken window and reeled back, his body rigid with repulsion.

Mrs. Simmons was out cold, her face mashed into the steering wheel, the deflated airbag acting as a kind of pillowcase. Blood dripped onto the floor from her shattered nose.

But that wasn't what made him have to choke back a ball of sizzling vomit.

Faith was in the passenger seat.

The impact drove the knife even deeper into her gut. Only half the handle was visible now. A pink sack that was some internal organ flopped out of the widened slash.

He didn't have to check for a pulse to know that she was dead.

414

Mrs. Simmons might be, too. He stared at her body, but it was too dark to see if she was breathing.

He jumped when he felt a hand on his shoulder.

"I'm sorry," his mother said. One of her eyes was filled with blood. "I'm woozy, but feeling better." When she saw Faith and her mother, she stiffened. "Look, that could easily have been us. It would have been if you hadn't saved me. I know you liked her and _ "

"Can you help me get them out of the truck?"

He didn't want to talk about it. Not now. Maybe not ever. He'd never get the sight of Faith's lifeless body out of his head.

Right now, he needed to keep busy. They came out here for a reason. He may have saved them from getting crushed, but they still had to go back for his father, grandfather, and James.

"West, I'm not even sure the truck can be driven."

"We have to try."

He had to use both hands to pry the passenger door open. Faith slumped sideways so fast, he had to dive to catch her from falling headfirst. His mother helped him lay her on the ground. Feeling her lifeless body in his hands, her blood mixing with his own, he thought he was going to pass out.

He took a deep breath, kneeling close to her, whispering, "Goodbye, Faith."

Mrs. Simmons groaned when they touched her, but she didn't stir. They got her out and dragged her near her daughter.

His mother insisted. "They may be bad people, but they're still family. I would want to be next to you."

When they got in the truck, West asked, "Are you okay to drive?"

She nodded, the flap of skin over her eye bouncing. "I'll be fine."

She put the car in drive. It shuddered briefly, then lurched ahead.

West pointed the way. "The old barn is just over there."

"I still don't know why you want us to go to a collapsed barn."

He told her why and she sighed. "I hope this works."

West stared straight ahead into the dark field, but as irrational as it seemed, his eyes only saw Faith, bloodied and gone forever.

# Chapter Thirty-Two

Matt was having a hard time making sense of the chaos around him. James was still grappling with Gregory Simmons's hulking son and surprisingly holding his own. His father was on the ground, bleeding out from a savage wound in his leg. And Gregory was shouting at Matthew to snap the hell out of it and help him.

Through a fog of vertigo and pain, Matt fought the opposing current. He stared hard at Gregory's bearded mouth, white spittle flying from taut lips.

"Help me tie this around his leg," he shouted.

Matt looked down. Gregory had wrapped an old extension cord around his father's upper thigh, right above the steady fountain of blood. "Just put your fingers there, unless you want to see your father croak."

"Wh-what?"

Gregory jabbed a thick finger at the knot in the cord. "There, there you cripple!" He turned to Abraham, his face just inches away. "You're not going to die yet. Not until you set Rayna free."

Abraham's face twitched. "Fuck...you."

Matt saw multiple blood soaked legs. He chose the one on the right and touched the rubber and plastic cord. Gregory finished applying the makeshift tourniquet.

"Fuck me?"

Matt watched several Gregorys slide from his distorted view. James was atop the man, pummeling his head with a flurry of blows. He felt his body rise as James lifted him up.

"Come on, we have to get the hell out of here."

His friend practically carried him up the creaking wooden steps. Matt's head swiveled on a neck made of hot taffy. Gregory Simmons must have hit his head on the bare concrete wall. He wasn't moving. Matt's gun was right by his fingertips.

"The gun," Matt said.

James tugged him hard. "We don't have time!"

Gregory's son was slow getting up, his face a mass of knots and blood. James didn't look much better.

"Where did you learn to fight like that?"

James gave a clipped reply. "I never fought before in my life."

And there was his father, lying so still in a pool of crimson.

*My father killed Stella*, Matt thought.

No matter who or what she was, she was still a child. How could he have done such a thing? So what if she was different. So what if she'd been hard to control. She was a part of Mom, which meant there had to be some good in her.

418

He should have never come back. Maybe none of this would have happened.

The Ridley curse was clear — they destroyed everyone around them, whether intentionally or not.

"West and Debi," he spluttered as James tripped on the top step into the kitchen.

Gregory said he had something in store for Debi.

His father had said that when they mate outside their family, monsters were born. Jesus fucking Christ. Was Gregory planning to do that with Debi?

James was breathless. "I don't know. I haven't seen them. If they're lucky, they're as far from this insane asylum as they can get. What the hell has been going on out here?"

Matt shook his head. It only made the dizziness worse. "I don't know. Not even when I was living right in the middle of it. I had no idea."

James huffed with each breath. Something wet and dangerous rattled in his lungs. They scooted down the hallway. Matt kept trying to get his legs under him. The way James was sounding, he didn't need the extra weight holding him down.

"I have to find my family."

"We will, buddy. We will. We just need to get the cavalry."

Matt tried to slip free. James had to lunge to grab him. "No. No time. I can't just leave them here."

James stopped and held him against the wall. "Look, I know exactly how you feel. The thing is, they could be long gone by now."

Matt squirmed under his grasp. "Or they could be right outside."

"You're in no condition to help them. I'm not much better right now." As if to prove the point, he started coughing, spitting a gob of red tinted mucous on the runner.

Matt was somehow able to break free. "You go. Get the cops. I'll wait here."

It was their only chance to get out of this alive. Matt couldn't drive. He could barely walk right now. The fate of his family rested with his old friend.

"Those guys aren't dead. They'll be coming up here any minute now."

Matt concentrated as hard as he could, trying to morph the three images of his friend's face into one. "I'll be fine. Go and give me one less thing to worry about."

James sighed with resignation, shaking his head. "Hide yourself somewhere, at least until they leave."

Matt gripped his arm. "I'll do whatever I have to do. Now go. We don't have time to waste."

"I'm not going to lose you, buddy. Not after all those lost years."

Matt stood straight as possible, trying not to weave. He hoped he was giving the impression that he was better than he felt. He needed James to think he wasn't leaving him to his death.

"The feeling's mutual."

Matt heard footsteps behind him. As he swung around to face Gregory or his son, there was a tremendous boom. Something sizzled through the air, just missing the tip of his nose. He turned in time to see James's right eye explode. His friend's head snapped back and his body fell forward, knees collapsing. His ruined face bounced off the floor.

"That was a very touching goodbye," Gregory Simmons said. The gun was now pointed at Matt. "I should have done that downstairs. But, woulda, coulda, shoulda." He motioned with the gun for Matt to follow him. "You're needed in the basement."

The vertigo released its grip on Matt's brain. For the moment, he could walk without needing to feel out for the walls. He didn't dare look down at James for more than one reason.

"What do you want from me?"

Gregory pushed him hard toward the cellar steps.

"You're going to get my daughter out of that damn room. Alive and well." He flashed him the key but didn't hand it over.

"Why don't you just open the door yourself?"

Gregory looked as if it was taking all of his self-control not to strangle Matt to death. "If I didn't think your father was a murdering son of a bitch, I would. But I don't trust him. Just like you don't trust me. You're going to have to talk him into giving her back."

They walked down the steps. Gregory's son had recovered, but looked like he'd need a doctor. He was missing several teeth and his nose was at an unsightly angle. He wiped snot and blood from his face with the back of his hand and painted the basement floor with a flick of his wrist.

Abraham was in the same position, arms at his sides, not moving. At least the corona of blood encircling him hadn't seemed to have grown much. The tourniquet must have worked.

"And what if I refuse to help you?" Matt said.

Gregory's son grabbed him by the throat. His hands felt like they were made of brick. They were rough and thick and felt strong enough to crush steel.

"Then I kill your wife and son in front of you."

Matt struggled for air.

Gregory cocked an eyebrow at him. "Think I'm shitting you?" He took a cell phone from his pocket, his thumb working the small screen. "I'll just have my wife bring them on down to the party."

He set the cell to speakerphone. It rang four times, then was answered by a voicemail message, "Hi, it's Sarah. Leave a message."

Gregory's air of cockiness deflated instantly. He put the phone close to his mouth. "Sarah, I need you to bring the bitch and her dumb ass kid down here right now."

Matt managed a smile, the fingers around his throat loosening. "Looks like... someone ruined... your plans."

He was released and hit the floor. His respite was brief. All the breath was knocked out of him by a swift kick to his solar plexus.

"Drag him over to his dying asshole of a father," Gregory said.

The meaty hand clamped over Matt's shoulder, dragging him along the floor the way children tote their favorite blanket around. His hands landed in his father's blood.

Gregory dialed the phone again. He said to Matt, "You better hurry. Doesn't look like time is on your side."

Struggling to breathe, Matt choked, "Just... give me... the... key... and I'll open... the door... myself."

"Not gonna happen. I bet you'd like to see my daughter dead. The apple doesn't fall far from the tree. Start sweet talking the old man."

His father's face was ashen, drenched in sweat. His mouth hung slightly open, the faintest of breaths whistling past his parted lips. He and Matt may have not gotten along, but seeing him like this was worse than the choking or the kick. He placed a hand on Abraham's shoulders, leaving scarlet handprints.

"Dad. Can you hear me?"

There was no response.

A shadow draped across them. Matt looked up and faced Gregory's son looming over him, his fists clenching and unclenching.

*He's waiting for dad to die. Once he does, I'm not far behind.*

With his back to them, Gregory said something into his phone but too low for Matt to hear. He did sense a twinge of desperation in the tone of his voice.

He gently shook his father. "Dad, I need you to wake up. West and Debi's lives are depending on you."

An eyelid quivered. Abraham took a deep breath, his mouth moving soundlessly.

"That's it. Come back to me. We need your help, bad."

A horn bleated somewhere outside. It sounded close.

Gregory pocketed his cell. "Damn phones aren't worth shit out here. Son, go upstairs and help Sarah."

Matt's heart sank.

*No! Not West and Debi.*

All along, he'd been hoping they'd somehow managed to get away, that they were in a police car or station at this very moment telling them what had happened. That help was on the way.

The son turned and went upstairs like a voodoo zombie heeding its master.

Matt tightened his grip on his father, jerking him harder.

"We don't have any time, Dad. Talk to me. How do we get the girl out of the room? I need you to tell me. No one else needs to get hurt tonight. Just tell me what I need to do."

Abraham opened his eyes. "Come closer," he whispered.

Matt knelt over him, his ear a hair away from his father's lips. He started to speak, and Matt prayed to God what he was saying was wrong.

# CHAPTER THIRTY-THREE

Debi was covered in sweat. Part of it was the shock and mild concussion. The rest was from working frantically to pile as much rotted and jagged planks of wood she and West could find within the rubble of the collapsed barn. The bed of the truck was loaded. Their hands and arms were pincushions for dozens of splinters. The large pieces were easy to pluck out. Smaller slivers just dug in deeper as she gripped the steering wheel.

She looked back through the small window to West who was standing in the flatbed atop the lumber. What she couldn't see were the trio of split boards that were sharp as spears resting on top of the truck's roof. West insisted he be the one to hold them down while she drove. Even though he was a couple of years away from being able to get his driver's permit, Debi had been slowly teaching him on back roads. Right now, though, they needed someone more than capable behind the wheel.

The entire thing was insane, but sanity had departed the Ridley farm hours ago. At least they were in a vehicle that could get them the hell out of here. Their Ford was toast. If nothing came of this, she was taking them straight to the nearest police station.

With the farmhouse in sight, she laid on the horn, flashing the brights. The truck jounced as it dipped into a deep hole.

"You okay, West?" she shouted.

He knocked on the roof in reply.

Debi looked at the passenger seat, the blood staining the tan fabric. She hadn't meant to kill the girl. But dammit, she wasn't going to let Faith hurt West any more than she had. Her death was an accident, but Debi was finding a hard time feeling bad. It worried her. She'd just taken a life and felt no remorse. Was that what this place did? Turned you into a cold-blooded killer?

She had to believe that the guilt would settle in later, once they were all safe and far, far from the farm. It was the first time in her life she craved regret, just to remind herself that she was still Debi Ridley.

Breaking through the overgrowth, she stopped the truck fifty yards from the brightly lit house but kept the engine running. She'd made enough noise to wake the dead. There wasn't a soul in sight.

"Come on Matt, where are you?"

Or if not Matt, at least one of the Simmons family.

She laid on the horn again, tapping the accelerator.

Someone was in the kitchen! She couldn't make out who it was, but their silhouette was plain to see. The back door slammed open.

*Who the hell is that?*

The body filled the entire frame of the doorway. Matt's friend James was big, but not that big.

428

The immense figure waved to her.

*He can't see that I'm not Sarah. He may even think that's Faith standing in the back.*

She kept the brights on so he couldn't make them out against the harsh glare.

West knelt down and spoke to her through the open half-window behind her head.

"We have to get him out of the house."

"I know. I'm thinking."

For the moment, whoever was waving to them was safe from their plan. They couldn't drive through the house to get him.

*He thinks I'm Sarah. I can't imitate talking like her. Why won't he just come over here?*

Debi stuck her arm out of the window and waved him over.

At first, he didn't move.

Not being able to see his face, there was no way to know his reaction. Was he wary? Confused? Upset that she wasn't driving to the back door to meet him?

She gave the horn two quick taps, then motioned to him again.

*Come on, King Kong. Just a few steps.*

The giant must have read her thoughts, because he took one careful step, then another. But he paused, hands at his sides hanging so low, resembling a gorilla.

Debi honked again, hoping he could detect her irritation. It was the way she urged West to get going when they were headed somewhere and he couldn't get his ass moving. She knew the horn itself sounded the same as always, but her intention always seemed to imbue a sense of urgency.

It seemed to shake the hulking man out of his indecision. He took several long strides toward the truck.

"Now, Mom," West said.

Debi mashed her foot on the gas pedal. The truck's tires spun in the grass and dirt, then caught. They shot forward with a tremendous jerk. In the rearview mirror, she saw West stumble backwards but he managed to stay on his feet and regain his position.

The man stopped but didn't turn to run back into the house, even though a four thousand pound vehicle was hurtling right at him.

When he appeared in full in the headlights, Debi gasped.

Everything about him was oversized, including the features of his face on a skull that appeared twice as big as it should be. His nose looked as if someone had taken a hammer to it. He stared at her with slack incomprehension.

She questioned whether she was doing the right thing, was about to make a sharp left and veer around him, when she saw the blood on his hands. He'd been hurt, but it looked like he'd done his share of damage as well.

430

She didn't need much imagination to consider who had been at the other end of those massive fists.

West shouted, "Stop!"

Debi slammed both feet on the brakes, her knees and elbows locking.

She saw the pointed slats of wood fly off the roof, guided in part by West.

Two of them sailed past the beastly man, disappearing into the dark.

But they only needed one.

And it struck home, right in his stomach.

Amazingly, he stood his ground, even as the makeshift spear pierced his gut, ripping through his back. He didn't scream. He didn't fold in on himself.

He just stood there, glowering at them.

"Oh shit!"

Debi started to shake all over.

*How is that possible? He should be dead already!*

Blood leaked from his mouth.

He started walking toward the truck, the rotted wood in his stomach pointing at her accusingly. *You did this to me! And now you'll pay!*

She put the truck in reverse, but couldn't seem to find the accelerator to back away.

"Finish him, Mom," West said.

Finish him.

Jesus.

This wasn't a wrestling match, choreographed for the masses.

But he was right. She couldn't just cut and run.

Dropping into drive, she found the gas and floored it, thinking of Matt and what had most likely been done to him at the hands of this monster.

His knees buckled and he pitched forward, the end of the wood sticking in the ground. His body hung forward, unable to fully fall.

It was too late to avoid him.

A split second before impact, he raised his massive arms, as if to stop the speeding truck. There was a brief, terrifying moment when it felt as if he had indeed halted its forward momentum.

Because somehow, he had.

In her panic, she took her foot off the gas. The truck moved backwards a foot or more.

"No, no, no," Debi sobbed, her foot accidentally smashing the brake.

"Punch it, Mom!" West shouted.

The giant was pinned to the ground on one side, the stake driven deep as a fence piling, and heaving against the truck on the other. No man could do that. She'd heard of adrenaline giving people temporary strength that defied logic, but this was beyond the pale.

"Go back! Go back!" West screamed.

She fumbled with the gearshift, pulled it down to reverse, and finally found the gas pedal. The truck roared away from the monster's impossible grasp. She backed up until the truck was a good thirty yards away.

He struggled to pull the stake from his stomach. Still on his knees, he wrapped his hands around the bloody end of the stake, inching his body forward.

Her stomach turned at the sight, his gore spilling from what should have been an instantly fatal wound.

She didn't need West to tell her what to do now.

There wasn't time to spare. If he somehow managed to free himself, God only knew what he was capable of. She'd have to leave the farm behind, which meant Matt, James, and Abraham would be at his mercy.

And he didn't seem the least bit merciful.

Screeching until it hurt, Debi sped straight toward him. If he tried to stop the truck again, she had no intention of letting up on the gas.

The crown of his skull was right in line with the grill of the truck. He looked directly at her, his uncomprehending black eyes chilling her to the core. She heard his skull shatter. The truck flew in the air for a moment as it rolled over his body. She braked hard as the four wheels touched back down, praying West had secured himself.

They came to a stop and she swung the truck around so she could make out the dead man in the headlights. His body was twisted like a pretzel. The top part of his head was gone. Brain matter oozed from his nose on down. Debi wanted to throw up. She could still feel the girth of his body as the truck rolled over him.

Her heart froze.

West was gone!

"No!"

She clambered out of the truck. "West!"

Wood thumped in the flatbed. "Still here," West said, pushing himself up from the pile of timber.

"West, are you all right?"

He looked over at the twisted man.

"Better than him."

West was bleeding from more places than Debi could count. The ragged edges of the wood had torn his flesh and clothes when he fell into it.

He jumped from the flatbed, grunting in some pain. Debi put her arms around him, unable to stop her tears. He rubbed her back, saying over and over, "It's okay, Mom. It's okay. We did it."

It was surreal, all of it, but more so her son comforting her after everything.

434

She kissed his forehead, tasting salt and copper.

"Now we need to get Faith's father and whoever else might be in there," he said.

He was so calm, she worried he was in shock. Odds are, they both were.

That didn't make him wrong.

"We don't know how many there are," she said, looking back at the dead behemoth.

"Yeah, but there's a way we can find out."

# CHAPTER THIRTY-FOUR

Whatever happened outside didn't sound good.

Gregory Simmons looked up the stairs pensively. He cocked the gun and pointed it at Matt. "Time is in short supply, old buddy. Get Rayna out of there, now!"

"I can't."

He fired a round that whizzed by Matt's ear. It pinged off the wall behind him, ricocheting into a stack of moldy boxes.

"Wrong answer. The next one goes in your wife's belly the moment she steps down here."

Matt moved away from his father. Abraham's breath was coming in short, shallow gasps. He wouldn't hold on much longer, even if they were able to get him medical attention.

"He said he has the room rigged with explosives. If we open that door, the whole house is coming down."

Now Gregory was screaming. "Then ask him how to deactivate the fucking thing! Does he want you all to die? Because that's exactly what's about to go down!"

Matt closed his eyes, trying to collect himself.

His father's confession chilled him to his core. How could he do such a thing?

"He can't answer me because you shot him, you asshole," Matt snapped. "He's out, Gregory. Even you can see that. He can barely breathe, much less talk. So if you're going to kill us, there's nothing I can do to stop you, least of all get your daughter out of that room alive."

Gregory kept stealing glances at the stairs. His face was a writhing mask of indecision.

"Or, we can stop this madness and find somebody who can. Maybe get a bomb squad down here," Matt said.

"A bomb squad? A bomb squad? What do you think this is, some kind of TV show? Ain't nobody going to come to the rescue here."

He suddenly rushed across the basement, grabbing bunches of Abraham's shirt and pulling him from the floor. "Wake up! Wake up you murderous pig!"

Abraham's head rolled to the side while Gregory shook him relentlessly. Matt grabbed Gregory's arm. "Stop it! It's over! All of it. These sick games our families have been playing are done."

Gregory pushed him aside, dropping Abraham back onto the ground.

"Where the hell is that boy?"

Matt felt a glimmer of hope. Gregory's beastly son hadn't come back, which meant Debi and West could still be free.

"I'm going upstairs out of this little bunker to make a call," Gregory said. "Pretend you're Jesus and bring that fuck back from the dead.

The basement door slammed. Matt slumped against Abraham's body.

The spins were in control now. All the times Matt wished he were dead when they came on like this. Now he was going to get his wish.

"I take it all back," he muttered.

There was no taking anything back. Not the infidelity of his mother, the killing of his sister, the kidnapping of Gregory's daughter, or James's murder. Insanity. All of it.

And all for what? Because an incestuous family had laid claim to this diseased land generations ago? It made no sense.

Perhaps evil didn't have to make sense. It just was. It festered and survived by its own rules.

And what did that say about his family that chose to live among such evil? Were they monsters themselves? Crazy, or possessing a kind of bravery that Matt would never be able to fathom?

He no longer cared about himself. Debi and West were all that mattered. Not knowing where they were or if they were unharmed ate away at him.

*I have to keep Gregory down here, focused on rescuing his daughter.*

There was no getting through to his father. Not where he was right now.

"Why, Dad? Why?"

For once, there wasn't a smartass reply or insult.

There was only one way to go now. He had get on his feet, fight through the vertigo that was tearing his brain in two, and kill Gregory. But how? And with what?

He looked around the basement. It was all boxes and cans, or at least that's what his jittering eyes could take in. Matt stood, felt his knees threaten to buckle, and willed them to stay locked.

There it was. Just under the stairs, he spied a garden trowel. Or several of them. It was impossible to tell. He weaved his way to the stairs, gripped a step and bent over. Bending when vertigo was at its worst sometimes led to short blackouts.

*Not this time. Not this time.*

Matt's hand shook as his fingers probed the cold, gritty floor. The trowel he thought he saw wasn't the one on the right. He reached to the left, felt the wooden handle, and snatched it up.

Swallowing back his gorge, he tried to settle down. Sweat poured down his face and back.

Now to find the strength to overtake Gregory. If his son came down with him, Matt's attack would be short lived. He had to make it count.

He crouched under the steps, the only place to hide in the basement.

Gripping the trowel with both hands, he focused on his father's still body.

The house suddenly shook. It sounded as if a bomb had gone off.

And it wasn't the one rigged up to Rayna's prison.

✚

West knew he had years, maybe decades, of therapy ahead of him.

If he survived.

With his mother's help, they managed to lift the broken giant's body onto the dented hood of the truck. When they were done, after dropping him several times, they were both covered in the man's blood. Now he knew what people meant when they talked about something making their skin crawl.

A steady stream of white steam boiled out from under the truck's hood.

His mother said, "Must have cracked the radiator. I'm not sure how much longer this truck is going to work."

West wiped his slick hands on his pants. "Hopefully, we only need it for another couple of minutes."

"Honey, I can take it from here. I want you to go find help. They'll be so distracted, no one will follow you. I'll make sure of it."

He shook her off. "I'm not leaving without you and dad."

His mother looked like she was about to argue, but sighed in resignation instead. They were both too tired and hurt to debate. And time wasn't on their side.

She reached into the truck and laid down on the horn again. West held onto the heavy rock he'd found in the field.

"Hey, we have something for you!" his mother shouted.

The dead man was a gory hood ornament, impossible not to see thanks to his mother shining a flashlight on the body. They needed Gregory Simmons to view their handiwork.

Most of all, they wanted him mad. Reckless.

"Come on, asshole!" West screamed.

The back door kicked open. And because they had moved the truck closer to the house, they could plainly see Gregory Simmons. He took one look at the truck and started to wail. West had never seen someone so angry before, not even when his parents were at their worst.

"What did you do?" he shouted, his voice heavy with anguish.

A second later, he was taking shots at them. West and his mother dove into the truck, keeping their heads low. Bullets shattered glass and pinged through steel.

442

"Put the rock on the pedal," she said, barely able to contain the fear in her voice. West dropped the heavy rock on the accelerator. The truck felt like a horse wanting to break free from its stable.

"Hand me that wood."

They had found an old plank that would be the perfect size to hold the steering wheel in place. His mother jammed it through the wheel, making sure the bottom end was securely on the floor.

Each thunk of a bullet made West jump. He had to be careful to keep his head down low, or one of those shots would find him.

Gregory Simmons was shouting something above the shooting and blaring of the engine, but he couldn't make out a single word. It wasn't so much he was saying anything specific, but speaking in tongues, a hidden language of mourning and rage.

His mother locked her eyes on his. "As soon as I put it in drive, I want you to slip out the door and stay low. You hear me?"

"Yes. Mom, I'm scared."

His mind was a tumble of what ifs. What if the truck stalled? What if the board didn't work and it veered from its target? What if Gregory Simmons managed to sidestep it and came straight toward them?

The last was the one that scared him the most. The moment the truck took off, they would lose any cover.

His mother poked her head up. A shot just missed her.

"He's right there, maybe thirty yards away. You ready?"

West nodded.

His mother shifted the truck into drive.

"Go!"

They leapt out of the open doors just as the truck shot forward. West tumbled in the dirt and high grass. He settled on his chest, slightly winded.

He looked up just in time to see Gregory Simmons running from the truck and into the house. He wasn't shooting anymore.

His foot just touched the bottom step into the kitchen when the truck barreled into him. It demolished the back of the house, cutting through the rotting structure as if it were made of balsa wood. The door, the wall, the entire kitchen exploded. The wood from the flatbed flew like dozens of arrows, impaling the walls and even the refrigerator.

"Holy shit."

West couldn't believe the damage. It looked like something out of a war movie.

His mother startled him when she touched his back. "Are you all right?"

He dusted himself off. "Yeah, I think so."

"Did it get him? I got an eyeful of dust. I can barely see."

West saw Gregory's Simmons's back a split second before the truck overtook him. If he wasn't crushed it meant he had to have been beamed aboard a starship.

444

"I'm pretty sure it did. It was right on top of him."

They cautiously walked to the ruined house. It groaned like a living thing – a wounded animal warning anyone near not to touch it. Plaster and dust rained through the gaping hole. The truck sputtered and died.

"We have to be very careful," his mother said. "It sounds like it could collapse any minute."

"We have to get dad out of there."

She held onto his shoulder. "I know, I know. Stay close to me and be ready to run like hell when I tell you."

Stepping into the kitchen was like walking into raw carnage. Everything in the kitchen was destroyed. Amidst the rubble were copious splashes of blood. The stench was unreal. West gagged.

It looked as if the big man and Gregory Simmons had exploded. There was no way to tell where one ended and the other began. They were a heap of meat and blood splattered against the far wall. His mother grabbed onto his hand, hard, as they stepped over the debris.

Thankfully, the basement door wasn't blocked.

West took a quick look down the hall, the floor warped upward as if a giant gopher had just tunneled underneath it. He saw James by the front door.

"Mom." He pointed to James.

"Stay here."

She ran over, tripping on the bunched up runner. She knelt by James, put her fingers on his neck. She covered her mouth to stifle a cry, got up, and came back to the kitchen. "He's gone."

West really liked James. He didn't have to come here and be a part of this. But he had. He was a good man, something that was in short supply. West wasn't sure how much a human heart or mind could take in one night.

He could contemplate all of that later. He tugged his mother's hand. "Let's find dad."

It took some effort to get the door open. The frame was warping as the weight of the house pressed downward on the shattered foundation. The sound of wood creaking and cracking was alarming. They only had minutes, if not seconds.

"I'll go first," his mother said, holding him back. She clicked on the flashlight.

There was a smell coming from the basement hauntingly similar to the one hovering over the bodies of the giant man and Gregory Simmons. West readied himself for the worst.

# CHAPTER THIRTY-FIVE

West's mother made it to the bottom of the stairs and groaned. He was about to ask her what she saw when a dark shadow darted from beneath the stairs. It tackled his mother, driving her to the ground. He jumped at the crack of bone on cement.

Without thinking, he ran down the stairs, unarmed and unsure how many more people were in the basement waiting for him.

He reeled back in horror when he saw it was his father who had attacked his mother.

"Dad!"

His father turned around, his eyes glassy, far away. His body wavered, ready to collapse.

"West?"

And then his father slid off his mother's body. West's heart stopped.

The handle of a trowel stuck straight out of his mother's chest. Her eyes were wide open, already starting to film over with the mists of gray death.

"No! Mom! No!"

West fell to her side, scooping her head in his arms and resting it on his lap.

His father struggled to sit up. "Oh God. What did I do?"

The wail that came from his father's throat made his blood run cold. It was the sound of a man on the brink of madness. He pulled himself across the floor, burying his face in her hair.

"I'm sorry, Debi. I'm so sorry!"

He and West openly wept over her cooling body, oblivious to the sounds of the house coming apart above them.

"West, I didn't know. I thought she was Gregory. I didn't know. You have to believe me."

West couldn't reply. The hurt was too much to bear. Of course he believed his father. But deep down, he knew nothing he said would ever help. There was no coming back from this. Not ever.

"Is that short stuff?"

For the first time, West noticed Grandpa Abraham laying on the floor. He looked and sounded as if he and the house were intertwined, both with very little time left.

He gently laid his mother down, his father draping his body over her. There was a lot of blood around Grandpa Abraham.

*This man murdered his only daughter*, West thought.

His actions had taken so many other lives tonight. Was it wrong to want to watch him die?

"What more can you want?" he said, standing over his dying grandfather.

Without opening his eyes, he replied, "The key. Get the key from your father. You can let the girl out."

West had forgotten about Rayna.

He went to his father. "Where's the key, Dad?"

His father wouldn't look up or answer him. West shook him as hard as he could. "I need the key! Hurry!"

He fumbled in his pocket and handed over a lone key.

West ran to the door and stopped from putting it in the lock. "What about the booby traps, Grandpa Abraham?" Calling him Grandpa felt wrong. There was nothing grandfatherly about the man before. Now, he turned West's stomach.

The old man shook his head and spluttered out a laugh. "There are no traps. No bombs. Sometimes… when you're good… noone calls your bluff."

He opened the door. The animal stench of urine, feces, and old sweat swept over him in a nauseating tide.

There was Rayna, unconscious on a thin, stained mattress.

Miraculously, she was still breathing. The same key that unlocked the door also unlocked the shackles. He scooped her into his arms, feeling her bones dig into his skin.

Her eyelids fluttered open, then closed. "Who… who are you?"

He carried her out of the room. "No one. Just rest for now."

Exiting the prison room, one of the overhead wooden beams cracked. West nearly dropped Rayna.

"Did you get them all?" Grandpa Abraham asked.

West tightened his hold on the birdlike girl. "Yes. No thanks to you."

Grandpa Abraham smiled, blood leaking from the corners of his mouth. "I thought you would. Told you… you're a lot like me. We… survive."

He took a shuddering breath, then a long exhale, crimson froth bubbling up from the deepest recesses of his lungs.

The man died with a smile on his face.

*This is what made him happy,* West thought with revulsion. He stepped over his grandfather, careful not to slip in his blood.

"Come on, Dad, we have to get out of here. The whole house is gonna come down."

"I can't leave your mother."

West wished he could carry his father, too, but the man had his arms wrapped around his mother in an embrace that would take the Jaws of Life to break. "You can't leave me, either."

The tears came and rolled freely, a torrent of sorrow that threatened to break him into a million little pieces.

"Please, Dad, I need you to get up and get outside."

It sounded as if looters were tearing the house apart above them.

His father finally looked up at him. "Go, West, and get her out of here. I'll be right behind you."

West took a step, then paused.

450

"You can't stay here, Dad."

"I know, West. I love you. You know that, right? I love you more than anything in the world. And I've always loved your mother. Even when things were bad, I never stopped loving her. Always remember that. Now, go."

The house rumbled and West nearly lost his footing. Out of abject fear, he ran up the cellar steps, navigating around the newly fallen detritus in the kitchen and into the safety of the back yard. He fell to his knees, careful to keep Rayna in his arms. Gently laying her down, he started to run back to the house.

*He'll come out any second. He will. He won't leave me alone.*

West was just outside the wide hole the truck had made when the house toppled onto itself. It came down with a great bone quaking rush. The force of it sent him on his back.

"Dad! No!"

In an instant, it was gone. The old farmhouse became a bookend to the disintegrated barn. Except it was also a grave for five bodies.

West watched the remains settle deeper and deeper into the foundation, knowing it was crushing his parents and grandfather more and more. They were probably unrecognizable now.

He couldn't stop crying, great heaving sobs that made his ribs ache, his heart sore.

A mushroom plume of dust and smoke rose up from the house, catching the first rays of the dawn.

People would see it and they would come.

West didn't have the strength to do anything more but cry and wait.

He turned back to Rayna.

Sarah Simmons knelt by her unconscious daughter. Her eyes caught West's as she was scooping Rayna into her arms. Without saying a word, she picked her daughter up and walked into the high reeds and grass. They disappeared, swallowed up by the neglected field.

The police would come, and West would tell them everything. They would believe him. They had to. When they dug through the rubble, they would find the bodies.

He knew no one would ever see Sarah or Rayna Simmons again.

There would be no one left for them to watch, to guard over.

*Let it rot, alone and unwanted.*

West collapsed onto his back, letting the dust roll over him, the overwhelming heaviness of sorrow feeling as if it could push him down into the center of the earth.

*Just let it rot.*

# AFTERWORD

Writing is a lonely profession. Writers make the Maytag repairman look like the DJ at a rave. However, it takes a village to help the village idiot turn his crazy idea into a real live book. *We Are Always Watching* is no exception.

My agent and force of nature, Louise Fury, is the one who planted the seed for the story back in the summer of 2015. She shared an article with me about some mysterious lunatic that was harassing a family who had recently moved into their dream home. In her wonderful South African accent, she said, "Ooo, I think this would make a great book. It's right up your alley!" Now, I get a lot of stories from a lot of people, but this one stuck with me. I talked to my editor at the time at Samhain, Don D'Auria, and he gave me the thumbs up. I was just about finished writing the first act when Don left, Samhain's horror line soon to follow. I lost momentum and the book was shelved.

Cut to four months later and I get a call from this Matt guy, a publisher at Sinister Grin Press. He wants to know if I have a book we can work on together. I immediately bring up *We Are Always Watching*. Now *he* gives it a big old Texas thumbs up and I was off to the races. The rest is history.

There are so many people during this crazy time that helped me in more ways than I can count, both directly and indirectly. Big thanks to my special Hellions – publicist and now editor Erin Al-Mehairi, first reader Tim Slauter (your input was invaluable), Jack Campisi, Jason Brant, Matt at Horror Novel Reviews, Rich at The Horror Bookshelf, David Spell, Zakk at The Eyes of Madness, Shane Keene, The Other James Herbert, Jamie Evans, Frank Errington, Jonathan Janz, Brian Moreland, Keith Rommel, Robert Dunn, Raegan Butcher, Mike Chella, Norm Hendricks (thanks for the house to work on my edits), Catherine Cavendish, Pam Morris, Nina D'Arcangela, my fellow damned at Pen of the Damned, Robert Stava, Mom, Carolyn and Tom, Rob Zombie, Ash Costello, the gang at Bloody Good Horror, Matt, Tristan, Travis, and Zach at Sinister Grin, cranky grandpas everywhere, Jim Harold, Kristopher Rufty, Ron Malfi, Russell James, Glenn Rolfe, Jackie Kingon, Stephen Combs, Tim Feely, Steven Gibson, Chuck Buda, Armand Rosamilia, Tim Meyer, and the guy who invented the My Pillow. Writer's need a good night's sleep. I just know I've forgotten some peeps. If I have, there's always the next book!

Most of all, thank you to my beautiful family - Amy, Star and Samantha. You've always been there for me, encouraging me, letting me have my alone time and the best of all, loving me.

# ABOUT THE AUTHOR

Hunter Shea is the product of a misspent childhood watching scary movies, reading forbidden books and wishing Bigfoot would walk past his house. He doesn't just write about the paranormal – he actively seeks out the things that scare the hell out of people and experiences them for himself. Hunter's novels can even be found on display at the International Cryptozoology Museum. His video podcast, Monster Men, is one of the most watched horror podcasts in the world. He's a bestselling author of frightful tales such as The Montauk Monster, They Rise, Island of the Forbidden, Tortures of the Damned and many more, all of them written with the express desire to quicken heartbeats and make spines tingle. Living with his wonderful family and two cats, he's happy to be close enough to New York City to gobble down Gray's Papaya hotdogs when the craving hits. You can follow Hunter and join his action packed Dark Hunter Newsletter at www.huntershea.com

25110568R00260

Printed in Poland
by Amazon Fulfillment
Poland Sp. z o.o., Wrocław